Disciples of Revolution

By: Christopher J Lloyd

Paperback ISBN: 979-8-9861910-0-3

Ebook ISBN: 979-8-9861910-1-0

To find more stories, check out fanart, or to be the first to know of upcoming releases subscribe to C.J's mailing list

Like C.J Lloyd on Facebook

ALSO COMING BY
C.J LLOYD

Titans: Afterlife (2022)

Her Icy Wrath: A Dragon Princess Novel

The Take Over: The Revolution Series book 2

Child Soldiers

The practice of child soldiers is far more widespread and more important than most realize. There are as many as 300,000 children under the age of eighteen presently serving as combatants around the globe. Their average age is just over twelve. The youngest ever reported was an armed five-year-old in Uganda. The youngest ever terrorist bomber was a seven-year-old in Colombia. Roughly 30 percent of the armed forces that employ child soldiers also include female soldiers. Underage girls have been reportedly present in armed groups in fifty-five countries.

These children serve in government forces and armed opposition groups. They may fight on the front lines, participate in suicide missions, and act as spies, messengers, or lookouts. Girls may be forced into sexual slavery. Many are abducted or recruited by force, while others join out of desperation, believing that armed groups offer their best chances for survival.

I condemn these heinous acts and plead that you help support groups that look to not only outlaw these practices but hold those who do accountable!

Protect Children Worldwide

1

Alex's fingers drummed over the frame of his cot, his lips moving as he counted the bullet holes scattered over the walls of his bedroom.

First-day jitters, that's what the upperclassmen lucky enough to be selected to attend New Hope Academy called it.

His chest was tight even in the soggy air of the bedroom. This was beyond plain anxiety. This was horror birthed from the stories of those who failed or didn't make it through the other side to graduate, those beaten mentally, physically, and spiritually by a system that considered them filthy street rats.

A shiver rattled his bones, but this wasn't about him. This wasn't about useless fears, the suffering he would have to endure, or the belittling that would come from the Exclusives who hoped to keep their ascendency over the less than.

His eyes rolled over to the ball of blankets that rose and fell with life. His baby sister, Olivia, lay in a tight ball, the Gore-Tex blanket he'd wrapped her in last night to stop her night terrors barely clung to her shoulders.

For her and for his dad, he'd conquer the brutality that awaited him at N.H.A. Mom would've expected nothing less.

Light caught the corner of his eye and pulled him back to the scattered dots on the wall. Those bullet holes served as painful reminders of the indifference Bourgeoisie citizens faced day to day. The thought of whom the bullets were meant for should've sickened him, but such an emotion had left Alex long ago. Now there was only acceptance.

It wasn't like he knew the previous tenants who lived there. He wasn't attached or invested in the outcome of what happened to them. They were dead, no doubt—the sentinels were efficient that way—and he didn't have a face to remember, or a broken smile to connect colorless dead eyes to. Nothing.

All the silent counting did was remind him of their morbid lives as Bourgeoisie citizens living behind the walls. A life where death was quick on their heels, where a father could be snatched up in the middle of the night during a raid and brought to the city's center for a televised public execution. A life where a mother could be accidentally killed because of misidentification, and no punishment or trial held for the ones responsible.

A sticky breeze putrid with the smell of rotting food and garbage whistled through the small gaps of the bedroom. The stench intertwined with the golden rays of the climbing sun that was warm against Alex's mahogany-brown skin. It helped fight the shivers of anxiety that made his body ache.

Through the bright gaps, Alex fixated on something greater, something immense over the horizon.

Mocking those on the other side of the wall stood the City of Constance, a smooth horizon of infinite metal structures crafted with a sensual smoothness. It was nothing like the cold sun-bleached block structures of the Suites. These buildings bore life, had urgency, and sang with the environment they rose from. The crown jewel was Venus Tower, a glittering gold double helix of glass and metal that shone so blue at night it made the Suites beautiful like the oceans he read about in school.

Around the illuminated metropolis was the massive inner wall that separated them from the lavish life of the Exclusives. The ones who lived within its borders. Since elementary school, he dreamt of what life was like in Constance. The enticing aroma of freshly baked bread and cooked meats wafting over the wall would do that to a kid.

He imagined honey-soaked ham, grilled short ribs falling off the bone, and Cornish hens. *Real* Cornish hens, like the ones seen on television, browned, rotating on a rotisserie, and decorated with herbs and spices. Nothing like the salted pungent entrails, gizzards, and fat scraps sold to Bourgeoisie citizens like him and his family.

But it wasn't just food. It wasn't the massive homes and apartments or the celebratory parties that Exclusives threw in their faces. Neither was it the freedoms and equalities that the Bourgeoisie thirsted for. It was something so simple and delicate.

Peace.

Alex rubbed the gunk from his eyes, turned from the rancid air, and breathed in the mildew drenched essence of the bedroom. At the end of the day, life was life, and there was only one thing that could change—

An abrupt snarl erupted from Olivia, interrupting his thoughts. Her nappy hair rose in odd puffs and shapes that gave their father hell when he tried combing through it. Eventually he stopped trying, and Olivia was all for it. His dad didn't have the slender brown fingers their mother had. She would massage Olivia's scalp with grease and oils. With hands and knuckles callused and scarred from working at the metal mill, there was no way their father could finesse his daughter's hair. As a result, Olivia's long messy coils fell wildly over her high cheek-boned face.

A subtle knock came to the door as their dad poked his head in. His glasses lay crooked on a wide nose, and his ebony skin shone with stress sweat. He was hunched over, trying not to crack his head against the ceiling.

"Time to get up, you two," he said, looking down at Olivia, who replied with a deep snort. Even in her sleep, her curved brows gave her the appearance of being pissed. They matched her personality.

"You want to give her a few minutes, Pops?" Alex sat up on his cot and looked down at her, admiring the resemblance she had to their mom.

He eased his brawny frame through the door. "Another bad night, huh?" his dad whispered.

Alex looked her over. He learned to block out what happened five years ago, it wasn't easy, but he got through it. Olivia, on the other hand ... "I thought she grew out of it."

His father rubbed his hand over his forehead. "The news, the attacks, the increased night raids . . . I'm not surprised. We can't afford to get her back on medication either. We can barely get by as it is."

"That's why going to New Hope Academy means everything," Alex said, looking down at Olivia, then back up at his father.

His dad smiled, gave a loose nod, and waved him out of the room. Alex slipped off the cot and tucked the blanket around Olivia's shoulders before kissing her on the forehead, then went out into the hall.

His father closed the door behind them and put his hands on Alex's shoulders. The barcode on his father's enormous right hand was a stamp of victory for most Bourgeoisie citizens, but everyone Alex's age saw the charagma as another way to keep tags and surveillance on their class.

His dad crouched low and whispered, "You sure about all this, Alex? You sure you want to put yourself through this?" He straightened his glasses, but it didn't hide the frantic glint of terror in his dad's deep brown eyes.

"Yeah, Pop, I'm good." Alex grinned big. "I'm excited about my selection. Honest. Only four years, right? Time will fly. I'll graduate and get my Exclusive class citizenship in no time. Then Olivia will go and graduate, and we'll take care of you. We'll be on easy street." He crossed his arms and raised his chin in confidence, hoping to calm the uneasiness in his father's heart.

"Easy street." His dad chuckled. "I know a lot of people who died on that intersection, good men. Young men like yourself, who can't repay the debts and costs of those retched potholed streets."

Of course, his dad didn't agree. Since that acceptance letter came, his father had glared at the piece of paper like it was a rotting dead cat on the sidewalk. When Alex first read it aloud, his dad dry-heaved as if the stench of a maggot-infested carcass had been laid in front of him on a dinner plate.

His father's forehead pressed against Alex's. "You know as good as anyone that they'll do all they can to make you fail."

Alex brushed a thumb across his nose. "So I won't let them then."

"You're a bright kid, Alex. You and Olivia don't get it from me. That's Myra all the way through. Look, just don't try to show anyone up, okay? Keep your head down, say nothing to nobody. And if you need to quit, quit. I'd rather have you home alive with Olivia and me instead of in a body bag. They're out for blood after what the Tanakas' oldest boy did."

Alex cleared his throat, fighting back bitter tears. Never could he have imagined one boy's actions could affect an entire group of people. Jason Tanaka had been loved and highly respected, and all the other kids in Eastern looked up to him. Then he did the unthinkable. The unforgivable. He committed treason against the United Nations of America by joining the Disciples of Revolution.

Once a close friend and the older brother to his best friend Nelson, no one knew what had pushed Jason over the edge. Not like it mattered now. After what he did, all the kids on the block were banned from having anything to do with the Tanakas, and Eastern Suites lost sanitation and garbage removal services as a result of his betrayal.

Initially, Alex hated Jason for what he did and wanted him dead like everyone else in Eastern. But those feelings faded when Nelson Tanaka was accepted into N.H.A. From there, Alex's hatred for Jason became pity for Nelson.

"Yeah … I understand, Dad." The words left a bad taste in Alex's mouth.

His father looked around the apartment cautiously as he always did when he spoke ill of UNA and its systems. He stood as tall as the ceiling would allow as his voice heightened with pride. "You'll be fifteen in a few months. In three years, you'll get your charagma, get a job, and even help out a bit around here." His father looked down at the barcode tattoo on his right hand. "You could get a job in the steel yard like me. Contribute to this great nation of peace."

"Maybe." Alex's eyes moved to the few cracks in the seams of the bathroom door. Who was Dad fooling? Since Mom died, he had long lost faith in the world government, like so many others. Everyone just stayed quiet, stayed in their lanes. That's all anyone could do anyway.

His father started whispering again as he crouched closer. "Lord knows I can't do this all by myself. If *they* would just let me work two jobs." He smacked a brawny fist into his palm, his voice trailing off as he looked over his shoulder to where the VEN-O rested on the kitchen table.

Nothing more than a black cylinder speaker, no matter what class you were, every home had a VEN-O quietly recording, gathering, interpreting. The fear came when it glowed a warm red. That's how you knew the sentinels were coming.

His father was biting his tongue, Alex knew. He loved his job at the steel mill. He was built for it. But any negative talk about the way UNA handled things could cost him everything. And that VEN-O picked up the worst parts of a conversation.

No, Dad, I can't do it. I can't live like that. I'd rather die. Alex was, and always would be, a tall, gangly boy built like a crane, and he walked like one too. With ashy elbows and knuckles, he was too bony and bird-chested to even attempt the thought of lifting up large sheets of metal, let alone carrying beams from point A to point B. Not happening.

His dad let out a drawn-out sigh. "We have to keep this place standing."

Alex knew his father was proud of the ruins of living space they struggled to make their own. The yellowing paint, white once upon a time, flaked from the walls, and massive brown spots stained the living room ceiling. One corner of the bathroom had its own ecosystem of black slime that he refused to go anywhere near.

Home and family can thrive anywhere with anyone as long as the love and compassion are there. Alex could still hear his mom's voice echoing through the frustration of their living conditions. If this was thriving, what was living?

His father's forehead ruffled as he wiped his eyes. "Go get ready for school. I'll get started on breakfast. Sound good?"

"Sure thing, Dad." Alex hid his disappointment behind a fading smile. No matter what, he had to press on at all costs. Olivia and Dad deserved that.

He dragged himself into the unnatural graying space that was the bathroom. The faucet knobs squealed, and a few brown globs of rusty sludge slapped the porcelain. The pipes rattled overhead like they always did when the 8 P.M. Sentinel patrol came grumbling down the streets in their huge six-wheeled trucks.

The sink was stained a strange blue and dull yellow, and Alex refused to look into the black abyss that was the corner of the bathroom. After about fifteen minutes of the faucet spewing brown, the water cleared and was manageable to the touch. He slid his toothbrush beneath, sprinkled a pinch of baking soda on the bristles, then went to work on his teeth.

He looked up at the long and narrow brown face that looked back. The horror stories Jason and other high schoolers told them about New Hope Academy crept in. He leaned over the sink and closed his eyes.

"Never show fear, right, Mom?" he whispered to his reflection in the mirror.

The door swung open, sending paint chips raining over the bathroom floor. Olivia burst in like she owned the place. "Hope the warm water's not all gone."

She stood in the doorway, hands on her hips, yet half his size. Alex spat in the sink, wiped his mouth, and moved past her. The moment he was out of the doorway, she slammed the door closed.

"Alex, be careful with that door!" his father called from the kitchen.

Alex didn't bother to defend himself. Olivia's shrieks of terror the night before had taken the fight out of him. How could he complain? Yeah, she was a brat, but she was *his* brat of a baby sister.

The kitchen was a little bigger than the bedroom. A small round table that could only sit two at a time took up most of the space. At the center was the black cylinder speaker with a bright green circular light at the top.

The VEN-O always gave Alex chills.

The soft dialogue of the kitchen's twelve-inch television caught Alex's attention as a news reporter spoke stoically. "Another terrorist attack rocked the south side of Constance. The fifth this summer due to another assault on a Venus lab. The midnight attack, which claimed the lives of five lab technicians and two sentinels, was claimed by the terrorist group known as the Disciples of Revolution. They tagged the remnants of the building with letters spelling DOR" A camera focused on the red abbreviations, which looked to be applied with a heavy paint resembling blood.

"Damn it!" His dad slammed his fist on the table, rocking the VEN-O. The green light flickered, changing from green to red. Definitely recording. His father took a deep breath, urging patience and peace as he rubbed the ridges of his knuckles. "Those cold-hearted, ruthless scum!" He said it loud enough for the VEN-O to pick up. He grabbed a slice of bread and stuffed it into the dented toaster, then pulled his glasses away and rubbed his eyes like he had something in them.

That's what Dad did when he thought about the night Mom died.

More night raids. The thought turned Alex's stomach. It added fuel to his drive to get out of the Suites and become an Exclusive.

His dad's eyes narrowed, and his mouth twisted as he glared at the TV. "Alex, turn that mess off. I don't want Liv seeing it."

"Okay, Dad."

Olivia inched her way down the hall, wearing her favorite faded jeans, old dirty sneakers, and a black windbreaker. In the thick curls of her hair rested the diamond-encrusted hairclip that once belonged to their mother. Though the stones weren't real, Liv never went anywhere without it.

She nudged Alex with an elbow and took a seat across from him. His father loaded her plate with eggs and sausage, and she added two pieces of toast. Alex did the same, minus the crappy attitude.

Between the anxiety of his first day and Olivia's savage attitude, Alex found himself counting the grains of black pepper on his scrambled eggs.

"Daddy." Olivia looked up with sad puppy eyes. "Do I have to go to school? It's been a week of insanity so far."

A veil of ignorance caked over their father's glasses, and he smiled through and through. "Honey, you know you have to go to school. What would your mother say?"

Olivia pursed her lips and shifted their mom's hairclip a bit before taking a bite of the toast.

It was already eight. The bus would be here any minute. "Dad, time to go," Alex said, shoveling a spoonful of eggs into his mouth.

His father looked at the digital blue numbers on the VEN-O. "I guess you're right. Alex, you sure you're ready?"

"Ready as he'll ever be," Olivia groaned. "He had an extra week to get prepared, unlike me."

"Unlike you, I'm going to New Hope Academy."

She stuck her tongue out. If it wasn't for their dad being there, she would've done something worse. A lot worse. Alex rushed to the bedroom doing all he could to control his breathing and hide his damp palms. He grabbed his backpack. The one good strap made it easy to slip it over his shoulders, then he slipped on his old worn sneakers their mom bought him a few years back before she passed.

His toes were coming out a little bit, but they fit like a sock. He reached under his mattress and pulled out an old family picture that had his mom in the center. *Let's do this,* he thought and kissed the picture.

Minus a few bends at the corner, it was in near perfect condition. He caressed her face and slipped the picture into his back pocket.

He and Olivia raced down the creaky wooden staircase where the halls smelled of Pine-Sol and old liquor.

"You two have a wonderful day," their father called out. "I'll be home by seven, no later." Dad smiled as he stood in the doorway dressed in his gray grease-stained coveralls with holes in the knees. "And Alex, remember what I told you. Remember what we talked about, alright?"

"Sounds good, Pop. See ya."

His dad wouldn't get all depressed and serious around Olivia as they both did their best to shield the truth of this world from her. A pointless attempt, of course.

Olivia waved as they made it to the bottom steps. "Bye, Daddy!"

His father returned the gesture and disappeared over the banister. The snap of the door shutting trailed from behind as they both headed out the main entrance of the apartment and down the streets of Eastern Suites.

Most of the apartments lacked proper construction and remained in bad shape. Some were boarded up with parts of the roof missing, yet people still lived in them. The packed complexes were several stories high, lifeless and passionless like the people, and riddled with old battle scars. But it was home, at least for the time being.

The sour summer humidity punched you in the mouth, but it still wasn't enough to turn Alex's anxiety away. Old furniture cluttered the sidewalks, and mountains of leaky garbage bags columned every corner. The sparsely populated streets were never as bad as they were now.

"Yo, Alex. What's up?" A tall and slender brown-skinned boy ran up behind them.

"Deacon. What's up?" They fist-bumped.

Deacon nodded to Olivia. "Madame. How are you?"

"Morning, Deacon." She scowled.

Deacon threw his hands up in defense. "Just trying to be nice, I swear."

Deacon Young and his family didn't have much to hang a hat on, just like the rest of them. So when Deacon also got his acceptance letter, Alex celebrated with tears in his eyes, knowing he wouldn't go through the N.H.A. experience alone.

Deacon's voice lowered. "Bro, did you hear about the attack last night? That means more rai—"

Alex elbowed Deacon and nodded toward Olivia, who didn't appear to be paying any attention to the conversation, but Alex cautioned him just in case. Deacon got the gist. "Yeah. DOR Again. I don't understand how they keep getting away. It's crazy enough they can operate within the inner walls."

Deacon shrugged. "Honestly, I think it's all a plot to keep us in check. Those who live 'below the line,'" he said, wiggling two fingers into air quotes. "Think about it. A terrorist organization led by teens. It's nothing but a lie."

Alex hoped Deacon didn't go on one of his rants. Sometimes they were over the top. And though it didn't seem like it, Alex knew it bothered Olivia. "Deacon, no more conspiracy theories. Just let it go," Alex begged.

They paused for a bit, watching a fat greasy-haired rat struggle to drag a bag of garbage into the crevice of a basement wall. They gave the creature a few yards of space, walking around it to avoid pissing it off.

Deacon sucked his teeth. "Conspiracy theories? Think about it, Alex. I'm telling you, the government is hiding something big! I know it. The increase in raids, entire Bourgeoisie families vanishing, then the unrest in the outskirts with missing people too. Who do you think's responsible?"

"The United Nations of America?" Olivia asked with a tone of frustration. "More make-believe stories, Deacon. And here I thought I was the youngest of the group."

Alex sighed, knowing that Olivia had been listening the entire time. His eyes narrowed on Deacon. "Kids run away all the time, Deac!"

Deacon shrugged. "Kids? Yes. Entire families? No."

Kids from all age groups swarmed the bus stop. Olivia mixed in with her crowd, which were a few kids from middle school. Deacon and Alex muddled into their own group as best they could.

"Check out the future wealthy class bootlickers," Tanner Gillespie sneered. "I bet you boys feel on top of the world right now. Like you'll be celebrating in Constance in four years. Don't get too excited. You'll be back with us in no time. Trust me."

Deacon wafted his hands in front of his nose. "Shut up, Tanner, and stop washing your mouth out with apple vinegar. Sheesh. Your mouth is running, but where are you going?"

The occupants of the bus stop erupted in laughter, and the corner of Tanner's mouth pulled, allowing a yellow tooth to show. Nobody reacted to Tanner's words. Truth was that every student at that bus stop—minus one—would've killed at the chance to be accepted into New Hope Academy. Even that tall toothpick of a boy, Tanner.

The laughter faded, ushering in a flood of whispers. The crowd of students parted unnaturally as that minus one, Nelson Tanaka, walked through with his head down.

"And what do you know," Tanner started, getting worked up again. "The boy whose brother might have gotten death warrants signed for all of us... Nelson, any word from Jason?"

The boy hovered over Nelson, making him look smaller than he already was. Nelson was silent. He shivered a bit but kept his head down with a blank gaze that rolled to Alex's feet.

Deacon stepped forward, and Alex saw his long dark fingers squeeze into a fist. It was Deacon's tell. He was going to throw a mean righty that would lift Tanner off his feet.

Alex grabbed his shoulder and yanked Deacon back. "You know we can't get involved, Deacon," he whispered.

Deacon lowered his gaze, dropping his shoulders. "Yeah, yeah."

An engine roared in the distance, breaking the tension as a bus came bouncing and screeching down the potholed littered street. It wasn't the old pale school bus Alex was used to. The large metropolitan bus hissed as its engine eased down.

A hush came over the bus stop, and the crowd broke apart, allowing Alex, Deacon, and Nelson to board. With a smooth clank of metal and plastic, the doors folded to the side.

Fumes of exhaust flushed from beneath with a muggy warmth forcing Alex to hold his breath, but once on, fresh air broke over their shoulders. The pristine leather seats filled with other Bourgeoisie students each had its designation: EASTERN, WESTERN, NORTHERN, and SOUTHERN, representing the four Suites that surrounded Constance.

Alex led the three of them onto the bus. The rows were filled with a mishmash of different kids. By herself on a row titled NORTHERN was a Black girl with long brown hair falling over her shoulders. Her black eyeliner and black lipstick were beyond outlandish in the Suites. She stared blankly out the window.

"What the hell is your problem?" Her eyes didn't move from the window, but Alex knew without a doubt that she was talking to him. "Read the signs. This is Northern. As far as I'm aware, you didn't get on the bus with me, so push on."

"Sorry. Sorry." Heat washed over Alex's face as he stumbled toward the empty rows which read EASTERN. While the other Suites had a few rows filled with students, the ones for Eastern could only fit four at the most.

The musty smell of "hard work," as his dad so elegantly put it, filled the bus and was leagues better than the torturous reek of garbage that amassed on every corner and sidewalk of Eastern. Alex plopped into a row just behind a boy who sat in the Western section. He eased closer to the window, and Deacon slid in next to him.

Alex turned to stare out the window and saw Olivia looking up at him from the bus stop. He stood and snapped the window down. "Have a good day at school, alright?"

Her mouth moved to the side. "Just hurry up and come home. I'll be waiting right here, okay?"

Alex gave her a confident smile. "Bet."

"Close that damn window," the bus driver yelled from the front of the bus. The row of students in front of Alex turned with an expression of utter disgrace.

He fumbled to get the window back up as he sat calmly in his seat.

"Starting the first day off right," Deacon whispered.

"Shut up."

From the window of the bus, the impoverished design of the Suites shifted as they drove through the different complexes. The walls grew taller and were more fortified the closer they got to Constance until he couldn't see Venus Tower overhead anymore.

Deacon nudged him and nodded over to Nelson, who sat by himself. "Dude, we should go talk to him," Deacon whispered.

"You can't be serious," Alex whispered, hoping no one heard. "If anyone saw us talking to Nelson, it would be over for us. We could be in the same boat as the Tanakas and labeled conspirators. I can't risk my life and family, Deacon."

Alex couldn't help but feel regret when he looked on at Nelson all alone, forehead pressed against the window. They had been friends for years, even before the death of his mother. In fact, after what happened, the Tanakas nearly adopted Alex. But in the Suites, blood was always thicker than water, and his priorities were always his sister and his dad.

"I know, I know. But it's Nelson. We've known him for years. We used to sleep over at his house. His parents made us lunch and dinner.... The three of us are like brothers."

Alex focused out the window. "*Were* like brothers."

"It's not right, man."

Thoughts of the raid that killed his mother overshadowed any warm memories Alex had with Nelson and his family. He wasn't risking Olivia and his dad's life on anyone. "Jason made a stupid choice. He did that to his family, not us. I feel bad for Nelson, I do, but there's nothing we can do for him."

Deacon lowered his gaze.

"Alright, you gutter rats," the bus driver barked from the front. "When we get to the wall, everyone stays in their seats, no sudden movements. If you do anything stupid, we could all get turned into ground buffalo. It only takes three minutes to scan my code, so shut up and sit still. Got it?"

"Yes," Every student replied robotically.

The bus came to a slow halt at the massive concrete gate, and the engine died. Large machine guns arched down at the bus, slowly focusing upon them.

There was a stillness in the air. But like they all agreed, nobody moved. Alex's fingers shivered on his lap. He hated guns, and these were the biggest guns he had seen so up close and personal. Deacon shook in his seat, sweat rolling down his face as his fingers clawed at his thighs. He looked a wreck, and Alex was sure he didn't look any different.

Alex squeezed his wrist till the skin became dry and ashy. "We got this. Four years," he whispered, face forward like everyone else's.

Deacon's Adam's apple bounced in his throat. "Four years, brother. Four years."

Alex remembered how excited he used to get watching the rising of the gate. Things were different when you got to the inner walls that separated the Suites from Constance. As he got older, the realization and meaning of segregation kicked in.

The silent calm of the other students shined a light on an unspoken rule unknown to him and Deacon, and their blank faces remained facing the front. Alex shivered as the rumors gnawed at his insides. His mouth was so damn dry all he could do was suck in his cheeks and bite down hard.

The engine rumbled again. A thick buzzing blared overhead, and the wall separated. The machine guns slowly rose in a robotic manner and panned left to right just like how he'd imagined.

Calm down, Alex. He snatched his wrist again, and his hand instinctively gripped the seat's edge.

They drove through the wall, entering a tunnel where small slivers of light at the top painted a picture of wires, pipes and a well-tarred street. At the front of the bus, a wide horizontal line of beaming light cut through the darkness and slowly grew into a semicircle.

The bus was quickly consumed by the brightness of Constance. What first caught Alex's attention was how smooth the road was, like driving on air. The skyscraper that was Venus headquarters was close enough that the sun gave it a golden sheen as it reached for the sky. The apartment buildings surrounding them were artistically sculpted and layered with floors that had plants hanging and growing from porches. People stood outside conversing, dining on patios, and living their best lives.

"Deacon, is this real?" Alex whispered. He hadn't noticed Deacon hovering over him in awe.

Soon, the apartments turned into parks as thick patches of trees and fields of grass and bushes erupted over the spaces of land as they continued on. The terrain evolved before Alex's eyes from flat grassy swards to gentle slopes and shady steep to rocky ravines. It was impossible to imagine, but there wasn't a single sentinel in sight patrolling the streets.

Tears welled in Alex's eyes.

It was the first time he'd seen his dream so close that he could smell the fresh-cut grass, taste the well-cooked meals and bakeries, and reach out and touch a member of the Exclusive class.

2

The bus swerved on a well-maintained road surrounded by grassy hills on each side. The only evidence of the city was a canvas of surrounding buildings and structures in the distance.

"Yo, this is wild, bro."

Alex wiped his eyes. "You ever see anything like it?"

"Not even close."

A boy in the seat in front of them spoke with a raspy tone, "You Eastern Suite boys need to shut up and sit down. Hate to break it to you, but you're not the most popular bunch in the Bourgeoisie clique."

Deacon arched over the seat, his fingers wrinkling the leather. "What the hell does that mean?"

The kid was dark-skinned, darker than he and Deacon, with tight curls more maintained than Alex's nappy head of hair. "Eastern Suite kids are always starting trouble. But when that Jason kid was caught with DOR bombing that Venus lab back in July, every kid on this bus almost lost everything. So yeah, your whole region is nothing but garbage. That's why you guys *smell* like garbage."

Deacon went to lunge at the kid, but Alex yanked him down. "Relax. We can't afford to mess this up for our families. Besides, we'd just be proving his point."

"Too late for that," the kid said crossly. "Just shut up and keep your head down like everyone else."

"Like mindless drones," Deacon mumbled.

They came through a large black metal gate. Unlike going through the wall, this stop was a lot more relaxed and less life-threatening unless machine guns popped out of the surrounding shrubs.

On the right side of the lawn was a small shed where three brawny men in blue and black uniforms stepped out and walked up to the bus. Two of them held black panels and went on to surround the bus.

Alex watched the one who made his way to his side. The man pressed on the panel, and it shifted into a long pole with a mirror at the end. He then swayed it carefully beneath the underbelly of the bus. He looked up at Alex with the face of a feral bulldog mad with rabies. There was no doubt he absolutely hated his job.

Alex pulled away from the window and kept his eyes forward like everybody else.

"What? What happened?" Deacon asked.

Alex pointed forward with a shaky finger. "Just look forward."

A bone-chilling squeak came from the bus as the doors pealed open. As if they were on a boat, the bus swayed as the loud clonking of boots moved in sync with the swaying; the poor suspensions raked painfully below.

Beneath a silver receding hairline, a man looked down the aisle of the bus. His facial expression reminded Alex of Olivia's whenever she didn't get enough sleep because of her night terrors. Unfortunately, a home-cooked breakfast with chicken gizzards and eggs wasn't going to fix this guy's face. This was him all the way through, a face radiating with ugliness like he'd stepped in a pile of dog crap and the smell permanently wafted beneath his nose.

The man scratched his bald spot, took a deep breath, then began calling out names from his massive gut. "Deacon Young, Alexander Quake, and uh, Nelson Ta–Ta—"

"Tanaka. His name is Nelson Tanaka," Deacon said, his shoulders back and his knees knocking into Alex's.

Every head snapped to the both of them.

Alex prayed Deacon would shut up and not say anything else the rest of the day. But he had to admit, there was something annoying about hearing this goblin of a man butcher Nelson's last name.

He gripped his clipboard tight and chuckled. "You Nelson Tanaka?"

"No, sir. I'm Deacon."

"Then don't answer!"

Everyone on the bus snapped forward. A chill crept down Alex's spine, and every muscle tightened. His bladder had strict orders to not give way at that moment.

"Unless I'm talking to you. Got that smart ass?" The man's fiery-red face grimaced. "You Bourgeoisie punks don't even deserve to breathe the same air as the Exclusives. You're lucky they're showing mercy to allow you to be educated with the future leaders of The United Nations of America."

Alex swallowed hard. His insides rattled from the man's voice. His cheeks didn't rise, and his lips didn't slant or pull in either direction. Although there was a slight tug of anger, there wasn't a snowball's chance in hell he'd act on it. Alex couldn't do anything, and if he did, his life would be over.

"So, the one next to the big mouth, your name's Alexander Quake, right?"

Alex exhaled as a terrible feeling that he'd somehow gained the attention of the wrong person filled his gut. "Y– yes, sir."

A barrel-chested laugh escaped him. "Well, my name is Officer Biggs. I'm the head of security for New Hope. I have a feeling you three and I are going to be the best of friends."

Alex's chin pressed against his chest. *Damn it, Deacon.*

"And Nelson Tanaka." Biggs hacked a laugh worse than the one Alex got.

Alex's stomach turned in knots. That laugh was nothing like the degrading lashing Biggs just gave Deacon. It was a laugh you gave to someone you hated as they crawled down death row on their hands and knees.

Biggs looked down at Nelson and tilted his head. "Boy, your brother didn't leave a good impression on anyone here. He had the audacity to join DOR" Biggs sighed and shrugged, then nodded softly. "People are gonna take that frustration out on you, and I have this feeling I'm not gonna see or do a damn thing about it."

Alex watched Nelson's eyes lower to the ground. His lips twitched slightly, and the sun gave away the tears that welled in his eyes. Biggs laughed and kept talking, but all Alex could do was focus on Nelson.

For a moment, their eyes met, and memories overtook him. Nights where they played hide- and-seek late into the evenings, the birthday parties, sleepovers where they stayed over at each other's houses, and of course, the scrapyard, their home away from home.

Life had changed so much for the three of them, Nelson more than anyone. Their lives would never be the same, their friendship over.

Nelson cleared his throat, rearranging his face into something more confident. "Yes, sir, I imagine so. For my family's sake, I'll take whatever punishment owed to my brother," Nelson said, keeping his voice steady.

"Oh, you will," Biggs snorted and grumbled. He turned to the large men outside. "Are we clear?" There was a slight pause before Biggs whipped his fat neck around, then slapped the shoulder of the bus driver. "Alright. Let's go!"

The doors squealed shut as the bus moved through the large black gates with a motorized groan.

A bad taste filled Alex's mouth. Every word his dad said to him earlier this morning crept in and dug into him like nails. *Four years of this. Just four years,* he thought, taking a deep breath. His heart pounded like crazy.

When they pulled up to the large building that had *New Hope Academy* written on the front, Alex's anxiety kicked into overdrive.

Kids their age in pressed, tapered uniforms jumped out of privately owned luxury cars and trucks. Nobody in the Suites owned a private car—it didn't fit within the rights of UNA's constitution. Something about the atmosphere and that vehicles were limited due to the fumes and exhaust thrown into the air. That's what they were taught in middle school anyway.

The bus moved to the front of the school and came to a hissing stop. Biggs clapped his hands. "On your feet, off the bus, and line up accordingly by Suite!"

As commanded, everyone jumped up and fell in line. Most of the students on the bus communicated with each other except the three of them. Alex, Deacon and Nelson slumped away, disappearing to the far back of the line as everyone drifted out the door.

Outside, Biggs led the group over a green, hilly field and down a concrete path where a few prestigious-looking students watched eagerly as the line came down. Up ahead, two more beefy men grumbled and laughed, but Alex couldn't hear a thing over his racing heart. He turned to look at one of the officers, a large dark-skinned man whose scalp shone in the sunlight.

"Eyes forward," the man barked.

Alex's gaze snapped to the head of the boy in front of him but drifted slightly to the campus. It was more beautiful than anything he ever imagined it to be. Like a lavish countryside dotted with trees, statues of the elite and successful, and of course, a statue of Cullen D. Roberts, the first secretary general of the United Nations of America, a title passed on to his granddaughter Dalia C. Roberts.

Teens swarmed the campus, turning it into a small community of young elitists whose varying gazes of disgust, frustration, and defensive pride made it easy to pick out the true attendees the school had been built for.

Exclusives wore navy-blue blazers, their golden buttons glinting like scrubbed gold. Accompanying the blazer, the males wore red ties and gray slacks, and the females gray checkered dresses, red stockings, and a red crossover tie.

"More pack rats, Biggs?" a light brown boy with curly hair who looked Hispanic called out. There were a few other kids around him of varying shapes and races who looked far from impressed.

"You know it, Manwell. Give them that New Hope welcome you kids are so used to giving," Biggs said, laughing from the front as they marched past. "We also got a special treat for you boys and gals too."

Biggs stopped and called Nelson forward. "This is our dear friend, Jason Tanaka's little brother. Nelson, right?"

Nelson nodded, but he didn't shy away from the shrewd threatening stares he got. He kept his face forward, chin up. Alex had never seen him this way before. Was he nuts? These kids, these people, probably wanted him dead. Why show courage now?

There was an awful stillness in the air. Even the students with their creased pants and uniforms were quiet.

"The asshole that joined up with terrorists?" one kid asked.

"Bingo." A greedy grin stretched across Biggs's face.

"Yeah ... we'll take care of him. A nice New Hope welcome. In honor of your brother, Nelson." Manwell stepped forward, mussed Nelson's hair, and smacked him on the cheek. "We all will."

Biggs called Nelson back in line, and they began to move forward as the pack of wolves in uniform laughed and spat at their feet. Alex wondered how long he could keep up the facade of calm.

He stared at the ground while the judgmental eyes stabbed him like blades as he drowned in the whispers of the ones who hated them. This was what his dad had been talking about. This was why so many Bourgeoisie students dropped out after their first year.

They came over another slight hill, and at the bottom, everyone grouped together, except for Nelson, who was left a few feet away. Everyone avoided him like the plague.

"Alright, Garbage Pail Kids, horseshoe around me, ASAP," Biggs bellowed.

The other two officers lined him, Deacon, and Nelson up front, facing the group.

"Help me welcome the new runts to the litter," Biggs grunted. He stepped behind Nelson and shoved him hard enough to send Nelson's pale, thin frame out of line and to the ground. "And dare I say it, one even lower than the rest of you, Nelson Tanaka."

The entire group whispered, and the torturous atmosphere they walked through a few yards back returned. There was fear in their voices. It was evident in the eyes of every student. Alex looked away from Nelson and hoped Deacon didn't do anything stupid.

A kid with orange-red hair and a pale face covered in freckles stepped out of the horseshoe formation and over to Nelson. He was so tall that he towered over the rest of them. Alex had only caught a quick glimpse of the boy when they climbed onto the bus as he had sat at the front.

The boy nodded to Alex, then to Deacon, and shook their hands before turning and smiling at Biggs and the other two officers. "We'll take it from here, gentlemen. Please, don't worry yourselves with Bourgeoisie junk."

Biggs sneered and nodded. "Sabastian, you're one of the few degenerates I can stand." He looked down at Nelson with a greedy smile and bumped Alex out of the way. "They're in your hands now."

The group went silent, but once the three officers crested the hill, they swarmed the two of them. Sabastian moved the group away from Nelson even further and pulled Alex and Deacon in as they all surrounded them.

"You Eastern Suite boys need to learn to keep it down," a pale girl with a round face and long tangled brunette hair said shrewdly.

Alex looked at Deacon, confused by the girl's statement. "I don't understand?"

"Between you and that damn window thing the moment you got on the bus, sticking up for *that* kid…" She thumped over her shoulder into Nelson. "You need to learn to stay low. We're not in the outer walls anymore; we're in Constance. It's not the same here. Those kids up there on that campus are different from us."

"Obviously. So what's the point of having us all together then?" Alex asked. "Isn't the whole point of social integration to help fight against division and the influence of terrorism?"

The girl who sat in the northern row and embarrassed him on the bus spoke from the back. "It's called the concept of assimilation." She flipped her hoody over her head, concealing her hair and face. She wore faded blue jeans that covered worn black sneakers, and Alex couldn't stop staring. Her eyes were a coffee brown, light enough to be different from his own, and shaped like almonds.

"W–what's that supposed to mean?"

"Never mind." She broke through the group and made her way over to a large tree.

Sebastian came over and smacked Alex on the shoulder. "And that's Yara. Don't mind her; she's a little on the edgy side. Smart as a whip, but beyond bitter. She's from the Northern Suites like me."

Alex watched as the girl leaned against the tree and looked up to the sky. When she looked back, he immediately turned away and focused on the group.

Everyone introduced themselves. Alex still wasn't sure if it was all a joke, considering how he and Deacon made fools of themselves on the bus. Alex greeted everyone as best he could, trying to remember the names getting thrown at him, along with the volley of questions.

"Can't believe you guys are from Eastern," said a short brown-skinned boy with dirt smeared across his cheeks.

"Sounds like we're not the most popular?" Alex commented.

"No, you're not. You guys are the worst," said the boy who sat in front of them on the bus.

"Guys, how about we ease the tension a bit, aye?" Sebastian wrapped his arms around Alex and Deacon. "Sebastian Milton, class leader, class president, at your service."

Another girl with black tangled hair that fell over her high cheekbones and had beautiful brown monolid eyes bumped Sebastian out of the way. "And I'm Jessica Shào, the *next* class president and the *next* class leader," she said with an eager sassiness.

Alex nodded and gave the best jovial expression he could. "Nice to meet you, and uh, everyone."

At Eastern Suites Middle School, it wasn't as strict, wasn't as beautiful, and didn't smell half as good. But the pros and cons still weighed in his head. At the end of the day, it was four years.

As they all spoke, Alex focused on Nelson, noticing how far the group had pushed him out of the circle, or rather brought the circle out from around him. He wanted to ask Nelson if he was okay. But even that could lead to being targeted.

Sebastian must have caught his gaze. His long pale arm wrapped around Alex's shoulders as they stepped a few feet out of the crowd. "You're obviously a smart kid, Alex. You wouldn't be here if you weren't going to be of some value to the Exclusive society. But you have to know … *he's* off-limits."

"I know." Glass bottles shattered in the dark crevice of his mind as another wave of memories surged. Back then, they stayed out late busting glass bottles, knocking on doors and running, and then playing Stick Ball with some of the other kids, Jason included. *How did things get so bad?* "I've known him almost all my life. He's like a brother."

"Not a blood brother, right?"

"Well, no, but—"

Sebastian took a deep breath. "When a kid gets accepted into New Hope Academy from the Suites, the game changes for them and their family. Sometimes that family is hated and envied. They'll be seen as traitors or worse. Then other times they're respected, the community congeals around them to help that person and their family succeed." He looked over his shoulder at Nelson. "His situation is like scenario one on steroids. And I'm pretty sure after what his brother did … I don't think anyone at New Hope is letting him drop out without suffering something big."

Alex tightened his fists.

Sebastian slapped his shoulder again. "C'mon, then. Follow me."

They flowed through the group of students toward Nelson. Alex's stomach turned and a shiver ran down his spine.

"You're Jason's brother, yeah?" Sebastian whispered.

Nelson looked over at Alex, then back at Sebastian with a nod.

Sebastian's expression became one of pain. His eyes sunk low, and even his posture of strength and confidence fell to one of mourning. "I was good friends with Jay. But when everything went down with him joining D.O.R, every single one of us had to abandon any knowledge of him. In our heads, we killed him. Buried him deep."

Jessica stomped over. "Sebastian, have you lost your mind? We can't be seen with him!" Her strong persona began to crumble, and a tear fell from her eyes. Then she turned to Nelson. "We can't have anything to do with you. It'll put us all in jeopardy and can put us and our families in danger."

Sebastian added. "Nelson, we're sorry. *I'm* really sorry. But you have to go. Anywhere but here. Do you understand?"

Deacon stepped forward. "No, man, that's not fair! Nelson is one of us, right, Alex?"

Sebastian grabbed Deacon by the collar and lifted him until he was on his tippy toes. "Listen, Deacon. Do you love your family?"

The atmosphere sent chills through Alex. It was now harsh and cold. Blood pumped heavily in his throat as he watched the horror on Deacon's face. He couldn't move. The look in Deacon's eyes made his heart race.

Deacon nodded, his eyes frantically scanning left to right. Alex's fingers trembled at his sides as he tried to grip what was going on.

"You love your mom, your father?"

Deacon nodded. "Yeah, man. I do, alright."

"Then trust me. Trust all of us when we tell you to stay away from Nelson. Do you understand?"

Deacon nodded, wiping a few tears away.

Sebastian's firm gaze fell on Alex. "Do *you* understand?"

Alex nodded like a broken bobblehead.

"Nelson ... Please ... go," Jessica choked.

Nelson nodded, not a word leaving his chapped lips. He turned and headed over the hill.

Alex couldn't help but hate himself for letting him go. Nelson, a kid he had been friends with since they were toddlers. Their moms took turns babysitting one another's kids. Nelson was right by his side with Deacon at his mom's funeral. In his darkest moment, Nelson was right there ... and now Alex was afraid to even look at him. Afraid to even be seen with him.

Sebastian pulled Alex with him, and Jessica grabbed Deacon as they were yanked back into the group. Alex watched Nelson vanish over the hill toward the schoolyard. The same schoolyard where Manwell and the other clean-dressed, well-nourished sons and daughters of the Exclusives waited.

"Listen, you two." Sebastian folded his arms, looking down at Alex and Deacon. The group surrounded them. "You already know what life is going to be like here. Don't make it any worse than it needs to be. New Hope can change you and your family's lives forever. Kids die trying to get accepted into this place because they know it'll lead to greener pastures. Jason almost ruined it for us. For everyone. The kid went ballistic."

Jessica shook her head and continued to wipe the tears from her eyes. In Alex's opinion, she was a little overdramatic.

For someone trying to be class leader, he expected she would hold herself together better.

"Joining D.O.R is a death sentence," a girl from the group said.

"Jay's lucky they didn't kill his entire family," said another.

Sebastian calmed the group. "Bourgeoisies stick together. If you don't screw us over, we won't shun you. Got it?" He threw out his fist.

Alex bumped it, and so did Deacon.

A symphonic chime echoed through the campus and even more so in Alex's chest. All the kids began to make their way up the slope. Alex followed behind Deacon, weighed down by a deep sense of cowardice.

He fought it with the images of his mother dying in the kitchen in his arms. It worked. It killed the cowardice. Killed the second-guessing of putting his baby sister and his dad in harm's way.

Sebastian waved them over. "Follow me. I'll get you guys to orientation. But fair warning, don't say anything to the teachers. Keep your eyes down the entire time and nod yes or no to every answer. Got it?"

"Got it." Alex's stomach fluttered. Who the hell was he kidding? Sweat ran down his chest and neck, and the day hadn't started yet. Who knew what other crappy situations awaited them as they entered the massive castle-like structure?

Inside, black and white marble tiles covered the floor, and the walls were smooth, glistening with finished redwood. Sunlight spilled through colorful flamboyant windowpanes, each detailed with art and breathtaking images, and every archway had an engraving. Alex's eyes narrowed, scrutinizing every word.

"Latin," Sebastian answered. "A dead language. A dead, dead, dead language with all things considering history."

"Sebastian, what's up?" a kid in uniform asked. A few other kids in uniform nodded and fist-bumped him.

Alex was slack-jawed, as he studied every interaction Sebastian had with the Exclusive kids.

"I know, crazy, right? You put in enough work, and you gain their trust. Life in N.H.A. isn't all that bad."

Thinking back to what happened in the schoolyard, Alex could see that Sebastian had pull with the security guards too. It didn't sit right with Alex.

They rounded a corner into a massive hall. Giant chandeliers hung from the ceiling, glistening like diamonds from the reflected light. Alex's reflection gleamed back from the slick, tiled floor.

He turned to Deacon and caught him eyeing a few girls in gray skirts. He obviously wasn't pissed anymore. "Bro, this place isn't so bad," Deacon whispered.

Alex didn't crack a smile like Deacon, though. Instead, holding on to his father's skepticism. Alex kept his mouth shut and his eyes away from anyone he walked by, refusing to let his emotions spill out of him.

"Well, here we are," Sebastian said, throwing his hands out as if to present some incredible creation.

They came to two large golden-brown doors, the knobs a rustic copper color. By the silence residing from the other side, Alex could feel the tension oozing from beneath the cracks.

"And where is *here*?" Alex asked.

Sebastian snickered. "Well, Memorial Hall, of course. The hall where kids like us have orientation."

"Cool, cool. Thanks." Deacon didn't look Sebastian in the eyes at all. "Appreciate the help."

"No worries. We're in this together, right." He turned to Alex, holding his hand out.

Alex gave him a nod but didn't raise his hand an inch. "Yeah, thanks for the support."

Sebastian gave that odd snicker again. "Alright then. Well, I'll be seeing you guys around. Good luck. And remember, don't say anything to the teachers. Eyes down, just nod yes or no."

Alex's eyes remained glued to the large doors. Chills raced over his shoulders, rippling down his arms. *One. Two. Three* … he counted in his head, taking in a breath.

"You ready?" he asked Deacon.

"No. But does it matter?"

Alex wrapped his fingers around the cold knob. It turned with a few clicks. For a moment, he heard his mother's voice, calm and loving, cheering him on. "*You got this. You know you can do this. I believe in you. Always have, always will.*"

The doors creaked with a deep whine as he turned the knob. Lights from above showered over him and Deacon. He threw his hands up to shield his eyes from the light.

Red felt carpeting stretched down to the platform where rows of chairs crafted from wood paneling lined both sides.

Fitted with leather cushions, the chairs slanted down to the center stage. The auditorium could easily fit a hundred people. As the light dimmed from above, a dome-shaped ceiling took life, and he looked up to see white with golden engravings and symbols of an ancient language were etched into it.

Whispers echoed from the first row which was filled with a mixture of people dressed as though they were about to visit Dalia Roberts herself. Three seats rested on the center stage. Nelson sat on the last chair on the end, closest to the staircase.

Alex took a deep breath, barely letting it out, and walked down the smooth carpet. A clean-shaven man with short cropped hair and a big smile ushered them down. Nobody else smiled in the front row, just him.

"Morning, gentlemen. Please take your seats," he said joyfully.

They did as he asked. Alex sat in the middle chair, making sure he didn't shift too much. He folded his hands on his lap, straightened his back, then kept his eyes on the ground.

A bright light cast over the three of them in a blinding flash. It dimmed just enough for Alex to see the people in front prep their notepads and pens. Their eyes were harsh with scrutiny.

An elderly gentleman rose to his feet. His voice sounded old and cranky as he said, "Welcome, gentlemen, to orientation. You will be asked a series of detailed questions by our panel in hopes of guiding you on the right path here at New Hope Academy. Unlike years past, we will be doing things differently. I'm sure you've noticed already that we have only selected three students to enter New Hope Academy this year, and all three students are citizens from Eastern Suites. This is due …" He cleared his throat, peering over at Nelson, and Nelson shivered. "This is due in part to our situation with a previous student. Are there any questions?"

Alex shook his head and, from the corner of his eye, saw Deacon and Nelson do the same.

"Well then, let orientation begin."

3

Fat globs of sweat rolled down Douglas Quake's forehead from behind his goggles. The glow from the soupy orange stuff lit up the dark space around him like the rising of a new sun. He hammered down on the cast, again, again, and again.

Another flash of Myra.

Bang!

A flash of their wedding day.

Bang!

Finding his wife in a pool of her own blood. He paused. The hammer slipped from his fingers.

A horn bellowed above. Right on time. He turned away from the glowing heap, which started to fade into a deep cherry. Another sheet of steel ready to be inspected then shipped to be added to the wall that separated the Suites from the outskirts.

Thank goodness for that. Bad enough, there were terrorists living within the walls. Hell of a lot worse if they let those disheveled ingrates known as the Pariahs over the walls too.

He shoved his work gloves and goggles into a raggedy locker, then hastened down the tight tunnelways of the mill, lunch bucket in one hand, sweat towel in the other. He slipped into a river of men and women whose faces were as filthy as his, if not worse. He loved every bit of it.

"Doug." Sidney O'Connor tilted his hardhat.

"Sid." He returned the gesture. "How's old Rita treating you?"

Sid winced at the opening above that showed the tall yellow crane that hung overhead like some overbearing mother. "She treatin' me good, ole fox, treatin' me good. How's life in the casting?"

"Not bad. Not bad at all."

They came to a line of people getting scanned through the cafeteria. Two men in black suits and faceless helmets stood like statues with rifles at the ready. Doug and Sidney both rolled up their sleeves, revealed their charagmas on their right hands, and passed through with a sweet jingle. Just a few cents taken out of their pay to enjoy the cool cafeteria and free water.

Doug unrolled his sleeve as the scanner read with a joyful gleam. The chime echoed like a lullaby compared to the latter. "More attacks. News said anyway."

Sidney snickered with a bounce of his head. Doug knew he wasn't too impressed. They set up shop on the same old bench they'd sat at for the last twenty years. It was a known thing that this was sacred space, and it belonged to them. Belonged to many others, too, at one point or another. They'd drink to them later.

Doug whipped out his chicken gizzard soup, rice, and a stale piece of bread. Sid had something of the same. It was more vegetable base than meat. Every conversation around them was low, subtle. Gazes jumped every so often on the black speaker that hung by the entrance. A VEN-O.

Sid cleared his throat. "Word on the street is another tax increase gonna be hitting us soon."

Doug tore into the bread that had a light crunch to it. His eyes rolled to the green glow of the Venus Oracle before falling down to his gizzard soup.

Sydney went on. "Heard it's gonna hit Eastern pretty good."

No surprise. Eastern Suites had lost everything from garbage disposal, water supply support, and food delivery to the local shops. Their punishment included an increase in raids and constant patrols. "Yeah, what else is new." Doug held his tongue from saying anything further, fighting back the curse and bitterness that wanted to spill forward.

The soulful chimes of those entering through the scanner continued. Doug's eyes rolled to the VEN-O again as a few others nodded in his direction. He obliged.

Sidney took one more spoonful of soup and paused. He went sickening pale. Fear, of course, Doug had seen many men turn that color when it came to money problems. He turned a few shades lighter himself after Myra ... "How many credits you away from not making it?" The words were barely words at all, more of a deep exhale.

"A hundred credits. Ninety if I can get Melody down to making two meals a day for me and the boys."

Doug hated to hear that kind of tone leave a good man. A family man. Sidney would pull the shirt off his back for anyone there. He helped Doug bury his wife when he could barely put food on the table.

"How much you need, Sid?"

Another songful chime cleared the air over the cafeteria. A few knocked back clear bottles of water. That would be the cleanest water some of them would drink for a long time.

Sidney shook his head. "I can't ask you to do that, Doug."

"Sid, how much?"

He was silent for several moments. "I appreciate it, brother, trust me. If this meal suggestion doesn't work, I might have to call ya on that offer, though. You got kids of your own you need to worry about."

"Ain't that the truth." Douglas dipped the crusty slice into the soup, softening it a bit. It didn't make it taste any better.

"That boy of yours is something else. He started New Hope today, right?"

Doug could only answer with a deep sigh of dissatisfaction.

Thoughts of his kids crept in. Hard to believe Alex's first day at New Hope was today. Doug loathed it more than anything. Truth was that this bull crap of an integration program was just a ploy to douse Bourgeoisies from joining Anarchy and keep the teens away from DOR Everyone knew it. Nobody said it.

He looked down the stretch of the table. Not too long ago, it had been filled with a dozen men and women, all people Doug considered family. All gone now. Taken away in the black of night, not even a note left. Zip-tied and gagged, he imagined. The children squealing in the dead of night, husbands and wives croaking with sorrow. Were they terrorists or sympathizers? He wouldn't know. Myra was neither, yet she was no longer there to raise her kids and see their successes.

His eyes zeroed in on the men in black uniforms, suited up like robots. Armor, helmets, guns, all completely uncalled for. Everyone at the cafeteria or those trying to get in were laborers, nothing more … nothing less.

Another soulful chime.

"That integration program is something else. It'll do wonderful things for our community," Doug said, lying through his teeth.

"More than you know. In time, there won't even be a Bourgeoisie class." That sly snicker came back. They both laughed, but the cackles died quick. "Speaking of that integration program," Sid's voice lowered as he inched over the table, "I heard they got Nelson still moving forward."

Doug nodded. "A damn shame. They're gonna tear that boy apart, no doubt. Make an example out of him."

One of Sid's brows arched. "Yui and Akira lost their jobs last week. Can't get no worse than that."

Akira and Yui Tanaka, the parents of the boy who lost his mind and joined DOR Doug treated Jason Tanaka like his own son, then he went and turned his back on everything and everybody. "The outskirts is a lot worse than that, Sidney. The worst of the worst live out there." Doug's eyes rolled to the outer wall that separated them from the wildness and the chaos that roamed about.

"It won't be long. They have a month at the most. You know nobody gonna hire them. Government has washed their hands of 'em, banned."

"Akira's a good man. He can bounce back from this, but . . ." Doug knew the Tanakas wouldn't come back from this. He rolled the thought of finding a way to share some of his credits with them. But the thought was quickly squashed by how he would be seen. He'd already lost his wife, and even though she was innocent, people still had their theories on whether or not he and Myra had something to do with Anarchy.

The Tanakas supported him and his children all the way through. But this was different. Their son joined a terrorist group. Jason had blood on his hands and a target on his back. The kid left his family hanging out to dry.

No way in hell his kids would do something like that. Alex was too laid-back. His kid hated violence and would never hurt a fly. After Myra, Alex had become a little distant. He didn't smile much, but what kid would after holding their dying mother with all that blood? And Olivia? Yeah, she was a spitfire and had her thoughts toward UNA, but she was slowly getting over everything.

A loud blare shot ice down Doug's spine. His eyes shot to the gate. A woman stepped back with a frantic fearful gaze.

"I–I'm only short by a few cents. I can make it up. Just take it out of my next pay?"

The sentinels snatched her from both shoulders. "Exit the premises, now."

"Please. I can work extra hours to make up the difference. Just let me get some water … please!" They buried the barrel into the woman's gut.

A metallic click shot fire into Doug's belly. He hadn't realized he was out of his seat and around the bench until the icy clasp of Sid's fingers dug into him. He looked down and met Sid's eyes.

"Calm down, brother. Alex and Olivia need you now more than ever, right?"

Douglas looked up at the woman getting a second barrel dug into her chest. She turned and left, crying hysterically. All for water, all for a cool place to relax before going back to work. She must have owed money, too much money.

He thought about the conversation this morning with Alex. At times like these, he really hoped Alex would make it through New Hope Academy, change the lives of him and his sister, and not settle for a life like this.

A life where *they* had their thumbs on your neck every day. Yeah, it was better in the other Suites. But no matter what, they would always have one thing in common. They were less than. They'd always be less than.

4

The halls of Eastern Suites Middle School were dead. Everything had been quiet since the spooks came asking questions, trying to find leads on those part of DOR

Like I'd tell, Olivia Quake thought.

The school walls were plastered with anti-D.O.R posters. One had a bunch of kids beating up a masked child. The title read *Those Who Hide Deserve to Die*. Other posters read *Do your part, speak up against radicalization*, and her personal favorite: *We fight for you, we protect you, help us help you* with a picture of a sentinel draped in imposing black armor, resting below it. Nothing human remained of the soldier, a helmet with a black visor covered any human emotion.

They struck fear into everyone. But not Olivia.

Sentinels were exactly what they looked like, mindless drones working for the very government that made it impossible to survive as a Bourgeoisie citizen. Orders. All they did was follow orders.

She thought about the patrol trucks that blew by on the cratered streets of dysfunction and filth. Streets she begrudgingly called home. The charcoaled six-wheeled killing machines had tires as big as garbage barrels, and on the hood was a gun bigger than she was. Each patrol truck carried squads of sentinels who would jump out on the corners at random times of the day.

But you were lucky then because, at least in the daylight, you could see them coming. At night was another story.

She gulped as a cold sweat encroached. Mom. Memories of her came rushing back, heavy and fast like last night. Olivia wished she was still on the medicine. At least then, she could grapple with it, but not now, not anymore. Daddy couldn't afford it.

Her heart pounded, and her hands trembled as her gaze homed in on the sentinel. She squeezed her eyes shut and focused on thinking about Dad, about Alex. Anything to keep her mind from going back to that place, that hell.

She jumped the moment she heard the first shot echo in her mind. Her bag and belongings fell as another two nightmarish bangs rattled off. Nothing but sounds of that awful night, but they were as real as if it was happening at that very moment.

Before she knew it, the smell of tangy pasta sauce and the gurgling of boiling water had their grasp on her imagination. Tears trickled down the sides of her cheeks as she saw Alex holding their mother. She was whispering something to him. Olivia didn't dare ask him what Mom said because she was always too afraid to remember. Mom's bloody fingers rose to her, and a gentle smile followed before ... Before ...

Olivia shrieked. No words, just the horrific wails of loss, pain, and anger. So much anger.

Every classroom door flung open as a few teachers came out to take hold of her. She wailed, fighting the memories that played in her mind like a horrific television show. It was all clear as day. That shattered doorway, five sentinels bursting through with their rifles raised. Mom picked up the spoon of pasta just as shots rang loud in the kitchen. Olivia still remembered how hard Alex held her after the fact. It hurt. Then a different smell overtook the pasta sauce, and it burned sweet.

Bang! Bang! Bang! The firing was so fast it sounded like three pops. Later she realized it had been a dozen bullets that rang in the air, shattering vases, framed family pictures, and killing Mom. Olivia remembered a few of the neighbors saying she and Alex were lucky to be alive at the time. Yeah, what luck.

The arms of two teachers wrapped around Olivia. She couldn't stop shaking. Her screams raked across the walls of the hallway. She looked back up at that stupid poster, the one that brought on the terror of her past. *We fight for you, we protect you, help us help you!*

Help? Sentinels didn't want their help.

We fight for you, we protect you, help us help you!

They sure didn't want Mommy's help.

We fight for you, we protect you, help us help you!

They wanted her dead. They thought she had some connection to some conspiracy to overthrow the government. Come to find out, it was all a mistake, an error made by superior officers. None of which were held accountable due to Mom's death being considered collateral damage. Daddy told her everything. He thought she was strong enough to handle the truth.

We fight for you, we protect you, help us help you!

Olivia became all the more hateful. All the more enraged. She wanted *them* dead. Her eyes focused on the sentinels. Dead. Dead. Dead. Every single one of them. They were the reason her family lived in that awful apartment. They were the reason she had night terrors to the point she couldn't sleep. They were the reason Daddy couldn't get more than one job. Restrictions.

She kept screaming as those awful words thumped in her head. *We fight for you, we protect you, help us help you!*

There was a sharp pinch in her arm. It stung, then went warm. Thick white clouds surrounded her, and her eyes became heavy. The whispers of teachers and students were all around her, but nothing drowned out the words of that poster. That terrifying lie.

We fight for you, we protect you, help us help you!

Olivia startled awake along with a wave of confusion that singed the sides of her head. She sat up to find herself on a green leather table. Snow white walls of painted brick were covered with colorful posters of anatomy, and the smell of bleach and plastic brought a strange comfort.

"Ms. Quake, we have to stop meeting like this." Nurse Fortin dug through her medical bag. She was young, real young, not old and angry like most teachers from the Exclusive community. She wore a sky-blue two-piece suit, the natural nurse's color. "Heard you made quite the stir in the hallway. You got all the teachers and your classmates excited."

Nurse Fortin didn't smell real. Nobody from Constance smelled real. Like flowers and fruits, fruits Olivia couldn't imagine, and her hair shimmered with colorful shades of yellow and brown. It didn't seem real either.

"Glad someone felt excited. It sure wasn't me," Olivia said, rubbing the sides of her face. A pounding headache was on the way, as one often was when they had to put her under.

Nurse Fortin handed her a cup of juice and an aspirin. "Was it about your mom again?"

Olivia knocked back the tiny white pill and slowly sipped the juice, savoring every sweet drop. "Something like that."

"Has your dad thought about putting you back on your medicine?"

"Nope."

"Well, maybe—"

"Can't afford it, Nurse Fortin," Olivia said harshly. "Not many families can afford to have assorted color shades of hair either."

Nurse Fortin hesitated. "You're right. That was very insensitive of me."

Olivia finished the cup of juice, then tossed it in the garbage. The headache was pulsing, but it wouldn't last long. "Can I go back to class now?"

"Of course, no one's keeping you here."

Olivia jumped from the table, opened the door, and went through. She didn't care how nice Nurse Fortin was. How could she since the woman was one of *them*? An Exclusive.

"Nurse Fortin, can I ask you something?"

A gentle smile came over her smooth face. "Of course."

"I heard that in Constance, there are no sentinels. That you guys have police. Is that real?"

"That's true. There isn't much violence in Constance, besides the rare terrorist attack by …you know who. So the need for sentinels really isn't required."

"But it's required in the Suites?"

"Olivia let's not go through this again. The Suites need the extra security. There's plenty of proof showing that Anarchy operatives and DOR supporters are coming from the Suites. Kids go missing all the time, just to join DOR"

Olivia didn't respond. She thought about Jason. "Thanks for the juice, Nurse Fortin."

She headed down the hall to world history. In class, dozens of faces of all colors, shapes and sizes whipped around to greet her. A hush came over the room. She found her empty chair in the back and plopped right in.

"You freaked again, huh?" asked Jada May, a fellow student with her hair pulled in a tight ponytail. She leaned over, keeping her eyes on the front of the room. "Mrs. Glass hasn't come back yet. I guess she's getting spun up on you."

Of course, she was. That's what happened every time Olivia had an episode. Whatever class she had—it didn't matter the teacher—there would be a small break, and the teachers would discuss how to *handle* her. All of it was a pain.

The door cracked open, and in came Ms. Glass, a pudgy woman with silver hair who waddled instead of walked. The room stood still. Olivia lowered her head, meeting the deep brown eyes that looked black behind her teacher's reading glasses.

"Class, let's return to the initial start of World War III, shall we." She didn't take her eyes off Olivia until she grabbed the raggedy history book. "We take notice that the war of ninety-five claimed the lives of billions, with nuclear and biological attacks at all levels, all world governments collapsed. What did this lead to?"

A dark-skinned boy with a thick mass of hair raised his hand. "The war of attrition. Like a last man standing."

"Correct, Donald. This last man standing," she smiled at him, "would be the deciding factor of who came through the ash first and who would take charge. And who came out on top?"

Olivia's eyes trailed out the window over the stack of old books piled high on a table. The last thing she wanted to do was get involved in the discussion. She was sick of it all. She knew the history of the world like the back of her hand; they taught it every year. Who didn't know the United States emerged through the destruction? Thanks to Cullen D. Roberts, no doubt.

"Olivia, are you with us?"

"No. Are you with me?" she answered, not taking her eyes off the window.

The class erupted in laughter.

Mrs. Glass looked appalled. "Ms. Quake, learning the hellish turmoil our country endured before becoming the fruitful nation we are today is very important. I would suspect you people—"

"Bourgeoisie people, you mean, Mrs. Glass?"

She gasped. "All of you should be overjoyed to be part of such lineage. Thanks to the unwavering leadership of Cullen D. Roberts, the United Nations of America has become the most successful world government in history. He was a man who accomplished something nobody thought was possible."

Whispers of agreement broke out amongst the class. Even Jada looked at Olivia strangely. There was a sickening turn in her stomach. Too much talking. She was way too jaded to be here today.

"Ms. Quake, with all regards to the unfortunate demise of your mother, it would behoove you to act like your classmates and not become too distracted by your pain. One could conclude you may not be satisfied under the leadership of the UNA."

Olivia shivered. "Oh, you're absolutely right, Mrs. Glass. I'm sorry. Sorry class. I guess ..." The thoughts of her mom dying flickered again. She curled her fingers beneath her desk. "I guess I got caught up in the past."

Mrs. Glass's face softened with sympathy. "Dear girl, of course. I do feel for you and the suffering of your people. We Exclusives see your plight, and we thank goodness for the implementation of the MLOL. In time we'll learn so much about each other, don't you agree?"

Olivia nodded unctuously, hiding the dread and fear from Mrs. Glass. In time, Mrs. Glass would get rotated out with another teacher from the Exclusive class who would have to do "their time" over the walls to teach bourgeoise students the victory and patriotism of being part of the United Nations of America.

Jason Tanaka didn't buy it, and neither did Olivia.

5

They barraged Alex and the others with questions that ranged from what their childhood was like, how they performed on exams, their hygiene, and to their parents' economic standing. *We're Bourgeoisie citizens. Why the hell does it matter?*

A grueling headache crept from the back of Alex's head, clawing deep within his skull. Sweat streamed down the sides of his face and armpits. His hands wouldn't stop shaking. To say he was mentally exhausted was an understatement, and by the looks on Deacon and Nelson's faces, they were feeling it too.

A tall woman with beautiful bouncing black hair and caramel skin rose from her chair. She stood proudly, her sharp green eyes glaring with cold indifference. "You, the boy in the middle."

Of course me. Alex swallowed. "Y—yes, ma'am?"

She flicked a strand of hair behind her ear. "How do you feel about the savages known as D.O.R.?"

Alex bit his bottom lip. He wasn't hesitating. It was just that the anger that came with thinking of his mom made his blood boil. "I hate them. I hate them with everything in me. They're the reason my mom's dead … So they can all rot for all I care."

Maybe it was the stress of all the questioning and the overall start of the day, but Alex had never felt that kind of blunt hatred. The woman arched a brow, and her expression softened a bit after Alex's answer, then she sat back down.

"Well, that's it for your orientation," the old man seated next to her said. He eased back in the chair, crossed his legs, and looked up at them with pity. "You may go on your way." He waved them off stage.

The auditorium doors burst open, and a younger man stumbled down the aisle. He was definitely a teacher. "Sorry! Sorry, I'm late."

The old man groaned with anguish, burying his face in his hand. "Principal Krate, so glad you can join us. But you're about two and half hours too late."

The man stumbled his way further down the aisle, nodding to the panel of ruthless teachers, and waved to Alex and the others.

Alex was too tired to wave back.

The man looked like he was a nervous wreck, sweating and fidgeting with his fingers. He adjusted his glasses on his nose and spoke in a calm reassuring tone that was like a glass of fresh water compared to the brutal fiery trials Alex had just passed through.

"Hey, guys. Principal Calvin Krate here. You can just call me Principal Krate, of course. This is my fifth year as principal of New Hope Academy, and I really hope you three find this place to be the bridge needed to unite our societies into one. My dad's dream is to create equality amongst the laboring class, and if all goes well, we can implement other lower classes too. I believe this is in line with the vision of our founding father, Cullen D. Roberts."

Equality amongst the laboring class? Alex wondered if Principal Krate really believed that. A smile crept across Alex's face, he didn't mean to let it slip, but after everything he witnessed and the chaos of their world today, the fumbling man before them couldn't be serious. This had to be some spiel that he said every year.

"You don't believe that either, huh?" Principal Krate's voice lowered as his eyes met Alex's. "That's what you're thinking, right?"

Alex's heart started racing.

"The principal asked you a question," said the woman who questioned him before, her green eyes sharpening.

"I–I–I…"

The old man uncrossed his legs and sat back, leaning his chin into his palm, and tapping his finger against his nose. "Not so funny now, is it, gutter rat?"

Sweat dribbled down Alex's face as he tightened his fist. His mouth was dry as all hell. Even if he wanted to say something, it would come out as a dry, raspy cough for sure.

"He's right to laugh," Principal Krate said.

The room went silent.

The whole row of teachers broke their necks to look him over in disgust and vile bitterness.

"You all heard me. He's right."

"Preposterous," one teacher exclaimed.

The beautiful green-eyed woman Alex had nicknamed medusa in his mind, rose to her feet with a leer. "You're seriously going to agree with a boy who can't afford to put a shirt on his back? A boy whose parents aren't even worthy enough to make our meals and wash our clothes?"

"Yes. Yes I am," Principal Krate said, nodding toward the three of them. "Until we start seeing these boys, and students like them, as people, the Middle-Class Lottery of Higher Living won't succeed."

A chill came over Alex. His anxieties and fears settled for a bit as he focused on this man of grandeur, wealth, and power.

"Can I have your name?" Principal Krate asked.

"Alex Quake, sir." Alex wiped his face to find his hands were cold and shaking.

"Alex, you're right to laugh. We're far from the dream of my father. There's a huge rift between the Bourgeoisie and the Exclusives, and an even greater one with the Pariahs. It makes my stomach turn." Principal Krate chuckled, looking to the row of teachers. "Unfortunately, my subordinates don't feel the same, but because of my father's position, they won't dare say a word. I can feel their disgust for the *other* students, though, and believe me, their hatred and brutality don't escape me either."

Was Principal Krate serious? Alex prayed it wasn't some cruel joke, some terrible lie, because the man's words gave him too much hope. An Exclusive with his prestige and his power would never speak to them like that, so why now?

"Alex, with the help of you and your friends, and the other students here from the Bourgeoisie community, I *know* we can make a difference. A difference that will end the hatred between the classes. Hatred that creates ruthless monsters and terrorists like the Disciples of Revolution and those like Anarchy."

A chest-rolling laugh broke over his words, and the whole row began shaking their heads, some joining the laughter. Principal Krate's face turned beet-red, and he hung his head a bit.

"Maybe the Bourgeoisie citizens. Maybe," one teacher replied. "But you want to rope the Pariah in with the wealthy?"

"The poor are poor for a reason, Calvin. Never forget that," the elder teacher, who seemed to be the ringleader of the row, spoke. "Your father knows that, and I'm sure you do too. So don't let Daddy's position get to your head. Even you need to know your place."

Principal Krate cleared his throat. "Right." A smile returned to his face as he stepped onto the stage. He held his hand out to Nelson.

A gasp stretched over the room.

Alex's lips quivered as he watched. From the corner of his eye, he could see Deacon's eyes about to bulge out of his head. Nelson looked at Principal Krate's hand, then back up at him. He did it a few times before finally shaking the man's hand.

"Jason was a great kid, Nelson, and I'm sure an even better big brother. Never lose hope and always remember that, okay?"

Tears rolled down Nelson's face. "Thank you.... Thank you so much."

Alex swallowed as Principal Krate turned to him.

"And Alex Quake." He threw his hand out. Alex received and shook it all the same. "I have a feeling I should expect remarkable things from you, kiddo. I'm rooting for you, alright?"

Alex nodded as he moved to Deacon.

"And you must be Deacon Young. I expect remarkable things from you, too, young man." Alex watched how Principal Krate studied Deacon's physique. "Keep up with your workout regiments and eat healthy. I'm sure you're going to go places, and quicker than you think."

"Awesome, Principal Krate. Thank you so much, sir. I … I thank you for the opportunity, and I know Nelson and Alex feel the same. It's been our dream to be here, our dream to even be considered, really. I … I just want to say thank you for everything you and your dad have done to look out for our community."

"Quite the talker too." Principal Krate laughed. "Well, I won't stand in your way, and neither will my subordinates." Principal Krate came closer and whispered, "If you have any issues with any of them, don't hesitate to tell me. Got it?"

"Yes, sir," they replied simultaneously.

He gave a terse nod and turned to the teachers in the front row. "Take diligent care of our future. I entrust them to you. Which means you will be as professional and courteous as if they were our own children."

"Yes, yes, of course," the older man replied.

Principal Krate trotted down the stairs and quickly walked up the ramp to the double doors. Once he was gone, Alex felt defenseless, like a toddler in a room full of wolves.

The teachers began to get up and collect their belongings. Alex and the other two remained seated.

Deacon rose from his chair. "Excuse me, can we go?"

"Go ahead, go ahead." The elder teacher with short white hair replied. He looked over the whole situation. "Your first class is with me."

"Seriously," Alex whispered.

Deacon shrugged. "Well, remember what Principal Krate said. Sounds like he's got our backs."

"Maybe," Alex replied, hiding the safety he felt. Deep down, he hoped more than anything that Principal Krate meant those words. The world needed more people like him, people who were above the classes and wanted unification.

Deep down, that was what Alex wanted. It's who he wanted to be. Someone of change. Someone who could break the shackles of the social glasses. But it could only be done from a position of power. As an Exclusive, he would have his foot in the door.

A difference that will end the hatred between the classes! Alex hadn't heard that kind of power and confidence in a voice since his mother. Not to mention, Principal Krate shook their hands. Alex looked down, rubbing his fingers together.

"Um, sir," Deacon asked, looking up to the rigid-looking man who spoke with a cross tone. "Can we please have your name?"

"Professor Threshfold is all you need to know," he said. "Now, follow me."

They followed Professor Threshfold through the radiant corridors of New Hope Academy. Many students nodded to the old man with a fearful gesture. It didn't matter if they were Exclusive or Bourgeoisie.

They walked into a medium-sized room where students whispered and talked amongst themselves. It was easy to see which social class was who, and clothes weren't the only reason. Half of the class sat on the left, while the other sat on the right facing each other.

"Seats on the left are for ... *your* class, of course," said Threshfold. He cleared his throat, plopped a brown leather bag on his desk, and fell into a black leather swivel chair that hissed as the cushions enveloped him.

Deacon, Nelson, and Alex found three empty desks. Two of them were directly next to each other, and the other a few rows over. Nelson sauntered away from them to the furthest desk. Alex was a little bothered that he didn't say anything to Deacon or himself. Who could blame him?

Deacon spoke under his breath. "Man, this is shitty. We can't leave Nelson hanging out to dry like this."

Alex pulled his bag over his chair and rummaged through it, pretending to search for something. "Deacon, what can we do? You heard Sebastian. Just look ..." Alex nodded to where Nelson sat.

The whole row of students began pulling their desks away from him. The loud screeching and groaning of metal over wood visibly rattled Nelson.

Alex ran his hands over his tight curls. "We can't afford to get wrapped up in his situation. We'll put ourselves and our families in danger."

"It's not right, man. It's not." Deacon finally dropped the conversation and focused on Professor Threshfold.

Alex pulled out a pencil and notepad and took a deep breath, finally ready to accept where he was and why. His mom would've been proud. She would've sent him off with an embarrassing kiss and words of encouragement if she were still around.

"Morning students, and welcome to Historical Studies, a new experimental study. Some of you know me from past history classes, but due to the rising of events and *concerns* from leadership, we have shifted the educational studies to focus more on major events that have led to the current social infrastructure of our world today."

A kid from the other side raised his hand.

Professor Threshfold nodded with a smile. "Mr. Hill, I'm sure you have quite the delightful statement to make?"

"Yeah, Mr. T. Does this have something to do with that gutter rat Jap, running off to get his nuts kicked in by the sentinels?"

Professor Threshfold glided his fingers through his white strands. "Yes, Bryan. You could say this new curriculum is due to Jason Tanaka's abandonment of his country to join terrorists." He strolled over to the boy's desk, glaring. The boy pushed himself against the chair like a mouse cornered by a viper. "But please refrain from such derogatory slurs as Jap. That's disgusting, and I will not stand for it."

The boy gulped, his face pale as snow. "Y-y-yes, sir."

"Good." He turned, though keeping his cold, scolding demeanor, his stride was more upbeat, and he even managed to smile. "As much as I begrudgingly hate to admit, Mr. Hill is correct. This class is to drown you all in the historic justification of why it's so important to support the United Nations of America. With organizations like the Disciples of Revolution and Anarchy, we as a people have to be vigilant, for we are all at risk of being attacked. Any one of us, Exclusive or Bourgeoisie, can be kidnapped and murdered. It happens all the time, more in other jurisdictions, but the influence has sprung in the northeast regions."

A girl from the Exclusive side of the classroom raised her hand. Professor Threshfold waved his hand, gesturing for her to speak. "Professor, what is it with DOR and these horrific masks they wear? Is it to hide their hideous faces from the public view?"

"Yeah, I heard they're monsters, not kids at all," a boy who sat right next to her added.

"Yeah, like that one member, the One-eyed Devil. She walks around with a sword, slicing and dicing." A dark-skinned boy leaned over his desk, his pressed blazer crinkling around the collar. "I heard she can walk right by you, and before you realize she's there, your head falls to the floor like a stack of books hitting concrete."

When he slapped his hands on the desk for emphasis, Alex jumped a little in his chair.

A deep groan came from the Bourgeoisie side of the room, followed by a sharp laugh. "You rich kids are so afraid of rumors and stories to the point that you make these terrorists out to be the wealthy class boogeymen. Is it because you realize mommy and daddy's money can't protect you from everything? Like justice?"

Alex gulped, his eyes rolled over to the girl from earlier, Yara. Her black eyeliner highlighted her intense eyes even from where he sat, and as she leaned over her desk, her long brown hair broke over her shoulders, spilling down her chest.

She continued, "Besides, I doubt people like the One-eyed Devil are anywhere near Constance."

A chill raced down Alex's spine at the name. One-eyed Devil. Considered one of the deadliest and most ruthless members of D.O.R, the One-eyed Devil was said to be a monster even though she had the body of a human girl. Like most of the members of D.O.R, she wore a mask, but hers was demonic and behind that mask was a single glowing red eye like a snake. That was what rumors said anyway.

The dark-skinned boy scoffed. "Like I'm going to listen to you, *Yara*. You wear the same jeans, black hoody, and black shoes every day. Talk to me when you get some new clothes. Scratch that. Talk to me when you get a life. Or maybe I can make it rain for you, and you'll show me something ..." He laughed as a few other boys joined in high fiving him.

Alex watched as she rolled her eyes and scrunched her face. "You know what? Maybe the One-eyed Devil is here ... I bet the Daughter of Death is, too." Yara made a popping sound as her hand expanded next to her head as if something had burst. "That's what it sounds like you know? When a round hits the skull, it pops." She focused on the dark-skinned boy who had been mocking her. "Just. Like. A melon, Justin. And all that remains is a pink mist."

The boy's eyes widened and watered, and everyone from their side of the room went silent. Alex was chilled to the bone himself. He didn't know whether to be impressed or piss his pants.

"Alright, that's enough, Ms. Miles. The sweet, flowery conversation of this class already leads me to believe this was the worst decision made by my boss." Professor Threshfold dragged a hand down his face. "Now, everyone, pull your history books out from beneath your chairs, and go to page fifteen."

Alex was still gazing at Yara; she sat a few rows over from him. Something about her was different. Maybe it was the skull-patterned hoody and torn black jeans or the fact that she boldly said what she felt. Or maybe it was the way her hair draped over her shoulders. Whatever it was, he couldn't stop staring.

She twisted in her seat and started digging through her backpack. Her left nostril was pierced, and a small skull glistened in the light of the classroom. Alex was surprised they allowed her to come to school with it in. He studied the curves of her lips and the smoothness of her skin.

Their eyes met again.

Oh, boy, he thought, looking away. A wave of heat rose from his shirt as sweat rolled down his back. He slowly looked back over at her. A middle finger slowly rose from her backpack as she cocked her head to the side.

Alex's shoulders slumped as his head hung over page fifteen. He chewed on his thumbnail, fighting embarrassment. Before the moment could consume him, Professor Threshfold's harsh voice broke over the classroom like a saving grace.

"Nineteen seventy, about a century ago, the United States was a country on the verge of economic collapse, social decline, and crumbling morals. Most of the country's leaders were bought and manipulated by massive corporations. Back then, politicians bought their way into positions, unlike now, where you must be elected by your peers."

A girl from the Bourgeoisie side of the classroom raised a hand. "Professor Threshfold, isn't it true that back then, they held national elections for leaders?"

"Yes, Ms. Carlson, absolutely correct. But in time, these elections were botched, and with the addition of the world wide web and social media, hackers and influencers were able to manipulate the masses. In fact, corrupt leaders utilized their money to buy votes."

"Kinda like now?" Yara blurted sarcastically.

Alex cringed.

Professor Threshfold sneered. "Ah, Ms. Miles, how I've missed your snarky sarcasm. You must be such a delight at dinner time with your parents and family members?"

She scowled. "My parents are dead?"

"Exactly. Anyway, unlike the events back then, the aristocrats now hold our elections. To avoid influence from the lower class, keeping electoral power amongst one class instead of the huge mess that crippled our country in the first place allows for a streamlined process that has no disgusting battles and barbaric arguments. Simple, clean, pristine."

"For whom?" Yara grumbled.

Alex snickered. His laugh must have been louder than he thought because his entire row turned, and so did half the class that faced them. Professor Threshfold tapped his chin, his eyes sharp as a machete. "Mr. Quake, is it?"

"Yes sir," Alex replied, defeat evident in his voice.

"Yara, my loveable little brat, has a pass to say what her heart desires. But you, on the other hand, don't have that luxury, Mr. Quake. It would behoove you to never speak again in this class. Never," he said in the most respectful way possible, but at the root of his statement was a threat. Nobody said a word, not even the Exclusive kids.

At Alex's expense, class continued on with no more disruptions from anyone, not even Yara. Professor Threshfold went from the nineteen seventies, a period of weakness for the then United States of America, in which the country's enemies saw an opportunity for attack. By nineteen-ninety, the USA had lost many of its allies due to poor decisions made by leaders and the inability to come to reasonable negotiations to keep the peace.

Iran attacked first, supported by what was once Russia. The USA responded with behind-the-scenes attacks utilizing cells from small terrorist organizations. Once the secret got out, Russia not only increased their support for Iran but was soon intertwined in the war leading to WWIII.

The bell finally rang, and Deacon and Alex packed their things to head out of class. But before he could reach the door, Professor Threshfold stopped him.

"Mr. Quake, a word if you will."

Deacon pressed his lips together. "I'll hang out in the hall for a bit."

Alex nodded. "Yes, sir, on my way," he said turning and making his way to his desk.

Professor Threshfold stuffed a few stacks of paper in his brown leather bag without paying Alex any mind. He cleaned off his desktop, ate a few crackers, and finally looked up with the foulest grin.

He dabbed a few crumbs away from his lips with the corner of a napkin. "Mr. Quake. What am I to do with you? Mr. Young seems to understand his place, and, well, Mr. Tanaka, that poor soul doesn't have a prayer to stand on. But you, Mr. Quake? You are cautious. You don't show much emotion, which is a card that has probably helped you get to where you are now."

Dad thought there was something wrong with him. Olivia thought he was broken and got pissed when he didn't cry at the funeral. But he did cry. He cried behind the locked bathroom doors when everyone was asleep in the dead of night, holding that picture of his mom in his hand. He cried when he missed the smell of her, her warm, boisterous laugh, and the way her hair tickled his nose when she hugged him.

Professor Threshfold was still going on. "Mr. Quake, I'm here to be that immovable wall placed in your way." He curled his fingers around the thickest history book Alex had ever laid eyes on. "For you to collide into. And I promise, you are not an unstoppable force, you little ant. You are nothing but a lowly spec in a chasm that is my world, and if you want to eat and drink in my world … submit yourself. If you want to learn and receive grace in my world … submit yourself. Otherwise …" He slammed the history book down on the floor in front of Alex.

Alex didn't budge. From the corner of his eye, he saw Yara slinging her backpack over her shoulder. She pulled some of her hair behind her, and as she squeezed by him, he could smell the sweet scent of a perfume that only compared to a wealthy girl's scent.

"I understand, sir." Alex shifted his stance, his body tensing just enough so he didn't tremble.

Professor Threshfold laughed. "We're going to have so much fun, you and I, Mr. Quake, you wait. Dismissed."

6

Alex bounced from class to class with Deacon.

Sports in Society class wasn't so bad even though Alex wasn't as physically gifted as Deacon was. After, they made their way to mathematic, a class where Alex was able to strut his stuff even amongst the Exclusive kids. He couldn't say the same for Deacon.

For most of the day, Alex kept his head low, and his mouth shut. But his eyes constantly searched for Yara, hoping he'd get another chance to see her again. "She probably thinks I'm a creep." He sighed, thinking about how she caught him staring on all three occasions.

Deacon nudged him. "Still stressing over that situation with Professor Thresh?"

Alex lied, but not entirely. "Yeah, I guess I shouldn't be surprised, though."

"Things could be worse. You could be in Nelson's shoes."

Nelson. It must have felt like the entire world hated him. Maybe after everything blew over with Jason, things would get back to normal for Nelson and his family. It's not like the Tanakas knew Jason would join DOR

They came to a lunch table filled with kids draped in worn, oversized clothes. A few Alex recognized from their initial greeting that morning. Sebastian was shoveling mac and cheese in his mouth when they came around the bench. He threw a thumb up.

"Boys! You're still alive," he yelled with a celebratory cry.

A renowned "Aye!" shook the table.

"Grab some chow and take up some seats." Sabastian slapped the bench beside him.

Alex got in line behind a few kids he recognized from the bus. The cafeteria was nothing like he had grown used to in Eastern Suites Middle School. The food looked fresh, clean, and more like something made for human consumption. Not the rotting apples, pureed peas and potatoes they got there just to keep them all full.

Alex stacked his plate. On the other side of the cafeteria was a portal to the world of the Exclusives. Shielded by a moveable wall, he caught a glimpse through the cracks that revealed a cathedral ceiling shining brightly over paintings of splendor.

Similar to the Bourgeoisie side, there were dozens of kids laughing and joking, talking about what they did last night, what they planned to do today, and how they wished they didn't have to share a school.

Alex laughed to himself thinking about Yara and what she said about the Exclusives making DOR out to be some boogeymen. It was no wonder they hated Jason, and it was no wonder they took that anger out on Nelson.

They feared him.

Exclusive kids knew nothing but power and influence. Of course, they hated feeling afraid. They never had to learn to sleep with their eyes open, with screams and gunshots echoing from outside their window as another house got raided. They never had to worry about having their doors kicked in and being shot dead because they got labeled as a terrorist.

Alex's eyes narrowed on the clean round faces, their eyes shimmering with joy. They slept in heated or air-conditioned homes on queen-sized beds. They had feasts and spreads bigger than he could imagine, then probably threw their scraps in the trash or fed them to the dogs because they'd made too much.

Alex looked over his shoulder at the other side and gritted his teeth. He wouldn't become like them once he graduated. He'd always remember where he came from. Never greedy or prideful, he'd stay humble and compassionate just as his mother taught him. He'd still visit the Suites every chance he got, no matter what.

"Take a seat, guys." Sebastian made room as a few kids left to clear their trays. "So, what do you think of N.H.A. so far?"

"It's aight," Deacon said. "Not going to lie about the food choices though. I'm stoked, no doubt." He crunched into a slice of cheese pizza. "I never imagined I'd be eating pizza right now."

Alex bit into his own cheesy slice, the gooey warmth a perfect balance of spice and tanginess. Herbs dusted the dough and topped the cheese with a fresh fragrance.

"Yeah, New Hope isn't so bad once you look the other way on a few things," said Sebastian. But he didn't look at them when he said that. "What about you, Alex, enjoying yourself yet?"

"If you call being patronized and threatened by an old man something to enjoy, then I'm having the time of my life."

The occupants left at the table laughed as a kid on his right slapped him on the shoulder. "Welcome to the club."

Sebastian raised a glass of chocolate milk. "Welcome." Sebastian's gaze shot from Alex to the doorway.

Alex followed his gaze, catching Yara strutting to a table of girls. Her hair had a smooth, natural bonce to it.

"Yara, happy Monday!" Sebastian yelled.

She turned, scrunching her face as if she smelled something rotten. "Oh, happy Monday, *dog* of the wealthy."

Sebastian's face reddened. Within, Alex laughed, thinking about her low, raspy voice. The same one she used to verbally lash out at the kids in their class.

She continued, "What awesome parlor tricks do they have you doing today, Sebastian?"

"Showing us new kids around," Deacon answered.

Shut up, Deacon! Alex wanted to say out loud, but he didn't want her to focus on him again. His eyes shifted, and this time he caught Yara's eyes burrowing into him.

"How lucky." She laughed and turned, heading to the table with all the girls.

"Man, she's rude, aye? A real depressing one that, Yara," Sebastian grumbled.

"Bro, she went in on a bunch of wealthy kids earlier, the girl's a savage!"

Sebastian slapped Deacon on the back. "The best description of Yara I've heard these last few years. A savage indeed, but a beautiful one at that."

Alex studied how she talked with the other girls. It was night and day. Her scowls were replaced by the devilish pull of her lips as she waved her hands sporadically, making the other girls laugh. "Yeah, she is beautiful,…" Alex mumbled.

A few gasps stretched over the table.

Alex looked up, snapped out of his hypnotic state and turned to Deacon and Sebastian. "Wha–what?"

"So that's why you were acting all weird after class? I thought it was because of Threshfold. It was Yara?"

"What are you talking about?" Alex's face became hot. "You guys are nuts! You said she's a savage, ruthless and cold-hearted to the core."

"Right," Sebastian said, arching a brow. "Just know if you go for Yara, you're competing with me, buddy. Don't think a freshmen's going to have much of a chance with a sophomore anyway."

Alex cleared his throat. "That's fine. She's all yours."

A few laughs blanketed the table, but everyone went silent again. Munching on a piece of crust, Alex looked up to see Nelson eyeing him and Deacon with a plate full of food in his hands. He looked like a deer in the headlights, and his silent cry for help glossed in his eyes.

Deacon rose from the bench. "Yo, Nelson, come—"

Sebastian ripped Deacon down into his seat. "Are you shitting me?"

Their entire side of the cafeteria went silent. Only the laughter and voices spilling from the other side clashed with the quiet.

Deacon shook his head.

Alex's heart pounded like crazy. Sebastian's scorched red and wide eyes looked like that of a madman.

"I told you before, leave *him* alone," Sebastian said, pointing to Nelson. "Or you'll be sorry. That's the last time I'm going to warn you."

Deacon looked reluctant. His hands trembled, and even as he nodded, he nodded like a boy who had just gotten chewed out by his father. Mr. Young never made him look like that, ever. Deacon turned to Alex, his eyes begging for support.

Deacon needed him, just like Nelson did. But all Alex could think about was Dad and Olivia and what would happen if anyone linked him with Nelson.

Alex turned from Deacon and bit into his pizza crust.

"Right," Deacon said. "Fear over friends I guess. Right, Alex?" Deacon slipped off the bench and tossed his tray into the garbage then left the lunchroom.

Nobody said a word.

Their last class of the day was Acclamation 101, and Alex struggled to focus. It had nothing to do with the dry, monotoned teacher who struggled to keep anyone's attention. It was more to do with what happened at lunch.

New Hope Academy was different than what they were used to. You had to know your place and play your part. Anything outside of that had dire consequences. Just by Sebastian's reaction, those consequences were severe. Deacon had to learn that.

The Acclamation professor rallied off a few more statements about how adjusting to Exclusive living could lead Bourgeoisie citizens to unknown stressors and using proper etiquette and mannerisms would save them from a lot of offenses.

The bell rang and class ended. Alex merged into the group of Bourgeoisie students, Deacon nowhere to be found. *Starting the first day off right, huh, dummy?* The thought pained him.

Sebastian nudged him, then wrapped a long arm around his shoulder. "First day suit you good or what?"

Alex shrugged his arm off him. "It was aight. Felt like a gazelle in the Serengeti for the most part. But I'll live to survive another day."

Sebastian laughed and slapped him on the back so hard he stumble forward. "Where's Deacon? I kind of wanted to apologize about earlier. I overreacted big time. I just … We've never had a kid do what Jason did, and the atmosphere around here is a lot denser if you know what I mean?"

"I don't. Maybe you can explain."

Sebastian stepped back and gave a nervous chuckle. "Think about it. You have two different social classes in one place. One social class think of themselves as gods compared to the other. Now, for the most part, we *peasants* know our place. We shut up when talked to, we eat when we're told to. But what happens if a peasant steps out of line? Not only steps out of line but jumps freakin' ship and joins the enemy. I know I kind of beat around the bush earlier …"

Alex was following, and for the most part, as much as he hated to agree with Sebastian, his point was already sinking in.

Sebastian continued, hands stuffed in his pockets. "With what Jason did, it put us all in jeopardy. We all look like backstabbers to the Exclusives. DOR is no joke. Those guys kill anyone and anything that moves. Class doesn't matter."

"Don't you think we know that?"

"Then why is it hard for your friend to see that your boy Nelson is a casualty of war."

Alex's eyes narrowed. "What do you mean 'casualty?' "

"I mean exactly what I said." Sebastian's voice lowered, and his eyes had that madman look again.

Alex broke eye contact, fighting the unease that rippled down his shoulders with a chill. "Is something going to happen to Nelson?"

"All I'm saying is stay away from Tanaka." Walking backward, Sebastian pulled his hands out of his pockets, then he smiled. "I'll see you guys tomorrow. I hope day two won't be as ridiculous. Good thing about N.H.A. is all your classes are in the same place. Different teachers, different curricula.

Makes it easier for us and the teachers." He turned and headed out to the yard where the day began.

Alex slung his bag over his shoulders and rushed to the bathroom. He furiously splashed water over his face, then looked at the boy in the mirror, struggling to catch his breath. His eyes were frantic, his hands shaking.

From the carousel of madness that bounced horrifying ideas throughout his head, Sebastian's words kept echoing. *Casualty of war. Casualty of war. Casualty . . .*

He turned the faucet back on and started drinking from it. The water was fresh and crisp. It didn't taste like the smell of rotten eggs like the sink water at home either. He splashed his face a few times, then stepped back.

Everything pieced together. A deep breath got him back into control, and he analyzed the situation. Nelson would be fine. But he'd need help from the shadows.

As everyone walked in line, Alex gathered with the others out in the courtyard. A bunch of the Bourgeoisie students already hung out just below the hill. A breath of relief came when Alex finally found Deacon. He was talking and laughing with another student.

Deacon looked up at him, but not for long. *Probably thinks I'm a sellout.* Alex made his way down the hill and over to Deacon. "Hey, bro?"

Deacon sneered. "Bro? Really? A bro wouldn't leave me hanging like that. Not someone I've known for a damn decade."

Alex pulled him from the group and out of earshot of any of them.

"Get off me!" Deacon shouted, ripping free.

"Deacon. Listen. We can't talk to Nelson or hang out with him like we used to, and we can't pretend like nothing happened," he whispered.

"So acting like a scared punk and not standing up for your best friend is the answer? What do you think Nelson would do, huh? You think he'd care if it were me or you in his situation?"

Alex looked away, focusing on a few glances the conversation was attracting. "I don't know. What I do know is you have a mom and a dad, and I have a dad and a baby sister that I have to look out for. Look … I got an idea that I think can help us connect with Nelson."

Deacon sucked his teeth, then lifted his chin. "What?"

"The scrapyard. What if we meet up there like we used to back in the day?"

"The scrapyard is always filled with people. Laborers, government contractors. Hell, even sentinels are out there patrolling. That's why we don't even go there anymore."

"Exactly. That's why I'm thinking we meet up after curfew when everyone's in bed."

Deacon folded his arms. "So you're willing to risk getting caught outside past curfew but not willing to talk to Nelson?"

"Getting caught past curfew is a stern warning, a reprimand at worst. We have our IDs, so if anyone catches us, we tell them we lost track of time … uh … working."

Deacon rolled his eyes. "Aight, man, I'll bite." He held his hand out, and Alex happily shook. Deacon pulled him in for a hug. "Nelson is one of us. Friends don't outcast friends when they need them. Alright. I don't give two dead rats what Sebastian says. Dude could squeeze a fistful of dog crap for all I care."

Alex laughed. "The first thing we've agreed on all day."

From the schoolyard, a line of limousines, flashy trucks, and other fancy vehicles lined up at the front of the school. An hour and a half passed before they were gone, and the bus came to pick them up.

Alex was the first on, Deacon right behind him. The bus driver gave a laugh that was more like a smoker's cough. "So you Eastern Suite boys made it through day one unscathed? Interesting."

The driver's laugh trailed behind as Alex found the same seats they had that morning. The moment he sat, he tore out two sheets of paper and started scribbling on one.

Nelson,
Meet us at the scrapyard at 2200 hours. Yes, an hour
after curfew. Don't be late.
Your friends,
Alex and Deacon
P.S Bring some of those awesome muffins your mom
makes!!

Alex folded the paper a few times, clutching it tightly in his left hand. He walked to the front of the bus, crumbling another sheet in his other hand, and made his way past

Nelson. He gulped, his eyes rolling around the bus, then flipped the note into Nelson's lap.

He continued down to the driver's seat where the garbage can was and tossed the crumbled ball in. The bus driver's eyes winced with curiosity. Alex gulped again and gave him a light wave, only to be answered by the jerking motion of the bus revving up.

When Alex made it back to his seat, Deacon was already asking questions. "Did he get it? Did he start reading it? What'd he say?"

"I don't know. I just sat down. You know as much as I do right now."

They both looked over their seats at Nelson, his head down. The decision was on him.

A couple of bumps down the garbage piled streets of Eastern Suites, the bus came to a rumbling hiss as it pulled over to the corner. They were the last ones to get dropped off.

Olivia was right there on the corner, book back tight to her shoulder, just like she said she would be. The look on her face was less than satisfying. Must have been a long day for her too.

Nelson lived a few blocks away, Deacon just a block shy of the scrapyard. They all got off the bus, Olivia tight to Alex's hip. She got clingy when she was emotional, even more so when it was about mom.

"Scrapyard," Alex said, watching them head home.

"Scrapyard!" Deacon yelled.

Nelson paused and rolled his neck low but didn't turn. Alex could've sworn he mumbled scrapyard.

Maybe it was the relief of the day ending or the fact that he'd finally reached out to Nelson, breaking the rules and status quo of how everyone treated him. Regardless, he had made his decision to see Nelson. To see his friend.

7

Broiled chicken gizzards, liver, and rice served as dinner—the fifth night in a row—and by the way his dad carried on about how good it was and "how a good thing never gets old," there was probably going to be a sixth.

At dinner, everyone talked about their day. Alex told everyone about N.H.A., the kids, and everything Nelson was going through. Dad wasn't surprised, and he warned Alex again about staying away from Nelson.

"It's unfortunate. Nelson's a good kid, and the Tanakas are a really good family. Everything with Jason is making them out to be traitorous terrorists. I heard his father was released from his job last week and so was his mom."

Why was he just hearing about this? Then again, how would anyone know if no one bothered to talk to him? The thought hit Alex hard.

Olivia's fork smacked the plate. "That's not fair!"

Alex jumped from the sudden outburst. He looked over at Olivia whose fist lay heavy on the table.

His dad's eyes buried into the VEN-O.

Olivia's fingers tightened around the fork till her knuckles cracked. She bit down on her bottom lip, and a tear rolled over her cheek. "The Tanakas were so nice to us after mom died," she said, wiping her face. "It's bull that they get treated this way!"

"Olivia, language," their dad said, his tone harsh, his eyes bouncing from her to the VEN-O.

"No, Daddy, it's true! Why are we always the ones that suffer? Why do we always get shafted?"

His father tucked his chin into his chest. Silent.

It was the truth that no one wanted to openly admit. The truth that every Bourgeoisie kept deep within themselves and feared to bring up. If you did, you were revolting against The United Nations of America. And once people got a whiff of that, better believe you would go missing.

"Olivia," Dad wheezed out, finally mustering up the courage to speak. "We are well fed, we are well taken care of and protected by the walls. The UNA does all it can for us, but it has to draw a line at terrorists. Whether we agree or disagree doesn't matter. We have to obey the rules, no matter how hard—"

"No! We don't!" she screamed. "I'm tired of being treated like a criminal in my own community by soldiers who don't even belong here. Because of who I am and my social class I'm treated like dirt. I didn't choose to live this life. I didn't want to be born into the Bourgeoisie class." She began sobbing uncontrollably. Alex scooted his chair over, and she fell into his arms. "I miss Mom. I want my mommy.... I ... I just want my mommy."

All Alex could do was hold her. Nothing came out of his mouth. His eyes were too focused on the vibrant green light of the VEN-O.

His father was sweating, his head facing the plate of gizzards as droplets smacked the plate.

No cool words of encouragement came like a big brother should have, not even kind words like *everything will be okay.* Alex just held her. That was enough. It was always enough.

After dinner, Alex helped her to bed. She was still a sobbing mess but coherent. It wasn't her worse day, far from it, actually. As she got older, she gained more control of her outbursts. Nothing like the hysterical crying that gripped their home after their mom died.

But Alex wondered if they would get "a visit" because of what she said in front of the Venus Oracle.

"Alex," she sobbed.

He leaned over from his cot. "What's up?"

"You think they'll come and take us away because of what I said?" she started sobbing uncontrollably again. "Do you hate me?"

Alex laughed, thinking about how much trouble she was and all the work of putting up with her. "Mom told me to love you no matter what, and to take care of you when times got bad, and to—" Before he realized it, he had tears of his own rolling from his chin.

He saw his mom laying on the kitchen floor, bleeding out. Three bloody holes in her chest. A roll of garlic bread at her side. The smell of sauce and the bubbling of pasta filled his head. He still remembered her last words.

"Take care of Olivia … your father."

"Mom, you're okay, right?"

Tears had run down her face. "Love them with all your heart.... Protect them, okay?"

He'd nodded as her grasp tightened around his hands. He had felt her blood squeezing along with it.

"Promise?" She'd given him a weak smile.

Alex had nodded, trying to block out Olivia's shrieking in the background. "I–I promise, Mama." His eyes had burned from the smell of gun smoke that filled the room. The pot of spaghetti had bubbled over on the stove. Blood had pooled beneath her, thick and sticky between their fingers as she held his hand.

"Don't allow this world to make you hateful, Alex." Her body had shivered, and her paling lips had moved a bit. "Don't ... become ... the ... world...."

Her hand had become heavy in his. If it hadn't been for the blood and her lifeless eyes fixed on him, he would have thought she was resting.

Alex thought deeply about Olivia's question. "No matter what happens, I'll never hate you Olivia. You're my baby sister. You and me forever. Right?"

She rolled over, looking up at him with watery eyes and extended her pinky finger. "Promise?"

Alex smiled, thinking of the last time they pinky swore. They were kids, maybe single digits. He stretched out his pinky finger and hooked it around hers. "Promise."

She nodded and turned back over.

Alex curled up on his cot and waited silently until Olivia's sniffling became drawn-out breaths of slumber. Dad checked in once or twice but soon even his snoring clawed at the bedroom door from the living room.

Alex pulled on his pants, slipped on his sneakers, and tossed a jacket over his shoulders. He slipped out the door and inched his way down the creaking steps of the apartment. A dozen others lived in the building, but everyone was asleep by now. Or at least he hoped.

He eased open the main door to the apartments and peeked out. A black six-wheeled truck, with windows so black you couldn't tell who was looking at you from within, crawled down the street. A patrol truck.

Alex slowly closed the door and pressed against the cold brick wall of the hallway. *One. Two. Three. Four … Damn it. I'm counting the missing tiles. Focus!*

He peeked out again, and after catching the beady red eyes of the brake lights as the truck made its way down a side street, Alex ran down the stoop, focusing on the massive wall in the distance. The city glittered beautifully, lights golden, with some buildings emanating a deep blue hue of sorts. Blinking red lights flashed from above. There was movement on the inner wall. Though the wall was far from where he stood, he still ducked behind a few piles of garbage.

He stayed low, avoiding streets, windows, and anything that could pinpoint his position. A stray dog burrowed its head into a pile of garbage. It growled as he snuck by.

"Easy pup, easy."

Once Alex was far enough away, the puppy stuffed its head back into a garbage bag, ripping out the foul contents of spoiled milk and rotting eggs.

He stumbled into the scrapyard where a small acreage of wasteland littered the area with pieces of metal from all over, utilized to help build and repair the massive walls and other structures. The yard was enclosed by a high wall of cinderblocks and razor wire, but they found an opening decades ago that copper thieves probably made.

Alex worked his way to the thin opening, avoiding the rusted wire and tangled heap of metal fencing that was a balled mess. The metal clanged and rattled a bit as he forced himself through.

Following the backside of the yard which kept him hidden behind tin containers and long slabs of tin sheets, Alex came to the area where they used to play as kids. The mountains of metal were a fortress they used to build shacks and hideouts when they played soldiers and terrorists.

Huddled with jackets on, Deacon and Nelson sat in a corner.

"Long time no see," Alex said, stepping into the moonlight that cast over the three of them.

Deacon nodded and high-fived him. "About time you made it. What happened?"

"Dog, patrol truck, everything, I guess. What's up, Nelson?" Alex fist-bumped him and brought him close for a hug.

"Hey . . ." A smile broke across Nelson's thin, pale face. He looked thinner than usual, especially in the face.

They were silent for a moment.

"So ... uh ... shitty day at school," Nelson said with a weak laugh.

Alex almost hated to laugh, knowing the joke was more of an effort to lighten how his day went. But it would've been awkward not to. "Nelson, I'm sorry about today—"

"No, we're sorry about today," Deacon said, cutting him off.. "We're supposed to be your best friends. We shouldn't have turned our backs on you. Screw what those kids say, man."

Nelson kicked a piece of scrap metal across the dirt. "I know you guys want to be there for me. I do. But I don't want to get you guys wrapped up in my family's mess."

Alex stuffed his hands in his pockets. Olivia's words ran through his head, stabbing him in the chest like a knife. "It's not fair."

Nelson bobbed his head. "Since when has life ever been fair? Nothing fair about the way we live. You know that better than anyone. This government, *their* government." He spat out the words, pointing over at the massive wall protecting Constance. "It's all built for them to exploit us. New Hope Academy is just another way to brainwash us into thinking we're so *fortunate* to be allowed to take part in their system. It's a trap. Jason told me—"

"Wait," Alex said, taking a step back. "You're still in contact with Jason?"

He could tell Nelson got nervous from his reaction. "Forget what I said, alright?"

Deacon stepped closer. "What'd he say?"

Nelson looked Alex over, then turned back at Deacon. "North America is the first continent to roll out the integrated school system. They're playing it off to make it seem like it benefits us, but in reality, it's all a lie. They lied to us and our parents. They say once we graduate, we're sent off to have better lives and families on one of the other continents. But it's a lie."

Alex chuckled in disbelief. "That's insane. UNA is trying to reestablish the world and expand. They need all the people they can get, civilized people especially. Why would they need to lie?"

"Because they're shipping kids to labs or worse." Nelson looked around, peering out into the darkness. He stayed on the balls of his heels the entire time.

"Labs?" Deacon's brow furrowed, and Alex could see in his eyes that the conspiracy gears were turning like mad. "What labs?"

"Jason didn't know exactly, but DOR has been shutting labs down and freeing people locked up like animals. They've been lying to us on the news about *terrorist* attacks. DOR is good; that's why Jason went with them."

Alex thought about his mom bleeding out and dying in their kitchen, all because they thought she was part of some terrorist organization. "Bullshit!" He shoved Nelson, tears welling in his eyes. "You think those sick bastards … those murderous monsters are good?"

Nelson shoved him back. "Are you stupid and blind? Are you a UNA dog? I just told you this government couldn't give a rat's ass about us, and you're mad about DOR?"

"You *know* why I'm mad!"

The scrapyard grew quiet under the brisk air of the pale moonlight. Alex's huffing and puffing became a white cloud. Nelson shoved his hands in his pockets and paced back and forth, combing his fingers through his short black hair. "Alex, you know—"

"You were there," Alex's voice cracked in the night air. He sniffed hard fighting the snot from rolling down his upper lip, then rubbed the tears away. "You were at the funeral with me, by my side. My side!" Alex pounded his chest. "All three of us looked in the casket at my mom. My mom who loved you guys like you were her own, made you guys cakes for your birthdays, had you spend the night … *My mom* who baby sat you and Jason when your moms had to work a little late at the food depository. *My mom* who was killed because they received a tip that we were caring for members of DOR and Anarchy. So yeah, screw DOR and if you think they're good, screw you ,too."

Nelson's face had lost what little color it had left.

A few sirens broke through the scrapyard, but the roar of patrol vehicles whooshing by didn't faze Alex a bit.

Nelson raised his eyes to meet Alex's. "I love you guys, just as much as I love Jason. And he loves you guys too. Alex, I called your mom, Mom every time I saw her. Don't you think that it hurt me when she was murdered?"

Murdered. Murdered? Nelson was the first person to call his mom's death a murder. Accident, mistake, collateral damage, but never murder. It had a different heaviness to it, a different sting. It made something burn violently in him.

"So you'd rather live over there," Alex said, pointing to the outer wall to the Outskirts. "That's hell. And you know it."

Nelson shook his head. "No. Hell is waking up every day knowing I'm less than a human because society classifies me that way. We'll never be like them, Alex. They're lying to us. We'll never be able to drive fancy cars, live in fancy homes with multiple bedrooms, kitchens with a refrigerator stocked with our favorite foods, in a city where the air doesn't smell like shit, and the people just as bad. They sold us a lie. The Bourgeoisie is nothing but pawns to keep the peace, because if we were to unite with the Pariahs in the Outskirts, they would be outnumbered."

Deacon was still silent, eyes low to the dusty ground of the scrapyard. Alex watched him kick a coil of copper wire, and exhale as their eyes met. Alex could tell he was conflicted.

Nelson continued. "We think hell is living out there in the Outskirts because we won't have the comforts of living off crumbs. It didn't hit me until I read Jason's journal, but we ignore the horrors of this world. We'd rather be blind than know the truth because it helps us sleep better at night. It makes us feel comfortable about not stepping out against what's wrong and what's right. Our parents make the easy decision to sit and live day in and day out as slaves to their minds, our society, and our government, then teach us to do the same. I'm tired of making that decision. I'd rather die."

Deacon finally joined the conversation. "Nelson, how did Jason get all this info?"

"I don't know, he never said."

"And I don't care," Alex said.

Nelson got in his face. "You can be so stupidly selfish sometimes, Alex. So wrapped up in your own beliefs that you don't care what others tell you. It's like you're afraid to decide for yourself. You'd rather be safe than sorry. Even if it means watching someone die."

Alex lunged and swung at Nelson. Nelson ducked and slugged him in the gut. Alex dropped to his knees, sucked in air, filling his lungs, and a dry heave followed.

Deacon pushed Nelson back and helped Alex stand. "Guys chillout!"

Alex broke away from them both and struggled to his feet. "Screw all this conspiracy bull! You're nuts, Nelson, and so is Jason."

Alex took off through the fencing, through the awful smelling streets, through the night sky where Constance glowed in the distance like some kind of prideful sapphire under the moonlight and slipped back into the apartment.

His father's snoring covered the opening door and the creaking of the floorboards. The moment he opened the bedroom door, Olivia sat up, waiting.

"It's past curfew...."

He jumped, snapping toward his cot. "I know." He took a deep breath and exhaled,

"What if you got picked up by one of the patrols?"

"I know."

"What if Dad caught you?"

Alex fell on the cot. "I know, I know, I know."

The moonlight beamed through the old bullet holes and poured onto the floor. He slung his jacket off and whipped his sneakers across the room where they slapped the wall. He didn't care if Dad heard. Thinking about Nelson and what he said tonight made him wonder why he even set up the meeting in the first place.

Olivia whispered. "Where did you go?"

"Went to meet up with Deac and Nel," he mumbled.

"Nelson? Is he okay?"

"Peachy. Insane and all about conspiracies like Deacon, apparently. Dude thinks DOR is good and that they're trying to stop some ..." Alex hesitated as he looked over at Olivia, whose eyes were swollen. She had been crying. He hanged the subject. "Just like you said, we're idiots, I guess."

"Alex, I'm sorry that I get like that. I really—"

"Olivia, there's nothing to apologize for. I know you're trying your best. You've gotten so much better. You're not beating me up anymore. That's a win."

She laughed a little. She came over and wrapped her arms around him. "You're the best big brother I ever had."

"I'm the only big brother you've ever had."

She slapped him upside the head, and went back to her cot, pulling the covers over her. "Night, Alex. And thanks for being there for me."

"Always." He turned on his stomach and faced forward.

Through the bullet holes, the moonlight took on the blue essence of the city afar. He pulled the covers up just enough that they wouldn't uncover his feet. It was going to be a chilly night. Soon, he'd have to stuff the holes with newspaper and cloth.

He thought of the future … he and his family's future. Nelson was wrong. Dead wrong. The path to living a life outside this one was possible. The path to be an Exclusive was right in front of him, and all he had to do was work for it. Keep his head down, and work for it.

8

The bus bumped and hissed as it grumbled through the first gate. Though they sat right next to each other, Alex didn't say a word to Deacon.

Once on campus, the three ogre-like men hobbled out of the little guard shed and shuffled their way over to the bus. One checked beneath, while another checked the sides. And Alex's favorite individual, Biggs, put the bus's suspension to work.

Here … we … go.

"Gutter rats, front and center!" Everyone on the bus leaped from their seats and stood proudly. "Off the bus, same as yesterday. Move it!"

The aisles cleared, row by row. Just like yesterday the three of them were the last ones off the bus. The moment they touched ground the doors shut, the engine revved, and the bus swerved through the roundabout, and disappeared beyond the gate.

Day two, Alex thought stuffing his hands in his pockets. They followed Biggs through the well-manicured lawn of the campus. The air pleasant with the fragrance of fresh cut grass and flowers was more than satisfying. Especially compared to the smell of Eastern.

Alex looked up to see Biggs slowing his pace to get to the rear of the line. He gulped as he met the cold blue eyes that widened gleefully from a red face. Biggs hacked a laugh and turned to the three of them.

"Got something special planned for you three. Well, one of you in particular."

Fear tangled in Alex's gut when he looked over his shoulder at Nelson, but after last night the games really didn't bother Alex much. Nelson could take care of himself.

The sun broke out behind New Hope like an egg sunny side up. Unlike yesterday the campus was silent and stiff as a dead rat. A few groups huddled together, a few girls were crying, and a couple of Exclusives watched with eyes so full of hatred it made Alex's skin burn.

They walked by the bench where those kids had gaggled yesterday, but they weren't there this time. Good.

They came to the top of the hill, but nobody went forward. Hesitation. But why?

"Well, go on, gutter rats, pile on down at the bottom," Biggs said, and they started down. "Ah-ah-ah, 'cept for you, Tanaka. You'll be coming with us. Got a few things to talk about."

Alex turned. He locked his jaw shut, but the shudder that rattled his body made his knees knock.

Deacon gulped so loud it caught one of the large men's attention and he chuckled greedily. Nel, snickered the same way, and in his eyes, Alex didn't see fear or sorrow. He saw a soldier full of pride and vigor about to face the firing squad.

"Why Nelson?" Deacon asked.

"What the hell did you just say to me, boy?"

Deacon shivered, but the words still rolled from his lips. "Why Nelson?"

Alex watched as Biggs unlatched a pouch on the left side of his hip—just before his pistol, thank God— and pulled out a sleek black rod. With a flick of his fat wrist it extended. He stepped to Deacon and hovered over him. This must have been what gorillas were like before they went extinct.

Biggs jabbed the ball of the metal rod into Deacon's Adam's apple. "Because I want it to be Nelson. Who knows, maybe next time it'll be you." Alex noticed the golden whiskers over Biggs top lip were wet with sweat. His red face glistened in the rising sun as if he had climbed a few flights to get to this point.

Deacon swallowed, and his throat nudged the metal ball.

"Will you two douchebags stop worrying about me," Nelson called out. "I don't need you piss heads to protect me or look out for me. I'm fine on my own. Right, Alex?"

The three men laughed with big brawny laughs, one even coughing and hacking in the middle of it. Alex looked at Nelson again. This time Nelson gave a cocky grin, one of assurance and gratitude.

Alex shook his head, but the thought still remained. *What are you thinking, Nelson?*

"You heard the kid. Get lost and join the other runts!" Biggs jabbed Deacon in the chest.

Deacon shook his head as he turned and made his way down the hill to the group. Alex looked back once and saw Biggs jabbing the metal shaft into Nelson's spine. *What was*

that? Why the hell would he voluntarily go? And with a smile?
Alex thought he imagined the whole thing. That confidence,
those firm eyes of victory, that smile.

"We've got to do something, Alex. We can't let them
hurt Nelson." Deacon kept shaking his head. "I don't know
what I'd do if ..."

"What do you mean?"

"You guys next to my mom and dad are the only family
I got; you guys *are* my brothers."

Alex's stomach started to turn. Thoughts of his mom,
thoughts of his dad and Olivia, and then thoughts of Nelson
began swirling. Nelson's words were loud in his head from
last night. *Are you a dog of the UNA?*

Alex shook the thoughts from his head.

"Nelson will be fine. That's why he said what he said.
Probably trying to rattle him," Alex said thinking about the
smile. "They won't do anything to us unless we do something
stupid."

"I just ... After last night, man, everything I've heard, I
know you think it's all fake and conspiracy garbage. But what
if ...?"

Alex scoffed. "What if the government is using schools
to kidnap kids and use us as lab rats? Come on, someone
would have said something by now. And the labs? That's
worse than the thing you told me about the black hole
sightings over the west coast last week. First of all, the west
coast is nothing but a wasteland of sand and a dead ocean
covered in radiation. You wouldn't last an hour out there.
Second, black holes?"

"Not holes, portals ..." Deacon blew a frustrated breath. "Maybe you're right, man."

They continued down to the group at the bottom of the hill.

Unlike yesterday the excitement of greeting them was lost on the group as heavy whispering and people racing from one conversation to the next replaced the hugs and cheers of yesterday. Their eyes were frantic and uneasy, some even teary-eyed. Alex took a deep breath. *One. Two. Three ...* His fingers tapped against his thumb over and over. Something was off.

Alex saw Sebastian shaking his head, and he leaped up to greet them. "Morning. I'm sure you guys are probably on edge too, aye?"

Alex looked at Deacon as if he had missed something, then gave the same look to Sebastian. "Why should we be?"

Sebastian paused for a moment and leaned in as if Alex didn't hear him clearly. "Are ... Are you serious?"

"None of you watched the news this morning?" Another spoke from the group.

Alex shook his head. After everything that happened yesterday and how upset Olivia got, Dad was afraid to get her riled up again, especially in front of the VEN-O. He kept the television off.

"Me neither," said Deacon. "Why? What's up?"

Everyone turned to them, eyes boggled, mouths unhinged, gasps of shock spread through a few people, and Sebastian cleared his throat. "There was an assassination late last night. DOR took out a highly influential aristocrat."

Alex's stomach dropped.

"What? In America?" Alex thought Deacon was going to fall. "But how?"

"Yup. Head shot from a sniper." Sebastian made both his hands do a popping motion from the sides of his head. "Head blown clean off."

Jessica came over, arms folded and tapped her foot, her hips shifting to the side. "They say it was the Daughter of Death."

Alex pressed into the conversation. "How's that possible? She's in Europe from what the last assassination confirmed. What is she doing in the Americas?"

Sebastian looked up to the sky. "DOR's making some serious moves. If she's here, I think they're gunning for the secretary general."

Now everything made sense.

And things got very scary.

The Daughter of Death was one of the most-wanted members of the DOR With a price on her head as high as a billion credits, the very thought of her being in America sent chills down Alex's spine.

Every kill was a head shot. Every shot taken was from an impossible distance. She even out-classed UNA's best.

Alex thought about what Yara said to get those kids scared. But now it was a reality. He remembered something some of the labor workers were saying a few years back when she really started gaining attention. *The Daughter of Death never misses.*

"I can't even imagine," Jessica said. "The Daughter of Death and the One-eyed Devil all on the same continent. No way that's a coincidence."

Night raids were going to get worse. Alex could hear the distant screams at night of families being torn apart, innocent people being blown away, killed. No. Murdered, like his mom.

"Maybe it's not her. Maybe there was a mistake, you know? I mean one assassination can't make it out to be this specific person. DOR has thousands of members. Probably hundreds of snipers. I mean, be realistic here?"

"There hasn't been an aristocrat assassination in a few decades in the Americas," said Sebastian. "Not even an attempt. Security measures in American cities are tight and impenetrable for all high-ranking officials on this continent, obviously since it's the home of the secretary general. I would agree with you, Alex, but then the calling card was found."

Alex shrunk away at the thought. Probably one of the most disrespectful, humiliating aspects of being assassinated by the Daughter of Death, was the fact she only needed one shot. And she left behind one proof of that shot. A hot pink brass casing deliberately left after the fact in the most obvious place, close to the victim's home. Proof that she didn't fear the government. Proof that she was untraceable, and proof that she could hit anyone, anytime, anywhere.

"Savage ..." Deacon said dryly.

The bell echoed snapping Alex out of his anxiety. He wasn't the only one. The whole group looked defeated.

Sebastian lowered his voice, but the firmness and grit was all there. "Everyone, keep your damn heads down today, and don't say anything out of place. If someone spits in your face, take it. Someone beats the piss out of you, take it. We can't afford anyone to retaliate. Is that understood?"

Without hesitation everyone agreed. No one batted an eye, no one spoke against Sebastian, or raised a hand, barely an inconvenience by the energy of the group. Sebastian's request rattled Alex, though, and by Deacon's horrific expression, he felt the same.

Nelson's voice was loud in his head, like a crashing wave: *the easy decision to sit and live day in and day out as slaves to our minds, our society, and our government.*

Alex shuffled to class. The eyes of the Exclusives fell on them like daggers. They needed someone to blame. The real threat, the real people who frightened them and caused them harm, weren't reachable, but Bourgeoisie students were.

It reminded Alex of the neighbor at their old apartment, old Mr. Testani. Mr. Testani had a dog, a mutt mix. He was a tall, tan man with deep wrinkles on his face. Because he lived by himself and worked till evening at the city dump, he would get home late. Talk about foul smelling. Not to mention the hard liquor. Thing was, Mr. Testani's dog would obviously crap and piss all through his apartment. Alex could smell it the moment he hit the hallway after school; the whole complex could.

When Mr. Testani got home, he wailed on that dog something fierce. He took out all of his fury, his failures, his sorrows, everything on that dog. A few months before Alex's mom was murdered, Mr. Testani hung himself. Dog found a loving home though. Unfortunately for them, Alex had a feeling they weren't going to have the same happy conclusion as Mr. Testani's dog.

Classes were awkward. Nobody talked much, and the teachers didn't complain, but they sent glares of discomfort to the Bourgeoisie side of the room. One teacher, the intimidating woman from orientation, actually had to leave class. She broke down crying halfway through. Nobody talked about the assassination, not even at lunch.

There was still no sign of Nelson. Heading into their last class, Deacon and Alex searched the halls and waited outside the door a bit. But nothing.

A mass of discomfort built in Alex's chest. His palms were sweating. *Get a grip. Get a grip, Alex. Nelson's fine. He's good.*

Deacon urged him inside. "Come on, we have to take our seats."

A chubby woman with messy brunette hair, graying on both sides of her head, rose from her chair and walked the aisle of the room, combing through the attendance roster. Every name called was a sharp "*here*" or a groan. Her chubby digits wrapped around a pen, checking with every answer of a student.

Alex's chair was uncomfortable. He wiggled, then slouched, then sat upright. His insides were going crazy, his thoughts focused on Nelson. *He's fine. Maybe he's in the principal's office. The guards scared him bad, and he felt safe enough to go to Principal Krate. I'd do the same thing.* He wanted to do that right now.

"Alexander Quake?" she called.

"Here."

"Nelson Tanaka?"

No reply.

"Nelson ... Tanaka?"

Silence gripped the room.

"Going once, going twice ..." Her digits wrapped tighter around the pen as she wrote in a steady motion on the notepad. "Moving on—"

"Ma'am?" Alex called out.

"Mrs. Cheadle, if you don't mind," she replied sharply.

"Sorry. Mrs. Cheadle, Nelson was with us this morning, but he got grabbed by the guards out front, and we haven't seen him since?"

Deacon added, "Yeah, I mean, isn't that against the rules or something?"

She shrugged. "Not my problem."

Alex's eyes narrowed. "But he's one of your students?"

"Oh my goodness. You really think I see you as one of my own students?" She started laughing then turned to the side where everyone looked to be grieving. "Class, isn't that a riot?"

A few laughed.

A student tossed his pen on the desk. "Nobody gives a crap about your friend. He's a traitor. Whatever happens to him he deserves. Bourgeoisie trash!"

One. Two. Three. Four. Five. Alex repeated his counting several times. He wasn't even counting anything, just counting for comfort's sake. His fingers cracked around the legs of his desk. His legs wouldn't stop shaking, and this heat … This burning in the pit of his stomach had him on edge.

Deacon looked him square in the face. "Alex, just relax, aight? Like you said, Nelson's fine, man. Don't let them get to you. You're the levelheaded one of the group, remember?"

Alex's head bobbed in agreement as he closed his eyes. Images of him jumping over his desk and punching the kid repeatedly flickered over and over. Alex could see the other kids trying to pull him off the guy then the guards coming in with those metal shafts. They would hit him over and over again.

Alex sniffled but didn't let a single tear fall. He shook those images out of his head. They came out of nowhere. As he focused on his desk, from the corner of his eye, he noticed Yara eyeing him hard. She gave him a nod, lips trembling, then turned to face Mrs. Cheadle.

Class continued.

The last bell of the day rang, and before the last chime could sound, Alex's books and notepad were stuffed in his backpack. He headed out of class, Deacon close on his heels.

"I think Nelson's in Principal Krate's office," Alex said.

"What makes you think that?"

"Cause if those dummies did something to him, it's the safest place for him to go for help."

Their brisk walk became a steady jog, and before Alex and Deacon got to the hallway intersection where Mr. Krate's office was, a high-pitched scream tore through the conversations that filled the hall.

Alex pivoted and bolted to the screaming. He wasn't sure if Deacon was behind him or not, and he didn't have time to check. He pushed through the crowd, heading toward one of the staircases.

Alex paused at the first drop of blood.

His jog became a shaking crawl until he came to a puddle. Then pain gripped him as he looked at the bottom of the stairs.

He could feel Deacon behind him, breathing hard. "Nelson!" Deacon jumped down the stairs and cupped Nelson in his arms.

Alex couldn't move.

More kids piled behind. A teacher screamed for the nurse to call emergency services. Alex's eyes rested on the bloody mess that was Nelson.

His left eye was swollen over, his face red with open wounds, already changing colors. His right eye rolled around the hall but fell on Alex, staring, unflinching.

"Alex, come on, man, help me!" Deacon screamed. "Help me!"

The last shout snapped Alex out of shock, and he raced downstairs to help Deacon carry Nelson. His mouth was wide open spilling blood. His front teeth were missing along with a few of his bottom ones, Alex surmised, although he could barely tell because of the swelling of Nelson's lips. Nelson was breathing, but it was nothing more than a wheezing gurgle.

"I got him, Alex. I got him...."

Nelson wheezed from his swollen mouth what barely came out as words. "Punched ... that fat troll ... in the face."

Deacon slipped his shoulder beneath him. "Don't say anything, Nelson. Just breathe and relax, brother. Just breathe and relax."

They carried him up the staircase. The only response they got from anyone was whispers, even from the other Bourgeoisie.

They came face to face with Sebastian.

He leaned in to help with Nelson but hesitated then lowered his gaze and stepped away, letting the three of them pass. If it weren't for Deacon screaming to come on, Alex would have stood there glaring at Sebastian forever.

The nurse was already ushering them into her office. They laid Nelson on the bed while a second nurse was on the phone with emergency services. Nelson was wheezing hard, his chest pumping up and down.

"What happened?" the first nurse asked.

Deacon answered, "I-I don't know. We heard some girls scream, and we found him like this." Deacon was on the verge of tears, digging his fingers into his scalp.

"Do you two know him?" she asked.

Alex could hear Sebastian's threatening words over the nurse's frantic conversation with emergency services, "*I told you before. Leave him alone!*" Tears raced down Alex's face, even though he tried to keep up a hardened expression. Nelson was lying there, tears streaming down his good eye and his hands shaking.

What kind of monster am I? Alex couldn't pull his eyes away from Nelson. What kind of person turned his back on his best friend, someone he considered a brother?

All of the excuses, avoiding Nelson to protect his family and fear of being seen as a terrorist or a DOR supporter melted away. And all that was left was Nelson, his best friend, his brother. Beaten half to death and left at the bottom of a staircase by himself.

"We need you boys to wait outside." The first nurse started coaxing them out.

Deacon tried to fight her. "Wait. Nelson. Yo, Nelson, say something, man."

Alex pulled him out of the office.

A bunch of kids crowded around them. Deacon punched a brick wall, his fist crunching on impact. He grimaced but did it a second and a third time till his fist was purple. It was easy to tell he'd broken his hand.

Principal Krate came racing down, and so did a few other teachers. They began breaking up the crowd and edging everyone outside. Principal Krate paced back and forth, sweating. "Wh–what happened?"

Alex shrugged, looking down at his feet. But that fire inside his belly, like back in Mrs. Cheadle's class returned when the three security guards came hobbling in. Biggs had a black eye and a busted lip, and another had a bruised chin. The third guy looked clean.

Principal Krate turned around and raised a brow. "What the hell happened to you two?"

"You!" Alex lunged at Biggs like an animal. "You did this to him!"

Biggs snatched him off his feet by his shirt, but not before Alex cracked him across the face with a right hook. His knuckles ripped open the cut on the bully's lip even more. Biggs threw him to the ground, whipped out that metal shaft, and was about to tear into him.

"Officer Biggs, drop that damn piton," Principal Krate yelled, "or so help me, I'll see you fired. Do you understand?"

His fat jaw dropped. "But, sir?"

"Do you understand me?"

Biggs collapsed the black shaft and stuffed it back in the pouch. He pointed to Alex and smiled. "I'll be seeing you again, Quake. Better believe that," he threatened. He and the other three guards walked out into the hall, yelling at every kid they ran into to clear out, even the Exclusives.

Principal Krate helped Alex to his feet. Alex began crying, burying his face into Principal Krate's chest. The man wrapped his arms around him.

"They did this to Nel, you have to believe me, it was them. They took him this morning when we got to school, we haven't seen him since then."

Principal Krate pulled back. "Alex, that's one hell of an accusation. I'll have a formal investigation done, but what proof do you have that it was them besides, they took him?"

Alex thought about the other students, Sebastian, Jessica, they'd saw the whole thing too. "A bunch of us gather at the bottom of the hill, it's where they bring all the Bourgeoisie. We all saw it."

He nodded. "I'll do what I can Alex, that's a promise."

Alex did all he could to keep it together, even with Principal Krate's support, but the pain the anger was too great. He hadn't cried like that since the night his mom was … murdered.

9

After fighting for his life these past few days, his parents decided that Nelson would be taken off life support.

Not even Constance's advanced medical care was enough to keep him going. They put him through multiple surgeries to control the brain swelling, but the damage had been done. Doctors told Mr. and Mrs. Tanaka that all they could do was keep him breathing.

Alex, Deacon, and Olivia stood in Nelson's hospital room. Mrs. Tanaka sobbed in the arms of her husband, her face long with misery and lack of sleep.

Alex could barely recognize Nelson. His face was so swollen, smeared with purples, blues, yellows, and cuts that disfigured him. He'd lost his left eye; doctors said the blunt trauma was so severe to his face they couldn't save it. Not that it mattered now. His head was bandaged tight, hiding the stitches in blood-stained gauze.

Standing at Nelson's bedside—as the world moved on as if nothing happened—Alex was frozen in time and space.

Agony crushed him in waves, along with bitterness and grief. For the last three days, he could barely get out of bed. He hadn't eaten, hadn't slept. Even now it felt like he was sinking into the floor and falling into a lake of blackness, drowning.

Mrs. Tanaka crumbled to the floor, her husband with her.

Nelson ... please forgive me. You probably hate me for leaving you to fend for yourself like that ... I—I just ... Alex couldn't say the words out loud. A tear rolled down the tip of his nose and slapped the pale tiled floor. *I take it all back. Everything I said about Jason, about you being crazy. I'm sorry, Nel! Don't go, man.... Stay. We need you. Your mom and dad need you.*

There was a steady knock at the door just behind them.

A doctor walked in with a few nurses. Alex cringed as Olivia's fingers wrapped around his to pull him away from Nelson's bedside. Every birthday, every sleepover, every joke, all the fun in the scrapyard flashed behind Alex's eyes.

It was like losing his mom all over again. An icy numbness turned his insides into a bitter cold desert, and blackness filled the edges of his hopes and dreams. Alex saw his selfishness revealed in Nelson's death.

In the hallway, his dad waited for them. He stuck out in his ragged overalls that were torn at the seams over his broad shoulders. Seconds passed before Alex realized his dad had his arm around his shoulders and he was talking.

"... but we'll get through this too. Right, Alexander?"

Alex's breaths were shallow, and the burning edge of his eyes yielded tears of self-hatred. His focused on Deacon, who stood in front of the door to Nelson's room. Deacon looked away like someone or something had smacked him across the face, and tears rolled down his cheeks, too.

A hoarse wail broke through the edges of the door and filled the hallway.

Nelson was gone.

Deacon scowled at Alex, and it lingered, harsh and hateful. Alex thought Deacon might have mistaken him for the guards that killed Nelson.

Principal Krate came down the hallway, his face red with eyes to match. He nodded to them. "Hello, everyone. I just wanted to visit Nelson and check—"

"He's gone," Deacon replied. "They just took him off life support."

Principal Krate's gaze fell to the floor. He leaned against the wall and gripped his chest. "Damn it!" He pounded the wall with his fist. "This isn't how it's supposed to be. Why? Why …?"

Why was right. Why were *they* so powerful, so influential? Why were *they* given everything on a silver platter? Alex peeled his father's hands from around his shoulders and began stomping down the hallway.

Every face he passed in the corridor was clean and bubbly, loving, and good smelling. Fresh. No deeply wrinkled foreheads or red eyes from being overworked, no sunken cheeks from lacking food. All supple and strong. All proud. Even in a hospital.

"Excuse me." Alex was whipped around by a tall woman with long hair that shone like silk, her bronze skin glowing under the bright light of the hospital. Her nose wrinkled. She smelled him, of course. Her voice was gentle, but there was something in her eyes, something patronizing. "Do you have an ID, young man?"

"I don't."

"Are you even from the inner wall?"

"No," he said robotically.

She snapped back as her expression changed to one of a woman who had just found a rat in her food pantry. "Well, I'm going to have to get security to escort you back to the uh …" She looked Alex over. His tattered jeans and shirt that hung loosely off his shoulders visibly disturbed her. "Outer wall, right?"

"Right."

"Umm, ma'am, that won't be necessary." Principal Krate came trotting down the hall. He showed her his ID.

"Are you seriously the son of Sean Krate? The same Sean Krate who's the governor of Constance?"

"One and the same," he said, blushing. "Please, I'm a principal at—"

The nurse couldn't stop smiling, eyes frantically looking Principal Krate over. "New Hope Academy. Yes, I know! My brother and I went there. We were so excited to hear that you had taken over and so warmed by your push to integrate Bourgeoisie citizens into our school systems."

Could've fooled me, Alex thought bitterly.

"Well, thank you so much. Actually, this is one of our students. Unfortunately, there was a terrible accident, and he … We lost one of our best students. Alex lost a best friend today."

She swallowed, and her eyes kind of softened. "I'm sorry to hear that." She looked up at Mr. Krate again. "I'm so excited to have met you. Please …" She whipped out a sticky note, scribbled on it, and handed it to him. "My name's Erica. Call me *anytime*."

"Oh, uh, thank you." He took it, slipped the note into his back pocket, and guided Alex down the hall back to where his father and the others were.

"Alex, please. I know right now isn't the time to bring this up, but you have to be careful in a place like this. You know *they'll* never understand."

The way he said it was like he was separating himself from them. "What do you mean?"

Krate stopped and turned. "Every class has monsters; every class has greedy, filthy representatives. And trust me, the Exclusives are no different. Bottom feeders on every corner." He threw his thumb behind him, pointing down the hallway from which they just came. "Like Erica. She didn't give a damn about what happened to Nelson. She didn't care you were distraught and in pain. All she saw were your clothes and immediately knew you didn't belong."

He wasn't wrong. "Were you able to conduct the investigation on Biggs and the other guards?"

Principal Krate cringed. "Looks like Biggs already has a lawyer, a damn good one, too. I talked to some of the kids down by where you advised, but they all refused to say anything." He sighed. "I could tell they were afraid too, but because of that, I can't move forward with the investigation."

There was a sourness in the pit of Alex's stomach. It was Mom all over again. Nelson died, and the ones responsible would get away with it. He looked down at the clean tiled floor, biting his tongue and holding back his tears.

"I promise, I'm going to change that. I'm going to change everything."

Alex looked up as a twitch hit Principal Krate's intense eyes. His fingers dug into Alex's shoulders, and Alex shrugged them off. "Sorry about that. You okay?"

Alex's gaze fell to the ground again. "No. No, I'm not."

Principal Krate had everyone from the other side of the wall dropped off at their apartments. The Tanakas stayed in the smooth black SUV as Deacon, Alex, and his family got out.

The door slammed closed behind them, and Alex looked at the blackened windows that were heavily tinted. The windows slowly dropped with a warm buzz, and Mrs. Tanaka held a pale, thin hand out. She waved Deacon and Alex over.

Her eyes were red and saggy. She wrapped her arms around both their heads, and whispered into their ears, "Don't let them take anyone else away from you. Fight, and make it through graduation. Do it for Nelson.... Do you understand?"

"Yes," Deacon replied.

Alex nodded. "Yes, ma'am."

She hid her face as a few more tears fell, and the window rose. The car glided down the pothole filled streets with a smooth hiss, not a rumbling groan like the school bus, blowing dust and garbage behind it.

Alex's father took Deacon and Alex by their shoulders and guided them toward the apartment. "You boys have been through a lot. Deacon, if you want to stay for dinner, we have enough?"

"No thanks, Mr. Quake. I need to get back to my mom and pops ASAP. They've been pretty strict with me being out since everything with …" Deacon closed his eyes.

"No, I understand." Dad nodded to Alex, and turned, ushering a sobbing Olivia into the apartment.

The wind blew as the pinkish sky of the setting sun cast over Eastern Suites in strips. The Venus skyscraper soaked in every glint and cast its shadow over the broken, torn streets mockingly.

Pain still stabbed at Alex's insides. It had been that way since they found Nelson, but fear twisted and entangled with it. Deacon was silent, which was weird for a kid who was always jovial and joking, the life of the party.

"Deacon, you—"

"You don't say anything to me." His gaze focused on the ground. A tear fell and was drank in by the filth of the concrete.

A weak raspy tone escaped Alex, "What?"

"Seriously, don't." Deacon's fists shook at his sides. "Right from the get-go, you were quick to turn your back on him. You didn't hesitate! Like a punk! Like a coward, you left him to those jerks at N.H.A."

"Deacon, we didn't have a choice."

"We did! Yeah, I let Sebastian step on me a couple of times, but at least it was because I was trying to reach out to Nelson. You made turning your back look effortless. Then when he opened up to you, you called him crazy and treated him like he was no one because he was calling out the government and calling out those who stood by and did nothing. People like *you*!"

"I know you're upset about Nel, but we can't turn on each other like this, not here, not after everything."

"You already did that!" Tears rolled down Deacon's face, and hatred filled his eyes.

Pigeons took flight and rats scurried from the piles of garbage that lined the sidewalk. Deacon's voice made Alex's heart jump, like Mrs. Tanaka's wail. But there was a silence to Alex's spirit, to his beliefs, and everything that he thought was right.

"You turned your back on Nelson. You turned on him when Sebastian told you to leave him alone, and like a dumbass, I listened to you," Deacon sobbed. "You said don't worry about it. That Nel was going to be fine. Now he's in a freezer. Frozen until his parents can come up with the money to bury him, or at least have him cremated."

Alex stood there with his mouth hanging open. Deacon's words killed a part of him, maybe the part that was clinging to life, struggling to breathe like Nelson was struggling to breathe when they took him off life support.

Deacon wiped his face and looked up at him like he wanted to kill him. "Don't talk to me. Don't come to my house. Don't eat near me." Deacon turned and walked away, heading down the avenue. But after several yards, he stopped and turned. "You know even the wealthy stick together. That's why they build those shitty cities. And here you are, someone who turned his back on his best friend, a brother. You're worse than they are."

Alex's knees buckled, his palms greeted by old paper and soggy newspaper caked with grease and grime. He knelt there on the street and cried just like he did at his mom's funeral.

A few people walked by, but they didn't say anything. It was normal around these parts. The echoing screams of loss were always the same. And the people around answered the same way. A hung head, a shake of disappointment, and a continuation toward their destination.

And what was that destination? A foul home, a job where you were paid nothing just to go back and purchase cornmeal, stale bread, rotting fruit and vegetables—if you were lucky—and the shittiest parts of what meat there was. The fat, the gizzards, the nose, the feet. Meanwhile, those with power ate like kings, and those above them drank the nectars of the gods.

What am I? Who am I?

He bathed in the rancidness of the garbage-covered streets, proudly inhaling the putrid air in clothes that barely got washed. He slumbered comfortably in apartments that barely stood, memorialized by the remnants of past deaths at the hands of those who "wanted" to help them.

A faint whisper cut deep through his misery, through his collapse, through the ashes that were Alex Quake. *But we ignore the horrors of this world, we'd rather be blind then know the truth because it helps us sleep better at night, it makes us feel comfortable about not stepping out against what's wrong and what's right.*

Nelson's words echoed strongly as if he stood right over Alex's shoulders, whispering in his ear.

He pulled himself up, then wiped the grime and nastiness from his pants. He wiped his face, uncaring of the filth staining his fingers. People had died from worse things than infection and disease.

Things like existing.

10

Alex sat on the bus by himself. Deacon was over in the other row where Nelson had previously sat.

A week had passed since they pulled the plug on Nelson, and that's how long it had been since Alex had been to school and seen Deacon. Douglas had allowed Alex to take some time off and Principal Krate agreed, at least until the investigation had been completed.

Nothing on the news told about the brutal death of a Bourgeoisie teen. Instead, the news echoed of the assassinations of high-ranking scientists and an aristocrat. Alex could only imagine the atmosphere at New Hope Academy now.

The bus came through the wall secured by machine guns before it rolled slowly through the city. The smiles, the lives of the successful, of those born into wealth, shone bright as the bus passed adorned statues of marble.

Alex watched the people consume delicacies that dripped from their lips like honey, and all he could taste was the sourness of bile on his tongue. The air stunk worse than the garbage piled on the streets of Eastern, and the people, these people, all seemed dead to him.

The bus stopped in front of the black gate. It leaned and shrieked as Biggs stepped on. "Quake, Young, Tana— Oops. Sorry about that." He sneered. "Off the bus!"

Alex's knuckles cracked at his sides. He kept his head down while following just behind Deacon. Oddly, the schoolyard was filled with laughter and joyful playing from the neatly dressed well-washed students of the powerful.

Alex focused on that pouch on Biggs's hips. If he did anything, if he reacted, Biggs had free reign to beat him senseless, maybe even kill him.

The curly-haired Hispanic boy from earlier tossed his head to Biggs. "Biggs, my dad said you and the guys will have a clean slate. He has an in with the judge on your case from the sounds."

"Mr. Bassett is the man. You tell 'em I said that, Manwell, you understand?"

"You know I will. Aye me and the guys will be skipping third period, going to head to the mall."

Biggs turned, laughing. "Hear no evil, see no evil."

The group high-fived and laughed as they continued their chatter.

They continued over the mound, and Biggs allowed them all to gather at the bottom of the hill, just as before. He held back Deacon and Alex for a moment and laughed. "Go on, join the litter. And no trouble out of either of you. Right, Quake?"

Alex stopped and turned to look up at the three large men. The sun fell over their shoulders in a warm glow. It sickened him. But not a word left his lips.

Deacon went his own way, off to a corner. The same place Nelson used to go after they dropped them off.

At the bottom of the hill, a few kids were chuckling, but silence consumed them once Alex mingled in.

How could they laugh? How could they even think of having as much joy as to laugh when someone they were aware of and had known was killed by the same men who grouped them together like cattle?

Alex got to the front of the group. Some of them had eyes of sorrow, and some looked at him with assurance and acceptance. Sebastian came over, giving Alex a shaky smile. Jessica wiggled to his side, but her excitement and energy were nowhere near the first day they met.

"Alex, I'm sorry," Sebastian said. "We're sorry about everything that happened with Nelson."

Jessica added, "This is the way things are. This is the way things have to be until we graduate. At least then when we graduate and get the opportunity to live better lives, we can live for those we lost on the way."

Alex's fists shook from their words. But how could he blame them? They were just like he was. Afraid, blinded by a dream cast over them to keep them asleep, and hoping for a better way of life. And by Jessica's words, Alex knew they were in too deep to care about anything else but that dream, that sweet lie.

He walked away from the group heading to another corner of the schoolyard.

"Alex, come on. You need us. We have to stick together. You still have the chance of a lifetime. Don't throw it away!" Sebastian screamed.

Screw them. Screw this school! Alex plopped to the ground, leaning up against the rough bark of a tree. A few apples fell and cracked open at his feet. He snatched one of them up and bit into it. The juice dribbled down his chin as the sweetness of its insides slid down his throat.

"Tired of the herd mentality?" a girl's voice said from above.

Alex looked up to see the long strands of hair spilling from a black hoody covered in skulls. Yara was stretched out on a few branches, crunching into an apple.

His fingers dug hard into the fruit. "Is that why you're never with them?"

"People dance to any tune these days as long as they're not alone. They'll eat each other too if you play the right song and castrate one another to keep the larger mass alive." She tossed a browning apple core across the lawn. "I'm sorry about your friend."

"Thanks. But I'm as much to blame as they are."

She dropped down from the branch effortlessly and inched her way down the trunk until she was by his side. "Fear makes you do stupid stuff. That's why *they* like it so much. It's easy to keep people in line."

"They?"

"The kids laughing and having a ball over that hill. The ones who've already forgotten the death of your friend or didn't even realize he existed. The ones who are probably celebrating it because they've chalked him up as a *terrorist*."

"Why did you say it like that?"

"Because they put the title of terrorist on anything that brings them fear. If I start a petition about bringing fresh food and vegetables to the Suites to bring home to families in need, I would be laughed at. But if one of our parents started something like that and enough people agreed and picketed, they would be labeled terrorists and poof! Suddenly they disappear."

Alex's eyebrows bunched as he listened to her words.

She raised a brow. "What?"

He hesitated. "Nothing. Just something you said kinda reminds me of what Nel was talking about."

She snickered. "I'm surprised you're not looking at me like you got to take a dump," she said, shooting him a glance.

His lips pulled a bit. "Not gonna let that go, huh?"

"Nope." She picked up an apple trapped in the roots of the tree and crunched into it. "If you want to talk to a girl, a simple hello is sufficient. Staring like a creeper will make you lose points."

Alex laughed again and nodded. "I'll keep that in mind."

She wiped her long black sleeve across her moist lips. "Another thing to keep in that big forehead of yours is that friends are hard to come by these days. I don't have a single one. Just because you lost one, you still got another. Don't let that slip through your fingers."

The bell for first period rang. Yara jumped to her feet and dusted the dirt and dead leaves from her jeans. She held her hand out, and long brown strands fell over her face, creating a soft shadow under her cheek as she leaned forward.

Alex took her hand as she pulled him up. She was a little taller than he was. She wore the same jeans every day by the looks of them and a pair of sneakers that looked as worn as the hoody.

Her brown skin was rich and deep even through the black eyeliner, and the pierced nostril that a skull grimaced on seemed so foreign to him. *Who was this girl?*

"Well, I'm sure I'll see you in class, fathead."

"Please don't make that a thing." Alex rubbed his forehead. As she walked away Alex hoped she would look back.

"I hope you're not staring at me. We just talked about this," she called out.

Alex's gaze immediately dropped to the ground. "Uhm, nope. Just still eating my apple."

Inside, the halls of New Hope Academy hadn't changed a bit. They were still overly crowded with students in blazers and leather loafers, girls in plaid skirts and stockings, all laughing, all talking about their prestigious lives. Nothing about a student being beaten to death.

An awful chill rolled over Alex as he walked past the staircase where they found Nel. Deacon was there. He stood on the edge of the first step, shaking. He turned with eyes so harsh that Alex looked away fearfully.

"Deac, can we—"

Deacon brushed by without a word.

Since Nelson died, Alex wondered if their friendship would ever be the same. Maybe they would never be friends again.

"Trouble in paradise?" the boy Biggs called Manwell asked. There were a few others with him, one red-haired kid with freckles, another dirty-blond with a combover. "Must be shitty knowing your traitorous friend got what was coming to him."

Alex bit his tongue and continued down the hall to his first class, convincing himself not to slug Manwell.

"Let it be a lesson to you and any of these other punks who want to join terrorists and attack our government! U.N.A! U.N.A! U.N.A!" Their chants echoed down the hall behind him.

Alex walked into his first class, Historical Studies, with his favorite professor. Yara shot him a smile, and he took the empty seat just behind her.

Deacon came in after him and took a seat at the far end. The room filled with whispers, and Alex saw a couple of glances shot his way from the opposite side of the classroom. They obviously had something to say but kept their conversations to a whisper.

"Morning, students, good morning, and welcome to the next episode of Historical Studies. Where I ..." Professor Threshfold paused for a quick second. "Well, well, well, Mr. Quake? So glad to see you with us. For some reason, I believed you wouldn't be back after *everything* that happened."

Alex cleared his throat. "Yeah, well, I have to see justice get served."

A boy laughed from the other side of the class. "Justice *was* served. Your boy was a terrorist or more than likely going to become one like his brother. Not our fault he decided to go nuts and attack the guards."

"Is that what they said?" Alex asked.

Yara jumped in. "Three fat police guards armed with a total weight of a ton are assaulted by a hundred-pound unarmed fifteen-year-old? Seriously, Justin?"

"I don't know what you gutter kids have up your sleeve or what drugs you guys are on. For all we know, he had a weapon that Biggs and the boys fought out of his hands, defending themselves," he said, leaning back in his chair comfortably as if he'd won the argument.

"Full of shit, every one of you on that side of the classroom!" Yara leaned over her desk.

A brown-skinned boy, rose out of his seat. Alex could see the disgust in his eyes. "Better watch your mouth."

"You Bourgeoisie kids been integrated into New Hope a few years and think you run the place. Let what happened to that kid be a lesson to you. To all of you," added another.

The classroom went silent.

Alex's insides raged with fire. He focused on his pencil and pad. Tears smacked the notepad. Yara slowly turned and looked him over, then faced forward.

She whispered, "Don't you dare let them see you cry." Her words were simple, but her tone brutal. "The moment they see tears in your eyes, it'll be like blood in the water, and they'll never stop. So wipe your face, now."

Alex did as she demanded and pretended to sneeze into his sleeves, blowing his nose and wiping his face at the same time.

"Well, onto the lesson then. Next topic is social media and its effects on society during the turn of the millennia. I'll focus on how our enemies utilized it to manipulate the masses," said Professor Threshfold starting his lecture. "The times were simpler back then, but technology was definitely at its finest. In fact, there's no telling where we would be today if it weren't for World War III. But thanks to the leadership of our great leader and founding father, Cullen D. Roberts, we came out strong from beneath the nuclear cloud that ravaged the many nations affected by the nuclear war, and its fallout."

Threshfold continued on, but the bitterness from what the students had said wouldn't let Alex go. Could he really do this every day? The mocking, the belittling? Hearing his dead best friend utilized at the butt end of a joke to put down the other students? It wasn't like the other Bourgeoisie cared anyway. They allowed Nelson to die.

Alex swallowed, knowing they weren't to blame. If anyone was, it was him.

Alex tried to remember the days when the three of them played tag with the other kids in Eastern all throughout the cluttered, ravaged apartments of the city. There were other kids in Eastern, a lot more, once upon a time. But they were nothing more than a memory now. Some went missing, and others ran away.

The bell rang, snapping Alex out of his daydream. If he could call it that. The tension of the conversations earlier broke as everyone headed into the hallways. He stuffed everything he had in his backpack and waited for Yara to finish.

"Thanks for that. For sticking up for me."

"Don't mention it. Nothing to be thankful for, to be honest. Your friend's dead. I just didn't want them to piss on his grave without a fight."

"Yeah," Alex said, thinking about what the one kid said.

He turned to where Deacon sat, but his former friend was already gone, his red shirt the last thing Alex saw heading out the door. Giving her a few feet, Alex followed Yara out. They had the next class together, and it wasn't a creeper thing, but more of comfort, really.

He didn't want to be alone, which made him feel even worse about what happened to Nelson because now he knew exactly what those first few days were like for him.

A slam up ahead caught Alex's attention.

Manwell shoved Yara against a bunch of lockers. Alex's heart started pounding. He could hear her lashing out at him and the other kids to let her go.

She shoved Manwell.

A few of the boys gasped and laughed.

Manwell smacked her across the face hard enough for the hallway to echo with a clap. Then he did it again a second time.

Alex saw those of the Bourgeoisie class standing there in horror, silently watching. Sebastian, the main one who supposedly had these feelings for her, turned away.

You're worse than they are. Deacon's voice was a surging pain in Alex's forehead. *Are you a dog of the UNA?* Another voice, Nelson's, surged behind. No, not anymore. Not this time. He wouldn't sit back and watch.

Manwell's hand came down for the third strike, but Alex held it back and wrapped his hands around the boy's throat.

Heart thrashing, it echoed in his skull. Nothing else mattered. Alex slid his foot behind Manwell's legs and slammed him to the ground. The boy's head smacked the tiles. He thought about Nelson and how Manwell and the others laughed and joked with Biggs.

Every cackle of a laugh was a blow to Manwell's face. To his nose, his eye, his nose again. *One. Two. Three. Four ...* Alex counted with each thrown punch.

A weight was lifted. He couldn't stop himself even with the wet smacks and the blood on his knuckles. He was no longer punching Manwell; he was punching the sentinel that killed his mother, and he was punching Biggs. He was punching himself.

They tried pulling Alex off, but he smacked them away. All of his anger, all of his self-hate went into each blow.

Everything around him became silent.

A wrinkled blood-stained collar crumbled in Alex's hand. Manwell's head dangled. He groaned as a few spurts of blood dribbled down from his nose, which was now positioned at an odd angle.

By the time they pulled Alex off, the damage had been done. He must have been a frightening sight. Even the kids that Manwell had been with backed away as Threshfold dragged Alex off.

Thank goodness Biggs and the other guards weren't there. Alex could feel the icy cold metal shaft crashing against the side of his face, the crack as his skull split open, the overwhelming pressure of his eye bursting from his head as Biggs hacked a laugh. He'd kill Alex like he did Nelson, and he'd enjoy it.

Alex's hands were cuffed as he sat in a small office. Dull green walls oddly covered in motivational photography in redwood framing gave little hope and added nothing interesting about the room. He just didn't have the stomach to look at the other occupant.

Barely able to fit in the fancy cushioned chair opposite him was Biggs, who couldn't stop grinning.

"Boy, you garbage rats sure know how to sign your death warrants, huh? First Taniki–ta–Tanaki or whatever the hell his name was, now you?" Biggs sat back in the chair that winced and bowed at the legs. The heaviest laugh erupted from his jerking stomach. "You are so screwed, and you don't even know it."

Not a word left Alex's lips.

His dad's voice echoed from the other side of the door, pleading with Principal Krate. He was near sobbing. The tone broke Alex's heart, but the thrill of beating up Manwell after he laid hands on Yara was the first—and possibly last—act of passion he'd ever act on in this miserable dump of a life.

"See, what's the matter with you kids and your generation is that since these terrorist organizations, your D.O.R. and

Anarchy members came in, you watched them do all these attacks and assassinations and think the high society is weak, that we're meek. But you and those other Bourgeoisie rats have no clue."

Alex snickered. "You're nothing but a tub of lard who wishes he could be on the same level as the wealthy. You're nothing but—"

A massive fist came across Alex's face. Split his lip on impact as blood poured from his mouth.

Biggs wrapped his gorilla-like hands around the back of Alex's neck and brought him close. "You know I killed your friend, and I'd damn sure kill you too. Unfortunately, that's going to be out of my hands because the father of the boy you pummeled has more money and pull in places you don't want to think about. That daddy of yours, that pretty little sister? I hope for your sake, all they do is kill you and leave it at that."

Horror broke through the adrenaline in Alex's veins. He kept it together. He wouldn't lose it, not in front of Biggs.

Alex's dad's voice went silent behind the door, and so did Principal Krate's. The knob started wiggling, and Biggs eased back, scratching the sides of his face. Alex's veins became ice. The door opened, and immediately, his father's eyes fell on him. He rushed over.

"What the hell happened here? He wasn't like this when I got here."

Biggs shrugged. "No idea. Apparently, the kid's clumsy. Right, Alex?"

"Can we go now?" Alex asked. He was ripe with fear.

His dad's hands trembled, and his eyes narrowed on Alex, fighting back tears. But Alex kept his confident expression. The one that kept his dad at ease. No need for him to lose it, not with Olivia right outside waiting for them in the hallway.

Principal Krate came over. "Biggs, get the hell out of here, now!"

"Of course, sir." Biggs smiled at Alex as he rose from the chair, the cushion permanently dented in.

When the door shut behind him, Principal Krate paced back and forth. He was sweating. "I wish I could spin it someway, with the loss of a friend and kids rough-housing and fighting. But what you did to Manwell, Alex … What the hell got into you?"

Alex stared blankly at the chair where Biggs sat. He thought about his mom over and over and over again.

"Alex." His dad's voice was a low groan as if he had given up on life ages ago. "Why did you do it?"

Nothing. The images of his mom bleeding out became his dad, then Olivia.

"Douglas, it would be in your best interest to take Alex out of N.H.A. It would be even better to keep him off the streets for the next month or so." Principal Krate's voice trembled. "Do you have a safe place to stay, to ride this out until it blows over?"

"I–I don't. How bad are we talking, Mr. Krate?"

"I fear Alex's life is in danger.… Possibly your whole family's lives."

Alex's eyes watered as Principal Krate's words hit him.

Hearing those words from Principal Krate's thin lips, his eyes frantic and his voice quivering, brought a stomach-turning feeling that made Alex want to vomit.

Everything he tried to prevent from happening, pushing Nelson away in order to protect himself and his family... It all meant nothing now. He was the one who poured the gasoline and lit the match.

He was the one who put his family in danger.

11

Principal Krate was a good man, a real good man. He had them dropped off back in Eastern without a word to anyone. They would need all the support they could get to get out of Eastern. Doug had already decided.

He looked over at Alex in the back seat. He didn't look like the same boy. Not since Nelson passed. It was like that boy's death took a large chunk of his son, just like when Myra ... He rubbed the stinging tears from behind his glasses.

Olivia leaned her head against Alex's shoulder. She held his hand. Doug was a hot mess in his head and in his heart. They'd come for blood, no doubt. Damn, they would come for blood. The black SUV pulled up to the apartment, and he quickly ushered the kids out.

He gave a terse nod to the driver, who returned the gesture, but something in the man's eyes chilled Doug to the bone. The SUV peeled off.

No, he'd imagined it, that's all, just imagined it. He got his kids inside, rushed them up the staircase. He fell, smacking his shin on the first three steps. Hurt like hell, but it would have to wait.

He swung the door open and pushed them both in. He scratched his scalp and began to pace back and forth. The apartment was quiet. Only the hum of the VEN-O broke the silence.

"Dad."

Something of a voice cracked in his ear, but he couldn't stop pacing. Where could they go? Any of the other Suites were out of the question. They would have to leave Constance. Only one other city in the Americas, and there was no room there from what he'd heard.

"Dad." The words were like the buzz of a fly.

There were the other continents. Europe had three cities, but he'd heard it was hard to be black in Europe these days even though racial differences were outlawed. Maybe Asia? Four cities there. Easy to get lost in the crowd. The only issue was the people didn't take too kindly to strangers. Not to mention the cost. But that was the same problem all around, wasn't it?

"Dad!"

He looked down at Olivia, whose eyes were teary with worry. "What is it, honey?"

"Dad, what's going on?" She looked at Alex.

The boy was a statue, his eyes expressionless, dead almost. There was still blood on his shirt.

Doug still couldn't believe it. His boy, the quiet one, the boy who strayed from violence, would rather cry than get into a fight, chose to snap on a child of another class. A child whose father swung a pretty big stick.

He ran his fingers down his face, trying to fight the sweat back. His heart pounded. He went to the window. A patrol truck crept down the road. His heart leaped in his chest. He doubled over with stomach pangs, gripping the back of the couch.

The truck crept down with caution. Fear had him imagining the sentinels inside getting their rifles ready with silencers, zip-ties on their hips for the kids. *No. Please no. God no.* The first tear hit the back of his hand, rolling between the creases of his charagma.

All the credits he'd saved up would be used to get the hell out of Eastern.

"Dad, are we in trouble, like the Tanakas?"

He wiped his face. His baby girl couldn't see her father breaking down now. He turned. "No. Nothing like that. I think it's just time to move on, you know?"

Alex finally looked up at him, but his eyes were hopeless. He missed his son's confident smile, never realized how it could make him feel. In a way, Alex was kind of holding them all together. He never let anything get to him. Not like things got to Doug or Olivia.

Alex got that from Myra. She had a stubborn passion for people, all people at that, from the leaders of this screwed-up world to the ones who lived in the Outskirts. Doug wasn't sure how much of that Alex or Olivia got, but it sure wasn't in him.

Especially now. He looked down at the couch. Beneath the middle cushion under the floorboards was a sawed-off shotgun. Ten shells. It was a stupid buy, but after everything with Myra there was one thought at the time.

He planned on loading it and waiting in an alley for one of the patrols to get out of their trucks and walk on foot. He'd take out as many as he could in the name of his beloved wife. But then he thought about Olivia and Alex. His babies. Myra's babies. She would kill him again if he ended up in the afterlife—if he left them alone in this world.

No. Revenge like that wasn't an option.

"Kids, come here a second." Olivia straggled over while Alex barely shuffled. Doug pulled them close, pulled their heads together, and whispered, "Pack up your clothes, all the essentials, nothing more."

Olivia whimpered. "Dad, what's going on?" Tears streamed down her face now.

"Do you trust me, honey?"

She nodded.

"You're still Daddy's little bugaboo?"

She gave a broken smile and nodded.

"Okay. Please, I need you both to do as I say. Please."

Olivia nodded and went to her room. He grasped Alex by the shoulder and whipped him around. His son's eyes were so empty. He wasn't this bad at Myra's funeral. There was nothing Doug could say to his son.

Alex nodded and walked to the bedroom.

Doug fell on the couch and started crying. Whatever strength he had in their presence crumbled. "Myra, please, send me a sign. Send me something, please. I don't know what I'm gonna do if they come to take our kids." All he could do was breathe the words.

With that damn VEN-O in the kitchen, he couldn't even get mad. The groaning of another truck made his flesh prickle. He wiped his mouth and took a deep breath.

South America! The continent where the largest chunk of America's produce came from. Mostly farmland since they destroyed the jungle and leveled the terrain for easy access. They could hide away in some of the more secluded areas, Start from scratch, live off the land, away from all this chaos.

He remembered that being one of the dreams of an old friend of his, a few discussed it at their sacred lunch table way back when. It was easy to dream back then. The truck passed as the howl of a dog broke the fading groan of the engine.

"South America sounds good, right, Myra?" He looked up to the brown-stained ceiling. The apartment looked disgusting now. Like the fear and terror of the whole situation had lifted some veil over his eyes, and he could see the world around him for what it really was.

Ugly. Broken. He tolerated it all, tricked himself into believing this was perfectly fine, but it wasn't. *Myra wouldn't have approved of this one bit, you big ole dummy.* He took a few more deep breaths.

Five thousand credits were saved up. He could pass them on to smugglers in the Outskirts. *Damn … the Outskirts.* He thought about Olivia. Thought about how lawless it was out there. He remembered the horror stories of how those who were once Bourgeoisie citizens got stripped of their class, then were forced to the Outskirts. They didn't last a day. Sometimes it was whole families.

He wrenched his eyes shut. He'd pack the shotgun. He'd have to show Alex how to use it. The boy hated guns. *He's gonna have to suck it up and take the mantle if anything happens to me.*

Doug got up from the couch dug up a pen and a notebook and started putting his plan into action. Resources, clothes, two days tops to gather everything he might need to find. No point in going to work. "Sorry, Sid. You're the king of the hill now."

12

Their bags were packed and on standby at the front door. His father hadn't slept since they came home in that SUV two days ago. All he did was gaze out through the windows. He hadn't said a word to Alex.

Sometimes Alex wondered if his dad hated him for putting them in this situation. The day they got home, Alex could barely function, let alone talk. After he packed his bags, Olivia came over and comforted him, but he couldn't fight the truth. All of this was because of him.

Alex lay against their bedroom wall, his thumb gliding over the picture of his mom. *Would you be mad at me like Dad?* He shook his head, thinking about how his dad hadn't even looked at him since everything happened.

Olivia was at the wall peeking through the bullet holes. "Still can't believe you laced a wealthy kid." She dug around the edges of the hole. "Didn't think you had it in you."

"It's not funny, look at all the trouble it caused. Dad hates me."

"I honestly don't care. Screw those Exclusive jerks. You should've done worse. Especially after what they did to Nelson."

Alex caressed his mom's face. "What's worse?"

"Kill him."

Alex jumped up from the cot, holding his mom's picture gently in his hand. "What the hell's wrong with you, Liv? Kill another student?"

"They killed Nelson without a care in the world, so why should we care? They obviously don't."

He lifted the picture of their mom to his sister's face. "You think Mom would've wanted me to kill someone, another kid?"

Her expression became emotionless. "Mom's dead. They murdered her too."

Murdered. There was that word again. Olivia was young, but she hid her true feelings well, even from him. Months of night terrors and screaming herself to sleep was only the exterior effect of watching their mom die, but he always wondered what the internal damage was like.

"Doesn't matter. We have to be better than them. I had a moment of weakness and couldn't control myself. Now, you and Dad are in danger."

She wrapped her arms around him and squeezed, burying her head into his neck. Alex laid his head on hers, hoping this would blow over and that this was a fear tactic to put him and all other Bourgeoisie citizens in their place.

But then, he'd thought the same thing about Nelson when Biggs took him away.

"I'm gonna talk to Dad," he said.

"You sure that's a good idea?"

"I just need to know where his head is. At least then I can gauge what I can and can't do and what I can and can't say."

She nodded, pursing her lips. "Good luck."

Alex arched his brows and headed out to the living room. Besides the low hum of the VEN-O, all other sounds came from the neighbor's apartment. He found his dad standing with his hands on his hips, a tattered black shirt on his shoulders, and jeans.

"Dad?"

"Shouldn't you be in your room?" he said gruffly.

"Yeah, but I just wanted to talk to you about all of this, about everything."

His father cleared his throat without taking his eyes off the window. Instead, he focused down the road. "Nothing to talk about."

Alex sucked his teeth. "Dad, we need to talk because maybe … Maybe this will be the only time we'll have to talk."

His dad turned and waved a hand toward the couch that was his bed. It was old, sagging in the middle, and cracked with the sounds of splintering wood when he sat down. "So, talk."

Alex fiddled with his fingers. "Dad, I didn't mean for all this to happen. Everything with Nelson just got to me, and honestly, it's been eating me alive."

His father took a deep breath, and Alex finally saw his dad taking an interest in what was being said. "I can understand that." His bulky frame leaned forward. "But did you ever once think about your sister and me? Did you think about the consequences?"

Alex's mind ran with the thoughts about how he'd treated Nelson for the sake of keeping Olivia and him safe.

"No, I didn't. I was … angry. I saw this girl get attacked, and I just couldn't take it anymore, Dad." His voice cracked a little.

His dad was silent for a while. He dug his fingers into his eyes and winced like something painful jabbed him in the side. He rose from the couch and looked out the window before pulling out the cushion.

Confused, Alex stepped back. There was a large hole, and he watched his dad rummage through the yellow fill of the couch. Then he pulled out a large gun. Alex stumbled back. When his father rested the silver barrel and brown handle in his hand, all Alex could see were the guns in the sentinels' hands.

"After your mom was killed, I went out and purchased this. It was a few days after everything happened. I guess I planned on taking justice into my own hands." His father wiped his face.

"Dad, what are you going to do with that?"

"Nothing stupid, trust me. Just listen. I knew then that if I left the house with this gun, I wouldn't be able to keep you and Liv safe anymore. They would've thrown you both out into the Outskirts."

Alex swallowed, calming his spirit. The barrel was wide and made his skin crawl. "So you stayed home."

"I did. And I shouldered everything that this world threw at our family from that moment on. I became selfless and long-suffering because that was the only way to keep you two safe. Then when the government came up with the integration program and you were selected, I knew this was your mom smiling on us. This was it. You would create a new path for our family."

"I guess I screwed that up then."

His father was silent for a minute, more silent than Alex appreciated, but what he did was unfixable.

"Alex we live in a world where we all make mistakes, but the margin of error is so finite and so risky, especially depending on what class you're in. I thought you'd learned that after Nelson's passing. But at the end of the day, you *are* my son, and I'll never abandon you. Got that?"

Alex nodded, and his father hugged him tight enough to feel the rhythm of his heart. "Thanks, Dad."

"Look, I have a plan that's finally coming together. Tomorrow morning, we're leaving."

"Leaving? Where can we go, Dad?"

He started putting the large gun back inside the couch, covering it with all the cottony insides. "South America. All kinds of fertile land there. We can build a house, live off the land. Be free of all this …" he whispered even lower than he needed, "madness."

Alex's tone matched his. "How are we going to do that? And doesn't that mean going into the Outskirts? I–I don't know, Dad."

His father laid a heavy hand on his shoulder. "Alex, I'm just as nervous as you are. But I'm looking on the bright side." He smiled. "We can make out there better than we'll make it here."

Sorrow and grief sunk Alex deeper into depression. Whatever life they had behind the walls was over. New Hope

Academy? That was done. He didn't even stand a chance at working at the steel mill.

He'd ruined their lives. "Dad, I'm sorry. I messed up bad."

His dad pulled him in for a hug. He couldn't stop crying. He was just as bad as Jason at this point. At least the Tanakas were able to stay within the walls. "We'll be okay, Alex. I know it."

Evening came slow and steady. For dinner, they had chicken gizzards again. Salty and chewy, Alex bit his tongue several times, trying to work the meat between his teeth. At the end of the day, it was food.

His dad discussed the plan over dinner. Alex wasn't a major fan of it, and neither was Olivia. But what choice did they have now? They were out of options. What really rattled Alex was the fact he'd have to learn to use that gun.

He wanted nothing to do with it. Not that it mattered now.

It was an hour before curfew. The streetlights shone through the bullet holes of the wall, and Constance gleamed triumphantly over the wall. It would be the last time Alex saw the emanating light.

There was a loud crack against the wall from outside. Alex stumbled back, nearly waking Olivia. A harsh whisper followed. "Hey, Alex! Hey!"

The voice didn't sound like Deacon. "Who's there? Deacon?"

"No, you klutz. It's me, Yara," she whispered.

Yara? His whole body shook from the thought of her being there. *What is she doing here?*

"Dingus, you there?" she whispered.

"I am," he whispered through the hole as loud as he could without making too much noise. "Meet me on the steps."

Dad's snarls echoed through the living room. It was the kind of snore he made when he'd worked too many shifts without time off. With the lack of sleep he had been getting, there was no way he was waking up anytime soon.

Alex crept downstairs and stood in front of the door. He covered his mouth and gave a quick breath. The last thing he needed was chicken gizzard breath. He patted his clothes and tried straightening them. He took a deep breath and exhaled slowly.

As the door opened, Yara turned, and her black hair fell stiffly over her shoulder. She wore jean shorts and her trademark hoody and sneakers. Something was off, though. She seemed jittery. Not strong and confident like she was in school, even her words were mousy.

Her left eye was bruised.

She smiled, grazing her hand over it. "Could've been a lot worse if it weren't for you."

"Oh, I just reacted, that's all." Alex slipped one hand in his pocket, the other he used to balance himself in the doorway.

"And because of that, life's gotten a little easier at school."

"Cool. Good to hear." He looked up toward the city and leaned against the doorway. "So, how did you find me? You stalking me or something?"

She snorted. Alex laughed as she covered her face. "I can't believe you made me do that."

"I can't believe you *did* that."

She caught her breath. "After everything that happened in school, rumors started springing up like crazy."

"What kind of rumors?"

"Like you're dead, or you're going to be dead. Scary stuff. So I talked to your friend, Deacon. The kid misses you, by the way, so don't let the act of brooding aloofness fool you. He told me where you lived and how to reach you."

Alex nodded, thinking about the times when Deacon and Nelson hurled rocks at the wall to wake him up in the morning to go hang out. "I see. Why did you want to find me?"

"Because it's been driving me crazy for the last few days. I want to know why?"

"Why what?"

She sat down and slapped the top step next to her. "Why did you do that for me?"

He joined her but gave her some space. He remembered Nelson's and Deacon's words loud and clear. "I guess I got tired of being afraid. Sitting by watching the people I care about getting stepped on for no good reason at all, just because of social differences ... I'm tired of it. " Alex thought about the last conversation he had with Nelson.

A soft sound came from her. A giggle. It didn't suit her. "To be honest, from the moment I met you, I thought you were a coward. You were just like the rest of the other sheep, following the line to the slaughterhouse." She wiped her eyes, looking up to the moon that glowed brightly. "But you shocked me, Alex Quake."

She rose to her feet and pulled him up with her. She trotted down the steps, then started walking through the darkened street that was only highlighted by the milky-white illumination of the moon. Alleyways were haunting black spaces where Alex feared evil hid, but when Yara turned, something in her eyes was assuring and alluring.

So he followed.

The dilapidated apartments did nothing but strengthen the bitter cold that whipped around them, causing Yara's hair to fall over her soft brown features. She was beautiful beneath the moonlight of the ghetto that was Eastern Suites. Powerful and so sure of herself with each step. Alex wished he had that kind of confidence. That fearlessness. It reminded him of his mom.

He asked, "So where are you from?"

"Here, like you. I'm in the Northern Suites." She pulled a few strands from her face.

"Isn't that like half an hour away? What about curfew?"

"Screw curfew," she bristled. "I'd rather hang out ... if that's okay with you?"

He hid a nervous chill. "Yeah ... Yeah, that's cool."

She smiled and lowered her head.

Alex's mind was all over the place. Fear, nervousness, joy ... anticipation. He didn't know what to say, yet he made it this far without mumbling and stuttering. It was all or nothing. This would be his last night stalking the streets of Eastern. Tomorrow morning they would be gone.

"Can I ask you something?" Her breath was a white haze under the streetlights.

Alex nodded.

"When you look at everything, how messed up the world is, have you ever thought about just giving up?"

Their pace slowed and Alex's throat became dry with thoughts of his mom dying and all those terrible feelings unearthed when Nelson died. It all sickened him. "Yeah. But I have to keep going for my little sister and my dad. I have to live for them."

"Have you ever seen that as a weakness? Caring for others?"

Alex sneered, listening to her pessimistic spirit return as they walked passed a blackened alleyway.

"No, I'm serious. Relationships are obstacles. I never knew my dad, and my mom ... she didn't want me. So, she abandoned me out there." Yara nodded toward the Outskirts. "For years, I felt so inadequate, like it was my fault. I hated myself."

"What? In the Outskirts? How did you survive out there? How old were you?"

She giggled, but not softly and innocently like before. It was more sarcastic than anything. "Five. And how did I survive?" She stopped and looked to the sky. "I did a lot of things a kid shouldn't do. Seems so long ago now."

Goosebumps swept over his arms, and it wasn't from the chilled air. "My dad told me the Outskirts were hell on earth. He said never ever leave the outer wall because that place will take everything from you. Your mind, body, even your spirit."

She wiped her tears away. "Your dad's right, you know? The Outskirts are a filthy place filled with death, injustice, betrayal. The worst of it is the pain of hunger. But here on this side of the wall, you have the same thing, don't you?"

Alex paused, searching for words.

"You want to know what makes the Outskirts better than life behind the walls?" She was obviously joking.

"What?"

She turned to him, and Alex caught a glint of moonlight from a tear rolling down her chin. "Freedom," she whispered.

Alex thought about his dad's plan. If this was the last time he would see Yara, Alex wanted to tell her everything. "Yara, I'm not going to—"

"You—" Yara's eyes widened as she backed away. What the hell are you doing here?" she asked, staring over Alex's shoulder and her voice trembling with terror.

A crack of pain smacked the back of Alex's head. The city spun as he collapsed, smacking the concrete. It smelled awful. Yara screamed. Alex's eyes rolled up just in time to see her being shoved to the ground by two large shadowy figures, then gagged and bound.

Everything was spinning. Yara's muffled scream reached his ears, but Alex couldn't focus. "Yara…" He groaned.

Another cold thud hit the back of his head. Yara's screams faded like a radio being turned low, and something warm rolled down his neck.

Then everything turned black.

Intense sobs and cries enveloped Alex as a sliver of light seared into his blurred vision. He winced as a painful ache reached from the back of his head. He started stretching his arms outward into the darkness, his fingers feeling around his environment.

The ground was hard, cold, cement maybe? He coughed, overpowered by the smell. The air was wet with piss and other pungent odors. All around him were the groans and cries of people, some begging for help.

"Hey," Yara's voice echoed in the darkness. "I'm glad you're okay. You had me scared for a little bit."

He groaned but was relieved to know she was okay. He rolled over onto his back and struggled to look up. Yara's hair fell over his face as she helped him sit up.

"What happened?" His fingers gently pressed over a warm egg-sized lump on the back of his head. It was sticky. He pulled his fingers away from the throbbing pain.

"Biggs and his goons hit you over the head, threw a sack over both our heads, and dragged us into a vehicle. I tried to listen and feel the movements of the truck."

"A truck?"

"The engine was too loud for it to have been a car, that's for sure. Not to mention it felt like we were thrown in the back of a container of some sort."

Alex winced again, pressing the spot on the back of his head. His father was going to be worried sick. So was Olivia.

"This isn't good, Alex." Yara's voice was hesitant and starting to crack with fear. "I think we're in some kind of prison."

Her fear made him feel even worse. She was the tough one. He scanned their surroundings as his eyes finally adjusted through the haze of a growing headache. They were in a cell of some kind, bars on the left, right, and in front of them. Behind was a rugged wall made from large, misshapen and cracked stone.

He stepped to the bars in front of them as his fingers grasped the rusty cold steel. There were cells all around them linked together side by side. People were screaming and crying. He even heard the voices of children and the squeal of a baby.

He looked a few feet across from them to where a boy and a woman looked back with sunken eyes. Their clothes hung loosely, the woman's face was frail and a sickening yellow beneath the dim light. It looked like they had been there for weeks, maybe months.

There were dozens of others. Some were bruised and bloody with welts and open sores down their arms and legs. One man stayed huddled in a corner, gripping himself.

Alex's chest tightened. His mind replayed everything over in his head. He could hear Biggs's laughter from when he was cuffed and waiting in the principal's office. The bully's words were sharp in Alex's ear now. *You garbage rats sure know how to sign your own death warrant, huh?*

Alex's breaths became rapid and shallow.

"Hey, hey." Yara wrapped her arms around him. "It's okay. Breathe. Breathe." She took deep breaths with him. "I don't need you losing it right now. We need to stick together. We're getting out of here, right?"

Alex's breaths rattled his body as he got a grip.

She patted his cheek. "Okay. From what I can remember, the ride was about an hour and a half. One thing for sure, I know I heard the gate of the inner wall open."

Alex hated to ask and suspected he knew the answer anyway, but . . . "You think this has to do with Manwell?"

"More than likely."

His fingers cracked around the flaking black bars of the cell, and he pushed himself away, pacing from one corner to the next.

"Hey, you guys from the outside?" a weak voice asked from the darkness of the cell next to them.

Alex stepped to the bars.

A boy, maybe six or seven, crawled over, his face thin and sickly pale. "Do you have any food?" he asked, barely able to finish his sentence.

Alex shook his head, and so did Yara.

Alex inched closer. "How long have you been here?"

"Two ... maybe three months." The boy hacked \.

"What?" Yara's face scrunched.

"Yeah, there are people who've been here longer. Mostly kids. We're easy to sell from what I've heard."

Alex slammed against the bars gripping them hard, his eyes wide with horror. "That's not funny. What the hell do you mean 'sell?' "

The boy jumped back, coughing and struggling to catch his breath.

"Are you freaking stupid?" a girl's voice asked sharply, breaking into the conversation from the cell behind them. "Can't you tell the kid's sick?"

Alex turned to see a girl with short pink hair and a bandaged patch over her right eye. She had light tan skin, and the one good eye was light brown. Even though from behind the bars she stood only at chest height, there was still something intimidating about her.

Her gaze sparked Alex's fight or flight. He cleared his throat, calming himself. "There's no way they can sell people like that. Not Bourgeoisie citizens."

She laughed. "Listen to you. You Bourgeoisie citizens act just like the Exclusives, you know that? Because you live behind the walls, you think you can live like the Exclusives. I'll bet you even dream of becoming a patrician."

Alex began to argue. "The integration program—"

"It's bull!" the girl yelled. "All of it! These people don't care about you. It's not about class. It's about power and influence." Alex shivered as she stepped closer, her eye scrutinizing him. Her voice softened. "Look at you. I popped your cherry, didn't I, Bourgeoisie trash?"

Trash? "Who are you? Where are you from?"

Her grin was near sadistic. "I'm from the Outskirts, a nobody. A Pariah, the bottom of the bottom, the lowest of the low. But oh, do I find it sweet when one of the high plummets to the earth. Sometimes you guys kill yourselves, or one of us kills you. But most times, you guys blow your brains out." She chuckled, pointing two fingers to her temple. "*Boom.*"

Alex shivered. She was nuts. "I don't believe you, any of you. It's all bull. You guys are in here because you messed up. Just like I messed up. Just like …" He couldn't finish. He turned to Yara. She shook her head in disagreement.

No. He thought about Nelson and Deacon. He thought about what Jason told Nelson about trafficking and New Hope being a setup. He thought about the labs. Insane. It was all insane DOR propaganda.

He collapsed to the floor on his knees. "It's not real.... It's not true.... Yara? It's not true."

She knelt in front of him and wrapped her arms around him.

"Anybody got a pistol for this kid? He's checking out?" the girl's voice echoed through the cells.

"It's not true."

She must have been about their age, but it was hard to tell in the light. He squinted and crawled closer to her cell, but she ducked back into the darkness.

"Believe what you want. Remain in that dreadful dream of illusions and false reality."

Alex turned to the boy, whose eyes were wide with tears and fear. "It's not true."

"Leave him alone." Alex turned back to the girl. Her top lip pulled at the corner as her eyes burrowed into him with bitter resentment. She flicked a vibrant pink strand over her hardened brown eyes. "He's obviously struggling to speak. They haven't fed us in a few days."

"Who are 'they?' That fat police guard and his friends?" Yara asked, disgust in her voice.

"Nah. They're nothing but cronies, not even worth their grain of salt. Nothing to worry about."

Nothing to worry about. Alex's eyes panned the massive bay of cells and walkways. They must have been deep underground somewhere. A loud screeching followed by a metallic slam made every head poke from the bars.

Dozens of hands of all shapes and colors reached through the bars. They trembled with fear and weakness. Alex gripped his mouth as the cries and wails rattled his bones and insides.

"Please, give us food," voices poured from the bars.

"Please, I miss my mommy and my daddy," a little girl cried.

"I swear I'm an Exclusive. I don't belong here. I can give you anything. I swear," a man's voice begged.

A joyful cartoonish whistle overpowered the misery and sorrow that filled the bleak darkness. The tune silenced everyone. A loud clacking started from one of the cells and worked its way toward them. Shadowy silhouettes backed away from the bars as the massive shadow casting on the floor grew with each crunch.

"Well, two for the price of one," Biggs said, scratching his scruffy chin. "Imagine us getting Alex and Yara. Oh man, won't the hallways of N.H.A. be less noisy without your yapping, gloomy, pettiness."

Yara banged against the rusty bars. "Let us out of here, Biggs!"

Biggs slammed a metal baton against the bar, barely missing her fingers. "Shut up."

Alex pulled her away. "Whatever Manwell and his dad want to do to me, that's fine. I'll accept it. Just keep Yara out of it, okay? Just let her go."

"Quake, you don't get it. If you're down here with the rest of these unfortunate degenerates and awful smelling gutter trash, you ain't nobody going nowhere. Well, 'cept for you two. They'll find your corpses in the Outskirts."

The massive metal door screeched open again from down the hallway.

"Biggs," a deep voice called. "Snag Quake and the girl. Bring them up. The amount has been paid."

Biggs rubbed his hands together, his charagma a stamp of victory. "Like music to my ears." His lips peeled back greedily, and he dug in his waist, then tossed two pairs of handcuffs through the bars. "Cuff yourselves."

"Screw you," Yara yelled.

"Cuff yourself, or I'll do it while you're unconscious. Pick one." He laughed.

Alex picked up the handcuffs and handed Yara the other pair. "Do as he says. I want to see if I can get you out of this. It's already too late for me."

Her eyes narrowed on him. "Are you insane? They want to kill you!"

"Yeah, but if it means keeping my family safe and you too, it'll be worth it."

"That's so stupid."

"And so touching." Biggs grunted with a laugh. "Now, please just put on the damn cuffs."

Yara took the cuffs and clamped them around her wrists. Alex clamped them tight around his own, the metal already rubbing uncomfortably around the bony parts.

Biggs opened the cell, ripped them from inside, and shoved them ahead.

The girl with the pink hair's shrilled voice echoed down the hall. "Don't piss yourself, hero. Not in front of your girlfriend."

"Keep moving." Biggs shoved him forward.

Alex's blood boiled. *What the hell's wrong with her?*

On the other side of the metal door was another world. A sweet fragrance of exotic fruit filled the air. Alex imagined something juicy and sweet from the tropical islands he read about in history class. His mouth watered. A large dark-skinned man dressed as if he was going to meet the Secretary General awaited them.

The dusty dungeon atmosphere was cut away as the floors changed to red wall-to-wall carpeting. The walls were decorated with portraits, and statues lined the hallway. Biggs shoved them forward, and the dark-skinned man snatched Alex by the collar and grabbed Yara by the arm.

"Bring them upstairs," Biggs grunted.

The man bunched his brows. "You sure the boss is going to be okay with that? What about the party?"

"Just do it!"

The man nodded and slung them forward.

"Alex, we have to do something," Yara whispered. "You can't just give up. Don't you have anyone who can help, connections maybe?"

"No." He wished he did.

"What about Nelson's older brother? He's part of DOR, right?"

"Yeah, but I don't have any contact with him."

Elegant classical music poured softly from down the hallway, large chandeliers gleaming like polished diamond, hung from the ceiling. Only the homes of patricians were as decorated, spilling with ego. Ahead, twisted in a perfect spiral, was a staircase, each step made of marble and lined with gold.

At the top, voices and laughter greeted them. Alex noticed a tan-skinned woman with dirty-blonde hair and the bluest eyes he had ever seen. She wore an extravagant champagne-colored dress, and the man whose arm she clung to wore a suit of the same color. When the man's eyes met Alex's, his heart raced with horror.

"T-that's Governor Krate, Principal Krate's father," Alex's voice was a near whimper.

The grip of Alex's tormentor tightened over his shoulder. He was shoved forward down the hallway and saw that Yara nearly lost her footing. "Don't you dare run," the man growled. "Keep your eyes forward, and don't say nothing to anyone," he barked.

The left side of the building opened into a massive ballroom. Pearly white marble floors and columns made of stone made the place look like a palace. Jade statues lined the archways, gold trimming sparkled everywhere, and the sweetest cool breeze set the atmosphere. There were dozens of people in the space. All of them high-class Exclusives.

A familiar laugh cackled, and Alex shot a glance to his left. There stood Professor Threshfold talking to a young woman who looked half his age. His eyes slowly rolled up to meet Alex's, but then he immediately looked away, continuing his conversation.

"What the hell is going on?" Alex asked as they were shoved forward.

"Sir," the brawny man called to another man in a suit with his back turned. He was entertaining a small group of women. "We have what you asked for."

The man turned, and Alex's stomach raced with excitement. He even gave a deep exhale of relief. "Principal Krate, thank—"

"Damn it, Conroy, not in front of the guests," Principal Krate replied with an elegant façade. "You know my father doesn't want my business spilling into his own. He's a crab that way," Principal Krate said, his tone shrewd.

"P–Principal Krate?" Alex muttered.

Yara snapped, "I knew there was something off about you."

Principal Krate shook his head. "It's more complex than that, Yara dear. Really it is. Conroy, bring them to the room. Manwell's father will be here soon. Get them comfortable, and I'll be right up."

13

Nothing made sense anymore. Why were they here in this place? Why didn't Principal Krate get them out of this situation? He was the one who told Alex's dad to keep him in hiding. What was all this?

They waited in a cold room strapped to two chairs surrounded by all kinds of gadgets and devices, the most disturbing being weapons. Yara struggled to break free. Her elbows bumped against his as she fiddled with the rope through her cuffs.

Beneath their feet and covering the floor of the entire room was a large sheet of plastic. Suddenly, the door swung open. In slid Principal Krate, fixing his cuffs and straightening a silk tie. He looked more confident than he did in school, more in his *element*.

"Yara, Alex," he said, nodding.

Yara wiggled in her chair. "Screw you and let us go!"

"Definitely not going to happen. You both saw my side business in the basement."

"Your side business?" Alex asked, trying to hide the terror in his voice and doing everything in his power to hold out hope for Principal Krate.

"Yeah, so I'm in the business of …" Principal Krate picked up a small surgical blade that reflected the barcode on his right hand, then glided its smooth edge over his thumb before laying it down carefully and collecting a pair of shears, the kind only found in hospitals. "Torturing, kidnapping, selling people … parts of people. Whatever the buyer wants, really."

"So many kids trusted you." Yara spat at his feet.

Principal Krate leaned over a table filled with more tools. "I know, and everything I told you, I meant. I love all of my students, and no matter how this looks, it's nothing personal. Alex, I had nothing to do with Nelson's death. And you can bet I'm going to take care of that as a final gift to you."

"What?" Alex looked up at him, wide-eyed and confused. He tried to rip free of the straps, but they were too tight.

"Conroy, you remember what we talked about earlier?"

The brawny dark-skinned man smiled. "Yes, sir."

"Good. Call Biggs in." Principal Krate scratched his smooth well-shaved face and smiled at the two of them like a man waiting patiently for a package to arrive.

Biggs came into the room and grinned as his eyes met theirs. "It must be my birthday or something because if I can—"

Bang!

A puff of white flared from the side of Biggs's head, and blood sprayed the wall as his heavy frame flopped to the ground.

Yara went silent.

Alex nearly pissed himself. He couldn't stop shaking.

Blood pooled in a thick puddle below Biggs's face. The plastic kept it from staining the smooth redwood floors beneath.

"I so hate removing good innocent people, no matter what class: Exclusives, Bourgeoisies, Pariahs.... But if you're a disgusting brute who throws your weight around and bullies? I love putting those types of people in the ground." Principal Krate gave a haughty laugh as he wiped the pistol handle. "Conroy, please clean this mess up before Manwell's father gets here, would you?"

"Of course, sir."

The large man cut a portion of the plastic sheeting and wrapped it around Biggs. Blood drained over his suit and head. His blue eyes were still frozen with a hint of excitement. The heavy-set man dragged Biggs's body out like the bag of garbage he was.

Principal Krate cleaned his glasses with a silk handkerchief and cleared his throat. "I know what you must think of me. I must be such a disappointment to you. Trust me, my father *feels* the same way."

Alex pleaded, "Principal Krate, please, sir, let us go."

A few tears rolled down from Principal Krate's eyes. Alex couldn't read him. Was he really this insane? Were all the people behind the inner wall this insane?

"You know, Alex, you remind me of myself as a boy. Quiet, *firm* in your beliefs. That's why it pains me so much to have to do this. You have no idea. I truly love everyone no matter the class," he sobbed. He came closer and leaned against the table that held a wooden bat studded with metal.

"What the hell is wrong with you?" Yara was shaking. Alex could feel her from his chair. "Why are you crying?"

"Because, like you two, I sought freedom. Joy. Peace," Principal Krate said with a tone that deepened and heightened into aggression. "Then my father ... He took everything from me. He beat this hatred into me. He took everything I knew and loved!" Krate slammed his hand on the table.

They both jumped, nearly toppling over.

Principal Krate took a deep breath, paced back and forth, and calmed. "I'm sorry."

Alex begged with sobs of his own. "Principal Krate, this isn't you. You want to unite the classes, remember? This isn't you! You said you wanted to end the hatred between the classes, right?"

"I-I did say that. Yes. End the hatred that creates monsters ..." He trailed off lost in deep thought as he looked over the table with horrific tools and weapons. "Did you know I was in love with one of our slaves? Not an Exclusive, not a Bourgeoisie, a slave girl. She was beautiful. Anastasia. She had soft fair features, silky, short black hair ... My father bought her and her family from Asia."

He's lost his mind. He's not even thinking about what he's about to do to us. Fear gripped Alex as he struggled to grasp reality. Principal Krate just went on talking.

"My mom, like me, loved and cared for our slaves. Anastasia and I fell in love. I would leave her flowers and love notes in my room when she cleaned. I'd make and sneak her and her family breakfast. They cherished me and my mother. The greatest moment of my life was when I told Anastasia

I loved her, and she said she felt the same way. Of course, the issue was society ... and father." Krate sobbed. His anger began boiling up little by little. "I told her we'd run away. I had a stash of money. I had everything worked out."

Alex tried ignoring his story. He wanted nothing to do with him or this awful grotesque reality. Maybe if he had just stayed home and gone to bed like Olivia did, neither of them would be in this situation. They'd both be home safe, not strapped in a torture chamber by some psychopath.

Principal Krate shrugged. "Father, on the other hand, thought my relationship with Anastasia was disgusting. To him, she and her family were property for the use of labor only. So," Krate said, rubbing the tears from his eyes, his face reddening, "he whipped me till I bled, then he pulled Anastasia into a room where all I heard were her screams."

Alex had tears running down his cheeks. Nelson's words, what Jason told him . . . It was all true. The inner walls were hell. They produced madmen like Principal Krate and Biggs.

"He got rid of Anastasia and her family. I never saw her again. Between my mattress, though, I found a journal she left for me, detailing our times together. On the last page, ink smeared with what I could only assume were dried tears, she left me a note saying: '*In another lifetime, you were my own, and I was yours. But in this life . . . in this hell, we are nothing more than flesh and bone, enslaved to society. But I will always love you.*'"

"You think we care about your messed up rich family? Let us go," Yara wailed, trying to force her arms free.

Her words appeared to cut deep into Principal Krate. He swallowed and shook his head a little like he was coming back to reality. "I guess. I guess you're right, Yara. After years of brutal beatings at the hands of my father, I became more like him. Mother eventually learned to hate me just as much as she hated him. I found her in bed, pills sprawled out next to her. She looked like an angel. She *was* an angel. And the last bit of *hope* in this world that made sense. Once she was gone . . . Well, you see." He waved his hands around the room.

There had to be some way to reach him, some way to convince him. "Principal Krate, sir?"

He looked up and gave a broken smile. "Yes, Alex?"

"I'm sorry about Anastasia and your mom. I lost my mother too, she was murdered in a raid. I never knew anything like that was possible in the life you live."

Principal Krate arched his brows. "Alex, the one thing I envy about the Bourgeoisie is your freedom. Freedom to love whoever you choose, freedom to strive. I dread my life. These women who come from money and come for money only want me for such. They don't know love. All they know of is palaces, cars, power, and influence. No, you and Yara are different, and it's a shame you both have to die."

The room and everyone within shook from a loud boom. The different instruments of torture rattled on the table a few feet away. Another explosion, louder than the prior, followed. The shattering of windows, yelling and deep shrieks flooded through the cracks of the closed door.

Principal Krate gripped his chest. "What the hell was that?"

An onslaught of cracks and snaps followed. Alex's heart thumped against his ribs. He thought it would burst from his chest. Yara started wiggling harder, begging for help as she cried.

The door swung open.

Conroy's black tuxedo was covered in blood, holding his guts in.

"What the hell's going on out there?" Principal Krate cried.

"We're under attack, sir . . ." Conroy fell in a corner, blood sputtering from his side. Governor Krate is dead sir, he was shot."

Principal Krate's eyes widened with horror.

Alex dry-heaved, trying to avoid looking at Conroy. He was a mess. What could do that to a man?

The cries of people didn't stop, and the gunfire continued on. A chain of explosions echoed from outside the room, this time a little further away but still close enough for Alex to feel it in the pit of his stomach. He dug his nails into the chair.

He looked over at Conroy, who was sweating bullets. His breaths were slowing and becoming shallow. His hand flopped to the side, and Alex saw the pink, bloody bit of his intestines.

"Is ... is he dead?" Yara asked with a cracking voice.

Principal Krate walked over and nudged Conroy with his foot. "No. No, he's just out cold. Conroy . . . get up! Conroy?"

Conroy's thick frame slumped to the floor as more blood drained from his torso, this time seeping into the cracks of the wooden floor. Principal Krate crouched next to him and slipped two fingers over his neck.

"Damn it," he said, stepping back.

A flurry of popping sounds cracked from the hallway, and a few *ping*s smacked the door. Alex's knees knocked, sweat poured from his armpits, and his guts wouldn't stop turning.

Principal Krate's demeanor crumbled as his body shivered. He pressed trembling fingers over his lips. "I–I don't know who's responsible for this, but they have to be idiots to attack the home of an aristocrat. Insane. They'll be executed for this!"

A chilling silence fell from behind the door.

It almost made Alex wish he'd imagined all the noise and horror that exploded from out there. But he knew better. The three of them waited, eyes locked on the polished bronze knob.

Fear fell harshly on him as he tried to keep his bladder tight. He glanced over at Yara. She wasn't a shivering, sweating mess like he was. Her eyes were locked on the door.

"What is it?" Alex asked.

Her lips quivered. "Just a feeling."

Principal Krate backed behind them. Alex could hear his long rattling breaths by his ear.

Then came the clonking of thick heavy boots down the hall. Closer. Closer. Then silence.

Tap. Tap. Tap. Metal against metal rattled the door.

Everyone jumped.

"Krate! You better come out . . . now," a young girl's voice demanded from the other side.

Young and oddly familiar, the voice put Alex strangely at ease. He was expecting the gruff, harsh voice of a man, a robber, coming to take Principal Krate for everything he was worth. And kill anyone who would be a witness.

"I know you're in there, Krate. Come out and answer for your crimes against humanity. You don't really want me to come in after you. Do you?"

"Listen, and listen well," Principal Krate yelled with a confidence and power that Alex thought died with Conroy. "You're attacking the home of the Governor of Constance, someone who has pertinent ties with not only the politicians, but the SGUNA as well. You're dead! You and your whole family are dead!"

There was a sinister cackle. "Funny you say that, because the governor is on the dance floor with a bullet in his head, so ... yeah, we took care of him."

Alex's entire body tensed as he tried to fight the shaking of his limbs. It was useless.

The door kicked open.

A flurry of pink mixed with the white fur of a mask came through. Alex closed his eyes when he saw the pink pistol.

Pop. Pop.

The grueling screams of Principal Krate made Alex force his eyes open, the grown man wailed like a wild animal, screaming about his "damn leg" from behind them.

Alex looked up to see a short figure, pink strands of hair sprouted over the white mask of a hare. A hood covered everything else around the head, allowing the ears to sprout forward long and firm. Another pistol rested at the person's hip, and a jean vest covered a pink hoody with leggings that slipped into thick black boots. They were the same kind of boots the sentinels wore.

"You guys alright?" the familiar voice asked. Alex couldn't make out the eyes through the mask. "Damn, and here I was hoping to find you pissing your pants. I guess I should've waited longer."

Alex's fingernails were bleeding from digging into the wooden arms of the chair. The girl came closer, her chin was a light brown, and her light brown eyes diligently focused on the ropes as she worked them loose.

She started talking again. "Yeah, I found both the bastards. Come get 'em. I'd hate for them to bleed out before being judged. Make it quick, too. Crude's going to be here soon, and you know she hates waiting."

Alex's voice shivered, "Are you talking to me?"

"Shh." She threw a finger up to her lips, eyes firm on him. Then she went back to talking. "No, not you, Brain, some Bourgeoisie kid. Yeah, about to piss his pants alright."

Alex studied the pink strands that peeked out from around the mask and thought of the girl back in the cell with the patch over her right eye. *It couldn't be, was she the girl from the cell?* He searched the eye holes of the rabbit, and there were two eyes. "Who are you?"

She yanked Yara up first, then helped Alex to his feet. He towered over her as it all began to set in. Even with the mask on and having both eyes open, the short pink hair and the height gave her away.

She shook her head. "Man, you Bourgeoisie kids suck at attention to detail. Too busy living like fat lazy rats instead of doing something with your life."

Alex spoke again. "Are you the girl from the cell?"

"Maybe I am. Maybe I'm not."

A hooded man came through the doorway and had to crouch to get in. A sculpted white porcelain mask detailed with black lines running deep into the facial features covered his true face. He wasn't as big as Alex's dad, but he was well on his way. The black hoody and armor that rested over his shoulders could barely hide the sculpted muscle bulging from the seams.

"Are the prisoners freed, babe?" the girl asked.

The large man nodded. "We got them all out pretty quick. Crude and I organized them so the strong could take turns carrying the weak."

The pink-haired girl sighed. "Good. By the way, this is the son of the governor, the one responsible for all the pain and suffering those people went through," she said, waving a hand toward a sobbing Principal Krate.

Behind the mask's haunting expression, dark eyes rolled over the room, then fell on Krate. He lurched to the bloodied man who coward in the corner.

"Please, don't kill me. Please don't hurt me. Please! I won't do anything. I won't say anything."

"Then shut up," a grizzly voice barked. "You've already got me aggy!" A brawny hand grabbed Principal Krate by his good leg, and the tall figure dragged him across the floor out into the hallway.

Principal Krate looked up with pleading, tear-filled eyes. "Please help me . . ."

Biting his lip, Alex turned away, focusing on Yara. "You okay?"

"I'm fine," Yara answered quickly, turning to the shorter girl. "It's you, isn't it? All of you guys. You're with DOR, right?"

Alex stepped back, holding his wrist.

"Bingo, kid."

Kid? Alex thought. His first instinct was to grab one of the pistols from her holster and get him and Yara the hell out of this place. It wouldn't be long before sentinels showed up, and when that happened, kids that looked as filthy as they did were shot on site.

"What are you doing here?" Alex asked.

The girl in the mask shifted her weight. "Saving your asses. And with a tone like that, I'm kind of regretting it."

Alex thought about his mother and the raid that led to her death. "Well, we didn't need you."

"Sure could've fooled me."

"Well—"

"Yeah," she said, pressing a hand against the lower side of her mask. "Yeah. Damn . . . Got it. Sorry. *Distracted* by some A-hole," she said, focusing once again on Alex. "Thirty minutes tops? Thanks, Brain."

The girl turned and headed out the door.

Yara was right behind her. "Wait! Take me with you," she demanded.

The girl didn't even turn around. "Not gonna happen."

"Why?"

She paused. "You two are the worst hostages I've ever saved, and I'm really not a patient individual," she said with a chuckle. She wrapped her fingers around one of the pistols and turned. "You can't handle this lifestyle. I don't care how much black you wear and how depressing you *think* your life is." She looked Yara up and down, then turned to face Alex. Her eyes rolled behind the mask. "By the looks of you, you're both Bourgeoisie pups who ended up at the wrong place at the wrong time."

"Yara, she's right. These guys are terrorists. Murderers."

The girl laughed, shaking her head. "So, you're one of *those* people, huh?" She took her hand off the pistol and strutted toward him. "The ones who think the politicians are making the world a better place, and *even though my life is rough*, if I work hard enough and keep my head down, I just might make it."

"It's better than blowing up labs and killing people for no reason."

"Are you kidding me? Do you know where you are, idiot? This was one of the largest human farms in the Americas. Those people in that basement were going to be experimented on for days, weeks, until they died, or if they weren't strong enough, they would've been killed and butchered for their organs. They planned on killing you, possibly slowly. Argggh. I only hope slowly. It's what I want to do."

Yara turned to him. "Shut up, Alex." Her eyes had tears in them. "Please."

He looked on confused and did as she asked.

"Look, I know life as a member of DOR is horrific, and it can be a short life span. Trust me, I wouldn't be making this decision if I didn't know the cost. I know almost everything about you guys."

The girl sneered. "Oh yeah, like what?"

"I know that you're the one the UNA calls the Daughter of Death. Your pink hair, the pink pistols, and the casings gave you away." Yara wiped her face and shook her head slowly in puzzlement. "I would've never dreamed someone as badass as you would be around my age."

"Well . . ." She shrugged.

Daughter of Death, right here . . . in front of me? The DOR member with a billion-credit bounty on her head? And she allowed me to talk this much trash and live? Alex couldn't believe how small she was, yet she was one of the most feared humans on the planet. There was no doubt now by her response, the way she talked, she was the same girl from the cell too.

"Yara, is this really the Daughter of Death?"

"Yeah, that's what the gov calls me." She took a deep breath. "Look, we really don't have time for all of this. Follow me."

A stinging acrid smell lay heavy in the air as they came to the lobby. Where there were once people enjoying themselves, drinking fancy drinks, wearing overly expensive suits and dresses, and partying at the expense of dozens of tortured souls, now lay nothing more than a blood bath with bodies sprinkled about the lobby.

Principal Krate was on his knees, begging for his life.

"Fifteen minutes," a feminine voice said sweetly from a white hood. Her face was covered by a grotesque mask that looked to be stitched together from white felt, like something a serial killer would wear. Hanging off her hip next to a large knife and a pistol dangled a blue plush lion key chain. "I have a few more bombs daisy-chained outside that'll definitely slow down the sentinels, but you never know."

"Fifteen is all that'll be needed," a toneless voice replied from above with a strange accent. Wearing a red demonic mask, a girl gazed over the bloodbath standing at the edge of the balcony that protruded from the lobby walls. Unlike the others, she was hoodless, allowing thick black coily hair to cover the edges of the mask that housed a horrific grin.

It was her. One of the most ruthless members of DOR The One-eyed Devil. Alex remembered the horrific stories of the girl with the red demonic mask.

She stepped off the ledge, a long black leather coat glided like a cape behind her.

"Wait," Alex screamed. *Is she insane? She'll break her neck from that height.*

She landed with the elegance of a panther, too inhuman to miss, too graceful to ignore. Without missing a beat, she drifted across the blood-puddled floor like a shadow.

Impossible.

Her coat dragged behind her, barely covering a black thigh-length dress with frills. Sleek black stockings rode all the way up her legs. What struck Alex oddly was the red teddy bear backpack pinned between her back and what looked like a sword.

She walked briskly over to Principal Krate who had been reduced to a babbling mess of emotions and hatred. The One-eyed Devil was short, about the same height as the Daughter of Death. There was a frigid heaviness in the air; there was no way Alex imagined it. It pressed all around him, on his shoulders, he could even feel it in his knees.

Was it coming from her?

She spoke sternly with that thick foreign accent, "Stewart Krate, head of the New Hope Academy institution, correct?"

Principal Krate looked up, his face wet with tears, snot rolling down his nose. "Y-yes."

Her left hand covered with a long fingerless black glove reached behind the ears of the red teddy bear and pulled a black blade from its scabbard. Even from where Alex stood, the light glinted from the blade's jet-black edges. He could swear it whispered.

"The same institution that has been sending graduates of lower-class students to be destroyed emotionally, mentally, and physically?"

"Please. I was ordered to do it. My father was the main one involved in that operation. He's connected with multiple officials, including the SGUNA."

"Like I said, we took care of him." The pink haired girl pointed to Governor Krate laying face down.

"Please. I have so much information. I can share it with you in exchange for my life."

Alex stepped away from them, from everyone, including Yara. "So everything was true," Alex stuttered. "The integration program isn't real? W-why?"

"I asked my father the same question when I was your age and found out the integration program was a broken promise." Principal Krate looked up with watery eyes. "'It's as real as they want it to be. That's the point. Hopes, dreams. Enough of that pumped into a community will keep everyone controlled and less aggressive.'" He took a deep breath as his body settled. "That's what my dad would say anyway. None of it matters now."

Alex's entire body shivered as everything Nelson told him set in. All of it was true. The horror of their reality was true. He looked down at his hands which trembled uncontrollably. "It can't be ..." he whispered to himself, holding back the tears.

"Please," Principal Krate sobbed. "Please. Please don't kill me."

The pink-haired girl laughed. "Funny how a life matters now. I was in that dungeon of yours for three days, and you never brought food down, never gave them water. You allowed those filthy guards to piss on us and beat us. You allowed them to do worse to the women. You'll have no sympathy from me."

"Me neither," the large man barked.

"None from me . . ." the girl with the stitched mask added.

The blade came to Principal Krate's neck. "Then judgment has been decided. By the cries of the dead, the meek, and the downtrodden, we DOR are the sword of the voiceless."

Principal Krate screamed, his cry cut short by the thumping of his head sliding off his shoulders.

"The deed's done. Ravens, move out!" The girl slashed the air, whipping droplets of blood from the blade to the ground then slid the sword gently back into the scabbard nestled by the red teddy bear. She leaped out the massive hole in the lobby that led outside.

Alex fell to his knees spewing pre-digested chicken gizzard and everything else he had for dinner. His hands shook, his body convulsed. It was more than just seeing the brutal murder of Principal Krate, it was hearing the truth about N.H.A. for the second time. Nelson was right. He was right about everything.

The pink-haired girl nestled up to the muscular man. "Babe, can you grab these two and bring them with us, please?"

He nodded. "You know it, beautiful."

The man snatched Alex up and hurled him over his shoulder.

Yara stopped him. "I can run."

Sirens wailed, and the beating of helicopters echoed overhead. Helicopters never came unless UNA got word that DOR was involved. That means sentinels had been dispatched.

Alex's mind raced. What the hell just happened? What would his dad say? What about Olivia? Even Deacon?

Into the night he went with one of the most feared organizations and enemies of the United Nations of America, the Disciples of Revolution.

14

They climbed down through one of the sewer drains. It was partially open and easy to get into and then cover it up. The dense wetness of sewage and waste clung to Alex like a second layer of skin.

He gagged with each step as the hulking man who carried him sloshed through the ankle-deep grime. With watering eyes, all Alex could think about were the poor souls who worked at the waste treatment facility, reeking of rotten eggs and an overwhelming funk that couldn't be explained.

"You can probably put him down now, babe," the pink-haired girl said. She tugged on the lower half of her rabbit mask. "I'd drop him too. He deserves to bathe in sewage."

The man stopped and gently slung Alex over his shoulder, careful to not let his hood and mask slip off. "Sorry about that, bro." He shrugged. "I'm sure you can handle your own, but desperate times call for desperate measures."

"Uhm, no worries. Thanks." Alex was thrown off by the laid-back response. He rubbed his chest, which ached from the constant jerking movements of being carried. His hands still shivered. "What's your name?"

"Code name's Kimbo. You?" He looked over his shoulder, his mask less intimidating now that he spoke like a normal person.

"Alex," he replied, trying to prevent sewage water from filling his sneakers, but it was a useless endeavor. Every step was a squelch in the dark tunnels. "What's a codename?"

"None of your business," the pink-haired girl shrilled. Her voice pinged off the dripping slick brick of the tunnel walls. "But if you were to have one, it would be P.B. for punk b—"

"Jo-Jo. Relax with all that," Kimbo's deep voice overpowered hers. "Give him a break, aight?"

Jo-Jo? Alex thought, watching her strut through the sewage as if it were a path of roses.

She groaned up ahead. "I swear, Kimbo. You're way too nice."

Kimbo turned. "She's awesome once you get to know her, I swear."

I'm sure, Alex thought, arching his brows. "She seems like a peach."

Kimbo laughed as they continued into the darkness.

In the cold, an orange glow up ahead revealed more of the rough, cracked walls. Old metal bent and curled from the water like a partially peeled apple. The rigged platforms seemed to rise on both sides of them as ancient wording from the old world took form. *A-line connection to the B-line.* Goosebumps rose over Alex's skin. The thought of making a run for it gripped his chest, but he needed to find Yara first.

He still couldn't believe she was willing to join them without hesitation like she had been waiting for the opportunity. Olivia and Dad rolled into his mind. He had no idea what time it was, but he needed to get back home ASAP. Dad wouldn't leave without him, but he'd certainly go bananas if his son was missing.

Could I even go back after tonight? Dozens of wealthy citizens had been murdered, including an aristocrat and his son. Alex had no part of that. They would understand. He'd turn himself in and share what he knew about DOR He might do serious time in the mines, but he'd have his life. Olivia and Dad would be safe.

Further, deep in the darkness, against the dribbling of gray water and their sloshing, brittle voices wove together. A mixture of men, women, and children. The tunnels opened up, and in the space filled with the orange glow were dozens of people. Abled bodies walked, and the strong carried the weak and sickly over their shoulders.

The voices cried with praise as they came out of the darkness, endowed with the flickering glow. The tall, slender girl with the freaky mask, Jo-Jo, and Kimbo, were immediately hugged and celebrated.

Alex finally found Yara standing a few feet away from them. He sloshed through the water while trying not to lose his footing. "Hey, you okay?"

"I'm fine, and you?" she asked watching the masked terrorists gather near the front.

Something about her eyes was different. They yearned for something. "Fine, I guess."

Her hand rolled down his wrist, then her fingers wrapped around his. Soft and gentle hands he didn't expect from Yara. They trembled for a second, and he thought it was him, but it was her.

He gave her fingers a gentle squeeze.

Yara's eyes were fixed on Jo-Jo and the others. "It must feel incredible. . . ." Her eyes glistened in the orange glow of the light held by the tall, slender girl with the creepy mask.

"What must feel incredible?" he asked.

"To be the ones who will change everything," she said softly watching the people around them look toward the ones who freed them. "Real heroes. I have to be one of them. I *will* be one of them."

She was serious. In her eyes, that yearning, that thirst was beyond evident now that Alex shifted his gaze. It made him want to know everything about her, this dark, gloomy girl who he thought hated the world and everybody in it.

"You are a real hero," Alex whispered. He tossed his head toward the light. "Better than they are for sure."

"Bullshit," she said.

"I'm serious. Tonight you were braver then I could ever be. You weren't afraid at all." He caught her confused glance in the dim light.

"Were we not in the same place?"

"What do you mean?"

"Alex, you were willing to sacrifice yourself if it meant me being released." She pulled her hair back and lowered her chin. "I guess you're two for two, right?"

"With what?"

"With putting yourself in harm's way for me."

Somewhere between hating to see anyone else die—which he got plenty of, unfortunately—and doing everything in his power to not see Yara get hurt, an unnoticeable courage was born. Better late than never, and it sure didn't last long.

"Listen up!" A harsh bark echoed in the sewer. It was the girl with the sword who cut down Principal Krate like it was nothing. Black curls stretched wide, and lose, bouncing over the horns of her mask.

She raised a bright light that glowed a warm red, just bright enough to give shape to six tunnels that opened behind her. She stood in front of the center tunnel.

"We may have gotten you out of that dungeon, but that doesn't mean your home free. Down this tunnel is freedom. Freedom away from the walls and into the Outskirts."

"The Outskirts?" a man's voice cried. "We can't go out there. We won't survive."

Jo-Jo yelled over him, "You'll be fine, trust us. We know some of you are Bourgeoisie citizens." Her mask turned to Alex. "Trust us, you'll be fine."

Another woman begged, "But our homes, our jobs...our lives. You can't expect us to leave all that behind."

"Well, go back," spat out the girl in her heavy accent. She pointed to the tunnel from which they all came. "Go back down that tunnel, back to that dungeon, back to that hell hole of a life you want so bad to cling to. But I promise they'll kill you. Because you know the truth."

Alex swallowed hard and finally gained the confidence to ask the One-eyed Devil a question. He had to know. He had to know if Nelson was right about everything. He already knew he was but needed to hear it again.

"And what truth is that?" he asked, his voice weak and low, his lips trembling.

She looked over and he couldn't see her eyes behind the thicket of curls. "The truth that all Bourgeoisie citizens are considered trash just like the slaves and the Pariah."

The crowd erupted in whispers as people disagreed. A few even broke away, heading back down the tunnel the way they came. Alex turned, looking down the abyss that was the tunnel leading back to the mansion. Through it all was Olivia and Dad. He'd tell the sentinels or whoever else would be back at the mansion the truth of what happened.

They would listen to reason. They had to. It was DOR, after all. They were monsters. Alex's insides swirled with grief, and his mind raced with confusion.

Yara didn't budge.

A tight squeeze around his fingers caught his attention. A smile slipped across Yara's face. "You should go, Alex. Your dad, your little sister, everything you've done has been for them, right?"

Alex hesitated, but he saw something in her eyes, something that was so far beyond him, it put them both in two different worlds. He looked down the tunnel watching the few people limp and dig their fingers into the wall to keep from falling.

"You want to stay?"

She glanced down the tunnel, looking uncomfortable. "I can't go back to that place. Not with those people. Not in that broken world."

"What about your family and friends?"

"C'mon. Friends? You know me better than that. My aunt and uncle adopted me, thanks to some soldiers coming across me in the Outskirts living off berries and roots. I cause them more problems than anything, trust me."

"But—"

"Go ahead if you *need* to go. But you know better than anyone, after everything we've seen … they'll kill you, Alex. You know that now, right?"

He did. But he wanted to believe that he could fix the damage he had done. He wanted to shoulder all the trouble he'd caused Dad and Olivia. He looked at the DOR members. It sickened him to be down here with them. Whereas Yara was right at home.

We'll never be like them, Alex. They lied to us. Nelson's voice prevailed over Alex's faulty hope in the system. He swallowed and turned to the few people who walked on, disappearing into the shadows. Back to the illusion, back to the lies and cover-ups. Principal Krate's voice was gruff in the darkness of his mind. *Hopes. Dreams. Enough of that pumped into the community will keep everyone controlled and less aggressive.*

He looked back into the darkness. He saw Dad and Olivia. Deacon too. He saw his opportunity to be an Exclusive crash and burn, along with the hopes of being so much more.

It was fake anyway. All of it. "Nelson and Deacon were right about everything."

"What do you mean?"

"We met up the night before Nelson was attacked. He told us that he was still in contact with Jason and that Jason told him everything."

Yara looked conflicted. "What's everything?"

Alex looked down at the foul ankle-high water that rippled with the steps of those around them. "Everything we heard today about New Hope Academy. From the UNA using people as lab rats, human trafficking…"

Yara was silent.

"I was so caught up in the lie. I should've listened instead of calling them crazy. Deacon and Nelson were right all along. About everything."

She wrapped her fingers around his chin. "It's not your fault. All of us were caught in the lie, Alex."

"But I sacrificed my friend, my brother, for an illusion. For a way out. And at the end of the day, it was all because I was afraid to do anything, afraid they'd kill my dad and sister like they did my mom. And it didn't even matter. They still killed someone close to me, and it hurt just as bad." He wiped his face.

She tightened her hand around his. "Well, let's go together…with them." She looked up to the masked individuals who were helping people stand. "The Disciples of Revolution are making a difference, or at least trying to. These people would be dead. *We* would be dead if it weren't for them."

He thought about Olivia and Dad. If the UNA found out he joined DOR it would be Jason and Nelson all over again. He looked down the hall where the others had started back toward the mansion. "I've got to find a way to get back home, but it can't be through that tunnel."

"Anyone else want to leave?" the One-eyed Devil called with a dry and apathetic tone. "Well, if there are no others, come with us. We won't steer you wrong. But first, Poachie?"

The girl with the white hood and sadistic white mask took point in front of the crowd. "Right. We have fresh fruits and bread for everyone needing it. Unfortunately, we don't have water right now. But once we get to the Outskirts, there will be plenty as well as more food where that came from."

The crowd grew anxious, and whispers broke over the slick tunnel walls of mold and filth. The last thing Alex wanted to do was eat, but for someone who hadn't had food in days, it probably didn't matter.

He chose a piece of bread and wiped his hands on his pants before digging in. He watched as some of the prisoners tore into the fruit and bread like wild animals, some with tears in their eyes, sorrowful groans of joy and happiness that made his stomach turn sour. *Did UNA really do this to them?*

Alex mingled with the masses along with Yara. They were about thirty to forty strong. It was hard to believe these people had been kidnapped. People who were probably from different parts of the city. Good people. Bourgeoisie people. People who were laborers and hard workers.

15

They took several breaks throughout their journey.

Alex's feet swelled and burned. The sneakers his mom bought him were reduced to a soggy mess, and the only thing beating back the pangs of hunger was the sludge and foul smell of the sewer.

Hours had passed. In the darkness an orange glow burned from the front of the pack. He didn't see any of the DOR members anymore, but Yara was still by his side.

It was hard to gauge what time it was, but Alex knew that by now, his dad would be losing his mind. He probably thought Manwell and his parents were trying to inflict social justice and had him kidnapped. It wasn't far from the truth.

The thought of the shotgun flickered in from the back of Alex's head. *Dad, I'm fine. Please don't do anything stupid.*

He scanned the long sorrowful faces of the others who had been without food for a while. Everyone was in bad shape, worse than him and Yara anyway. The only thing pushing them on was freedom.

The movement slowed up front to a stumbling shuffle until finally it halted. Alex turned to Yara as they both sloshed forward.

A dry emotionless voice cracked over the crowd, "To those who made the journey, know that we are outside both the inner and outer walls. We're no longer in Constance or the streets of the Suites, but in the Outskirts. Freedom is in your grasp. Start anew, be merry, be whatever you like. . . ." she said, her voice fading.

Twisting metal waned as gears knocked and bounced off the walls of the sewer. Whispers and gasps fell over the crowd until light crept over a circular shape in front of them. With a deep groan, the circle rose and became a golden crescent. A breath of warm fresh air blew dead leaves and debris into the tunnel.

Alex filled his lungs.

Before them stood an array of shacks and broken buildings that had been fixed into homes and living spaces. Some of the shacks were anchored into the outer wall, attached like an unwanted conjoined twin. On a crumbling road, a few people gathered, talking and laughing. The smell of food being grilled and other scents permeated the air.

A blue sky cast a golden aura over the surroundings from a thick forest just behind the structures. Everything smelled incredible and mouthwatering.

This was the Outskirts?

Everything came to a standstill once they poured out of the sewer drains. Alex stumbled forward, legs trembling as the stories his father and others told him of the Outskirts took flight.

Jo-Jo's voice echoed over a growing crowd of the inhabitants. "Everyone, welcome these new citizens to the

Outskirts. Please treat them well. Give them jobs, give them food, spare whatever you can. They're going to be needed for the future."

What the heck does that mean? Alex wondered, swallowing hard.

The crowd broke away into groups. Some met other members of the Outskirts with tears and wails of excitement as if they had been long-lost friends. Others slumped away, disappearing into the murky underbelly of a new world.

Alex looked up to see the DOR members grouping together. The One-eyed Devil was talking as the others listened and nodded. Yara hurried over to the group. Hesitating, he followed a few paces behind her.

The girl with the demonic mask turned, tilting her head to him and Yara. "You two, come here." Her hair was like a wild shrub of black curls that fell over her mask, covering the eyes.

"M—me?" Alex pressed a finger into his chess, shivering. He couldn't take his eyes off the pistol on her hip and the sword she utilized to cut down Principal Krate and his father.

"Yes."

Alex nodded to Yara, and they both did as she commanded.

"Jo-Jo tells me you're both interested in joining the revolution?"

Yara gave a terse nod, her hardened expression was just like it was back in school.

Alex looked down at the crumbling streets where large roots bulged from the earth like tearing seams. "I'm just trying to get back home," he said, looking over his shoulder to the large wall that reached to the sky. It was higher from the Outskirts and made him queasy looking up.

"Alex, this is an opportunity to make something of ourselves," Yara argued. "We can finally make a difference in this messed-up world. Revenge Nelson."

Alex thought about Biggs and how Principal Krate blasted him without a second thought. "That was taken care of last night, wasn't it?" He looked up as the sun formed over the horizon, giving the Outskirts life and color. "Why are you so anxious to join them?"

"I'm tired of watching those arrogant, pompous bastards treating us like garbage. I thought after everything that happened to your friend, you would feel the same. Well, don't you?"

Alex didn't know what to feel. He looked at the outer wall. It was more intimidating than the one separating Constance from the Suites. Years of weather deteriorated the cement structure revealing the metal rebar skeleton beneath. Some of the exposed area was utilized to make tarp shacks and reinforced homes.

"What happened to Nelson was terrible. He's gone. As much as I want to blame everyone in Constance for that, I had some part in that too." Alex looked up at the masked individuals behind her. "But how can I join a group of murderers, Yara? How will that help change anything?"

She threw her hands out in disbelief and groaned with frustration. "They aren't murderers!"

Jo-Jo stepped in, her hood allowing a few pink strands to fall from the crevices of the mask and down a narrow light brown chin. "Well …"

"Not helping," Yara said wide-eyed. "They're going to change everything. DOR will set things right. They'll make it so we don't have to bite our tongues around the wrong people. Where Bourgeoisies and Pariahs aren't used as slaves or worse. What do you think they planned to do to us last night?"

Alex gave a blank stare. In the light, he caught a glimpse of Yara's deep brown eyes glossed over with worry. It reminded him of the gaze they shared back at the Krate's mansion. In that underground dungeon, they saw true horror, a true hell worse than what his dad described of the Outskirts. And from the lips and mouth of Principal Krate, Alex heard the truth.

As his fingers curled into a fist he thought about Olivia and Dad. All that really mattered was finding a way to get back to them as soon as possible. He looked back up at the Outerwall which was a pressed mess of concrete blocks reinforced with steel in the lower areas, grass and foliage grew from cracks and wrapped around rusted rebar.

"It's a tough decision, honey, I know," A tall heavy-set black woman came over holding a basket of apples. "You all should take it easy on him. Few people can give up the only life they've known at the drop of a hat. Especially if they still have family over there." Her eyes rose to the wall.

The One-eyed Devil ran over like an excited toddler. "Big Mama Erving," Her voice softened in a comical unrealistic manner that took Alex by surprise. Her hair bounced over her shoulders.

The whole group came running over, dug their hands into the basket, then stuffed their pockets. They were all laughing and hugging the woman like children who had just gotten off the bus and greeted their mother.

He was shocked. The One-eyed Devil lifted her mask enough for Alex to see her smooth ebony skin.

"Oh, my children. Another big haul, huh?" asked the woman, laughing with jubilation.

"You spitting truth, Big Mah," said Kimbo as he wrapped his brawny fingers around a shiny red apple and crunched into it. Juices rolled through the thick black curls of his beard. "But ain't nothing like the snacks we come home to."

The old woman tapped him on his shoulder, grazing over the linked bullets that chimed over Kimbo's broad shoulders. "You children do more than you'll ever be appreciated for."

The girl with the scary white and black mask tossed the husk of an apple to the side. "Tell that to the leaders of Anarchy."

The old woman's face softened as her gaze searched Alex. "Is it your folks on the other side, honey?"

Alex's gaze fell to his feet, refusing to answer. He owed nobody here answers, no matter how nice they were.

"Big Mah asked you a question." The one-eyed Devil's fingers slipped over the handle of her pistol.

"My father and baby sister."

The woman nodded. "And your mother?"

"Dead."

"How child?"

He wiped his face. "Killed in a sentinel raid. There was an error in the system or whatever. They got the wrong house, wrong family, wrong everything."

The old woman nodded and gently placed the basket of apples on the ground. The others continued digging in and grabbing more apples.

She wrapped her arms around Alex, bringing him in close. She smelled of sweet cakes and bread and other good foods with salts and spices. He wanted to cry. Years had passed since he'd been hugged with that much warmth.

She stepped back. "I was a slave once. Gonna leave it at that. But I will say this. I don't think anyone is worthy of death, especially those people behind that wall, whether they be Exclusives, Bourgeoisie, or whoever. But I do believe that when you fight for the right thing, people are going to perish."

He looked into the woman's old tired eyes. "Were you treated badly as a slave?"

She smiled. "Not by the family that owned me, no. I was given a bed and freedoms that a lot of slaves weren't. I learned to drive and had the opportunity to go grocery shopping. But once I stepped foot out the door of that house ... Let's just say life changed quickly for a slave woman."

"Is life better as a Pariah, then?" Alex hated to have the words fall from his mouth.

"Than a slave?" She chuckled. "It wasn't easy at first. The family that owned me released me, but because I was a Pariah previously, I wasn't able to become a Bourgeoisie like yourself. But I made a way."

She had a genuine smile. Alex looked around at all the people in the Outskirts. There were no slender faces of starving, dying people, no sunken eyes of disease and suffering like he had expected. These people adapted, made a place for themselves, and survived.

"I won't leave my dad and sister over there. And if they find out I'm with D.O.R ..."

"Imprisonment, outcasted by their own community, and worse punishments, I'm sure," the woman replied. "I know you have a hard decision to make. But if anyone can help you with that decision, it'll be with this group of young heroes right here."

She pointed to the masked faces, the bottom jaws munching and moving behind them. A group of terrorists, murderers, and assassins, some having bounties that could put him next door with aristocrats if he turned them in. They'd kill him before he got the chance.

She wrapped her arms around Alex again. "The name's Big Mama, honey, and you come see me if you need anything."

He nodded. She bent over, lifted the basket of apples, then made her way back to the shack where a few people wearing aprons appeared to be working inside.

"Alright, we got some pies to bake and rolls to make, too." Big Mah limped to an old apartment where the first floor had been set up like a store front. A sign hung outside made from slabs of old that read. *BIG MAH'S SOUL FOOD.*

A sturdy hand consumed Alex's shoulder and nearly knocked him forward. "Everyone loves Big Mah. Thieves, murderers, the worst of the worst. And because of us, nobody messes with her," Kimbo said from behind the mask.

Alex looked up to see the brown eyes watching him. The others behind Kimbo stood waiting for a decision. The One-eyed Devil stood with her arms folded, the sinister red mask making his skin crawl.

"So?" she asked.

Alex looked to Yara. She nodded, eyes pleading as her lips moved without uttering the words. He thought about his family and everything that had happened with Nelson after Jason's decision. Alex wondered if Jason was in the same predicament.

But Alex did have a choice where Nelson had none.

"Crude," Kimbo said with his deep voice, looking at the One-eye Devil. "I think we can trust him. Besides, Jo-Jo trusted him enough to bring them both along, right?"

Her real name's Crude? What kind of crazy name is that? Alex thought watching the girl with demonic mask.

She tilted her head. The handle of the sword glistened with a gold covering. "Jo-Jo?"

Jo-Jo tucked a few strands of pink behind her rabbit mask and sighed. "Yara's fine. The other one . . ."

Kimbo turned to face her. "Come on, Jo."

A deep groan escaped her small frame. "Fine. But if he dies in a ditch somewhere, let it be said that I, Joanne Jo-Jo Rossi said it first."

Kimbo lowered his head and groaned. "You didn't have to say your real name, though."

She shrugged. "Screw it. Let's go already."

Kimbo turned, shaking his head. "So, you coming? Once in a lifetime chance, homie?"

Alex looked back at the wall. Memories of his childhood with Nelson and Deacon crawled in, but even more was the fear for Olivia and Dad.

He'd be right back. He just hoped Dad would be patient enough to wait up. "Let's go."

They followed a thin trail into the thick woods. There was a strange serenity to the forest, Alex's footfalls died in the echo of crying birds. It wasn't like the puttering of pigeons and clawing ratchet squeals of rats or the growls of runaway dogs that molded Eastern, but more like a song of freedom carried by the warm scent of pine needles.

An intricate trail of assorted wildflowers led between the patches of deep green. Blues, whites, and oranges faded into yellows painted the forest the deeper they went. Only in the middle school biology books had Alex seen such colors. Blotches of white floated through the deep blue above and darting from tree to tree were birds of many colors and sizes.

How could the Outskirts be so beautiful? he thought.

"First time leaving the exterior walls?" the tall girl with the white hood and creepy mask asked. Her mask was more grotesque up close, detailed with crying black tears that made the lips run black. She had a strange smell about her. Like the tar they used to pave the streets entering the inner walls for the delivery convoys.

"Y-yeah. It's pretty amazing."

Partially lifting her mask, she buried her teeth into a juicy red apple. Her skin was fair, her lips thin and pink.

"Yeah. Something about the smell of pines gets me all excited. It's the hunter in me."

"My name's Alex."

"Yeah, I remember. Everyone calls me Poachie," she replied, holding out a black gloved hand. "Maybe I can be your first friend in the group."

Alex looked down at her hand, hesitant to reach out. What was she like under that twisted mask? Her long cold fingers wrapped firmly around his. "Nice to meet you."

She snagged a bottle of water from her backpack and began taking short sips. "What was your occupation back in the inner walls?"

Occupation? "A student. Just a student, like Yara."

"Nice." Her tone perked up with strange excitement. "Student life. I always wanted to go to school. Never took a step near a campus or anything, but I always pictured these extravagant libraries and labs and classrooms filled with other kids. I bet it was awesome. Was it awesome?"

Alex arched a brow, he cleared his throat. "I wouldn't say awesome. Elementary school and middle school were okay. I mean, it was all Bourgeoisie education, so it was nothing compared to New Hope Academy."

"Is that right?" Crude replied from the front. Alex was surprised she heard them. His voice was low the entire time especially over the birds, or so he thought. "Explains why you two were easy pickings then. Yara, you went to the school of the damned too, correct?"

"Uh, New Hope? Yeah."

Jo-Jo butted in. "We met a kid from New Hope. Jason, I think his name was."

"Jason?" Alex rushed to the front where Jo-Jo was. She jerked around, her hand gripping the knife attached to the armor over her shoulders. "Was his name Jason Tanaka?"

"Yes." Crude turned. "You know him?"

"We're friends. I mean, were friends. I grew up with him and his . . ." He thought of Nelson. "Do you know where he is?"

"He's rolling with the Sandstorms down on the southern border in South America," Kimbo answered. "They help with getting food to all the Outskirts around the other cities and other areas in the Americas."

South America. Alex thought of his dad's plan. He looked up to the rising sun, his insides wrenching with worry. "Is there any way to contact them?"

Jo-Jo shook her head. "Those guys are shadows like us. I think of them as the Robin Hoods of DOR, providing food and essentials for the people of the Outskirts to survive."

"I see." The excitement of thinking he would see Jason faded fast.

"We can reach out to headquarters and see what we can get for sure." Poachie rushed up front. "We'll take care of you."

They continued down the half-beaten trail for another half hour, Alex's legs throbbed and burned. Yara seemed to be doing fine. She kept up with the rest of them like it was nothing. Crude threw a leather-gloved fist in the air.

Everyone stopped.

The symphony of birds continued overhead, and Alex's heart was the bass that kept it all in tune. Kimbo, Jo-Jo, then Poachie took position behind trees, weapons drawn. One darted up front while the other two separated behind them, forming a triangle.

Alex watched as Crude dropped to a knee, and everyone in the group followed her actions, Yara and Alex along with them. A strange buzzing came overhead. A small black helicopter smaller than a sparrow glided down to them, pausing in front of Crude.

"Any trackers, Brain?" She pressed her fingers against her ear. "Good." Crude gave a sharp whistle that silenced the birds above, and the others came hustling back. "All clear. Kimbo, take point."

Kimbo flicked the side of his rifle and slipped it back over his shoulder. "Word, heading home. Back to Gilligan and hitting the gym."

Kimbo walked in a zigzag. His lips moved steadily. Alex could tell he was counting. He stopped and pulled away a net entangled with dead leaves, stones, and branches, revealing a metal trapdoor. He clipped the netting back to a latch crafted to look like a dead branch and lifted the doorway with ease.

"Ravens, let's go," Crude commanded.

Everyone followed suit and climbed down a handmade ladder of bark and rope. Jo-Jo, Yara, and Poachie went without hesitation. Alex looked down below, studying the concrete floor that awaited.

"Do I have to shoot you first?" Crude replied with a dry rasp.

"N–no, I'm good." He grabbed hold of the ladder and eased his way down. Crude came in the moment Alex made ground. He looked away, fearing what she would do if she caught him looking up her dress.

Jo-Jo giggled. "Smart move. She'd remove your eyes from your skull."

Alex gulped, stepping as far away from the ladder as possible.

Crude dropped. She was just chest height and intimidating beyond belief. Her presence was something to behold. Made sense she was the leader.

Kimbo lingered above a little while. Alex heard something dragging grittily above near the hatch, then Kimbo finally made his descent. A loud clank and a rusty slither of metal clicked overhead from the ladder.

"Alright, area secured."

Crude nodded. "Area cleared and secured. Doff your masks."

A heavy sigh of relief fell over everyone as they all removed their masks and pulled back their hoods.

Alex stumbled back, lost for words. Everything they had been through these last hours, the shooting, the explosions, the deaths...the murders. Nothing could speak to the soft faces of girls and a boy with the body of a man.

Behind Jo-Jo's mask was light brown skin and soft features that were more detailed now than they were in that basement prison. She moved a finger's worth of pink hair behind her ear to get a better look at Alex and Yara.

"What happened to the patch?" Alex asked.

"Oh, that thing? I wear it over my non-shooting eye when I'm incognito. Nobody would expect a girl with one eye to be a sniper."

Nobody would expect a girl to be a sniper in any case, he thought, but didn't dare say the words.

As Poachie lifted her mask and removed her hoody, two long brown braids fell down her shoulders. Her skin against the light was as white as the finest pearls. She must have been fifteen or sixteen at the most. Despite how ghostly pale she was, she was pretty, beyond pretty. It was hard to believe a girl like her wore such a grotesque mask.

Then there was Kimbo. Behind his muscular frame rested a square-jawed boy, young and tired looking. He must have been Alex's age, maybe a little older. But no one brought more shock than Crude—the One-eyed Devil herself—whose gentle ebony skin and cherub-like features were like that of a child.

As impossible as it was, she couldn't have been older than Olivia. A pre-teen at best. Her thick fro still fell over the cold, dead coffee eyes that Alex barely got a glimpse of. Her face was a permanent expression of unearthly concentration. Cold. Calculating.

His heart surged. Every muscle in Alex's body screamed run. He pressed against the cavern like walls and did his best to not draw too much attention to himself. Escape wasn't a possibility at the moment anyway.

Except for Jo-Jo, black paint caked around their eyes. For once, Yara shared the same shock as Alex. They were like them. Kids. Yet ruthless and cold. Deacon was wrong. DOR *was* a terrorist organization of kids.

"So, let's show them around," Poachie sang with excitement.

Kimbo slapped Alex on the shoulder. "Aight, well, y'all go do that. I'm gonna hit the weight room and clean Missy-E."

"Missy-E?" Alex asked, looking up at him.

He swung his machine gun from over his shoulder. "If one ever could exist, this is my side piece, my mistress." He shot a glance to Jo-Jo. "No offense, babe."

She rolled her eyes. "Trust me, none taken," she said with a snobbish tone. "I'm heading to the showers."

Kimbo went on, "Missy-E is an M300, the great, great, great, great, great granddaughter of the M249 light machine gun." He glided his thumb over a glowing tab, letting a few empty rounds drop to the ground.

Alex pressed harder against the wall, beads of sweat rolled down the sides of his face as images of his mother flickered. Looking at the barrel alone caused the nightmarish scene of her death to spring to life.

Jo-Jo growled and stomped off down the hall. "Boys and their toys."

Still, Kimbo continued, eyes wide with excitement and passion as he spoke of his weapon. "Both battery and gas-powered, just in case of an EMP. Missy is the most effective weapon of her time. Made from the lightest and strongest metal discovered back in the new millennium. She weighs about twelve pounds, fifteen with a canister of rounds if things get funky, if you know what I mean?"

I don't. Alex nodded as Kimbo went on talking about the massive gun like it truly was his significant other. The raid came crawling back, and Alex fought with all his might, controlling his breathing, struggling to fix his thoughts on something else. Kimbo hadn't even noticed.

Poachie pulled him away, Yara right along with them. His racing heart had already started to calm, and the cold sweat was just starting to let up. Even as they made their way down the concrete hallway, Alex could still hear Kimbo going on about Missy-E.

"Wait, hold on a minute, I didn't even tell you about the different rounds you can put through her. It's righteous!"

"Jo-Jo and Kimbo ..." Poachie sighed. "Between those two nut cases, things have sure gotten livelier around here."

Yara cleared her throat. "How long have they been here?"

Poachie's fingers skimmed across the smooth concrete walls. The structure was cavern-like and made with great care and engineering. There were deep cracks in certain areas, damp spots from where water got through, and tons of roots coming in from above.

"Well, Kimbo and I have been here the longest. Kimbo's been here since he was ten, and I've been here since I was eleven?" She looked up to the ceiling. "Yeah, that sounds about right. Five for Kimbo, six years for me."

That long? Alex thought. "Wait a minute, that would make Kimbo fifteen."

Poachie laughed and turned with reddening cheeks. "Duh. How old did you think he was?"

"I don't know. In his twenties?" he said and Poachie looked at him like he was crazy. No way Kimbo was the same age as him. How? The kid must have grown up near an impact zone. *Fifteen?*

Poachie let out an angelic giggle. "I'm kidding. Kimbo gets that all the time. He's always been a big kid. Must have been all the good eating he had growing up behind the walls of Fort Roberts."

Alex stopped.

So did Yara. "Kimbo's from where?" she asked.

Poachie gulped. "Oops. I've said enough already. Forget I said anything. And *don't* tell Kimbo I told you that. Alright?"

They looked at one another, then nodded.

Poachie continued on as they came into a massive room surrounded by more natural stone, but structured and secured by concrete. It was set up into a living room. Alex had never seen anything like it. Couches, a sixty-two-inch television, and on the other side was a kitchen with a large dining table. Nothing like the tight space of the apartment where his father made the kitchen and living room his bedroom.

"Welcome to the hangout spot. We relax, study the ridiculous propaganda that's fed to you people in the inner walls, but also—and thanks to Brain—we have the ability to watch movies and old TV shows made prior to World War III."

"How's that possible?" Yara asked.

Poachie placed her hands on her hip and scanned the area with a smile. "From what I understand, this place has been a DOR headquarters since 2025."

Alex looked all around, slipping his hands into his pockets. "Forty-five years … DOR's been around that long?"

"Oh yeah, the originals were a lot more badass than us. More cutthroat. But this place was an old World War III bomb shelter, so the foundation is pure concrete layered with led. No one can track us on any kind of network."

Yara smiled. "That's incredible. No wonder nobody's been able to track you, amazing."

"Glad you think so." Poachie brought them down another hallway that had doors on each side. "My room is on the left here. On the opposite is Kimbo's." They walked a few feet down. "There's Brain's. Over there's Jo-Jo's, then Crude's. Right next to hers is an empty bunk room and on the opposite side, three more empty bunk rooms. Since you guys are going to be staying with us until they get you into the DOR system and shipped to your unit, I assume you two will share a room?"

Alex's legs felt like rubber. He could barely fumble the words out as the thought of sharing a bed with Yara was way too much for him to consider. "Oh, uhm … we're not—"

Yara looked uncomfortable. "Oh, no, no, no, nothing like that, we're not together. Just friends."

Poachie shrugged. "Too bad. Alex is kinda cute."

Alex swallowed hard, immediately feeling a sensation of warmth come over him. *Relax. Murderers, remember?*

Crude's door swung open.

She wore black sweatpants, sneakers, and a white tank top. Her face was clean of the black face paint around her eyes, but it didn't take away the deadpan expression. Her skin was a beautiful black he hadn't seen before, much darker than his dad's. Her coffee brown eyes narrowing on him sent a chill down his spine.

"Crude, how's it going? Just showing the new recruits around. Any words of wisdom from the Ravens' commander?"

"Don't die." Crude's eyes rolled from Yara to Alex. "Have you decided on whether or not to join us?"

"Yes," Yara announced. "No way in hell am I backing down to join, that is, if you'll accept me."

She turned to Alex with an expression of cold belittlement. "And you?"

"N–no." Alex's mouth was too dry to get the word out. A heavy silence settled over the hall. His eyes searched the floor, trying to avoid catching her cold dead glance. "I–I just want to help my dad and little sister. That's it."

Poachie laid a gentle hand on his shoulder. "We get it. We'll do what we can for you while you're here, okay? That'll give you some time to figure it out."

Alex nodded.

"What a shame." There was no life in Crude's tone. "I guess if you don't figure it out soon, I'll have to execute you."

Alex jumped to life. "What?"

A nervous giggle erupted from Poachie. "She's just kidding. Really, she's just kidding."

"No. I'm not. If you give me any reason to believe that you'll betray us or compromise our efforts in this region,

I will kill you. No one person is more important than the freedom of the enslaved and subjugated. Isn't that right, Po?"

Like back in the mansion the air became cold and heavy. There was no doubt about it, this was coming from Crude. How was that possible?

Poachie nodded unctuously, clasping her hands together. "Yes, ma'am," she said, her voice soft and broken.

Yes, ma'am? He thought watching how Poachie's body language shifted as if she were talking to someone with renown and respect.

Crude's gaze drifted down the hall. "I'm going for a run. Any of you want to join?"

Alex's lips pulled, the nerves in his face going crazy. *Was she seriously asking me? She just threatened to kill me.* "Were you asking me too?"

"You have legs, don't you?"

She's insane!

"Crude, maybe once I'm done showing them around, they can connect with you?"

"Fine. As long as it doesn't interfere with dinner."

Sweat glistened from Poachie's forehead as she laughed again. "Of course not."

The little girl, who was just chest height, continued down the hall. The heaviness in the air went with her. Alex couldn't have been imagining her energy like icy needles digging beneath his skin. She was a monster.

Poachie scratched the back of her head. "Sorry about that. Crude gets really angry when she's hungry."

"Is she hungry all the time?" Yara snickered.

Crude's attitude didn't seem to change much from when she decapitated Principal Krate. The only emotion or jolt of life that took Alex by surprise was the way she acted around Big Mah.

"Crude's a little different," she stated while continuing to walk down the hall. "But I promise you, she's the most loving person you'll ever meet once you get to know her."

Yeah right. "How old is she? She looks young, but I assume she's the oldest here, right?"

"Nope. Actually, I'm the oldest. Seventeen. Crude's the youngest. She's thirteen."

Alex eyes widened. "*Thirteen*! Why are you calling her ma'am then?"

"She's the current commander of the Ravens, put in charge by the leader of D.O.R herself, Valkyrie."

Alex clenched his fist so tight his knuckles cracked. His head was spinning, he had so many questions, but he knew he had to relax. Valkyrie, the Ravens, finding out this girl was a commander and a ruthless killer. Crude was only a year older than Olivia, yet she could lop a grown man's head off with the flick of her wrist, and without hesitation, command the respect of the most lethal people he had ever encountered.

These people were monsters.

16

Poachie brought them through different areas, including a gym equipped with old rusted equipment. It was pretty big and smelled like mildew and cheap cologne, but it was better than the poor excuse of a gym Alex remembered at Eastern Suite Middle School.

Crude was at a dead sprint on the treadmill, wasn't even breaking a sweat. Her breaths were calm, her facial expression cold and emotionless. She was looking down at her fingers and digging through her cuticles.

Poachie guided them to the showers, then looped Alex and Yara back to the living room and kitchen area. "So, what do you guys think?"

Yara smiled and shook her head. "You guys are everything I thought you would be … and what I want to be. DOR's the voice of the ones who have gone to the grave, the rusty gear that won't allow the establishment of corruption to grind forward. Ever since I was a little girl, I dreamed of joining."

"Well, thank you. I've never heard anyone say it that way, but awesome." Poachie's brows rose. "I assume when we connect with leadership. They'll find an available unit for you after some training and evaluation."

Yara bit her bottom lip. "We won't be here?"

"Oh no. New recruits get shipped off for evaluation, training, then sent to a field platoon."

Alex watched the growing disappointment on Yara's face. "Why can't we stay here?"

"Raven is a more specialized unit. We barely make a squad, let alone a team. A platoon has at the bare minimum thirty-two troops. But that works best for us because of the missions we go on."

Alex arched a brow. "What do you guys specialize in?"

A devilish grin overshadowed Poachie's soft innocence. Like a switch deep within had flipped. "The Ravens are a covert division of DOR We're the best of the best and quite merciless."

Alex couldn't argue there. He could still see the frozen face of horror on Principal Krate as his head rolled away. The man he believed in so much, only to discover he was a psychopath.

"We function in, let's see …" Her fingers rolled over the curve of her bottom lip. "Handling reconnaissance for one. We're sometimes ordered to capture or eliminate high-level targets. And the best part is, we gather intelligence behind enemy lines."

That was impossible. There was no way they could manage all those tasks. "You guys are so young. It doesn't make sense. How do you do it all?"

"Well, all of us on the team are the best at what we do. Jo-Jo is the best sniper the world has ever seen, and she's only fifteen. Kimbo is our weapons expert and covers for Jo-Jo on missions. I'm second in command and the explosives expert, and then you have Crude, who's … Crude."

"Who gives you guys orders?" Yara asked.

Poachie's lips pulled as she looked to the corner of the cement ceiling. "Kind of a complex answer to that. DOR has a well-organized leadership chain, but we're technically a sub force of Anarchy."

Anarchy …. There hadn't been many attacks from Anarchy, maybe two or three Alex could remember growing up, but DOR had taken over the scene, causing the most damage. All along, it was Anarchy pulling the strings.

A nervous jitter came over Alex, but he fought the words out of his head. "All I want to do is go home. My dad and little sister have got to be worried and to be honest, I don't belong down here with you guys. I'm not a soldier. . . . I'm not a terrorist."

Poachie hummed a bit, then started laughing. "I'm sorry. I just love that innocence about you. You're so oblivious. You'd be surprised how easy it is to label someone a terrorist." She stretched out on the couch, bringing her hands behind her head. "Do you know what a terrorist is, Alex?"

He thought back to his elementary education at Eastern Suites, remembering the definition given by his teacher in his antiterrorism class. "It's the use of violence and intimidation, especially against citizens of the United Nations of America to cause chaos and destroy political balance throughout the one world order established by UNA."

"And how much do you know about the history of your precious UNA?"

"Well, everything. They teach us history in school."

"Like what?"

"Well, after the utter defeat of the Terrible Nations—"

"Russia, China ..."

"Well, yeah?" Alex raised a brow.

She looked on inquisitively. "Go on."

He shifted his lips to the side. "Well, UNA survived WWIII, and Cullen D. Roberts was elected as SGUNA. Then, on July 4, 2020, the UNA was born." He studied Poachie's face, checking to see if she was satisfied.

Yara shrugged. "Are we missing something?"

"Plenty. Like the massacre of C13 and other cities prior to the walls being created. Just stuff like that. Stuff they remove from your history books altogether."

Alex watched Yara's puzzled face. "What are you talking about? There was never a massacre."

"Unlike you two, I was abandoned when I was three," Poachie said, appearing to change the subject. "So I missed the 'education' you guys received. Instead, I learned everything from the streets, by the people and the whispers of the past. Taught from nights sleeping beneath houses and days living off scraps." She paused and snickered. "And the one thing that was consistent across every continent was the massacre. A day when a city of hundreds were obliterated."

Alex shook his head in disbelief. "I'm sorry. I don't know what you've been told, but that's obviously not true. It's a blatant lie that someone told you, Poachie."

She tilted her head. "What about you, Yara?"

"I was abandoned, too. I kind of remember my mom telling me something about the massacres a long time ago.

That even people from far-off countries who came to the mainland's had witnessed it. But after a few generations, the massacres became nothing but echoes. Just like you said, vanishing as if they never happened. Then once I came over the walls, I never heard anything of the massacres. Again, it was as if they never happened."

Poachie's gaze softened on Alex. As beautiful as she was, he had this stinging in the back of his throat. There was a dark side to her, minus the odd smell of gunpowder and motor oil that seemed to flow from her.

"You might not trust us, Alex, and you know what? We may be terrorists in the eyes of the United Nations of America, but I'd be more frightened of the ones who hide terrifying lies than the ones who are using violence to awaken the sleeping."

Jo-Jo walked in from down the hall, drying her hair. She was in shorts and a tank top, revealing her toned body. She didn't miss a day at the gym, that's for sure. "Poachie, would you be a dear and do one of those fruit salads you're killer at?"

Poachie stood and stretched to the ceiling, her fingertips barely grazing. "Sorry, Jay, no more fruit. We'll have to wait for the next convoy to come by."

Jo-Jo groaned with a tone that shrunk into a whimper until her eyes fell on Alex. "*You're* still here?"

"Where am I going?"

"Sounds like you were going home or something. Or do you need us to escort you home too?"

Alex jumped to his feet. "I don't need you to do anything for me."

Her lips pulled to the corner. "Oh, so tough now, are we? Back in that mansion, you were pissing yourself. Now that you're safe and standing in front of someone almost half your size you got balls I see."

"Shut—"

Before Alex could get a word out, Jo-Jo leaped over the couch and threw her legs over his shoulder. He was on his back with her legs tightening around his throat before he could get a cough out. His arm seared with pain and grew worse the more she pulled on his shoulder.

"Jo-Jo enough," Poachie commanded.

She released and kicked him in the face with her heel.

Bloody drool oozed from Alex's lips as he hacked and struggled to his feet. A sharp ache shot up his shoulder. What the hell had he been thinking? She was right. He forgot the girl he continued to talk down to had a billion-credit bounty on her head for assassinating government officials.

Alex remembered how Yara described the Daughter of Death in class that first day. Giving the gruesome details of a man's head exploding.

Jo-Jo mused. "Aww, are you gonna cry?"

Instead of feeding any further into the situation and getting his ass handed to him again, Alex marched out of the living room and headed to the gym. He prayed Crude wasn't down there, but at this point, it didn't matter.

Before he made it to the doorway of the gym, he could hear grunts and metal rattling. The steel bar was just smacking off Kimbo's chest when he came in.

"Aye, bro. What's up with you?" he yelled.

You're sociopathic half-pint girlfriend, is what he wanted to say. Alex rubbed his shoulder and shook his head.

"C'mon, man. Something's up. What you got?"

"What's Jo-Jo's problem?"

Kimbo took a deep breath, exhaled, then busted out four more reps on the flat bench, the bar bending from the weight. The four plates on each side rattled as he set the bar. "Yeah, she can be a lot. She's a lot to handle even for me."

"Why does she hate me?" Alex rotated his shoulder clockwise, then counterclockwise.

Kimbo sat up, pulling on some of the long locks of his hair. "She doesn't hate you, man. You just got to earn her respect first. She's survived a long time being a sniper and a go-to kill shot for DOR and Anarchy."

"About Anarchy," Alex sat down, rubbing his shoulders and trying to gain some of his pride back. "Sounds like DOR works for them, huh?"

Kimbo's head bobbled a bit as if he were unsure. "I'm sure after everything you've heard on the news about us, then what happened last night too, you probably think we're these bloodthirsty killers, but we're not. If I were to look at the difference between us and Anarchy, it would be that the Disciples want to influence change step by step. Anarchy on the other hand, wants to force change through chaos. We actually bump heads a lot."

"That's weird. But I haven't heard anything from Anarchy until now. I kinda thought they died out."

"That's what the news wants you to think. We've never kidnapped a Bourgeoisie citizen, ever. Anarchy sure has. Sure we've killed some Exclusives, some aristocrats and politicians, but we've freed thousands of slaves and Bourgeoisie citizens from labs in the process and brought them to the Outskirts."

"Then how do you explain last night?"

"Easy. DOR has absolutely no remorse for people that celebrate and take part in human trafficking, selling, murdering . . . you name it." He picked up a bottle of water and guzzled. "Evil people are everywhere. It's got nothing to do with class, trust me. I've lived on both sides of the wall."

Thoughts of last night came back hard, swirling in Alex's mind as all the conspiracies turned reality came at him at once. *This whole world's awful.* Thoughts of all those people locked in that dungeon long before he and Yara got there made him sick. "How are people that evil?"

Kimbo took a long swig of water and wiped his mouth. His forearm bulged over his nose. "I wondered the same thing growing up. I hated watching the proud and powerful treat the lowly like garbage because they could. I've seen people do terrible things to each other, and nobody did anything."

Alex wondered what Kimbo's life was like living in Fort Roberts. If Constance was the crown jewel, Fort Roberts was the crown. It was the most fortified city, the wealthiest out of the six continents, and of course, the place where Dalia C. Roberts made her home.

"Crazy to think the world is this messed up. Crazier to think that I tried to ignore it. It took my best friend dying and me and Yara getting locked in some dungeon to realize how screwed up everything was. All the Exclusives are evil."

"You're wrong, Exclusives are no eviler than any other class. Class has nothing to do with it." Kimbo looked down to the ground lost in thought. "Sometimes people are evil because of the evil done to them. Think about babies and little kids, right. They don't come out evil and hateful, but if you grow up around nothing but evil, nothing but nastiness and foulness, even if it's not being done to you, you're seeing it being done to others in that environment. Sometimes that leads to people knowing nothing else but that evil perception."

"As crazy as it sounds that makes a lot of sense."

"Nah, man, what's crazy are the evil people who think they're doing good. Those are the really crazy ones. Those are the ones to be afraid of. Those are the ones who got to go." Kimbo laid back down on the bench and knocked out a few more reps.

Alex's fist tightened. "Kimbo, where did you grow up?" Just as Poachie asked, Alex didn't say anything about what she told him and Yara.

"Fort Roberts," he spat out in between a rep. He took a break and sat up again, looking at Alex as if waiting for him to ask another question. "Nothing to say?"

"What's there to say?"

"First off, like how does someone who grew up in the richest, most fortified city in the new world end up in an organization plotting its downfall?"

"Well, you said it."

Kimbo laughed. "Yo, you're funny, Alex, real funny."

"Why are you in DOR?"

Kimbo took a deep exhale, forcing the air from his lungs, and looked down at his feet. Whatever he was thinking about, it must have been painful. Kimbo's lips moved, and the way his eyes searched the concrete floor was a little concerning. "Wait. You got a little sister, right?"

"Yeah, I do." Alex thought about Olivia and couldn't help but smile.

Kimbo smiled, too, showing a mouthful of pearly whites. "Pain in the butt, I bet, right?"

Nothing like Jo-Jo or Crude's attitude, but Olivia was up there. "Yeah, she's something."

"I'm a big brother, too," he said, using the front of his shirt to wipe the sweat streaming down his face. "My sister's a pain in the butt too. A *real* pain in the butt."

Alex arched a brow. "Olivia once hid my backpack from me, raced to the school bus, and told the bus driver I was sick. So I got left. I had to walk all the way to the middle school—about three miles—with sentinels watching me like a bad habit the whole way."

"Not bad. I'll raise you," Kimbo said, lifting his shirt over his head.

Thick risen strips of scarred flesh covered his back. They were the type of scars left from wounds so deep the body did all it could to seep into the gashes, strengthening and refortifying the wounds with extra tissue.

Alex's eyes fell away.

"Yeah. I'd look away too if I could see it. I can still feel the pain sometimes. The nerves in my right leg still twitch like it's happening at that moment."

"W—what happened?"

"My sister." He draped the shirt back over his shoulders. "Like I said earlier, sometimes people aren't born evil, but the world has a tendency to make them evil."

"Your sister did that to you?"

"Nah, not by her hands, anyway, she's—"

Poachie walked in, hands behind her back, looking down at Alex. "Hey, you okay?"

His face warmed from embarrassment. "I'll be alright."

"Good. Well, dinner's ready, so you guys should hurry along. Alright?"

"Yeah, buddy!" Kimbo's voice deepened. "What are we having today, Poachie, chef extraordinaire?"

"Roast pheasant. I got it a few days back and had it marinating in some of the herbs and spices I traded for back at the wall. I've got a side of wild rice and veggies as well."

Kimbo tensed and slapped his hands together in excitement. "Man, life is good!"

The words of what dinner was going to be didn't hit Alex at first. Pheasant? Wild rice and vegetables? Where were the over-salted chicken gizzards and stale bread? His stomach cried from her words alone. "You guys have food like that down here?"

"I pride myself in my cooking. Maybe it'll be so good you'll stay a little longer?"

Kimbo gave the deepest laugh. "I bet you will!"

Poachie gave Alex a hand and pulled him up from the chair. Permeating the air was an aroma of spices that were completely new to him. It smelled even better than the food in N.H.A. "Wow, that smells amazing. Did you really cook?"

"Of course. You think I'm a joke?" She nudged him.

Poachie took Alex's hand again and pulled him down the hallway toward the kitchen and living room. Assorted cups of orange liquid waited on the table. A pitcher of the same liquid rested in the center. A roasted bird browned and dressed in green and red vegetables brought the table to life, but besides all that, it was the laughter and conversation that took Alex by surprise.

Yara and Jo-Jo looked to be getting along great. Crude nodded and shook her head every few seconds, then her gaze fell on Alex.

He stepped back and thought of finding a corner deep within the gym to hide in. Poachie tugged him forward.

"So, have you made a decision yet?" Crude asked.

Alex shook his head, looking away.

She sighed, closing her eyes. It was the first time he saw her face soften. She kicked a chair opposite her. "Is that better, Poachie?"

Poachie nodded with excitement and brought Alex to the chair. "It's been a long time since we had guests at Raven Headquarters. So I wanted to go a little overboard with cooking."

"At the cost of our rations, I see?" Crude growled, lowering her gaze. "But food is food." Crude snatched a fork and knife and slammed her fist on the table. "So, what are we waiting for?"

Alex jolted back by her intensity, too nervous to sit. At the most, back at home, his dad's words were a gentle whisper. All of the conversations at the dinner table were whispers with that VEN-O listening. It felt like the conversations were scripted. Nobody could share their true feelings. Otherwise, *they* would hear, and the sentinels would come.

Crude's entire demeanor changed. Her edge dropped off some, and it seemed like all her attention fell on the array of food.

"Crude!" Jo-Jo yelled. "You need to relax. Until Kimbo gets here, we don't need you wolfing down everything like last time." Jo-Jo's voice softened as she clasped her belly. "I didn't even get a sliver of that damn turkey."

Everyone laughed except Crude, who gave a childish frown and poked at the grilled bird's breast.

A smile slipped across Alex's face.

Kimbo came from behind with a bear hug, nearly squeezing the breath out of Alex's lungs. "Welcome to dinner! Crude, you want to fight me for a drumstick?"

"I'll kill you," she rasped.

He went over and pulled her out of her chair, hugging her tight, taking her off her feet. The room filled with laughter and an energy Alex hadn't experienced in a long time. Not since his mom anyway.

"So, what's taking you so long to sit?" Jo-Jo's eyes burrowed into Alex. "We can't eat until everyone sits at the table."

Alex nodded and sat down, scootching himself closer to the table. Everyone held hands, said grace, gave a moment of silence for those lost, and even a moment of silence for their enemies. Then everyone began eating.

Crude nearly jumped over the table as she tore a wing off the pheasant. She ripped into the meat like a wild animal, shoveling rice and vegetables into her mouth. Never in his life had Alex seen a person eat like that.

The bowl of rice was gone, the wing of the pheasant picked clean, and veggies nothing but remnants. She pulled off a drumstick and ripped the seasoned crunchy skin clean away like a magician removing the covering off a table then devoured it.

Everyone laughed and talked about stories of survival while Crude inhaled food. Nothing personal, just events that entertained. Nothing about killing, nothing about destroying UNA or bringing it down.

The food was incredible and the pheasant's breast juicy. The rice was soft, and the vegetables were cooked just right, not brown mush like at the middle school. Alex's tastebuds went crazy.

Tears broke from Alex's lashes as he tried to control his laughter as he listened to Kimbo's storytelling. After watching Poachie's comical reaction and how Crude inhumanly consumed food, Alex was bent over cradling his stomach. Yara was in tears too. Laughter and joy soaked into Alex's bones, and he didn't want it to end. But Olivia and his dad were a sharp pain that needed his attention.

His eyes searched the kitchen counter, where a separate plate of food lay covered in plastic. Poachie poked him in the ribs. "Everything okay?"

Alex nodded to the food. "Leftovers?"

"Oh uhm . . ." She rushed over to the plate of food and placed it into the refrigerator.

The clanging of eating utensils silenced along with the laughter. It was as if he'd walked into an uncomfortable conversation as eyes searched one another. Even Yara's gaze became one of concern and uneasiness.

A nervous laugh slipped out, and Alex followed it up with the best fake yawn he could muster. "I don't know what time it is, but being underground is exhausting," he said, stretching to the ceiling. "Going to head to that room."

Everyone nodded as he rose from the table. He placed the empty plate in the sink and headed down the hall. He counted the steps, pacing himself till he came to the door.

Inside there was a wooden framed bed, old and craggy, and a mattress that had been stripped of its plastic covering from age. Yellow stained sheets and dark green covers were neatly folded at the foot, and a pillow he wouldn't dare lay his face on was set at the head of the mattress, which was covered in brown and green stains.

He made the bed as best as possible and chucked the pillow to the corner of the room. He checked the seams for signs of bedbugs, flipped the mattress, and finally fell onto the bed, letting his back sink into its rough embrace.

An ease of relaxation fell over him. Small but oddly perfect, the room was encased in white stone walls, the floor concrete like everything else in this place unless it had a rug thrown down, but it was perfect. He hadn't had a room to call his own since . . . *Yeah.* The thought of his mom crossed his mind. Thoughts of Dad and Olivia too.

A knock came on the door.

"Come in."

Yara crept in, lips pursed as she closed the door and leaned against it. He should've been excited, sweating with a racing heart. But that nervous phase was wrung out by the chaos of the previous night. "Hey."

"So you might want to take a shower before you get all comfortable and relaxed in bed. I don't think you want to sleep with sewer clothes on."

Alex jumped out of bed, the smell finally kicking him in the face. With everything going on, he couldn't believe he'd forgotten about a nice shower and a fresh pair of clothes. "You're right. Things have just been crazy, you know?"

"Yeah, I know. Any more thought about how you're going to get to your dad and sister?"

He sighed, leaning against the wall. "No idea. My dad's got to be losing his mind right about now though. I don't know what he's going to do or what's going to happen after everything that happened last night."

"What do you think he'll do?"

Alex thought about his dad's plan to leave the walls and venture into the Outskirts. If he followed through with the plan, he could catch up with them somehow. But that was wishful thinking. Knowing his dad, he'd stay put until Alex returned.

"My dad wanted to leave the Suites and head to the Outskirts today."

She lurched forward. "Are you serious? Why are you just telling me this?"

"Well, I started to tell you last night, then …" He felt the large lump on the back of his head.

"Oh." She folded her arms. "Do you think he would leave without you?"

"I'm starting to hope he does, but knowing my dad, he wouldn't do anything like that. For all I know, he probably thinks I've been picked up or something, and that makes me nervous."

"You think he'll do something he'll regret?"

Alex thought about the shotgun beneath the couch. "Not with my baby sister around, no. That's the only saving grace." He thought about the story Dad told him and the reason he had the gun.

"We're going to figure this out, Alex. If anyone can help you get to your family, it's these guys. And I'm with you all the way."

As much as he liked Kimbo and Poachie, he still wasn't sure about the Ravens. Not to mention there was still a lot of hiding going on, and that made him nervous.

17

The air was dry and from the blackness behind Alex's closed eyes came the soft gritty grind of metal above him. His eyes peeled back, immediately every bone and muscle tensed.

Standing at the foot of his bed, rolling a lollipop gently between her teeth was Crude, her black blade at his throat. The blade was strangely warm against his Adam's apple.

Her brown eyes were focused, her nose scrunched. She wore a black sleeveless dress with a thick leather black and red belt around her waist, black calf-high socks stretched down to the same black rugged combat boots she'd worn yesterday.

Alex raised his hands. "W-what did I do?"

She placed the point of the blade just below his chin. The lollipop moved to her left cheek. "What's your decision?"

Alex gulped. *Not this again.* "I don't belong here with you and the others, Crude. I've decided today that it's time for me to go back to Eastern. My dad's most likely worried sick."

"Belong?" Her eyes narrowed. "Belonging has nothing to do with it."

He looked down the shaft as she used the edge of her blade to lift his face back up to hers. "DOR is obviously for a different type of person. I'm not a soldier or killer. I can barely fight. All I want to do is make the best life I can for my dad and baby sister. I can barely look at a gun, let alone hold one."

Her frown put a bad taste in his mouth. What was she thinking? For all he knew, it was about food.

She pulled the lollipop from her mouth. "I agree. You're definitely a coward, and I wouldn't trust you with a gun if my life depended on it. But . . ." She sheathed the sword and stepped down, placing her hands on her hips. "Jo-Jo vouched for you."

"No, Jo-Jo vouched for Yara, not me," he said, rubbing his throat. He swung his legs off the bed. "I'm not who you think I am."

She crunched down hard on the lollipop, munching on the shards as she watched him intently. "Jo-Jo said you were willing to sacrifice yourself for Yara if it meant getting her out of harm's way."

Alex thought about the other night, and everything that happened. Yara didn't deserve to die. She was the courageous one, the one who fought for what was right and spoke her mind no matter what. It was him who bent a knee and cast his best friend to the wolves and allowed him to die. No, sacrifice wasn't the word. "I just wanted to protect her, that's all."

"Self-sacrifice is a trait only found in a few. Most people cling to life because they're addicted to it, living off the drunkenness of its spoils uncaring of who they harm. All that matters is *them*. This is a cold world, Alex, and if you're willing to sacrifice yourself for anyone that isn't family . . . that means something."

Crude didn't know how wrong she was. He thought of Nelson and could still see his body hooked up to tubes, his eye gone, and a face so swollen and disfigured it was unrecognizable. "I let my best friend die. I abandoned him because I was afraid if I got caught up in his drama, that his situation would affect me and my family. When he needed me the most, I turned my back on him. Now he's dead. That's not self-sacrifice."

"No, that's what a coward would do. And back then, you surely were a coward. But if you had the opportunity to relive that situation again, would you stand up for your friend? Would you die for him?"

"Of course I would!" Alex jumped at her question. He hid his face as tears fell. Memories of him, Nelson, and Deacon playing in the scrapyard came as swift as a summer's breeze. "In a heartbeat."

"That's all I needed to know."

Alex took a hard sniff and looked up to see Crude with her hand out. Covered by a fingerless leather glove, it was the same hand she used to wield her sword. She said, "I'll increase the time for you to decide. I'll only do this once. After that' I'll begin taking fingers."

He gulped. "What makes you think I'll be a good member, Crude?"

She stepped down from the foot of the bed and swung the door open. "Just remember, I'll be taking fingers." She slammed the door shut.

Well, that was a unique experience. If he didn't know any better, Crude had just shown some form of trust. Her words sunk in as he started getting dressed. If they wanted him to join so bad, he had questions, and more than likely, they had answers.

When he opened the door, Yara was right there. He stepped back. "Oh, hey."

"Hey," she said sheepishly, her gaze rolling away. It wasn't like her.

"Good morning." He thought about how he'd reacted last night. "How did you sleep?"

"Fine. Thanks for asking." There was a strange expression on her face as she stuffed her hands in the black hoody that was her signature article of clothing. "So, Crude coming out of your room isn't weird or anything."

"Oh, uh, she just … she just wanted to extend her offer to join again."

She smiled, looking away. "How did that go?"

Alex looked down at his hands. "Sounds like I better figure everything out or else I'm gonna find it pretty hard to eat with a fork."

"That bad, huh?"

He nodded. "So what's up, did you need me for anything?"

"Oh, uhm, yes. I ugh, *they* want to talk to the two of us in the living room. I think it has something to do with what happened back at the mansion. You … want to walk together?"

"Of course."

They made their way to the living room.

Poachie sat on the kitchen counter, Kimbo on the arm of the couch with Jo-Jo by his side. Crude sat at the table gnawing on something, then there was a new face. A pudgy dark-skinned boy with hair kept in a nappy fro sat at the head of the table. His eyes darted away when Alex looked him over. He looked young, younger then he and Yara were for sure.

Poachie jumped down. "Great, everyone's here." She clapped her hands together and took a deep breath. "So a few things. First off, we haven't been on the up and up with you two. First, I want to introduce the brain of Raven, who we call, all jokes aside, Brain."

He raised a trembling hand as he lowered his head. He muttered something, but it was too mousey and weak to break the air.

Alex nodded, then his mouth twisted as he shoved a brow to the ceiling. "So why didn't we see Brain yesterday or on the mission?"

Jo-Jo hung over the couch loose and uncaring as if she dreaded to be part of the meeting. "Brain's not the *shoot em up kill em type*. He's the guy who helps with planning and strategizing and getting us out of sticky situations. If you noticed, the night that we saved your butts, we were talking to someone on our mics, he's that someone."

Alex nodded, studying the boy who looked to be uncomfortable in his own skin. He didn't look up at anyone, instead just locked his eyes down on warn sneakers that seemed too small for him.

Poachie picked back up from where she started. "Thanks Jo. Just like she said, Brain holds down the fort and feeds us intel during our missions. He keeps us alive. But on to that second part of us hiding things from you. We've been monitoring the both of you from the beginning. At first contact in the mansion, we utilized facial recognition and sent it to Brain." She nodded to the boy who looked too ashamed to look Alex in the eyes. "He did a full background search on you that went back to the day you were born. Everything about you checked out, Alex. A Bourgeoisie boy who lost his mom when he was younger. You focused on your education and got top scores in your studies. That's how you got accepted into New Hope."

Alex snickered. "You guys were just what, testing us or something, pretending to be our friends?"

"Are you seriously that stupid?" Jo-Jo rose on her elbows on the back of the couch. "You seriously thought just because you showed interest to join, we'd take two randoms into the top-secret base of the most badass, most wanted soldiers in the world?"

Poachie leaned back, folding her arms. "Everything that happened yesterday with showing you around, feeding you, laughing and talking . . . None of that was an act, Alex. But you better believe we did our homework, especially on you," she said, turning to Yara. "You weren't born into the middle-class slums were you, Yara?"

Alex's turned. His thoughts ran about the little she told him the night they were kidnapped, about how she was really from the Outskirts. How the heck did they pull up all this information on them?

Yara shook her head. "No. I was born in the Outskirts and abandoned there by my mom. She—"

"*Aaang.* wrong," Jo-Jo blurted. "Try again."

Alex's gaze went from feeling sorry for Yara to scrutiny. He took a step back from her. "What are they talking about, Yara?"

Yara's brows furrowed, and she looked over the room as if she had just heard the worst news possible. "What are you guys talking about? I don't understand. I was abandoned in the Outskirts by my mom."

"Wrong again," Crude said, rising from the table. She drew her sword. The thin, strikingly black blade had a strange bow to it. She gripped the black handle firmly in her hands. "And I don't like liars. If I can't trust you here, I can't trust you when bullets start flying, and people start dying. Answer the question."

Alex tried to understand what was going on. He watched tears well in Yara's eyes.

"Please," she begged.

"Tell the truth, Yara," Crude commanded.

Yara wiped her eyes. "Alright!"

Alex faced her fully after the outburst. "What's going on?"

"I told you I was born in the Outskirts, but that's not one-hundred percent fact. Actually, I was born within the inner walls of Fort Roberts. But I swear it's not what you think."

Alex's mouth filled with a bitter taste. He shook his head in disbelief, remembering how much hell she gave the Exclusives at New Hope Academy, how she chastised them and belittled them. "What? You were one of them the whole time?"

Yara stepped closer. "It's not like that at all."

"So what is it then?" he snapped back.

Crude lowered the sword between them. "You need to listen before you jump the gun, fool."

Alex silenced and slipped his hands into his pockets. A carousel of thoughts from the first day he laid eyes on Yara bounced around in his head, and he wondered what was real and what wasn't.

"I'm not some snobby prick, I swear." She looked at Alex with tears rolling down her eyes. "I swear."

Alex leaned against the wall of the kitchen, thinking about the girl who sat in that row on the bus for students from Western Suites. "So what's going on then, Yara?"

She sniffled. "Yup. I was born in the inner walls of Fort Roberts. Surrounded by the wealthiest of the wealthiest, the grand city. Home of the Secretary General herself," she said as if giving a grand entrance. "I was born a secret, hidden in the pantries of a slave shack till I was three. My mom was a slave, a maid servant who did more than just *clean*. My father? Just some aristocrat piece of dog crap who couldn't keep his pants on."

An awful sense of shame made Alex's skin crawl. "You don't have to say anymore."

"It's fine. Really. Hid it long enough, to be honest. When I was three, the wife discovered me while I was trying to dig out scraps from the garbage can. All I remember was my mother being hanged on my father's command, and I was driven out to the furthest part of the woods and left there in the wild." She sniffled, wiping her nose. "So yeah. I was born in the Outskirts. Was all that in your background check?"

No one said a word.

Crude placed the blade back in its scabbard and yawned. "Alright, so now that we got that out in the open, let's move on. You two already know Poachie, Kimbo, and Jo-Jo. You *think* you know me, but who you don't know is Brain." She thumbed over her shoulder to the boy, who lowered his head. "I've known Brain since . . ." She tapped her chin. "Since we were five, right?" She turned to him.

He swallowed hard, shrinking into his chair, and gave a subtle nod.

"You guys grew up in the Outskirts?" Yara cleared her throat, trying to fight through her pain.

Crude looked up at the corner of the room in deep thought again. "Well, I know I did. Brain, not so much. He's a test tube baby."

Alex's neck snapped back at her words. "A what?"

Poachie nodded. "So Brain was born in a lab, some kind of experiment UNA was running to create highly intelligent humans. Then they started taking in children for a more *exciting* project." Her eyes rolled to Crude.

Crude looked up with dead eyes. "They wanted to create a super soldier. So here I am."

"Crude," Kimbo spoke with a deep voice, "time to call in the Raven's SITREP."

She rolled her eyes. "Right. Brain, open up the O.C.."

The boy nodded and raced down the hallway.

"You guys are coming, too. You get to meet the leader of DOR." Crude began marching down the same corridor they initially came down in the beginning.

The leader? Alex thought. For some odd reason, he pictured Crude to be the sole leader of the organization. With her harsh nature and the way she dealt with people, it only made sense.

This leader must be far more frightening compared to Crude to keep someone of her nature in line.

18

Douglas Quake paced back and forth. His skin crawled, and his mind raced with the thoughts of what had become of his son.

His tears from this morning dried up in the gleam of the rising sun, and every word, ever curse he wanted to scream, he swallowed.

He turned and looked at the green ring which pulsed on the cylinder black speaker. Silent. Listening. Gathering ...

"Daddy?" Olivia's voice was a brittle leaf in a raging wind. "When's Alex coming back? He's coming back soon, right?"

Doug swallowed hard. He'd have to come back. There was no way Alex would just run off, abandon his old man and baby sister. No. That boy had more sense than that, more strength than . . . *Unless he thought running away would keep them safe?*

Doug took a deep breath and exhaled. He turned to Olivia with a smile. "Of course he is, honey. Alex went to pick up some supplies for us. He'll be back soon."

"Dad, you said we were leaving this morning." She wasn't buying it. "I don't think Alex would take this long."

His daughter's eyes focused on him, and Doug almost gasped at the similarities to Myra's. Olivia wasn't buying it. She knew her brother all too well.

"Dad, something's not right."

"I know things are scary right now. But I promise, everything will work out, honey. I promise. You trust your daddy, don't you?"

She nodded.

"Good. Let me make some breakfast."

Like a ghost she slunk away into their bedroom.

He headed to the kitchen and pulled out the hidden pork belly he had been saving for their birthdays. It was cured and salted to perfection and had been bathed in maple. The smell alone would calm the atmosphere. For Olivia, anyway.

He cracked three eggs. Slathered the pan with fat and tossed the chunks of belly in. But the sizzling only added a heaviness to his heart.

There was a clump in his throat. He took another breath, stepped away from the pan, and tried to center himself. Where was his son? Doug's hands trembled, and the silver wedding ring on his left hand clattered against the table.

He eyed the VEN-O.

A strange sound echoed in the distance. Couldn't be helicopters. UNA never used helicopters unless they were going after high-value targets or someone important was coming into the city.

No, they didn't take my boy. His jacket was gone, along with his sneakers. He left of his own will. Would have heard a commotion otherwise. Douglas's eyes rolled to the couch. *Alex is fine.*

He flicked on the television, took another breath, then turned to mix the eggs. Olivia loved scrambled eggs, and Alex loved fried pig belly. He'd be happy to come home to the smell.

Doug looked up to the brown blotches on the kitchen ceiling. He had been harsh on Alex. A little too harsh. The boy lost his best friend, had a weight on his shoulders like no other, and finally got a taste of what life was truly like out there over that damn wall.

"Citizens are calling it a massacre...." The stern voice of a reporter crept into Douglas's ear.

He scrambled the eggs furiously, glaring down at the stamp on his right hand that made him feel ill. "It's always a massacre when it comes to you people," he said under his breath then took a quick glance at the VEN-O. "When it comes to us, you tend to flower up the statement."

"Two dozen Exclusives dead, amongst them Governor Krate and his son Stewart Krate, principal of New Hope Academy."

The fork fell to the floor chiming with the sizzling and pops of fat. Doug slowly turned, his eyes focusing on the television, his heart thrashing. He swallowed.

"A party in celebration of the strides made toward the unification of the classes was brutally interrupted as bombs went off all around the street, destroying vehicles and killing those trying to escape. It's considered the most brutal DOR attack in history."

Doug sat down hard. A trembling hand went to the knob to turn the television down. He hung on every word of the reporter. The body count of the attack was still rising. No survivors.

No. No. No. His fingers pressed against his forehead, sweat rising in beads. The Suites would be flooded with sentinels now. The raids were going to be bad.

"We got visuals on perpetrators," the reporter said with a nod. Her cold brown eyes were stern and hardened with anger. "DOR operators, of course. We believe, based on characteristics, the One-eyed Devil and the Daughter of Death are currently working together within our walls."

Doug sat back in his chair. "The worst of the worst."

There was only one reason they would be paired together. DOR was more than likely planning an assassination for the SGUNA. There was no way around it. And if he thought so, government officials were probably thinking the same thing.

"We also have visuals of two others, unmasked individuals who we believe have recently joined the ranks of DOR The first photo is coming on screen now."

The first photo was of a girl with long hair and brown skin. She looked like any other girl from the Suites. Based on the wanted poster now flashing on the television screen, Doug suspected she was from the Northern side. That place would be torn apart.

"And the second photo …"

Doug threw himself back. He fell out of the chair and hit his head off the counter. "No! No! This is a mistake. They're wrong. No!"

Blood pulsed through his head, through his face, and behind his eyes. His skin was on fire. His heart smashing was painful now. He clawed at his chest. Deep thuds came in waves.

A boy with tightly curled hair, a nose like Myra's, eyes like his own, and a scrawny build looked back with a broken smile. "Alex. It can't be...."

Olivia came running into the kitchen. "Dad, you okay? What happened? What's wrong?" She turned to the television.

The echoes of the reporter pinged off the walls of the kitchen and living room. An unbearable heaviness hung over them. Doug thought about the Tanakas. No, not Alex. His beloved son, his legacy wouldn't do that to his family. Not like that Jason Tanaka.

"He wouldn't...."

Olivia exhaled. "Good."

Doug turned to her, horrified.

"They all deserve what they got. I'm surprised Alex had the guts to join them. I didn't think he had it in him to fight, to stand up against *them*."

Doug watched the streams flow down Olivia's face, and he saw peace, joy, and hope. Not the horror and fear that radiated from him. He felt disgusted with himself. What had happened in the last few years after Myra's death that he had become so detached from his children?

All this time, he'd been trying so hard to teach them to accept their place in this world. To follow the rules and regulations, to not end up like so many others. To not end up like their mother. To play the safe route. But internally, he had been caging them.

He had never seen his daughter so proud. And it killed him to know she could feel this way about this decision her brother made. Doug hung his head as he leaned back against the kitchen counter while sitting on the floor.

I'm sorry, Myra. He wiped the tears away. Maybe this was how Akira and Yui felt when Jason joined D.O.R, and again when their second son Nelson died. Weak, worthless, and like failures.

How could he have not seen the damage and pain inflicted on his children? The brutality of what this life inflicted on them over the years should have raised red flags. He thought he had them under control, that they were different than most kids. That they would overcome the stigmas of this world, just like he and Myra did.

But he'd failed them. Alex turned his back on them because he failed them as a father. He saw only what he wanted to see with his children. Not who they were ... not who they were becoming.

The VEN-O started blaring. The hair on his neck stood on end.

"Please be prepared to receive sentinel support. Please be prepared to receive sentinel support. Please be prepared...." The soft robotic voice was feminine yet cold.

Douglas looked to the couch. "Olivia, did you know?"

She shook her head and wiped her eyes. "Alex hates guns, Dad. I honestly thought he hated DOR too. But I guess everything with Nelson changed that."

Douglas believed her. She didn't need to lie. Everything was laid out now. He forced himself up. The blue smoke of burnt pork belly and the grease spilling over the counter added to the chaos, the robotic voice overpowering.

They'd be here soon.

His steps were heavy, slow, passionless. He went to the couch.

"Dad, what are you doing?"

He didn't answer. Instead, he asked, "Olivia, would you leave if the choice came to staying with me or joining DOR?"

Her watery eyes rolled away from his.

His heart shattered. He took a deep breath as his eyes rolled around the room. He'd failed his children. Failed his wife. What kind of man was he if he couldn't have created an environment where they felt safe and wanted to stay together and not with murderous terrorists?

"Dad. We love you." She looked at the news, tears streaming down her eyes. She rubbed them away with a trembling hand. "But we're not like you or the other parents. We're not even like Mom I guess. We can't accept ... this." She looked around the apartment. "This life is too suffocating."

"They're going to come for us, okay."

She nodded.

"I want you to go into your room and close the door. No matter what you hear, don't come out. You hear?"

"Dad, what are you going to do?"

Doug pulled out the cushions, pulled the shotgun from the cushioned cotton, and loaded it.

"Dad!"

"Do as I told you, Olivia."

"Dad, no, please. I'm sorry. I take it all back! I take it back! I'd rather stay with you!"

"It's okay." The roar of engines growled from outside. He peeked out the window as three large trucks pulled up. Dozens of men in all black jumped out. A turret swerved to the window. He pulled back out of view. "Go, Olivia."

"Dad, you don't have to do this. Turn yourself in. Please!"

He shook his head. He thought of all the empty seats back at the table in the mill. Their table. All of them were picked up during night raids, whisked away, never to be seen of or heard from again. They were erased.

With what Alex was involved in, this would be war. Not only would Alex face public execution, but so would Douglas. Olivia would be imprisoned for a little bit, but because of her age, and if she kept quiet, she would be sent to the Outskirts. Hopefully, that's where Alex was.

He loaded a few more shells, then wrapped the shotgun in a blanket. "Follow their instructions. Don't make any sudden moves." He hoped they would take her out of the apartment first.

The blaring sound of VEN-Os all over the apartment building could be heard, the robotic voice soft and patronizing. "I love you, honey, with all my heart, mind, and soul. You know that, right?"

She nodded. "I do, Dad. I do. Please! Please don't do this. I'm sorry."

He walked over and held her tight. He kissed her cheeks and her forehead and pulled his fingers through the kinks and curls of her hair. "They're gonna send you to the Outskirts. Find Alex. You understand?"

She buried her face in his chest and cried.

"I know. I know. But this is it for me. I'm just sorry I wasn't more for you guys, that's all." He fought back tears of his own. But he had made his decision. "Keep moving forward. I love you."

She held him tight.

A blaring speaker echoed from outside. "Apartment 22A, prepare to receive sentinel support."

Heard that one already, "Go to your room. Do as I say."

Olivia let go and rushed to her bedroom. The door slammed shut behind her. He kept the blanket tight on his lap, hands on the trigger. They wouldn't kill him without a fight.

There was a strange silence. Then there was a thunderous pop from downstairs and the sound of boots trudging through the hallway. The staircase rumbled with footsteps. His heart raced. Fingers tightened around the trigger.

He could hear the radios now, the still voices. Blank, emotionless. There was a gentle chime from the VEN-O, one that nearly reminded him of lunch at the table.

"Mr. Quake," a human voice, a woman's, softer, gentler than the robotic tone, came through the speaker. "We would advise you to put the shotgun down if you want your daughter to walk away from this."

A cold sweat chilled him to the bone as his eyes rolled around the room.

"Mr. Quake, please. Do as we say, the gun you have wrapped in the blanket, toss it to the side. Give yourself up, and you and your daughter will have rights to a speedy trial."

He fell forward on all fours. They had been watching him all this time. "How long," he called out. He didn't look up. "How long could you see us?"

"Since you moved into the apartment, Mr. Quake." The voice had gained a patronizing tone. "Now, please, toss the gun several feet away from you."

He shoved the shotgun away and kept his hands on the ground. Eyes on the ground. Tears dribbled over the grooves and deep crevices of the wooden floor. All this time ... All this time they had never been free.

The soft chime broke over the kitchen. A loud pop burst through the front door as a wave of blackness swooped in. He looked up to see the faceless black visors spilling into the apartment. Olivia's shrieks echoed.

"Olivia, calm down. Calm—" A crack of pain rushed from the back of his head. His vision spiraled as a black sack went over his head. Another crack clapped against the side of his face.

The sounds of Olivia's shrieks and cries for her daddy were a distant echo in the aching pain of his skull.

He felt his hands and feet get bound. He felt his body get picked up. He thought of Myra, Alex, Olivia. His family. His friends, the Tankas. How could he have been so cruel to have turned his back on the people who supported him most in this world? To teach them to submit. Like a dog. Like a slave ...

19

Alex followed them past the ladder that went up to the entrance of the base. Everyone bunched by the stone wall.

Brain placed his hands on a scanner and a side door slid open, revealing a dark room. As they stepped in, the place lit up, coming to life with all kinds of machinery that blinked, beeped, and flickered. Half smoothed concrete, some craggy rock, and the rest steel framing was what made up the room. Multiple large screens hung from walls.

The key piece of equipment—a black metal chair with all kinds of gadgets and thick cables connected to the computer system beside it—had multiple bright lights focused all around to highlight it. Alex studied it from afar, taking note of the leather straps. Knowing these guys, he assumed it was some kind of torture device.

"Over here," Poachie said, pulling Alex over to the group who stood in front of a massive screen.

Brain plopped his chubby frame deep into a leather chair and began typing away. *Searching* came across a bright blue screen. A steady beep intertwined with the other sounds that filled the room. Then the screen turned black, and a silhouette sitting comfortably in a chair came on the screen.

"Ravens, good morning," said a girl's voice.

Alex watched as Crude and the others stood straight and saluted. "Ma'am!"

"At ease." Though in a dull lit room where you couldn't see her in great detail, a girl sat back in a large leather chair. Her skin was a warm brown, long black hair fell over her shoulders, two short bangs hung over her face, one of them covering the right side. She raised her chin. "I see two unfamiliar faces. Who are they?"

"Two recruits, ma'am. Background checks were completed along with surveillance." Crude saluted again. "Both are Bourgeoisie caught up in the rescue mission to free those from that prison run by the Krates."

The silhouette leaned over in the chair. Alex squinted, catching the smoky black eyeliner that sheltered eyes and even blacker lipstick that glistened. Her hands folded on her lap, showing black fingernails, and her voice was smooth and steady. "Interesting, I trust your judgment, Crude, leader of the Ravens. But I'm interested in why you trust random civilians to join our ranks. That's not like you?"

Crude swallowed. "It's all based on a suggestion, the background checks, and a conversation I had with—" she turned to Alex "—him. I think they can be trustworthy members with potential in the organization."

"Understood," she said, leaning back in the leather chair. She was well hidden at times, and as Alex looked deeper, he noticed two silhouettes behind her. Guards maybe? "I'll have them pushed through to the recruitment team for training and selection into a proper occupation, but for the time being, I'll leave them in your care. I hope that's okay. I know it's a little unorthodox, but things are starting to get a little lively."

"Thank you, ma'am." Crude stood strong, her back straight, still saluting, never taking her eyes off the screen.

"Okay. Report for the day?"

Crude lowered her hand and nodded. "Mission redemption was a success. Zero casualties, and one-hundred and eighty civilians freed and released outside the walls to make a choice for themselves as to what they want to do. Though I'm not sure about the undercover Anarchy member who was supposed to be there."

"The Anarchy member was able to escape. I contacted the commander of Anarchy late yesterday afternoon and he confirmed. But I'm concerned, especially for the ones you have with you. I assume they were amongst those imprisoned?"

"Uh, yes, ma'am. Looks like torture and murder for a revenge scheme connected to New Hope Academy. What's the concern?"

"I assume you haven't watched the news. That's unheard of for the Ravens, Crude?"

Crude bristled.

Alex watched the anxious twitch of her eye and nearly smiled at the first sign of normalcy from her. Her fingers curled into a shaking fist at her waist. He thought of the person in the shadows, the one Poachie called Valkyrie. She was young too, it was in her voice, but why was she hidden from the ones she was in charge of?

She shot a glance down to Brain. "Pull up the television, now!"

Brain went to work, typing away as two of the massive plasma screens came on, blaring news reports. On one screen were reports of what happened in the city, and on the other, reports from dozens of other cities spouting about the same event. When Alex's middle school photo came on the screen of the news broadcasting, his heart stopped.

"Shit," Yara whispered as her photo appeared on the screen too.

The panic started out like a slow-moving mudslide, then barreled down his insides as the next scene showed a live video feed of Alex watching the execution of Principal Krate and his father. His heart was heavy. His entire body felt like ice as the video continued, showing him running with the group. He cupped his mouth to keep from vomiting as he read the News title: *DOR Mass Murder*.

In a peach pants suit, a woman with a stout build and curly orange hair looked to the screen with horror and anger as she read from a document. "Members of the Disciples of Revolution stormed a charity event organized to celebrate the successful integration of Bourgeoisie students into New Hope Academy. DOR murdered school representatives and teachers, along with our beloved governor Sean Krate and his son, the very ones who established the integration program."

A cold grasp tangled with his hands, but Alex couldn't look away from the screen as his picture popped back up. Even in the photo his brown skin looked ashy, lips dry, and hair unkept in tight curls. How embarrassing.

"Alexander Quake is shown with DOR members during the brutal murder of a government official and is also involved in the mass murder as well. This terrorist was not only a student at New Hope Academy, but he was on suspension for attacking a fellow student from the inner walls. What's most frightening, is this young man is also friends with a past Bourgeoisie student, turned terrorist, Jason Tanaka."

Terrorist? She called me . . . a terrorist?

Alex was shaking. He felt large brawny hands fall on his shoulders. For a moment, he thought it was his dad. Oh God, Dad and Olivia. What about Dad and Olivia?

Yara stepped in front of him talking, her fingers curled around his, but he couldn't hear a word she was saying. Everything was pounding. A thud, a horrible heavy thud like a sledgehammer smacking the bare chest of a poor soul, over and over and over again.

Below his picture were the words *most wanted*, with a bounty on his head for over five million credits. Yara had the same amount.

The leader of DOR spoke over the news. "Sounds like we can trust you, after all, Alex Quake."

He stumbled a bit, the room spinning.

Jo-Jo's voice was stern and brutal. "What's wrong? Not used to having a bounty on your head?"

Alex dug his teeth into his bottom lip, tasting the metallic saltiness that mixed with his spit. "You think this is funny? Some kind of joke?"

No one said a word.

The second television screen showed sentinels—fifty men strong—some on trucks fixed with machine guns bigger than Kimbo's. Helicopters glided above. They were all over Eastern Suites.

All in front of his apartment.

His dad was yanked out of the apartment. Even with a black sack over his head, Alex recognized the warn grease-stained overalls. Behind him, bound and crying hysterically, was Olivia. "Alex! Alex, help! Where are you?"

Tears streamed down his face. "Olivia! Dad!" He dropped to his hands and knees, slamming his fists into the concrete floor, repeatedly. Blood trickled from his split knuckles. "No! No!"

"Cut it!" Crude yelled.

The television screens went black.

All his fears, everything he tried not to be and to be associated with, it all happened. His father, his baby sister, the only family he had left were being dragged away by men in black uniforms and helmets, dressed just like the ones that came and killed his mother. Faceless men.

The leader spoke from the shadows. "Alexander Quake, look at me." His eyes rolled, narrowing on the ghostly shadow tears trickling from his face. "Look behind you. That pain you feel? Every single one of the people behind you has felt that helplessness, that pain and suffering."

Rage consumed him. "Is this some kind of contest? Huh?"

Poachie went to place her hand on his arm. "Alex, all she's saying is—"

"Screw what she's trying to say!" He ripped his arm away, wiping his forearm across his face as he tried to fight the sobs that rippled from each shaking breath.

"Alex Quake—"

"Oh no," Brain groaned, typing at his desk and staring at a screen that had more info on what was being reported. "UNA is organizing a public execution."

"What?" Crude's gaze furrowed as she went to the screen, scanning the report that just came in.

Poachie moved quickly to the both of them. "Damn it! What are they doing?" Her voice caused Alex's heart to skip a beat. It cracked as if she was fighting back tears of her own.

"What is it?" Alex hated to ask.

Jo-Jo and Kimbo rushed over as they all slowly turned to him. Not even Jo-Jo could look him in the eye. In fact, she looked broken in a way, disappointed.

"Tell me, what is it?"

Crude raised her head to the screen and looked into the darkened silhouette. "They plan on executing anyone tied with DOR," she said, turning to face Alex, "including family members."

Alex's shoulders fell. His mind and body didn't seem intact anymore. Too much was happening at once. Every breath was quick and shallow. The room was spinning faster. The floor came quick. Hard, heavy, cold.

But the ground didn't smell anything as bad as the foul streets of Eastern Suites.

Alex jumped up in a sweat.

Yara cupped his head in her hands. "Relax, I got you."

The living room was bright, and on the other side of the couch was Poachie. Alex looked around frantically; his thoughts were scattered all over, his brain trying to pluck them from the static cloud of confusion. "What happened?"

"You passed out during the SITREP," Poachie spoke softly. "Kimbo brought you in here, so Yara and I stayed till you were back on your feet. How do you feel?"

His mouth was like cardboard. But his memories were coming back harsh and fast. "Everything that happened on the news, that report that Crude read ... That wasn't a nightmare, was it?"

Yara shook her head, her eyes wet as if she had been crying for a while.

No one said a word. It didn't make the situation any less real, any less dire. There he was, trapped in suspended horror. All he had in this cold, hateful world was his father and baby sister. The baby sister he promised to protect at even the cost of his own life.

"I have to go." Alex jumped up and headed down to his room to get his sneakers, his mind churning to find any feasible way to fix what he had started. There was no reason for him to be there in the comforts of this place while his father and Olivia were in some fortified prison, held up like terrorists even though they had nothing to do with what happened in Constance.

Yara rose from the chair. "Alex what are you going to do? What can you do against UNA by yourself? Think!

Thousands have tried, whole towns; they were all wiped out. Now they're nothing but bleached bones. So what can you do by yourself?"

"I-I don't know, but I need to get my dad and sister out of this situation." He looked up at her as if she were stupid. "Who did they take from your section of the Suites?"

"My adopted parents. But I mean, they only kept me around for the extra income that came from the government, but . . ."

Alex thought about the pity party he had given her after hearing the truth of her life and upbringing. "You can't even feel sorry for them, can you?"

"Nothing to feel sorry for. Those people don't love me. They saw me as more trouble than anything else. Barely fed me."

Dread slammed into Alex's gut. "They're people! Bourgeoisie people, like you, like me. Don't you care about anyone else besides yourself?" She shook her head and rose to her feet, bolting down the hall to her room. "That's what I thought."

Poachie rose from the couch. "Yara was worried about you, Alex. Why would you say that to her? Don't you think she feels the same way you do right now?"

"Obviously not. You heard what she said."

"But, you've known her longer than I have. Can't you tell?" She shook her head.

"Tell what?

"Yara isn't like you. She's kinda like Crude in that she doesn't show her emotions. She hates it. Of course she would say those things about her adoptive parents."

Of course, he thought, fighting the chaos surrounding his life. With every passing second, the fear tightened in his chest, and he could barely breathe. He could see Dad and Olivia meeting their fate at the hands of some kind of firing squad or whatever capital punishment UNA would subject them to.

"I just don't care anymore," Alex said with a tired voice. "The only ones that matter to me are my family."

The clonking of boots came from down the hallway.

Alex turned to see Jo-Jo approaching with a nervous expression on her face. "Crude wants to speak with all of us in the operations room."

Poachie nodded. "Got it. Can you go get Yara? She's in her room, I'm sure."

Jo-Jo nodded. Alex caught her gaze. She gave him a terse nod before turning away. "You got it."

"Let's go," Poachie said, pulling him down the hall back to that room.

Inside, Brain was still hard at work on the computer. The screens were still on, the same reports flashed with latest updates and information about what was happening. The news painted the Krates as a humble, loving family who cared about uniting all classes. The slaughter of everyone in the Krate mansion was said to be a terrorist attack instigated by DOR to cause civil unrest between the classes and to strike fear on both sides.

"That's not true!" Alex's fist tightened. He winced and gripped his wrist, searching the origin of his pain, only to see his left hand was now the size of a glove, throbbing with so much pressure, he had to let it go.

Kimbo looked up at the screen. "UNA propaganda at its finest." He gave an expression of assurance. "How are you doing? You hanging in there?"

Alex grabbed his head. "Besides knowing my family is on death row, and my hand's probably broken?"

"That's fair. I can't imagine how you feel right now, man. I wish—" Kimbo cleared his throat.

"Kimbo, enough!" Crude yelled from the computer screen hovering over Brain's shoulder. She didn't even look back to make eye contact with Alex.

Jo-Jo came in with Yara, and Kimbo jumped up and yanked a metal table over, snagged some chairs and arched them around the table.

Everyone took seats.

Poachie pulled Alex down next to her.

"Commander, everyone is here and accounted for," Poachie replied.

"Good," Crude rasped with a deep sigh. She stepped away from Brain, who continued to keep his eyes locked on the massive computer screen before him. "I'm just going to get straight to the point. We got information in regard to the public execution. The executions will take place ninety days from now between the intersections of Eastern and Southern Suites. It'll be broadcast all over the world. Thirty days from now, government officials will release the style of execution to the world at all levels. During the second month, security will be tightened, after that . . . a count down."

A deep relief came over Alex. "That gives me plenty of time to go and turn myself in then."

Jo-Jo rose, slamming a fist on the table. "You can't be this stupid. They'll kill you before you get to the gate." His gaze burned into her, but she shrugged it off. "This isn't some exchange where on good faith they'll accept your submission. If they don't shoot you on sight, they'll capture you, then torture you for days to get information on us. Information you won't have because you won't remember." She looked to the metal chair with lights shining over it.

"Jo-Jo's right." Kimbo sat back in his chair, folding his arms across his wide chest.

Poachie leaned forward. "They'd torture you for eighty-eight days. On the eighty-ninth day, they would allow you to see your sister and dad again, only to execute them while you sat in a prison cell."

Crude added, "Then they would talk about how much of a coward you were for not turning us in, blast it all over the world news in more propaganda, and after a few more days of killing you mentally and physically, they would execute you."

Alex's bones rattled at the thought. His withering hope took another blow. Three months, about ninety days at the most. Alex ran his limited options through and through, and nothing was good.

Well, except for one.

"Please … I know all I've done is talk about you guys." He whimpered, eyes glued to the table, blurring with tears. His fingers dug into his thighs as he lost all control of his body. "But please, help me save my dad and sister."

He couldn't look them in the eyes after everything he had called them, after everything he considered them to be.

And even now, their sympathy lay heavy on his chest. They genuinely cared about him and his situation.

"No," Crude replied. "We can't, unfortunately."

Deep down, Alex wanted to ask why, but he didn't deserve to. Instead, he licked his lips and nodded, fighting as hard as he could to not burst into tears again and beg on his hands and knees.

Poachie added, "We're not supposed to go on missions without orders from the leader. And missions with personal vendettas and bloodline attachments are not allowed. It puts the organization at risk."

"But screw orders," Crude said. "I won't stand by and let someone lose everyone they would risk their lives for. Especially family."

Kimbo smiled and slammed his fist on the table. Tears in his eyes. "Damn right. We're Ravens!"

A deep sigh escaped Jo-Jo's lips. "I've only known you two a few days, and you're already causing more than enough trouble. . . ." She let out a low apathetic groan, raising a weak fist. "Ravens ho."

Alex raised his head as he listened to them, then he turned to Poachie.

Her two thick braids fell to one side. "I know for as long as you can remember, you were taught to fear and hate us. UNA made us out to be the reason the Bourgeoisies suffered. But in reality, all we've ever done is try to free you from the fake reality they painted over your eyes. Honestly, it doesn't matter what class you're in, if you're fighting for freedom . . . then you're already on the right side."

Alex sobbed like a child who'd heard the best news of his life. "After everything I said about you guys, you're still willing to help me?" He thought about Nelson and what his friend had been trying to teach him back at the scrapyard. "Thank you for everything."

With a right eye burning a strange crimson red, like that of a reptile, Crude leaned against the table. Alex rose from the chair, eyes widening, teeth tugging at his cracking lower lip. She wasn't human. How else could her eye do that? *The One-eyed Devil.*

"So, what's your decision? Are you with us or—"

"Yes," Alex said, not missing a beat. He knew the question. She didn't need to put that blade against his throat. They already proved themselves to him over and over again. "I want to be a member of DOR"

The room roared in celebration.

Even Yara smiled a little from the other side of the table. Kimbo jumped up and lifted Alex with a bear hug. Alex thought he would squeeze the life out of him. Jo-Jo's mouth pulled to the side as she gave a respectful nod.

Poachie's face became serious. "Alright then, you both start training tomorrow."

He looked at Poachie as if she had a second head. "Training? We should be getting ready to save my dad and sister. Why are we training?"

"Because in order for you to work effectively as a member of Raven, you need to be physically fit, trained and proficient to handle weapons. You need to develop the instincts of a killer." Poachie pointed to the chair. "The downloader can cover about thirty percent of that. Everything else will depend on how hard you train. But don't worry, yours truly will be one of your trainers."

Alex looked Poachie up and down. "You?"

"Yup. We have eighty days to get you to where you need to be. You won't be as good as we are, but you'll be better than your current state."

"Hella lot better," Jo-Jo said with a chuckle. "You guys are pretty squishy right now. Probably can't even handle a pistol, I bet."

"Of course I can't." Alex looked at Yara. "You?"

She shook her head, raising a brow.

Poachie cracked her knuckles. "Good. Because Jo-Jo will be the one to train you in arms combat. Kimbo will get you physically fit and prepared, and Crude will be the hand-to-hand combat expert. Brain and I will get you both set up for the downloader."

Alex turned and looked the machine over. It was intimidating, alright. It looked like something you would get the lethal injection in. Massive cables protruded from around it, and the straps alone made him think twice.

"What is it?"

"Brain?" Poachie looked to the boy.

He spun comically on the swivel chair, missing the spot where he wanted to stop. He slowly worked himself around again. "Everybody calls it the downloader. Quick, easy, simple to remember, I guess. In reality, it's a cerebrum cerebral cortex amplifier or a 3CA system."

"And what's that?" Yara shifted in her chair.

"The human brain is like a computer, the supercomputer of all supercomputers. Now picture each brain cell working as its own mini-computer. You take that and times it by the hundred billion cells an average human has, and it's not hard to realize why we're the most superior species on Earth."

Jo-Jo laughed hard and obnoxiously. "Wow, no wonder we bombed ourselves into extinction. We're geniuses."

Brain folded his hands in a pyramid. "Well, being smart doesn't mean anything when people want power and greed. But that's beside the point. The downloader treats the human brain like said computer and allows the user to upload skill patterns into the human brain. So you want to master hand-to-hand combat? Sure thing. I'd program the right skills into the feed, get you in the chair, and hit enter."

Alex shook his head. "That's impossible. Neural engineering is not even close to that kind of technology."

Brain leaned back in his chair with a keen look near to being impressed. "How much do you know about neuro engineering?"

"Just a little from what I've read about from books I found in an old library. But, I know forcing that kind of data into the brain would fry a person and make this machine what it actually looks like. A torture device."

Brain rolled his eyes. He rose from his chair and walked over to the table. "Before World War III and the past governments blew themselves back to the stone age, scientists were already utilizing brain-computer interfaces. They just didn't have the equipment to utilize it safely."

He could do things Alex and Nelson only dreamed of. But even this training would be a lot for him.

It wasn't long before Yara's scuffling overtook him as she strode by on his left. She trotted a bit and turned around. "You got this or what?" she asked, pulling a few sweat-soaked strands from her face, her hair already starting to frizz.

"How are you in this good of shape?" Alex winced, trying to fight the sharp pain radiating through his legs.

She jogged in place and smiled. "Just good at running, I guess."

"Another trick you learned living in the Outskirts?" he wheezed, each step heavier than the last.

She threw her head back with a laugh. "Oh, I get it. You're pissed because you can't hang, so you get mad at me because I'm physically gifted."

Alex sucked his bottom lip in. His mouth was so damn dry there was no spit to spit with. "Gifted? Whatever." *We'll see how confident you are when we get to that cliff's edge again.*

She rolled her eyes. "Seriously, Alex, you good or not?"

"Just go ahead." He sucked in a breath. "Right behind you."

She nodded and continued on at her steady pace, bouncing up and down, gripping the straps of that fifty-five-pound pack close. *Gifted.* He sucked his teeth.

There were eighty-three days left, and he had to make the best of it. Feeling sorry for himself and complaining about how tired he was or how much it hurt didn't mean a damn thing. All that mattered was Dad and Olivia.

He exhaled, clearing his burning lungs. A few salty drops seeped into the cracks of his lips before he quickened his stride to catch up. Where the soil was soft, it was easy to tell someone ran a path clean through the hillside and through the thickly green branches that arched overhead like a tunnel.

The green canvas broke away as they came to the cliff's edge just in time to see the dark blue of the morning brighten with golden light. The rising sun was ripe and bright over the horizon. Alex's stomach already thought of Poachie's breakfast that would be waiting for them back at base. But that was easily still two hours away and down below.

"Yara's really smoking you in the foot race, Alex. First few days you had a full head of steam. Now you're losing focus," Kimbo said, dropping his bag and downing a bottle of water. He stretched his legs a bit more and tugged on the three ropes that awaited them. "You alright to climb down?"

A few more deep breaths filled his lungs. Alex nodded, dropping the bag, unable to get a word out. Yara shot him a glance that was a *don't be an idiot* type of expression. He downed a bottle of water and crunched into an apple, the sweet juices running down the cracks of his mouth.

"Let's go!" Kimbo yelled, his bag already on his shoulders as he pulled the straps high up on his back. "I didn't give you a break, recruits!"

Come on. The thought broke Alex's exhaustion momentarily. A weak part of him wanted to cry, while another part—the part that knew Olivia was in a prison by herself, suffering from her night terrors without him—wanted to strangle that weak part. He slung his bag over his shoulders and pulled the carabiner from his waist.

"You guys remember what I told you about the Swiss seat?"

Alex thought about the first day of cliff climbing. He was scared half to death back then. "Kind of."

"Well, snag your rope and get to work." Kimbo leaned back against the tree.

Alex looked up a few times, catching Kimbo's studying eyes. Sometimes Kimbo would sit back and watch them struggle with getting the harnesses right, well him more than Yara. Every time he looked over, she was checking her safety points and tightening the straps around her waist.

"Done." She smiled, taking a deep breath.

"Damn, Yara, you're on fire today." Kimbo walked over and checked her harness, making light adjustments. "Good to go. You ready to go down?"

"Now or never, right?"

Alex could hear her gasping. When he looked over, she was on all fours crawling back to the trail. This happened the first few days. Yesterday, she mustered up the courage to stand over the edge, but it was a whole new ball game to go straight down.

Besides that time when she told everyone her true backstory, the second time Alex saw Yara crumble from within was when they made it to the edge of the cliff.

Kimbo checked Alex's harness and laughed. "Dude, you want to die before you save your family?"

A knot formed in the pit of his stomach. "What?"

"Yeah, man, your harness is all sorts of ate up. At the least, you'd end up with one testicle getting a clean divorce from the other," Kimbo said, laughing. "Don't worry, don't worry, I got you."

He completely re-did Alex's harness and walked him through the setup all over again. After what Kimbo just said, Alex wondered if he could make it down that cliffside today.

Rivers of sweat ran down Yara's face. Her bottom lip quivered. She took her position with her rope and carabiner secured. Alex did the same. Kimbo was in the middle of them.

He shot them a glance. "Alright, slow and steady, step back to the edge."

Alex's legs shook terribly, but it was nothing compared to Yara's chattering teeth that echoed from the other side of Kimbo.

He turned to her. "Yara, hold it together. You got this."

Her sobs broke over the rocky face of the cliff. "I–I do? I mean, I do."

Alex looked over his shoulder. Below was a sea of green from a dizzying height. There was a strangeness to being this high up. A simple missed step could send a person into the grips of gravity, but you'd enjoy the pure weightlessness before sure death.

"How you doing over there, Alex?"

"Gravy. Just gravy."

"Yara, you got this, right?" Kimbo yelled, his voice echoing all around the cliffside.

"Y–y–yeah, I do. We got this!"

"We don't have a choice. If we die here, doing this, then we never stood a chance of saving our families, right?"

"Right. You're right."

Kimbo laughed with excitement. "Alright, let's do this. Hang over the edge until your back's perpendicular to the ground."

Alex walked back till he faced the bluest cloudless sky he had ever seen. He turned and finally saw Yara. She nodded, tears falling as they caught the morning rays.

"Now, take your first jump. Use that break hand, keeping it close to your back like I showed you guys a few days ago. Trust your equipment. Trust me, nothing else is going to save you."

Alex kept the rope to his back and did his first jump. He threw his hand out and snapped it into place behind his back. He followed Kimbo as best he could, but he was moving fast. He repeated the movements, the sneakers barely able to get a grip on the cliff's edge. He cushioned every jump.

Before he knew it, he was getting slapped on the back by Kimbo as his feet graced the soft cushion of grass.

"Great job, Alex. Come on, Yara, you got this."

Alex looked up. He could kick himself for not trying to help her or give her some motivation up there. She was frozen.

Kimbo placed his hands on his waist. "Damn, I think she seized up. Yara!"

"Yara," Alex cried. "You got this, okay? If I can do it, you can do it."

She shook her head and held the rope tightly. Her sobs echoed over the mountainside.

"Yara, breathe," Kimbo shouted. "You wanted to be a part of DOR, then this is your first taste of fear, girl. You got to eat it. You're gonna be put in situations that will be far more dangerous than this, so you got to move."

She nodded.

"Alright, listen to my voice." Kimbo began walking her through the motions again. She struggled to get her footing back on the cliff's edge. "I'm coming up."

"Wait," Alex said. "Yara, if anyone can do this, it's you. You're the first person I've ever seen put an Exclusive in their place. You're not afraid. You're angry. Use it. Don't think about this cliff. Think about why you wanted to join DOR in the first place. What was your drive? Remember that."

Her head bobbed up and down, and even from the ground, Alex could see she let her body loosen a bit.

Kimbo began giving commands.

She got her foot and the rope to where it needed to be, then began descending. Alex grabbed her rope and balanced her as she came down. The moment her feet touched the ground, she whipped around and wrapped her arms around him, burying her face into his chest.

"I, uh …" Alex was lost for words.

She pulled away, wiping her face. "Sorry, I was just . . . Sorry."

"No, it's fine. We're good. You good?"

Kimbo didn't even try to hide his smile as he collected the rest of the rope.

She nodded. "Thanks for that. For saying all that. It's what I needed to hear."

"Glad I could help."

"We're not done yet, recruits." Kimbo wrapped the rope and stored it in his backpack. "We got another four-mile run, back to base, so get ready."

Alex nudged Yara, and she chuckled as they got their backpacks ready. Alex did some more stretching, but the only thing that would ease the pain was ice and a hot shower. He straightened and put his focus on Olivia and Dad. He could hear Olivia crying for Mom in his head.

"Alright, let's go!"

"That's more like it," Kimbo said. "Let's go."

After breakfast and a hot shower, Alex found himself on his stomach, stretched out on his bed. His body had long since gotten used to the grooves and knots that plagued him the first few nights.

His muscles were too busy trying to deal with aches and pains of other discomforts, like his bruised and blistered feet, shin splints that made it difficult to stand up straight, and his all-time favorite lower back pain that only stopped aching when he lay on his belly.

Nothing more could be done, and he had to recover quickly because in about forty minutes, he was heading to his next event of hand-to-hand combat. With Crude. He was never the type to throw hands with anyone. Fighting was the last thing on Alex's mind. What happened at New Hope with Manwell was something he still couldn't explain, but ...

"Are you stupid and blind?" Nelson's tone was harsh in his head. Alex could still feel the chilled air in the scrapyard. Stupid and blind. Nelson was right. Back then, he was stupid and blind. It took Nelson's death, the experience at the Krate mansion, and the news of his father and sister being taken away to accept what was going on.

"I hope they're all alright," he said, thinking about the Tanakas and Deacon and his family. If what Crude and the others said about what UNA is doing was true, then they would be in the same situation as Dad and Olivia. Nobody deserved that.

A knock rattled the door.

He pulled his face out of the bed sheets and turned. "Come in."

Yara came in dressed and ready to go, her stance strong as ever and the fear of heights long gone. She came in fighting with a comb to get her thick hair straight.

"Hey," he said, rolling over onto his back. "What's up?"

"You as nervous as I am about hand-to-hand?"

"My heart's pounding just thinking about it. Ever since I saw what Crude did to Principal Krate ..." Alex shivered. "We don't stand a chance."

"You still think about Krate?"

"Don't you?"

"Hell no," she scoffed. "Those guys were murderers and worse. They deserved what they got."

"Yeah, they were messed up. But Principal Krate, what if he was a really good man at one point, but because of his upbringing became messed up in the head? He wasn't born evil."

"Look, Principal Krate was a grown man who made a grown man decision to orchestrate and manipulate a system to kidnap hundreds of people, including children. Selling, killing, who knows what else he was doing to those people." Her fingers curled tightly around a bunch of her hair as she struggled to comb through. "I have no sympathy for people like them."

Yara was right. Deep down, he wondered why he still felt sadness about watching Principal Krate and his father die. When Biggs was killed, there was a strange relief, but it was different with Principal Krate. Alex thought he'd genuinely cared about their wellbeing at one point.

Alex thought about his own relationship with his father. His dad always taught him to be kind to everyone. "*It's too easy to be nice to the people you like. The work comes when you're kind to the people who hate and despise you,*" Dad would say. "*And don't be like them. Never ever judge anyone by their class. Even if they treat you badly, you do all you can to treat them with respect.*"

His dad was about working together and being longsuffering to build relationships. What if Principal Krate had his father, and Alex had Governor Krate as a father? Would he have ended up like Principal Krate? A broken, confused boy who didn't know right from wrong anymore. Someone forced to accept a frightening, disfigured status quo.

Alex rolled his legs off the bed. They were still tight and burning, every muscle cursing him out. "It's almost like brainwashing or something, isn't it?"

"What is?" Yara gave up hope on combing through the thickness of her hair.

"Everything. The news lying about DOR, hiding and ignoring the fact that Principal Krate and his father engaged in some messed up stuff. There's no way they don't know about that. They're covering up the dungeon and everything else to push the UNA agenda. No one will know the truth."

"But we know. The people Crude and the others saved know too." She sucked her teeth and made her way to the door. "Stop trying to understand them. They're all like the Krates. So why try to figure them out?"

"Kimbo's not like them."

"Kimbo's different."

"Different how? What if there are more Exclusives like Kimbo, people who don't agree with the government? You heard what Principal Krate said. He hated the division of the classes. And deep down, I think he really meant that."

"You go ahead and hang on to the words of a dead psychopath. I got hand-to-hand combat to attend. Coming?"

Alex sat back for a minute, wondering how it was so easy for Yara to see things so black and white. He wasn't built like that. His mind couldn't see it that way. "Yeah, let's go get beat up, I guess."

They headed down to the gym where the weights and flat bench had been cleared out, leaving behind the worn carpet imprinted and dented from where each individual piece of equipment sat for months on end.

Crude waited in the center of the mat, legs crossed, and hands on her lap. Her sword was to her left at arm's reach. All Alex could think about was that night and all the blood spilled from that blade.

"You guys ready then?" She looked up, her eyes hidden in the thicket of her fro.

"As ready as we'll ever be," Alex replied, fighting back the jitters in his fingertips.

Crude didn't wear her black boots. She was barefoot, her toned ebony legs shimmered beneath the UV light. From the material of her black dress and the frills, Alex could tell it was the same one she wore the night he first laid eyes on her, minus the hoody coat. The dress was sleeveless, revealing her ebony skin and toned arms.

Kimbo walked by and laughed. "Take it easy on them, Crude. I put them both through a lot."

She gave a devilish grin. "They'll be fine."

Alex shuddered. *Oh, hell no. She's smiling.*

Kimbo shook his head. "Alex don't let her frame fool you. It's like if Hercules was reborn in the body of a teenage girl. The longest any of us lasted on the mat with Crude is two minutes."

Alex swallowed, anxiety crept in. "Who holds the record?"

Kimbo pounded his chest.

Yara chuckled. "I'm sure you're strong, Crude, but not that strong."

"Sounds like you want to be the first on the mat then?" Crude asked monotoned.

"Why not?" Yara looked Alex over mockingly. "Alex would probably piss his pants if he went first."

Yara slipped off her shoes and stepped onto the mat. Something about what she said didn't bother him. Before he could get a word out, she swung at Crude. Crude caught the punch, smiled, then shoved her back.

"Not bad," Crude said, lifting a brow. "But I thought growing up with a background like yours that you'd have more bite in you."

Yara lunged forward, faking a swing with her right but throwing her left. Crude dodged, grabbed her hand, then had Yara on her back twisted up like a pretzel.

"You give yet?" she asked, giving Yara time to recover.

"Hell no, I'm not letting a little girl beat me."

Crude tilted her head, looking up at her side-eyed. "Whatever gives you courage."

This time Yara went to kick her. Crude absorbed the blow, grabbed Yara by the throat, and lifted her off her feet. Alex stared in awe. Yara kicked and struggled in the air as Crude laughed, then slung her across the mat.

Alex stepped back, looking down at Yara. She scurried back to him, not taking her eyes off Crude, rubbing her throat. Her eyes were watering as she coughed to get air. "What the hell was that?"

Crude tilted her head robotically. "What, this little girl too much for you?"

"No little girl can do that." Alex's voice was low; he didn't want Crude to hear. Yara looked up, and he helped her stand.

When Crude stepped forward, Yara jumped off the mat. "Alex, you're up."

No boy—or man, for that matter—would get into the ring with her. *Like if Hercules was reborn in the body of a teenage girl*, Kimbo's joke lingered. Obviously, it was far from a joke. Between her eyes changing colors and becoming like that of a demon, it only made sense to ask.

"What are you?"

She clenched her fists, cracking the bones in her hands. "A demon, a devil, a monster . . . whatever UNA made me to be."

Alex thought about her and Brain. "Were you really experimented on in a lab?"

"I'll tell you if you get on the mat."

Alex grudgingly nodded, accepting the offer for knowledge, although the price would be expensive. But he had to know. That night back in the scrapyard, the last real conversation he had with Nelson and Deacon, right before Alex blew up on them, Nelson had been talking about kids and labs.

With a deep breath he stepped on the mat.

Crude sighed. "I wasn't always like this. I smiled a lot. I laughed a lot. There was joy back then. When I was four years old, sentinels came into my city and wiped out all the adults. Both my parents were killed, including my baby brother."

"That's terrible," Yara said from behind him.

"Not the best part. All the children from four to ten were taken to labs and experimented on. We were told that we would be the future of the world and usher it into a new peace. Lies, of course. There were hundreds of us. Only five made it to the next phase in The Dark Ones Project. I was the youngest."

A chill came over Alex. How could the United Nations of America approve something so horrible? "I don't understand. What were they doing to you?"

"Trying to create enhanced humans. Brain called it black-blood infusion. It was this black stuff, thick and inky. We had to have transfusions five times a week until our bodies got used to it. As painful as it all was, it was good to be with those who were of my people."

"You're serious then?" Yara stepped onto the mat. "You're some kind of enhanced person?"

Crude nodded. "After the five of us survived, they wanted to destroy all existence of who we once were. That way, we would swear our allegiance to *them*, and if we didn't, we'd be exterminated. So they made the five of us fight to the death. The winner would have their minds *cleansed* and live as a knight amongst the Exclusives."

"You won." Alex's fist wouldn't stop shaking. "I don't understand. How did you survive?"

"Won? Hell no. The others agreed that I would carry on the legacy of my people and live on. They refused to kill me. So . . . they sacrificed themselves, allowing me to kill them.

And in my tears, I promised to do everything in my power to survive."

By the time Alex heard the first sniffle, rivers of tears streaked down Crude's face, but her expression hadn't changed. She walked over to him, used his shirt to wipe her tears, and slammed a fist into his chest that sent him to the other side of the room.

Alex's mouth jarred open as a sorrowful groan crawled out. *How many times will I end up on my back like this?* he wondered.

Yara was by his side helping him stand.

Crude walked over and stood over him. Through her hardened expression and through the thick black curls, Alex caught a glimpse of her softening gaze over him. Her voice broke through the sound of being underwater.

"You better get ready, both of you. Because it's going to be a long few months."

21

Olivia rested behind the bleach white walls of her prison cell, the single fixed window showing a life of leisure and peace over the rolling green hills. Venus Tower looked to be just an arm's reach away.

Her hatred grew. How could a prison cell be more comfortable than her own home? It wasn't hard to guess where she was. Not to mention the three meals a day provided by the strange woman in the blue jump suit.

Without missing a beat, the heavy steel door squealed open, and in came the woman. She plopped a tray of food down and brought in her cleaning supplies. Olivia eyed her as she began scrubbing away at the floor. She looked too clean and too full to be from the Bourgeoisie's class. She was tall for a woman, a little shorter than her dad with wide shoulders and a square jaw. Her black hair was intertwined in a long thick braid that fell down to her hips.

"Hi," Olivia's voice was a near whisper. She did it often, trying to make conversation, but she was ignored at every attempt. It was just like an Exclusive to do so, and honestly it had gotten the best of her.

The woman paused for a moment, keeping her eyes on the well-waxed floor, then continued scrubbing away with the rag.

"Can you tell me where I am? Where my father is?"

The woman continued scrubbing.

"Please, if you know anything ..."

"I have nothing to offer you," she answered without missing a beat, still scrubbing.

Olivia lay against the wall and took in a deep breath. She brought her white slip-on shoes to the side of the bed as she tucked her knees under her chin, watching the woman work. "You're an Exclusive, aren't you?"

"So, what if I am?"

"Why do the powers at be have you scrubbing away in a Bourgeoisie cell?"

The woman scrubbed some more, then looked up to the corner of a room where a green circular light pulsed. "Because it's what I deserve," she said crossly.

"What you deserve, huh?" Olivia did her best to fight getting angry. She was frightened, and it was hard to tell how long she had been in this place. On top of that there was no sign of Dad or Alex. "Sounds pretty lame to me."

The woman shook her head.

"Do you know what I'm in for?"

Olivia watched as the woman's head pulled to the corner of the room. She was as afraid of the VEN-O as everyone else. But not Olivia. She was on death row, set up for public execution because her dork of a brother finally grew a pair.

But she wasn't worried. The one thing she knew about Alex, he'd never let anything happen to her.

Olivia continued, "I'm in here because my brother joined the most hardcore group of rebellions the United Nations of America has ever faced." She snickered under her breath. "When they take down UNA and get rid of those stupid VEN-Os, maybe you won't be afraid to talk. But then again you're an Exclusive, you guys are heartless, greedy pigs anyway."

The woman paused from scrubbing and cleared her throat.

Olivia waited for a response, anything.

The woman grabbed her rag, the bucket of cleaning solution, and left. The tray of food still sat on the counter. Olivia looked up at the pulsing green light. It mocked her. But that was fine. She wouldn't shed a tear. Not in front of that damn green light. She stayed strong like Mama would've and like she hoped Dad was doing.

Nothing to worry about. Alex would be coming soon enough. She knew it in her bones. Her big brother would never let her die. She had never been prouder of him. Now more than ever, she wanted to emulate him.

She would.

Once she got out of this place, she'd join the ranks of DOR, too. She would be a freedom fighter like her brother, like Jason, and so many other kids throughout the Suites who grew tired of being treated like filth. Tired of the ones who could take whatever they wanted and not be held responsible for their actions.

PART II

22

(Seventy-one days after Alex had his sternum partially crushed)

Gleaming over the trees, the sun glimmered in a way that brightened the pines and oaks below. Four jumps, that's all it took for Yara and Alex to be halfway down the cliff. Scaling the grooves and finding his footing, Alex enjoyed every bit of the scenery.

At the bottom, Kimbo was nothing but a spot acting as their anchor. This was the tenth time in the last four weeks they'd descended the mountain. It was four times the height of the one they originally started on.

Yara smiled, looking below, then turned to give him a nod. "How are you feeling?"

"Not bad!" yelled Alex. He released his hand, giving the rope some slack. "Check you out, though. Looking like you know what you're doing."

She did. They both did a ton of growing over the last few weeks. Yara's dark dress code became a blend of camo and black, she kept her hair in tight braids, moving away from the wavy straightness Alex had grew accustomed to at New Hope.

She laughed, still fighting back a hint of anxiety. "After going up and down that small cliff for the fifteenth time, I guess heights aren't so bad anymore."

Alex could say the same for working with guns. The way Jo-Jo and Kimbo forced weapons on him, whatever nightmares and fears he had before drained into the black hole of a gutter that was his self-consciousness. Not only guns, but everything had changed since he decided to join them. He watched the news more; he heard the lies fed to those like him on the other side of the wall. UNA propaganda was extremely powerful and at times he still believed.

He drowned out his old self with training. It was easier to have your body broken than accept that all your life you had been lied too by your own government. Every day was a battle. When his old mindset crept in, Crude beat it out of him thirty seconds flat in hand to hand, or he'd hit the gym with Kimbo until physical pain drowned it out.

Before he knew it, Alex was digging his heels into the soft soil, breathing in the fresh pine air. Songbirds chirped all around them. As much as he wanted to enjoy it, Alex had to focus on the six-mile run back to base.

He coiled his rope and crouched over, stuffing it in his backpack. Kimbo nudged him with his boot. "Aye, homie. You nervous about sitting in the chair? Just a few more days."

Three days to be exact. The closer the time came, the more Alex wondered if sitting in that chair would result in his brain getting fried from overload. Five percent chance of that happening by Brain's calculations. But if it meant getting an edge over the enemy and saving Olivia and Dad, nothing else mattered. "A little, but whatever it takes, right?"

"Whatever it takes, I'm all for it." Kimbo gave him a fist bump, then played with the small earpiece on his left ear lobe.

Yara reached for Alex's hand and gave a tight squeeze. "Whatever it takes."

They broke away and began the run back to base, their boots crunching over the rocky trail. Unlike the unbearable pain from when he first started, running came easier. Alex found his pace and stride, which he had to adjust after retiring the sneakers mom bought him, an emotional release for sure.

He got a pair of black sturdy tactical boots. He'd traded for them back at the small village outside the walls for a rabbit he trapped while hunting with Poachie.

Kimbo froze mid stride, then threw a hand up.

Alex froze as his senses took over. Birds chirped madly, and the rustling of chipmunks as they raced around the pines gave no distraction, not even the snaps of grasshoppers popping and flipping from the wild grass that grew in patches around the road. He took in the sweet scent of pines and dandelions. There was nothing out of the ordinary around them. *"That doesn't mean a damn thing."* Jo-Jo's voice was a harsh pull from the back of his head. *"Head on a swivel and never lose details on your surroundings."*

One. Two. Three. Alex bolted behind a grove of trees. Yara went left while he kept every breath steady, his eyes studying every inch of the hill and brush around them. When Kimbo added tactical stops to the training regiment, Alex could barely hear the sounds of birds, let alone the rustling of leaves over his thudding heart.

Relying on instinct out in the wilderness improved his attention to detail, even more so after hunting game with Poachie in the early mornings on his days off. If Alex had his weapon, Kimbo would have them picking out target reference points.

Three sharp whistles broke his focus.

They fell back on the trail, continuing their jog back to the base behind Kimbo. Not bad. Clean and sweet. A heck of a lot better than the sweaty mess they both were last month. Between their complaining about hunger, exhaustion, and the unforgiving blisters at the bottom of his feet, Alex respected the patience Kimbo had for them.

Even though life had changed, Alex still found joy in his new lifestyle as a DOR member and an operative of Raven though the lingering factor was pulling a trigger. There was a stark difference between aiming down a scope and shooting a clothed plastic dummy than pulling the trigger on a person who had their whole life ahead of them.

They made a few more tactical stops. On their last one, Alex was sent to scout a hilltop on the edge of a clearing. He came to the edge of a dense thicket and hid his bag, covering it with a few branches and leaves. He took note of a strange tree that looked to be covered in what must have been a thick net of spiderwebs, then admired the sea of green that rolled over the hill and hissed like a crashing wave as the light breeze gave the land life.

He imagined what the enemy would do in the setting, *Like I would know*. But that's what everyone else beat into his and Yara's head the last month and a half.

On his return, Kimbo and Yara set up shop for a short morning snack, applesauce and left-over biscuits from last night's dinner. Poachie broiled some venison, boiled some wild rice and topped it off with the thickest golden brown buttermilk biscuits. Alex didn't say anything to anyone, but she made a side dish of six extra that he kept hidden in his pack.

"Anything?" Yara asked, shoveling a spoonful of applesauce in her mouth.

Alex shook his head as he crept back through the trees. "Nah, nothing but the birds, open skies, and a good day to go hunting."

Kimbo wiped his mouth. "A good day to catch a round to the face, too, if you're not careful."

Alex ducked low and posted up behind a tree. "Sorry about that."

Kimbo shook his head as he devoured his biscuit. "Don't be sorry, be smart. Just because we're training doesn't mean you don't take it seriously. There are only twelve more days till the execution. Remember, these people see you as a terrorist now. Think about how you saw us not too long ago."

It was a long road, but ever since he found out about UNA's propaganda and how they planned on executing his dad and baby sister, the world had changed. That life he lived previously was a lie. Nelson would've been proud. It's too bad he still hadn't gotten word about Jason and his unit down on the South American border. He hoped they were good.

"You're right." Alex dug his fingers into the rich, loose soil. Two chipmunks raced between the three of them, chasing each other around the roots of a large oak.

Yara licked her spoon. "You think we'll be able to pull it off?"

Kimbo leaned back on the stump. "The hopeless optimist in me says we're going to kick ass, stack bodies, and save your family."

Alex leaned forward, adjusting his boots. "But?"

Kimbo exhaled, interlocking his fingers behind his head, and looked up to the twisting branches of the oak tree above. "But, the soldier in me says to count your blessings and take joy in knowing you may have seen your last sunrise."

Alex gulped, letting a handful of soil sift through his fingers.

"You two are rolling with the most dangerous members of DOR, though, and I'm not bragging. Crude and my wifey are no joke. And you can't leave out Poachie and me. We're the anchors." He laughed a little, but it trailed off into the atmosphere.

"Kimbo, you and the others don't have to do this for us," said Alex.

"You're damn right we don't. But what kind of big brother would that make me if I allowed your baby sister to come to harm?"

Alex smiled, still in disbelief that they were willing to sacrifice themselves for someone who hated them at one point. It's hard to believe he blamed them for his mom's death back then. Only UNA was responsible.

"Aight, recruits, let's boogie."

They snatched up their bags, stuffed the garbage in their pockets, covered up any traces, and disappeared down the trail back to base.

The run slowed to a trot once they made it close to the entrance. Kimbo called Brain on his earpiece, and the buzzing sound of a small drone copter glided overhead. It did a couple of flybys and vanished into the branches above.

Kimbo pulled the camouflage away. Alex worked on getting the trapdoor open, and Yara kept watch.

"Aight, let's go," Kimbo commanded.

Yara made her way down first, Alex second. As usual, Kimbo hung out a little longer, more than likely securing the camo netting on the trapdoor. A deep groan above, followed by the rusty clank of the bolt racing forward, ended the morning workout.

Yara nudged Alex gently, and Kimbo high-fived both of them. "My little fledglings aren't so little anymore."

Yara rolled her eyes. "Oh, please."

"So, what's on the docket today for you two?"

"Marksmanship." Alex nearly spat the word out.

"Ah. With my pink-haired goddess, my spitfire vixen, my deadly femme fatale, my—"

"Augustus, they get it," Jo-Jo's voice barked from down the hall.

"Jay, come on, not my real name ..." Kimbo walked away, hanging his head.

"Well, stop going over the top then, Auggy."

He threw his hands up. "No, we *are not* making that nickname a thing."

Yara laughed, but Alex stayed focused, not knowing what to expect from Jo-Jo. Some days, she was peachy, then there were the days where she acted like someone pissed in her cereal. But damn, he would be lying if he didn't admit she provided the best training.

Alex had never fired a weapon in his life. In the beginning, it felt like the blood froze in his veins just from the sight of them. Thoughts of his mom would come rushing back, the horrific memories reaching and clawing at him. But three weeks of Jo-Jo slamming a rifle into his hand or taping a pistol to his palm as she locked him into the weapons vault changed everything.

When it came to firing at targets, Jo-Jo's commands, knowledge, and guidance made him even more comfortable, no matter how belittling and retched they were. After a month, he didn't feel like he'd shoot himself.

Kimbo was right about them. They were the deadliest members of Raven. Crude, some kind of super soldier, and Jo-Jo, a weapons prodigy.

Jo-Jo placed her hands on her hip. "What do you guys want to work on today?"

Yara looked up at Alex. "What are you thinking?"

Alex scratched the back of his head and thought about how they would go about freeing everybody. UNA had all kinds of weapons and soldiers at their disposal. "What will be the most dangerous thing we face when we go to save everyone?"

She tapped her index finger on her lips, humming. "Armed guards, tactical units trained to track and destroy DOR operatives, gun trucks . . . Ooh, my favorite. Me!"

"You?"

"No, no. I mean snipers, dummy."

I'm the dummy?

"Snipers are the most frightening enemy on the battlefield. Besides surveillance, our sole duty is to make sure the enemy is pissing their pants scared and make people feel like there's no hope of survival. I love it," she said in the bubbliest voice.

She's insane. "What's the best way to battle a sniper?"

Jo-Jo looked all googly-eyed. "Run. Hide. Crap your pants, run some more?"

"Seriously, Jo, give us something," begged Yara.

"Alright, alright. Meet me back here in an hour. I'll give you guys some pointers that might keep you safe from these government lames who couldn't hit an apple off the roof of a moving train."

Alex's eyes narrowed. "And you could?"

"Air conditioners are alright. It's not too hot, and I find myself the perfect spot." She gave a moan of satisfaction. "Finding the perfect spot is like … I can't even explain it. What is something that fills you with overwhelming ecstasy and joy?"

Alex shrugged. "I don't know. Poachie's cooking?"

"Idiot." She turned to Yara. "You?"

"I uh …" Yara's gaze fell on Alex, then rolled around the hallway. "I got to go."

"What got her all hot and bothered?" Jo-Jo asked as they watched Yara speed walk down the hall to the kitchen.

"Beats me. Something about you not brushing your teeth, I think?"

Jo-Jo's lips pulled to the corner, and her eyes narrowed on him. She laughed hard, eyes rolling to the weapons room. "You know I could kill you and make it look like an accident, right?"

"I'm just playing."

"Children play. I'm the Daughter of Death. Spraying brains over the pavement is how I have fun. See you in an hour."

As Jo-Jo rounded the corner of the living room, she brought her hand close to her mouth, and he watched her take a few sniffs.

After a well-deserved shower, Alex slipped on a fresh pair of socks and boots and bloused the torn camo pants that had been handed down from Kimbo. An all-black thermal went over his shoulders. His gut wrenched knowing Jo-Jo would have them in the woods all evening.

In his backpack, he skimmed over an extra pair of socks, underwear, shirts, and bypassed some old brown pants to find the prize. A nicely wrapped biscuit. He broke it in half and tore into it before heading down to the gym.

Deep grunts followed by loud thuds echoed from down the hallway. At the squat rack, Kimbo was throwing up four forty-five-pound plates on each side of the bar, and on the treadmill across the room was Poachie. Alex made his way over to her, and she graced him with a smile the moment their eyes met.

"Thanks for the biscuits last night. Man, they're good."

"Of course," Poachie said in between breaths. "I'm glad you like them. How was the workout this morning?"

"Great actually. Hunting in the early mornings has helped. I'm getting my footing down, and my focus on the environment's gotten a lot better. All thanks to you."

Even though she looked to have been running for a while, her breaths were controlled and effortless. She whipped one of the long braids over her shoulder. "Nothing to do with me. It's all you. Focusing on saving those you care about is making you better. I'm just giving you steps and knowledge."

"Well, I'll let you get to it. I got to catch up with Yara and Jo-Jo."

"Marksmanship?"

"Yup, with yours truly." He groaned.

A hand raced to her mouth to fight back laughter. "Jo-Jo's one of the world's best marksman. Cut her some slack."

"She's a pain in the ass, though. I can't believe she has a billion-credit bounty on her head."

"This coming from the kid who used to be afraid of her at one point, right?" she asked sarcastically.

"Yeah, but . . ."

"What?"

"I was wrong about you guys. One of my best friends told me about everything happening in UNA, and I didn't believe him. His death was what woke me up."

She slowed her jog to a steady walk and exhaled. "Sometimes life has to break you and steal something from you in order for your eyes to open." She stopped the treadmill, then gripped the handles of the machine. She breathed heavily. "Sometimes it's not a thing, but someone."

In her eyes, Alex saw she went to a dark place, and he followed the breadcrumbs she left as he thought of Nelson, the Tanakas, and Deacon. "I hate myself just thinking about how I dissed Nelson. I accused him of being crazy. I should've done more. Said more. Just been a *friend* and not a coward. Now it's too late for Nelson, his parents, even Deacon."

Poachie slung one of the large braids over her shoulders. Her pale skin almost bright red from all the running. "When I was younger, I was taken in by this sweet elderly couple. The husband worked the mines a lot, 'looking for gold,' he'd say. They never had kids of their own. I was from an Outskirt spot close to Fort Robinson. They never delivered food to us. This started a famine that hit everyone in our region hard. We made it work for a little while. They shared as much scraps as they could with me, and for a while, we were happy."

"What happened?" He wanted to force the question deep down and not ask.

"People got desperate. When people get desperate, selfishness kicks in. People become monsters. A gang of thieves broke in and killed the couple. I hid beneath the floorboards, listening to their screams, and I remember seeing the old man looking at me through the cracks, putting his fingers to his lips as he bled out. I remained silent, listening to the blood trickle and smack the floor in front of me. After a few days of sitting there, the smell of death overpowered my fear. I got up and ran. You wouldn't believe it, but for the longest time after that I was a mute. If it wasn't for Kimbo, I'd probably still be a mute."

Alex's eyes gleamed over Poachie. Her smooth, slender unblemished face looked as if they had never seen those kinds of horrors. Besides her external beauty, she was kind and selfless. It was hard to imagine a girl who had been through so much could turn out to be so . . . like Poachie.

"Well, don't let my story take you off your game. You better be at your best when training with Jo-Jo," she said with a gentle gaze.

"Right." He stepped back from the treadmill. "Well, I'll see you later. And thanks again for the biscuits."

"Good luck, and don't let her get under your skin."

As he passed his bedroom, Alex saw Yara leaning against the doorway of the kitchen and living room entrance, chewing on her nail.

"You ready for this?" she asked, not looking up.

"If it means saving my dad and sister, I'm ready for anything." His fingers were deep in his pockets, fumbling with balls of lint.

They made their way down to the armory. Yara was oddly quiet. Alex noticed a few glances from the corner of her eye, but he didn't say anything. There was only one thing to focus on. Family.

Jo-Jo waited in the middle of the hallway, rolling a long pink bullet between her fingers. She was decked out in her camo, which was a mixture of greens, browns, and blacks. She tossed the pink bullet to the ceiling and snatched it out of the air. "About time you two showed up," she said with a greedy smile. "You ready to become deadly precision killers like moi?"

Alex nodded unctuously while Yara snapped her fingers at her side. She was more jittery than usual.

Jo-Jo pressed her hand against the scanner, and the massive bolt lock pulled back. With a loud clank, the armory door slid open grittily, and they stepped in. Overhead, the flickering light greeted with an annoying buzz. A breath of gunpowder, oil, and metal exhaled from the doorway.

"Choose your weapon. You guys already know what I'm going with."

Alex eyed the multiple variations of machine guns and rifles all lined up and well organized on the walls. On the opposite side were dozens of variations of submachine guns and pistols. After spending a few nights in the armory, he memorized the sections of calibers, pistols, and automatics. His focus was on the AR, an MX-23, to be exact. The same weapon that was used against his mother.

He wrapped his fingers around the hand guard and pulled it from the shelf. The MX-23 was one of the sleekest ARs on the shelf. It had a digital ammo reader, automatic target acquisition, and round suppressor. It was standard issue for the sentinels.

If all else failed, he could use their own weapons against them. Of course, he didn't intend to get that close.

"I'm going with this one," Yara said, snatching a Reaper X10. The same sniper variation Jo-Jo used minus the pink camo. She held the weapon as steady as she could. It was already a little over half her size.

A muffled laugh escaped Jo-Jo as she held a hand to her chest. "Are you serious? You really think you can handle a reaper?"

Yara tightened her grip around the hand guard. "If you can do it, why can't I? Is it because you used that stupid brain machine of yours? Is that what makes you so special?"

"I thought I told you pup' before. I've never touched that 'brain machine.' My skills are learned from experience, all *naturelle* over here. I'm what you get when you cross a prodigy and a badass."

Alex rolled his eyes.

Yara grabbed the reaper and continued to the ammo point. She scanned in her weapon of choice and the number of rounds required. Alex did the same, holding the MX-23 over his shoulder like Kimbo did with Missy-E.

"Thirty rounds for you, Alex. Fifteen for the wannabe," said Jo-jo, snatching her backpack. "Let's change things up a bit." She eyed Yara. "How about I show Yara the joys of being a sniper, at the same time showing you both how to possibly *survive* an encounter with one?"

Alex immediately got the feeling this was going to be a teaching moment for Jo-Jo to put Yara in her place. Daughter of Death or not, if she went too far, Alex planned to put a stop to it really quick. "Fine."

Yara clenched her jaw. If she were a wild animal, she'd be baring her fangs right about now. "Fine."

"Good." Jo-Jo grabbed her rifle and locked the bolt forward. She slipped a small earbud deep into her lobe. "Brain, you reading me? … Good. … Yup, heading to the Outskirts. Going deep woods … Got it."

Alex's insides fluttered, thinking about the training and what it would entail. Thoughts of Jo-Jo and her nickname struck fear into his heart, but knowing the kind of person she was and the fact she was on his side brought more comfort than fear.

She continued talking through the earpiece. "Let's keep surveillance up. We're gonna start losing light soon, so, yeah. … Alright, awesome." She turned to them. "Let's move out. Hope you got everything you need for the next few hours."

They came through the opening above. Brain waited below the ladder with a full headset on and gave them a thumbs-up before locking up the hideout. Alex ran over and covered up the entrance just like Kimbo taught them a few weeks back.

"Alright, follow me." The suitcase with the sniper gun was easily longer than Jo-Jo was tall, but she carried it with pride, holding it closer than how she held Kimbo's hand during movie night. "First things first. C.S.T. Thoughts on the meaning?"

Alex looked to the sky, a deep blue through the reaching branches of oaks. The sun was bright but becoming a deep orange as the methodical chirp of birds began to calm as their heavy footfalls broke through nature's hymn. "Combat sniper tactics?"

She gave a symphonic hum of surprise. "Not bad, Alex. Not correct, but actually pretty close." She turned, walking backward, eyes bunched, and mouth pushed to the side. She shot Yara a confident glance before turning around to continue down the trail. "Yara, since you want to be the next Jo-Jo, you obviously have the answer, right?"

The X10 banged against Yara's lower back and neck. She was stumbling and constantly wrestling with the barrel. She looked up at him for support. "I don't know."

"Oh, no, no," Jo-Jo said with a tone of endearment. She turned with widened eyes, smacking her hands against her cheeks. With heartless sarcasm Jo-Jo said, "I can't believe she doesn't know." Yara looked away, focusing down the trail again. "Counter sniper tactics, geniuses."

Alex sighed deeply, feeling sorry for Yara. She looked embarrassed. Her eyes shifted to the floor as she grabbed the shoulder strap close. "Maybe—"

Yara snatched his hand and shook her head. "Don't," she whispered.

"What was that?" Jo-Jo asked.

"Maybe you can go into more detail." Alex nodded to her. She answered with a broken smile. "You know ... about C.S.T."

Jo-Jo trudged forward through the uneven terrain as they climbed higher on the rocky trail. "I'm getting there, I'm getting there. The important thing I look for personally are high-value targets. I usually keep a book of my targets handy." She slipped out a black and white notepad from her backpack, covered in all kinds of childish stickers and doodles. "Check it out."

She tossed it to Alex. He fumbled with it before finally getting a grasp on it and opened to a beautiful woman, tan, with deep blue eyes and flowing long brunette hair. A deep red X was etched across the entire picture with the word ELIMINATED at the top of the page. He flipped through more pictures of different men and women of varying ages, even a few of kids their age.

It was the next picture that brought a tightening grip around his chest. A shiver made it hard to grasp the pages. It was the picture of the assassinated politician that enraged everyone back at New Hope Academy. The man was smiling big, his family around him, a fat red X was etched across the entire picture, along with a poorly drawn face with a tongue sticking out comically. ELIMINATED.

Alex hated to ask. "This is a hit list, isn't it?"

Up front, Jo-Jo threw a thumbs-up. "I call it my *Got 'em* book, but sure, hit list is the bland, boring notion."

"And all these people are dead?"

"Yup, I got 'em all. I already have my fresh notebook ready and raring to go." She turned around with the softest smile, tapping her backpack.

"But there's got to be at least sixty pages." Alex flipped through all the Xs.

"Seventy-five. Some pages I kinda got bored and started doodling in, but I got sixty-eight confirmed kills. I've been on fire lately," she exclaimed, her hands raising in victory.

"You okay?" Yara asked. When his eyes met hers, the bleeding concern that painted her face wasn't for Jo-Jo's targets. She wasn't horrified like Alex was by the deaths either. "Are you thinking about your dad and sister?"

Her question awakened him in some way to a frightening reality. He closed the book and thought about his dad and sister. *You got to stay focused. You can't get distracted, not now. Not when you're this close.* He handed Yara the book. "Yeah, thinking about the plan, that's all."

Yara changed the subject to how childish and yet organized Jo-Jo was when it came to killing. Alex's thoughts of all those people continued to jab at him. What could turn a person . . . no, a kid his age into a killing machine that doesn't find anything wrong with what she does? How was it possible?

Alex's legs lifted higher, and his steps shortened to avoid falling or rolling his ankles. During those long runs back to base with Kimbo and Yara, he learned that a path on rough mountainous terrain wouldn't show mercy to your body. It was up to him to control and deal with the loose gravel, thick tree roots, slippery surfaces, and prairie dog holes.

Narrowing into a rocky pass, the trail drifted, and the thick foliage opened into beautiful scenery that overlooked a valley. It was shocking that the trees could conceal the vastness of the open terrain.

A female moose and her calves grazed below, and a group of turkeys waddled freely. The valley was a side of the world Alex wished Pop and Olivia could see. Once he got them back, he'd teach Dad to hunt and Olivia the same.

All around, green shrubs and foliage bobbed up and down around them with an abundance that made him forget all about the city life behind the walls. The Outskirts was true freedom. No garbage-covered streets, no wild dogs and large rats, no beds or cots, and the rage of dealing with a bed bug infestation. The Outskirts had a breath about it, fragranced with the pines and wildflowers of the countryside, both enticing and rejuvenating.

"Alright, pups, let's get down to business." Jo-Jo opened her backpack. She pulled out a long green mat, a notepad, and a few other pieces of equipment, then started assembling the parts of her rifle. "So, I'm gonna start being a little more of a hard ass, so bear with me. Yara, I appreciate you wanting to learn to use a sniper weapon, but it's more than something to *try*."

Start, huh? Alex scoffed beneath his breath, thinking further into the attitude and persona that was the Daughter of Death.

Yara laid her rifle down gently next to Jo-Jo and homed in on every word. "What else can you teach me?"

Jo-Jo paused for a moment. A sliver of a smile made it halfway across her face before being killed by the scrunching of her nose. She snapped the barrel into place. "First of all, here." She handed Yara one of the many gadgets she pulled out of her backpack. "That's a range finder. Gives me what I need for comfortability level and how I gauge a target."

Yara placed it up to her eye. "Whoa. What are all the numbers?"

"Number and measurement overlay. Put it down to where that moose is grazing."

Yara got up on her elbows and focused down the valley. The moose and her calves were substantial size dots across a stream. "Are you seriously going to shoot the moose?" Alex asked, developing a sour swelling in his gut.

"Maybe. What's the distance? I'm banking nine-hundred ninety meters if not a thousand?"

"Thousand . . ." Yara pulled her eyes away from the range finder in awe. "How did you know?"

"Badass remember?" Jo-Jo took out another gadget that looked like a handheld fan of some kind.

Alex knelt down curiously behind her. "And what's that?"

"Wind meter. Not that I'm going to need it this close." She pulled out another notebook and began writing in it. "Thousand . . ." she whispered. "Wind . . . Range . . . Alright."

Yara looked down from the range finder to focus on Jo-Jo. "What's that?"

"My dope book."

"Oh, another *cool* terminology made up by yours truly," Alex mocked.

"Sounds like it, right? It's old-school terminology for data on previous engagements. Every great sniper keeps track of every kill. That's how you get better." Jo-Jo sunk into the mat, adjusting the small knobs on the scope of her rifle. Her breathing slowed, steadied.

Alex's stomach sunk as her breathing was drowned out by the distant trickling of the stream. His eyes rested on the moose and her calves.

A thunderous crackle consumed his insides. The echo stretched on over the valley sending everything below running. The two calves scattered. The mother dropped amidst a pink cloud.

Alex jerked forward, grabbing Jo-Jo's arm. "Wh—?"

"What the hell is wrong with you?" She swung around with a pistol dug into Alex's chest. "Don't you ever touch me like that again."

"Why did you shoot her? You saw she had two calves."

"Calm down. The calves are at least two years old by the size of them. They'll be fine."

"That's bull." Alex thought about the notebook with all those pictures. "I'm done. I'm tired of training with some kind of psychopath."

Yara grabbed his arm. "Alex, we need this. What about the rest of the training?"

"No. I'm done. I can figure out a way to save my dad and sister without killing animals just for the hell of it."

"Brain, can you tell my hubby and Poachie that I got us enough meat to last us the rest of the year?" She looked up at Alex with a devilish glare. "And tell Poachie to get some dessert started. It sounds like we're going to have a crying session with one of the pups."

Alex grabbed the MX-23, slung it over his shoulder, and hiked back down the trail. Yara pleaded for him to stop, but he didn't turn back. The flashes of those photos were engrained in his head now.

What the hell was wrong with her?

23

At dinner, Poachie made moose brisket. The most terrifying thing about the meal—besides the ruthlessness of Jo-Jo's kill—was that it smelled absolutely delicious. With the mixture of salts and spices and the addition of sauteed peppers and onions, how could Alex not find the aroma mouthwatering?

Nobody cared that the moose had two calves out in the wild. Nobody cared that it was just out doing its thing, living life, being a mother. Instead, they all feasted, Yara included. Alex's way of protesting was eating the salad with leftover fowl, silently hating Jo-Jo, even himself, for wanting to take part in the feast.

"What is it with you and this mother moose that's got you pissed, bro?" asked Kimbo as he wiped grease from his lips.

Jo-Jo slammed her fork on the plate. "Don't even bring it up. I can't stand to hear him cry and get upset about it again. It's bad enough that he left the butchering to you, Poachie, and Crude."

Crude jabbed her fork into a few slices of moose, juices smeared on one side of her cheek. Her eyes were as narrow and mean as a wild dog who just found a juicy steak in an alley. "Let him cry. He's not getting any."

Poachie scootched closer to him. "I hope you're not mad at me for making the brisket, but that moose is going to keep us fed for a long time. And it'll be more than enough for you, your dad, and your sis when we save them."

Alex watched the subtle nods of everyone at the table. Even Jo-Jo rolled her eyes with a terse nod. It was impossible to hide the joy and optimism they were already accounting for his family being saved and that they could stay with them.

"For a kid who's lived off scraps his whole life it's kind of odd to see you cry over a fresh kill like that." Jo-Jo shoved a slice of brisket into her mouth smacking and chewing loudly.

"It's not fair." Alex moved a slice of vegetables around his plate. Before he could catch himself, the warm dribbling of tears came breaking over his cheeks. "Why kill her when she was innocent? All she was doing was keeping her children safe, feeding them. She was being a mom, right? Just . . . like my mom."

Everyone stopped eating.

"Shit," Poachie said sorrowfully. "Alex, I—" She started snatching plates and meat from everyone. "Everyone, turn your plates in. We're going to have salad instead."

"Oh, come on," Jo-Jo barked.

"Now," Poachie demanded.

Alex watched as she grabbed Crude's plate. "Poachie . . ."

"Crude," Poachie replied, not backing down. "You let me have this win, and I promise I'll make you any dish you want."

"All of them," Crude answered.

"Deal." Poachie snatched the plate away.

In the awkward silence and while everyone patiently waited at the dining table, Poachie went back to cooking. Instead of moose, she made more fowl with a side dish of salad and wild blueberries.

Though nobody said anything about his outburst and attitude Alex felt so bad that he headed back to his bunk. The passing voices outside his room kept him at bay, and he wondered if he'd pissed Kimbo off and the others. He already knew Crude and Jo-Jo were angry.

Unable to find comfort, he got up and went to the gym, focusing on weightlifting. It was quiet and empty. Perfect. He hit the flat bench first and did a few reps just like Kimbo taught him. It was nothing like the impossible weight Kimbo put up, but enough to get a good burn and release some stress. Alex moved to squats and finished with a slight jog on the treadmill.

As he hit mile three, Jo-Jo came in.

She was still pissed, he could see by the look on her face. Alex's heart raced faster. He turned up the speed.

"Can we talk?" she asked sharply, cocking her hip to the side.

"Sure." He powered down the treadmill and grabbed a towel, wiping his face.

"Follow me." She snatched his hand and pulled him through the halls. They went past the living room where everyone was watching a movie.

Kimbo looked up and gave Alex a terse nod and a thumbs-up hidden from Jo-Jo's sight. Alex should've known he had something to do with this. Unfortunately, Kimbo's help could do more harm than good.

She placed her hand over the armory scanner, and the door clanked open. *Oh great, she's locking me back in here again. Another long night of organizing the weapons and reading the manuals.*

Inside she allowed the door to close and lock. A deep flutter of nervousness made his insides sink. She groaned, scratching the long pink strands of her hair, pacing back and forth, talking to herself. She was pissed alright, but it didn't seem to be directed at Alex. Or so he hoped.

"Look, I'm sorry, okay?"

His head snapped back. "Oh, okay."

"You know? About the damn moose and her babies and how it somehow connected to your mom and what not. Sorry, okay?" She said it as if she were looking for Alex to accept her apology.

"Yeah . . . I accept your apology."

She cleared her throat. "Good, because I mean I got food, for us, for you and your family if we get them back."

"Not *if*, when."

She lowered her head. "When."

This time he didn't hide his thoughts. He just laid into her without fear of retaliation. "Why are you like this? Like you hate everyone and everything?"

Jo-Jo leaned back against the wall of weapons and sighed looking up to the ceiling. "Don't be so dramatic."

"You know what I mean," he said, trying to stay composed. "I get that Crude allowed me and Yara to join you guys because she trusts you. But if you trust us, why treat us like garbage? Yara obviously wants to try her hand at being a sniper like you, and you crapped all over her the entire time."

Jo-Jo shrugged with pursed lips. "She didn't seem to mind."

"It doesn't mean she liked it."

"Kid—"

"I'm the same age as you."

"Age means nothing!" She slammed her fist against the wall, rattling the rifles and pistols. "You think just because you did a little bit of training with us you can talk down to me? How many lives have you saved? How many people have you fed and provided a better life for? How many people have you killed in order to save a life and end tyranny?"

He lifted his chin, feeling the weight of her words as she scowled. Alex saw the eyes of a killer: ruthless, monstrous, devoid of hope. Eyes he feared would become his someday.

She sneered. "People like you will never understand. You lost your mom and think all the pain in the world and pressure of life has just plummeted on your shoulders. Compared to the poor and those enslaved, I bet you had no idea you lived in an ivory tower behind that freakin' wall. You make me sick."

"Shut up!"

She glared. "What did you say?"

"I said shut—" Before he could gurgle any more words, his head cracked off the corner of a table, sending bullets everywhere. A pistol was buried firmly beneath his chin. Tears trickled down his cheek, but they weren't his.

Jo-Jo dug the pistol harder into his jawline. "I freakin hate people like you. You're so damn spoiled. You don't realize how good you have it." The pistol shook in her hand as more tears fell on his face.

Alex's heart raced with the unsteadiness of her hand. A single mishap, a hiccup, and his brains would paint the floor.

"You know what life is like for people of our skin complexion outside the mainland? Huh?"

"What are you talking about?"

She spat on the floor next to his face. "Exactly. Who cares if you're Bourgeoisie, and so what if you get treated like shit every now and then by people who have more money? You still get to go home, a place to lay your head and fill your belly. It's nothing like being a pariah, being hated, spat on, and killed because of the color of your skin."

Jo-Jo lifted the barrel from his chin but kept it on his chest as she rose to her feet. Sweat trickled down the sides of Alex's face. There wasn't a doubt in his mind that she'd pull the trigger. Her breath was as steady and calm as it was when she shot the mother moose, eyes empty. She slipped the pistol into her waistline.

He winced, feeling the warm stickiness on his scalp. "What are you talking about?"

She wiped her face. "As crappy as the world can be, there's always someone who has it worse than you. Try growing up in Europe. Yeah, when you're wealthy and have influence people will let things slide no matter what skin color you are, but over there, when you're a pariah, you're fair game. My father was an olive-skinned Italian, and my mom was beautiful with skin like mahogany. Even being mixed, it was like people knew to hate me, to be disgusted by me."

Alex's body still trembled, his shirt stuck to every inch of him. He leaned against the table, trying to stand. "You were treated differently," he looked down at his deep brown hands and arms, "because of the color of your skin?"

"Like I said, there are worse things than being judged by how much money you have."

"I don't understand. Racism is outlawed in the UNA?"

"In the Outskirts, there is no law, no UNA, just survival. If you're lucky enough to find someone to hang tight with and who won't stab you in the back or sell you to the highest bidder, you're lucky."

"I'm sorry. I didn't know."

"Of course not. You're so high on that horse of yours, calling me a monster. Mama told me there were people like you. Blacks who have no idea about the tragedies and hatred that were so subtle. Even as a Bourgeoisie, you would be too blind to see it. She called you the *fortunate ones*."

Fortunate ones? Alex rubbed the back of his head. The wet stickiness trickled down the back of his neck. Everything he had been through in the Suites was all based on his class, never his color. That's how it was, the Exclusive class was made up of all. Colors, genders, beliefs none of that mattered, only the class you belonged too.

He lowered his head hating himself for judging Jo-Jo by her actions. "My dad told me years ago how bad racism used to be, even before the world wars and the bombs being dropped. He never talked much about it, but you're right. I never experienced that kind of hatred."

Jo-Jo dug deep into her pocket and tossed him a rag. "Press it hard against the back of your head. It'll stop the bleeding."

"Thanks." He groaned, doing as she said. The dull ache produced an egg sized lump that throbbed with his calming heart. *That's going to be there a while.* "Where are your parents in all this?"

"Dead. And that's all you need to know."

Disappointment took hold of him. "Jo-Jo, can we agree to chill out on both sides? I'll stop being over the top on my end, and you—"

She cocked her head to the side. "No, you're right." She crossed her arms and blew a few pink strands from her face. "You and Yara are pretty cool, and it's not that I don't like you guys. I do. And I think you can do a lot for DOR It's just that you can't be soft. And you, Alex, are freaking squishy. It drives me crazy."

She was right about that. Deep into the crevices of a persona he tried to build amongst the others of Raven, he wondered if the choice had to be made, could he pull a trigger to end another person's life?

The thought frightened him to death, like some hellish rite of passage that could never be reversed. Would he become like Crude or like Jo-Jo? Would Olivia and Dad be able to look him in the eyes again without seeing that black abyss, that emptiness?

"I'm afraid, Jo-Jo."

"Of course you're afraid. That's normal. You'd be considered a psychopath like me if you weren't."

Alex hung his head thinking about what he'd said to her. "Look, about that—"

"It's fine, dummy. And I'm sorry about everything with your mom, dad, and sister. Losing my parents almost destroyed me. In a way, it did. But I promise, we'll get your dad and sister back, alright?" She held out her fist.

Alex bumped his knuckles against hers. "Thanks."

She threw her head back and let out another deep exhale before pressing her hand against the reader that unlocked the armory door. "Look, if Kimbo asks, tell him you slipped on some loose rounds or something."

Alex snickered. "Right. Got it. Will do," he said, following her out of the armory. He wasn't going to dare add any more fuel to a fire that had burned down to cinders, and he didn't need a second knot on his head.

When they made it through to the kitchen, Kimbo met them both with open arms, and hugged them. "I'm glad you two could . . ." He looked Alex over and saw the back of his head.

Jo-Jo flashed Kimbo a smile that faded when she turned to Alex.

"Yeah, I slipped on some bullets in the armory. Clumsy move on my part. But we had a friendly conversation about everything. Real good."

Jo-Jo nodded. "Yeah, really good, babe." She tapped Kimbo's broad chest.

"Oh, okay." By his tone alone, Alex guessed that Kimbo didn't buy it, but he left well enough alone.

Crude turned to lean on the backside of the couch from where she sat. "So with all the foolishness over, can we go back to eating the moose?" she deadpanned.

Alex was beside himself that the leader of a band of child militants had such a priority for food, particularly meat.

"Crude, how are you still hungry?" asked Poachie.

She shrugged and turned back around to continue watching television.

Yara came over. "Can we walk for a bit?"

"Sure thing."

They walked down the hall and she ushered him into his room. Inside, she closed the door, leaning against it with her eyes closed and an expression of relief. He watched as she took a deep breath. She looked more stressed than usual.

"I just needed a break, if that's okay?" Yara moved gracefully across the room and with two steps, she had her face buried in his chest. His heart fluttered.

Her fingers wrapped around his. So much had changed since New Hope. Yara had gone from a bitter sharp-tongued girl to someone he'd follow into battle. She'd be the one saving his life more than likely, and that made following her all the more easily.

She turned her head up, her face close enough that he could feel the warmth of her breath. The girl he couldn't stop staring at, the one who stuck up for him, and the one he destroyed his life for was in his arms.

"What do you need a break from?"

Her eyes were closed as she said, "Everything just seems impossible, right now. I don't know if it's just my nerves or the fact that I feel like I'm not cutting it. But I feel like I'm struggling bad, Alex."

"You never look it." A trembling hand reached for her face, and she leaned into it. His heart raced. "Yara, you're one of the strongest people I know. You're doing a heck of a lot better than me. You're stronger, faster. I'm just trying to keep up."

In the dim light, her skin glowed bronze, smooth and soft without a blemish. Her nose and curved lips had him mesmerized. Worry gripped him. He couldn't afford to lose his focus on Olivia and Dad, not this close to executing the plan. And besides, they were soldiers now.

The warmth of her breath on his face, sweet and comforting gave the chaos storming in him peace. She laid her hands on his shoulders. "Do you regret what you did in the hallway back at New Hope?"

His lips quivered. The thought of Manwell brutally smacking her as everyone watched, some even laughing, made his blood boil. Especially after what they did to Nelson, he'd never stand by and do nothing again. "No, never."

She wrapped her arms tightly over his shoulders. Her nose was cold against his neck, and he could feel her shaking as gentle sobs rolled from her body. Her tears trickled down his neck and soaked his shirt. He gripped her tighter.

"I'm sorry Alex. This is all my fault. If it weren't for me, you wouldn't be in this situation, risking your life to save your dad and sister. You'd still be at New Hope Academy and at home with your family."

He pulled her away and lifted her face. His gaze focused on her brown eyes. He had never seen her this way. "Stop crying. A strong person once told me, 'Don't you dare let them see you cry.' "

She sniffed hard wiping her face. "Why don't you hate me? You should be blaming me for all of this."

"It's not your fault, Yara. This world is broken and messed up. Just like what everyone here keeps saying. All we can do is fight now." He wiped her face with his shirt. "You're still with me all the way, right?"

"Always."

24

It was the day of the helmet. The day where either their brains got cooked like scrambled eggs, or they became some kind of hardened killers with whatever skills they chose to have put into them.

Alex and Yara sat in the living room, everyone around them silent, their eyes locked on the both of them. There was a tightening in his throat as Alex took in two huge breaths.

Kimbo broke the quiet. "So what are you guys choosing?"

Alex rummaged through the nine downloader chips Brain sat before them the night before. Hard to believe the thumb size pieces of plastic and metal could have such an effect on the human mind. "I'm not sure. I guess to be a better fighter, handle weapons better . . . and anything on being stealthy."

"You only get two options. Nobody wants you guys to be a smoking vegetable after it's said and done because Brain overfed your cerebral whatever," Kimbo said.

"Cortex, babe. Cerebral cortex," said Jo-Jo soothingly.

"Yeah that."

Kimbo folded his brawny arms across his chest, veins bulging from the skin as he sunk deep into the cushions of the loveseat. Jo-Jo was hanging off him like some lovesick puppy, and Kimbo was just as bad burying his face into the side of her neck.

"I guess I have to think on it some more." Alex turned to Yara, who sat at the table with her chin in her hands, knees bouncing off the leg of the table. "What about you?"

"I'm thinking something with medical, and I like the stealth idea. Whatever will make me a better warrior, I guess?"

Jo-Jo chimed in. "You guys should ask Crude. I'm pretty sure she did some crazy stuff, and she was able to get three slots thanks to her enhancements."

"Three?" A shiver ran down Alex's spine. "What were they?"

"I think mixed martial arts, swordsmanship, and … special ops mastery?"

Alex bristled. *A true killing machine.*

"She got all of those downloads while she was still with the government though. They programmed that into her."

Alex nodded. "So what if I get tired of my skills? Can I wipe and reset?"

Poachie was glued to a book. It looked old with a blue hardcover and the pages looked brown and aged. "That would be a Brain question for sure."

Footsteps cracked down the hall from the armory. It had to be Crude and Brain. Every muscle in Alex's body tensed, and his insides cramped and gurgled. He took a few controlled breaths because his hands wouldn't stop shaking, and his heel tapped sporadically on the floor. He slipped his hands into his pockets and made his way to the kitchen table, then took a seat across from Yara.

Crude came into the light, Brain right behind her.

To think this kid was some genius. No one would have thought it by the looks of him. He was round, shy, and avoided conflict like the plague, but he did start to talk more the longer they'd been there.

"You two ready?" Crude asked with a dry uncaring tone. "Doesn't really matter if you are or aren't."

Alex clenched his jaw and squeezed his hands tight in his pants pockets. The slow crawl of beading sweat came quicker than normal. He prayed nobody saw, especially Jo-Jo. She'd pounce on him without any remorse with heckling and trash talk. He made his way over to the kitchen and plopped beside Yara. "I'm ready."

Everyone's eyes fell on him.

Kimbo threw a fist up. "That's my boy!"

Poachie gave a worried looked and tilted her head down. "You sure?"

"Yeah, I'm good." It felt like a rock had slid down his throat. Alex pulled his hands from his pockets, wiping the sweat down the legs of his camo pants. "Why wouldn't I be? I look fine, right? I feel fine."

A smile pulled from the corners of Crude's lips. "Right. You'll be up first. But first things first." She buried her sword into the middle of the kitchen table.

The black blade emitted a strange vibration, the handle curved and spiked at the edges. The blade itself was strangely beautiful with a sheen that gave way to the craftsmen of such a weapon.

He reached for the handle.

"No!" The whole room cried.

Kimbo had somehow leaped over the couch and yanked Alex back into his chair just in time.

Alex's heart leaped up his throat as he searched the room frantically trying to keep from falling out his chair. A few streams of sweat connected at his chin and fell. "Wh–what is it?"

"No one can touch that blade, Alex. No one but Crude," Poachie pleaded with those same eyes of worry she flicked his way when he volunteered.

"I get it. It's her blade. Sorry about that."

"No, you don't," Crude commanded. "This blade was made specifically for me. It's special. It talks to me. If you were to touch it, you'd be turned into a pile of blackened ash and bone. We'd have to have Yara scoop you up with a shovel and dump you outside."

Alex sighed and rolled his eyes, confused as to why they still messed with him, especially on a day as serious as this one. He played along. "Okay. Sorry."

Crude tapped her palm on the hilt of the blade. "Anyway, it's time for the commissioning of you two into DOR"

Alex looked up at Crude, then turned to Yara with a raised brow. *Commissioning?*

Yara's eyes lit up like the moon on a cloudless night, bright with excitement. It put his heart at ease to see some joy come back to her.

Crude wrapped her fingers around the handle. "Though you have earned our respect over the last several weeks, making it through some of the most strenuous training and situations that would make others quit or wish they were dead, you continued on with passion and vigor. No matter how uninspiring some of you were."

Crude's mahogany brown eyes burrowed into Alex. *Of course, you look down at me.*

She continued, "Now it's time for your devotion."

Alex gulped, his eyes searching the room. "Devotion? What the heck is that? What is all of this? I thought we were already part of DOR"

"Not yet, brother," Kimbo barked. "You both got to read the creed. The creed is the blood seal. It's the pact."

Brain walked over and handed Alex an old rolled-up scroll. By the browning of the words and lettering, this wasn't just regular ink. He looked up at Brain, who nodded. It wasn't much to say, but the words . . . something about the words.

Crude commanded, "Disciples!"

The kitchen filled with barks and howls.

"Cease," Crude barked. They all silenced. "With the authority granted to me by the current leader of the Disciples of Revolution Militia, Valkyrie, I, Crude, put my name on the line as a tribute to push these two recruits into full discipleship. My second in command?" Crude snapped a stony gaze to Poachie.

"Recruits rise!" Poachie shouted. Alex and Yara immediately jumped to their feet. "I, too, Poachie, second in command of the Ravens, put my name forward as a tribute to have these two recruits pushed into full discipleship. If anyone disagrees, remain standing, and plead your case."

Alex watched as Brain knelt, then Kimbo, then Jo-Jo, and finally Poachie. She looked up at Alex with a wink.

"Then, by the articles bestowed to me by Valkyrie, the current leader of the Disciples of Revolution Militia, I call first recruit Alex Quake to read "The Disciples' Creed." Alex, what is our creed?"

He swallowed hard and nodded. His fingers gently unrolled the scroll. Some of the letters had crusted away, and there seemed to be a brown smudge of a fingerprint. It was then he realized the wording was written in blood. The blotches of brown at the end of the creed had flaked a bit. He began reading with all his heart, with all his soul, the words written in dried blood:

"We will expose the sins of the new world.

We will crush the ones who feed off the meek and innocent.

By our blood-soaked hands, we will bring peace and lay down our lives for justice's sake.

Our parents are the people who we call our mothers and fathers,

And for them, we give all that we are.

We are the hand of fate, the warring hands of freedom, protectors of the lowly.

We are the Disciples of Revolution!"

Crude nodded, then gestured to Yara. Alex carefully rolled the scroll and handed it to her. She was shaking, her hands clammy and wet.

"You'll be alright," Alex whispered.

She smiled.

"By the articles bestowed to me by Valkyrie, the current leader of the Disciples of Revolution Militia, I call second recruit Yara Miles, to read The Disciples' Creed. Yara, what is our creed?"

Yara snapped her head toward Crude, her back straight and her shoulders strong as she began reading the words from the scroll with a confidence and pride that gave Alex goosebumps. Like a real soldier. A real warrior. There was an ambiance about her that filled him with confidence in her own abilities.

Why was she so nervous? She didn't need to be. She handled herself these last few weeks as if she had been through plenty of battles. Joining DOR was obviously a piece of cake for Yara. This was her dream. No doubt about it.

"… *We are the Disciples of Revolution!*" Yara yelled the last line passionately.

Crude ripped the blade from the table and twirled it around effortlessly, showing her mastery as a swordsman before letting it slide back into the red teddy bear holster over her shoulder. "By the power vested in me, welcome to DOR"

The room erupted in howls and barks that shook the table. Alex felt it deep in his chest. It was overwhelming. Kimbo wrapped his arms around him, accidentally putting Alex in a choke hold. He looked up to Yara, who had tears of joy in her eyes, her hands clasped together as her bottom lip quivered. Alex smiled as Poachie gave her a hug, and Jo-Jo gave her a high-five.

There was no doubt in his mind that this had to have been one of the greatest moments of Yara's life. As if she had been created for this moment, for DOR, a beaming smile consumed Yara's face. Her eyes softened, and her cheeks bubbled as she used a hand to wipe away her tears.

Crude jumped down from the table, looking up with those cold mahogany brown eyes, emotionless and hardened. Never had he met a girl seemed to hate to smile. He thought Yara was bad back at New Hope Academy, but Crude was a whole new level of disdain.

"So, I won't have to kill you after all Alex Quake," she said with a brooding rasp.

Instead of fear, he smiled. "Not this time around. I'm sure I'll give you an opportunity eventually."

"Sooner . . . rather than later." She eased her way by him in a tender manner.

He placed his hand on her shoulder as she brushed by and smiled.

"We're not so different from you, brother." Kimbo looked over at the others celebrating Yara. "We may have had different experiences in life and chosen different paths, but we aren't monsters. Imperfect, broken, struggling to find our way? Believe it. But we want the best for everyone even those in the deepest inner walls. I mean, they're people too, right?"

Alex nodded and looked up at Kimbo, slapping him on the shoulder. He thought about the other kids back in school, the ones who mocked Nelson after his death, then about the kids who refused to mourn him out of fear. In reality, they were all equally horrible, but Kimbo was right. Imperfect, broken, and struggling to find their way. As wrong as they were, they were just like everyone else.

Poachie nudged him from behind. "Congratulations, Disciple."

"Yeah, congrats," said Jo-Jo, shoving him. "Knew you had it in you all along. Seriously."

Alex scratched the back of his head, looking away. "Thanks, but if it wasn't for you guys getting us ready and going over and beyond to get me to where I needed to be, I don't know where I'd be."

Jo-Jo sneered. "Don't get all mushy and humble. Just take the thank you and drive on, alright?"

"Alright."

Crude shouted over the celebratory words and excitement. "Now that that's out of the way," she began, looking up at Brain, "it's time for our new members to go with Brain to the downloader. Everything's good and ready, right?"

"Y-yeah, we're all good on my end. Just need them to select their skills, and we can get the 3CA started."

"Alright, let's go." Crude began walking down the hall.

As a group, they all moved down the hall toward the tactical operations center. Fear swarmed Alex's insides. Thoughts of backing down and delaying the process ate away at him. His canines sunk into his bottom lip. The salty taste of blood and the sharp pain pulled his focus to the room ahead. *Dad and Olivia need me to be at my best. Not at my weakest. No fear, no backing down. I'm a DOR member now.*

He walked beside Crude. If anyone knew the right skills to select to save Olivia and Dad, it was her.

"What?" she asked, keeping her eyes ahead.

"I want to know . . . I need to know … What skills do you have?" He'd half expected her to either cut him down or rock his chin with an uppercut but asked anyway.

"S.O.M., that's special operations mastery, master swordsmen, and M.V.O.E., motor vehicle operator expert."

She really did have three. *Incredible.* "So I need two of those to save them then?"

"If you go with my skills, you'll die, Lux."

"Lux?" Alex asked, his face and nose scrunched.

"Yup, that's your codename. I wanted to mash together Alex and suck. Yara's is Enyo."

"But wouldn't my codename be like luck or something then?"

"Nope. That would be too cool for you, and frankly, you're not that lucky. So I smoothed it out with the 'ux' at the end. So, Lux."

"Okay, whatever. What do you mean I'll die?" They entered the room that housed the downloader. The machine was humming, and the helmet looked more frightening than ever, but he was too focused on Crude.

"Do you have superhuman strength?"

"Well no."

"Do you have regenerative power?"

"Of course not." His eyes goggled in disbelief. "Wait. You do?"

"Do you have a sword that talks to you and gives you the ability to do the impossible like cut down dozens of soldiers in an instant?"

He cleared his throat. "No."

"Choose skills that are going to make you great with your own abilities. Don't choose skills that your body can't handle. You'll either injure yourself or get yourself killed. Regardless of what you can learn from the downloader, you're still limited by your body and brain. Got me?"

Alex nodded, looking down at the girl who spoke to him like she was seven foot six. He chewed on the inside of his cheek, thinking of her words.

"She's right, Al—I mean Lux," Poachie said. "That's why we've been training you guys to get used to weapons, getting you in shape, exposing you to the different tactics we utilize. The downloader is what we call a combat amplifier. It helps improve our strength and abilities, but a five-year-old with the skill to wield any weapon still won't be able to properly utilize a shotgun if they can't lift it."

"Got it." The skills he needed had to be perfect for him, but perfect enough to have him save Olivia and Dad. He scanned the room, lost in thought, studying all their faces. Everyone had their different skills and abilities. "If you guys don't mind, can you share your skills with me? It'll help me understand what I should choose."

Without hesitation Kimbo and Poachie gave their skill masteries. Kimbo: weapons expert and stealth mastery. Poachie: Engineering and explosive expert. Brain didn't have anything just his enhanced genius.

Alex turned to Brain. "Give me weapons expert and . . ." He thought about his own past and experiences. "Mixed martial arts mastery."

Kimbo raised a fist in excitement. "Yeah! That's my boy, right there. Don't even worry. I'm going to get you in the shape you need to be in to even take on Crude. I promise."

Crude monotoned, "He's lying. You'll die. I promise."

Alex laughed. "Good." He took a deep breath and blew it out, looking at Yara and Poachie. "Wish me luck."

Before Poachie could step forward, Yara hugged him, then kissed him on the cheek. He was taken aback. "Thank you, for everything. I know you're going to be alright."

He cleared his throat, playing it off like it was nothing, but his heart raced just like it did when they were in the room together. "Thanks."

She smiled and looked away, moving back to the others as Poachie took her place. Poachie fixed Alex's shirt and patted his shoulders. "You got this, okay?"

"I know."

She hugged him. "It's going to be crazy at first, but trust me, you'll get used to your new skills."

He exhaled. "Thanks, Poachie."

Alex turned to the machine and sat in the poorly cushioned seats. It reminded him of a wretched dentist chair with leather wrist bracelets. The helmet went over his head. A leather strap went beneath his chin and snapped over his left ear. Brain cinched it tight. A thick piece of foam which had a piece of a branch jammed in it, was slipped into his mouth.

"Bite on this." Brain nodded. "You're going to need it, trust me."

From a metal arm that was connected with wires and other metals and plastic came a strange visor that robotically went over Alex's eyes. He couldn't see anything but blackness.

"Strapping you in now, Lux," said Brain. The cold leather tightened around his wrists first, rough and worn, then he felt his legs get tightened down.

Then silence.

Footsteps faded away from the chair. Behind the blackness of the visor Alex closed his eyes. He thought of his mom and her smiles, her hugs, her cooking. He thought of Olivia. Olivia, before their mom's death, the girl who loved her big brother, and wanted to be like her mother. He thought of his dad, the man who worked hard but had hope in the world and in his government, not fear.

Brain called out, "Weapons expert and mixed martial arts mastery, correct?"

Alex nodded feverishly. His hands trembled at the arms of the chair. He dug his fingernails into the material.

"Alright, on my count, okay?" Brain's voice sounded just as nervous as Alex felt and that sure didn't help.

Alex nodded again, fingers squeezing into the material of the armrest.

"Starting download in three ... two ..."

Metal clanged and banged as the chair rattled. A chime radiated over the room. Alex tried to break free as he lost control of his body. *I'm doing this for Dad and Olivia. Dad and Olivia. Dad and Olivia!*

There was a heavy vibration that rocked the chair. A terrible sizzling radiated from the crown of his head to the base of his neck. Images and videos flooded behind the visor. Visions of weapons and men fighting. They came like memories. A burning jolted into his skull that nearly forced him out of the seat. The pulses overwhelmed his body with rolling, searing pain as he bit down on the foam wrapped branch, and his jaw cracked.

Memories, images, a knowing.

Like contractions, the waves increased, burning his skull and searing his eyes. There was a fear, something that was so deep and hidden from years of evolution that had bubbled to the surface. Alex didn't just think it was possible to survive this. He *knew* his brain was going to explode.

Another pulse made his back crack. Another made him bite down on the foam so hard he cracked a tooth. The humming grew with intensity. He gave a drooling wail, then everything went black.

25

With the swirling thoughts and the echoes of a distant headache, Alex managed to flutter his eyes open. Images of dozens of rifles, pistols, and carbine modifications flickered behind each blink. It was like someone had shoveled the memories of a hardened soldier into his brain, the weapons, the fighting....

He looked around. The space was dark and gloomy, but he could see it was his bunk he lay in.

He rolled over, wincing, fingers pressing against his forehead. A painful pulse and ringing ebbed from the back to the front of his skull. He pressed harder, but nothing helped. Sweat droplets formed over his forehead and rolled down the sides of his cheeks. A frigid chill followed.

"Poachie—" he called with a voice hoarse from thirst. His feet hit the floor. The sensation was like sand and a flush of warmth. When he went to stand, his legs folded beneath him.

He took a deep breath before trying again. As he stood, his legs wobbled. He braced himself on the mattress, using it to inch to the foot of his bed. The room began spinning, and a cold sweat overtook him. He dropped to the floor and puked nothing but water until he was dry heaving. The ache in his chest was on par with the headache.

The door swung open, and light hit him in the face. He gave a deep groan of anguish and threw his hands up.

"Shit, Alex. I mean, Lux. You're up?" The voice was a girl's and familiar as the silhouette edged over. Metal clattered. A warm arm went beneath his shoulder and helped him back into bed.

Yara's face smoothed out from the blurriness, hands on her hips with an expression of worry. She looked good, better then how he felt anyway. Her hair was in a ponytail, and her stature looked more confident than before the chair.

That's right, the chair. He forced a dry, gritty rasp. "Yara, what happened?"

She closed the door, preventing the light from entering, and sat a metal tray at his feet. "Enyo. My codename."

He groaned again. "Enyo?" That's right, Crude talked about that before he went to the chair. And his codename was Lux. But … *That's right. My name is Alex. . . . Alex Quake.* His memories and thoughts were all shattered pieces. He remembered things from his past and some things from his present, but they were all mixed up. Intertwined with the new memories. "What happened?"

"The downloader's what happened," she said confidently. "Yours didn't take too well. They honestly thought you were going to die." She lowered her head as worry broke across her face. "You kinda had me freaked out for a little bit."

He rubbed the sweat away. She handed him a glass of water as he sat up. As awful as he felt, their was a little joy to know she was worried about him. "Didn't you have to go in the chair too?"

She leaned against the wall, arms across her chest. "I did, and everything went perfect for me."

Of course. "What did you select for your skills?"

"Medical expert and M.V.O.E."

"Motor vehicle operator expert," he said, remembering Crude's skill set. He looked up with bunched brows.

"Exactly. I can drive almost any vehicle, aircraft, and marine craft. Pretty cool, right?"

"What happened with trying to be like Jo-Jo?"

"I'd rather try to keep you guys alive longer. Be that support person, you know?" She handed Alex two pills. "Take these. Eight milligrams each of aspirin."

He popped the two tiny pink pills into his mouth and washed them down with the glass of icy water, finishing the whole thing. "Looks like you made out just fine. No harsh reactions or blacking out. How long was I out for? Two hours?"

"Two days."

"What?" He jumped up, and the world around him began moving awkwardly again.

"Calm down." She seized his shoulders and eased him back. "Alex, you didn't take too well to the downloader, but you're alive. From my understanding, your brain cells needed more time to absorb the currents of knowledge they received."

Alex managed a chuckle, trying not to let her words feel too offensive. "So what you're saying is that I was too dumb for the downloader?"

"Take it how you want. I'm just your nurse for the moment." She pulled a container of homemade applesauce that was Poachie's specialty.

He looked down at the sprinkles of cinnamon that she always topped it with. "How is everyone?"

"Fine," she said following his eyes down to the container.

Thoughts of Olivia and Dad flickered. Fear crawled up his throat. "We don't have much time left."

"Ten days."

"Ten . . ." He winced. And here he was out on his back for two days. Two days that could've been used for more training and getting him ready. He slammed his fist against the bed frame.

"Hey." She handed him a spoon and the container of applesauce. "I need you to eat so you can get your strength and focus back. We need you at your best to pull this off, right?"

Alex licked the dryness away from his lips and nodded. With four whopping spoonfuls, he finished the applesauce and woofed down a bacon, lettuce, and tomato sandwich. There was a cup of wild blueberries left, and he finished that too.

"So . . ." Yara lowered her head to make eye contact with him. "How are you feeling?"

"Better. Just this crazy headache." He pressed the sides of his temple. "Really, you didn't feel anything after?"

"Well, I had a little bit of a headache and some dizziness. I slept for about twelve hours. But nothing like what you're going through."

A bitter laugh slipped out as he shook his head.

"What's that look for?"

"Honestly, just you. Right from the beginning, this whole journey has been so easy for you. Like you've done it all before or like you were made to be here with them." He nodded to the door. "I think I'm just going to get myself killed when it's time to save Olivia and my dad. If . . . If I do, just promise me you'll make sure they follow through without me?"

She snatched his hand. "That's stupid, Alex. You're going to be the one to save them. And you'll survive, and once we do that, we'll make UNA pay for what they've done."

"See, that right there?" Alex smiled. "That leadership, that confidence . . . That's something I don't have. But that's who you are, through and through. You're strong, Yar—I mean Enyo. Who knows? Maybe you'll be Raven's next leader after Crude."

She smiled, hiding her face. "Pfft, a girl can dream, right? But Crude, she's so much more. She's strong, focused, and has everyone's respect. I don't know how I can earn that. Funny to think she's a few years younger than us and an absolute powerhouse."

Alex slung his head back. "Hard to believe a lot nowadays."

She wrapped her fingers around the tray and collected the jar and spoon. When she went to leave, Alex grabbed her hand. "Everything alright?"

He looked deep into her coffee brown eyes. "Do you regret talking to me under that apple tree?"

She bit her bottom lip. "Do you regret throwing your life away for me?"

"Still asking that question?" He turned away sheepishly.

"What's your answer?"

"I'll never regret it."

Her eyes welled up a little, and she nodded. "Good. I'll check back in on you in a little." She walked to the door and opened it. "I'll let everyone know you're awake. So, expect visitors."

"Thanks."

It didn't take long for everyone to come and visit. Kimbo burst in first, with Jo-Jo closely behind. She had to slap him on the shoulder a few times to keep his voice down, and even when he apologized, he did so in a booming voice.

"So you're still alive, huh?" Jo-Jo shifted her mouth with an unimpressed expression. "Well, what doesn't kill you, I guess."

"Thanks for visiting guys."

The door cracked open, letting a sliver of light in from the hall. "Okay, okay, my turn," said Poachie as she wiggled her tall, slender frame through the doorway. Her olive skin glowed from the hallway light.

Kimbo slapped him on the back. "Alright, bro, get better soon. We're gonna need you at a hundred for this mission."

Jo-Jo sneered. "What he said. And Poachie, please let the kid breathe."

"Oh, relax, *Joanne*."

"Poachie," she groaned before getting yanked into the hall by Kimbo.

Poachie sang with laughter as she made her way by his bedside. Her soft brown eyes searched as her long braided hair fell down the back of her black tank top. "So ... how was your first meal after the chair?"

"The best . . . as always." Alex clasped his fingers together as he sat on the edge of his bed. The concrete floor was cool and nice against the soles of his feet. "You spoil me."

She smiled, but it faded gently. Her brown eyes were bright even in the gloom of the room and her lips shifted to keep the smile up, but her face was sad and beautiful. She came to the edge of the bed and sat next to him. "I was worried."

Alex curled his fingers.

"I've lost way too many friends and so much more than that these last few years. I should be used to it. I should accept it. I *have* to accept it," she sobbed. "But it doesn't make it any easier. So please. Don't die on me just yet."

His words were a murmur. "I'll do my best."

She wrapped her arms around his shoulder and pulled him in close. It reminded him of his mom's hugs. It was deeply loving, like she was somehow trying to transfer all her love and protection into him.

"You should come out into the hallway. You can walk, can't you?"

"Well ..." He went to stand, and his legs wobbled. The room seemed to slide, but Poachie kept him upright. "Stood up way too fast."

"Yeah, I think so," she said, wrapping his arm over her shoulder.

"Did the chair have this kind of effect on you?"

"Oh, no, not at all. You're the worst I've seen, to be honest."

He couldn't help but laugh at himself. "Why am I not surprised."

"Don't be too harsh on yourself, Lux. It could be worse. You could be brain dead. Or just plain dead."

"And that's why I love you, Poachie. Always looking to the brighter side of things."

As she moved, the stuffed blue lion key chain fell from her belt loop. She nearly let him fall as she bent to pick it up.

"Sorry, sorry." She cradled the stuffed lion gently and with great care slipped it through her belt loop. "This thing means the world to me."

"No, it's fine. Sorry for being all over the place myself. Between the chair and thinking of my dad and sister, it's been hard to focus on anything else. I just don't know what I'm going to do if I lose them."

"We're going to save them, Alex. I know it. Don't worry about anything else."

Suddenly the door was kicked in. The doorknob cracked the concrete wall hard as both Alex and Poachie ripped around. Crude stepped in, her thick curly hair hiding her eyes. "Poachie. Lunch. Now."

"Seriously, Crude, you can put a please on the end of that, you know?"

"Please, now?" her tone softened like a pleading child. It reminded Alex of Olivia whenever she begged Pop for something.

She sighed and walked toward the doorway.

"You are the leader," Poachie replied.

Crude hugged her as she passed, then turned to face Alex from the doorway. Silent. He swallowed, looking around the room. "Can I help—"

"Shut up. Glad you're okay. Alive anyway."

He didn't know how to take it. Was she serious? "Thanks?"

"Focus on getting your strength back. We just got a mission from Valkyrie. We're heading into the outskirts, the *bad* parts of the outskirts, and meeting with an Anarchy spy who has some highly sensitive information. What he has will change the pace on how we go on the offensive against UNA. So I need you ready to go, alright?"

"Y-yes, ma'am."

She turned to head out, but then slipped back through the doorway. "Don't die until you save your dad and sister," she said. "That's an order."

There goes the old Crude. He tried hiding his smile. "Yes, ma'am."

She marched out of the room, that sword strapped to her back. She went everywhere with that thing. Ate with it, most likely slept with it. He shivered at the thought of how she'd executed Principal Krate. All that blood spilled in just one day. How could she sleep with something like that?

After a few hours of rest, he was back on his feet. Just as Crude had discussed, the plan was to go into the outskirts to gather some information on a mission that would be coming down in the next several months, one that could do some severe damage to the heart of UNA. He still didn't have all the details.

Still a little groggy, he shoved on his black combat boots, tightened the laces, and jumped to his feet to test his balance. The spinning and awkward movements of the world were gone, but there was still a slight nausea. He'd muscle through.

Alex threw on a black long-sleeved thermal and headed down the hall. Yara came out of her room. "Hey, wait up," she said. She rushed back into her room, then came back to walk with him. "How are you feeling?"

"Good, all things considering."

"So the shanties ... From what I understand, we're going to a pretty rough spot. Nothing like picking up food and stuff from Big Mah."

"Yeah, we'll be fine, though."

He drifted off, thinking about Olivia and Dad. His heart started racing as the what-ifs poured in. *What if I fail? What if I can't save them? What if I die?* His heart thudded in his ears. The voices, the questions. They were maddening. He rubbed a tear away before it could fall.

Yara's hand fell on his shoulder. "You sure you're up for traveling? Maybe you should get some more rest. I mean, you need to be at a hundred, and we start going over our strategy tomorrow."

"I can't. How can I just sit around knowing my baby sister and my dad are in some UNA prison? Who knows what they're doing to them?"

She stepped in front of him. "Lux, we got this. We're going to save them. I promise. You trust me, right?"

He nodded.

"Good. Let's go. You need the fresh air anyway after being locked in that funky room for the last few days."

"My room doesn't smell that bad."

"It does, trust me."

Everyone waited in the living room. Crude rolled a pheasant bone between her teeth at the table. Jo-Jo was messing with a pistol, looking through the chamber. She clapped a clip in, and the chamber snapped forward with a metallic click.

"Pups are rearing to go. Even the sick one?" Jo-Jo asked, not taking her eyes off the pistol.

"I'm fine. Let's get this over with so we can work on the strategy to get my family and everyone else out of prison," Alex replied.

"Good," said Crude. She tapped the bone on the table, then stopped. "We're going to meet with an informant. An old member of Anarchy, so the information should be solid. The only thing is we're going deep into Playground." Her eyes focused on Alex and Yara. "You two keep your heads down, eyes on the dirt."

Alex looked to the others, then back at Crude. "What? Why?"

Kimbo posted up on the wall with his arms folded across his chest. "Playground's rough territory. It may not seem like it, but there is some order to the madness. The one thing we don't want to do is cause trouble and bring unwanted attention to us."

Poachie spoke from the other side of the room. "Kimbo's right, you two. The Outskirts is an ecosystem balanced by hierarchy. In order to remain hidden, we flow with that balance."

"Alright, whatever. I won't say anything."

"Yeah, right. Because I'm gonna believe that tone." Jo-Jo slipped her pistol into a holster, then flung a jacket over her shoulders. "The last thing we need is to get on Beanie's bad side. This is an in-and-out mission. That means avoiding sentinels and not getting caught up in dumb shit, *Lux*."

Beanie? A seed of thought vanished before it could take root. "Wait. Why are you looking at me?"

"We rescued you from being tortured and murdered. You got caught outside past that stupid curfew, didn't you? So keep your face to the dirt."

He threw his hands up. "Alright, alright."

Crude rose from the table. "Jo-Jo and Kimbo will carry pistols, no one else. Lux and Enyo, you're both wearing hoodies. I would say wear masks, but it would draw more attention than anything. We move as a unit. Tight, no breaking rank or you'll be dealing with me. Got it?"

"Got it." They all stood up straight. Alex struggled to keep up.

Crude shook her head, eyeing him. "Let's go. Brain, keep that recon drone high in the sky."

They left base, bypassing the old rusted yellow sign that read *high radiation.* A deterrent, of course. The thing struggled to remain upright in the dirt. They traveled up the winding trail of overarching branches and the hissing of leaves. The breeze brought on the sweet scent of nature's perfume and cooled the dampness of sweat that remained on his back and arms.

The scenery changed from forest and rocky trails to clumps of scrap metal littering the ground. Lean-tos covered in old tree branches and leaves were sparingly dotted close to the woods. Densely packed improvised buildings and shacks made of rusted metal, concrete, and plastic tarps were closer to the wall, then spilled over the land.

Dozens of people were about, moving from one shanty to the next. A line of shabbily dressed people were outside of Big Mah's store, but Alex and the others went to the opposite side, to a more densely populated area. The air changed. It became heavy with smoke from different causes, some sweet, others pungent with a harsh musky skunk funk.

Alex watched a man tip a bottle to the blue sky as he guzzled a yellow liquid while another took a puff from a pipe and blew rings. The voices became gritty, the language harsh. In a well-fortified building, a man was thrown out of a window. He jumped to his feet, threw up a finger, and went on his way.

Tension crept over Alex's shoulders, heavy and cold like a blanket of ice. It wasn't as crippling as being back at New Hope, but that didn't stop him from studying everyone who walked by. These people weren't like the ones back at Big Mah's. Their eyes followed, searching hungrily. There was a violent desperation in them, something that went beyond just surviving. He remembered Poachie's story about the famine.

Jo-Jo jerked his head down to the ground. "The one thing you need to know is if Crude gave you an order, that's an order. You're DOR now, right?"

He nodded, keeping his eyes on the dirt.

"Then follow orders," she grunted.

Alex's eyes rolled to the front of the group. He saw the red teddy bear backpack strapped to the jean vest Crude wore and the sword's handle hidden beneath the thickets of hair. Poachie on her right, Kimbo on her left. Yara was in the middle, and he and Jo-Jo made up their six.

Every other word from the conversations around them was a curse, the men hardened with scarred faces and hopeless eyes. Most of the clothing was tattered, grayed and browned by the earth, yellowed by their own bodily fluids more than likely. The women smoked too, and those with young faces were tucked close to groups of men. Their eyes sad.

This was the Outskirts he had expected, the place that gave him nightmares. He watched a woman get smacked to the ground, and a man began yelling over her. Alex's eyes snapped forward. He paused.

The man looked up with his only good eye, a blue eye wrinkled with age, yet his tan face didn't look that much older than Pops. "What the hell you looking at boy? She ya sister or something?"

Alex shivered at the thought and looked down to see the sorrow in the girl's eyes as tears filled them. *Help*. Her eyes said help. Jo-Jo slapped the back of his neck and yanked his face down.

A hush fell over the chaos and rugged conversation. In the distance, the cluttered streets parted for an all-black truck. It road high, gliding over the garbage cluttered road.

sentinels … Alex shoved his hands in his pockets.

"Faces down, remember. Don't draw any attention," Poachie spoke loudly enough for only them to hear.

Alex controlled his breathing as the warm breath of exhaust wafted from the truck. The vehicle sat on three pairs of large tires. The vehicle had an angular belly with strange panels beneath that glistened in the light. A horn blared. Alex could hear the grumbling of a few men who cursed the truck just behind.

He breathed more easily.

Jo-Jo sniffed the air. "You smell that?" Her voice was a near whisper.

Alex sniffed, taking in the remnants of exhaust. "No. What is it?"

"The smell of you crapping yourself."

He focused back on the ground, keeping his hands stuffed in his pockets.

They walked down a few more roads and came to a building that had women hanging out front. Some wore high-riding shorts and dresses high above their knees. Pop would've killed Olivia for even considering wearing anything like that.

"Eyes on the ground, lover boy. You don't want that kind of action."

"What action?"

Jo-Jo giggled as the group paused in front of a building. At one point, it looked like it had been a portion of an apartment complex, but now only the metal frames and a concrete block with windows and a wooden roof remained. A blue painted sign read Baily's Goods.

Crude whispered, "This is the place. Same rules apply. Keep your faces down, hoods over your head for Lux and Enyo."

Everyone gave a terse nod.

Filled with the smell of wood finisher and oil, the store was covered in broken, dirty tiles. The walls were covered with old world knick knacks, things Alex thought no longer existed. Some of which were outlawed by the UNA, things like old newspaper clippings, books, and pictures from a time long ago.

He stepped outside of the group, his eyes hungrily devouring the images. It was all alien to him. Pictures of people, the way they dressed, their eyes, their smiles. Jean pants and jackets, wild curly hair, peace signs, and loud vibrant colors. Pictures of sports teams and of cartoons like the ones Brain watched.

"Crazy, right?" Poachie asked.

"Yeah. I mean, sorry, I broke from the group, but it's just …"

She nodded and smiled. "Sometimes when we have goods to trade, we get Brain new cartoons and videos to watch. He doesn't get out often, so it makes things a little easier on him. He doesn't show it much, but I know it can get lonely."

Alex nodded. He started reading the dates: 1970, 1988, 1990 . . . "Why do you think it all happened?"

"What?"

"The wars. Why did people hate each other enough to blow each other up into nothingness?"

Her eyes goggled a bit. "Well, it's not like we don't exist anymore. I mean, you and I are here. The people out there are here too, right?"

"But it's the same thing, isn't it? The hate?"

"Yo, Lux, Poachie," Kimbo called them to the front.

Crude was nodding to a tall, wrinkled man with worn leathery skin. His eyes were black. A few strands of wiry silver hair fell over his forehead like a dirty mop.

They were guided into the back, and there sat another man. Tan and bald with a beard that seemed to burst from his face, he was old but not like the man outside the room. This guy was aged by something else.

"Glad DOR could grace me with their presence today, and the renowned Ravens, no less. It's an honor," the man said sarcastically, hanging off his chair as if he couldn't care less.

"The prints." Crude's tone didn't change from its cold monotone.

"Straight to the point, huh, youngin?" The man spat a blob of black on the ground and snorted. "Makes sense why they have you kids doing the heavy lifting. Got no brains."

Poachie, ripped forward and slammed a large knife into the table. The man nearly fell out of his chair. "My commander asked for the plans."

"Well, sheesh, I didn't hear her. She could've asked again."

"She doesn't ask twice." Poachie's voice was venomous, no longer sweet and warm. "Give her what she asked for."

The man nodded, throwing his hands out in a calming manner. He eased back in his chair, and his persona changed quickly. "Forgive me. I have to test the new generation to see the resolve. Unlike this *new* Anarchy, the use of ..." he looked over the room, "kids to do a man's job is still mind-boggling. But I heard a few things about the Disciples. Especially about the Ravens. Heard y'all have a hell of a leader. A merciless killer. That you?"

Crude didn't answer.

The man nodded and gave a wrinkly grin. From beneath the table, he pulled out a satchel and slapped a thick manilla folder on the table, his charagma tan and wrinkled by the bulging veins in his hand. Papers burst from the folder. "That's fifteen years of my life on that table. Fifteen years I'll never get back."

Alex eased over to see what the fuss was about, but Poachie snatched the folder before he could get a clear look at the papers. Crude pulled out the chair across from him and plopped into it.

The man eased back a little. "I can usually tell what a person's about when I look them in the eyes. But with all that hair covering up that pretty face of yours, it's hard for me to get a glimpse darlin'."

Crude leaned froward. "Funny, I can tell what kind of a man you are by the way you sit in that chair."

"Oh really?"

"Yeah."

"What kind of man am I then, *darlin*?"

"You're the kind of man who pisses himself if he sees one of his own troops killed. The kind of man who avoids death at all costs. The kind of man who stays fifteen years sleeping with the enemy, only to run when his secret reaches the surface."

His eyes became like fire. He stood, kicking the chair back. He leaned over the table toward Crude, who didn't even flinch. Two Berettas were planted firmly against the man's forehead by Jo-Jo and Kimbo.

The man put his hands up again and eased by. "Joking, joking."

"I'm not," Crude replied apathetically.

The man shrugged. "I'm sure some rumors are going around about me tanking the mission. But everything I did in Fort Roberts was for a reason. Shit, everything I did brought light to the labs, the testing, the human trafficking. All of it."

Kimbo snickered. "Thank you for your service."

The man hacked a bitter laugh. "The Disciples of Revolution are nothing more than the boot lickers of Anarchy. You know that, right?"

Everyone in the room was silent.

He smiled greedily, licking his teeth. "In war, children are only good for a few things. Especially girls. I can tell a fe—"

Poachie slammed the man against the wall, the knife at his throat. She was breathing heavily. Alex had never seen her move so quickly, so furiously. She was different. Almost animalistic.

"At ease, Poachie," Crude commanded. "It's not like my second to get shaken up."

"Yes, ma'am," Poachie said, shoving the man and removing the blade from his throat.

He straightened his jacket and cracked his neck a few times.

"We're leaving." Crude grabbed the documents and slipped them into her red teddy bear backpack. They all began to leave. "No matter what they said about you, old man, no matter how true it is, what you've given us, and what you've provided DOR and Anarchy with has saved hundreds of lives."

Alex looked over his shoulder. Crude didn't turn to face him, but Alex saw a tear drop down the man's face as he silently nodded.

Alex couldn't help but study the realm of vintage he'd stumbled into. He was the last behind the group when the man came out from the back.

"Wait!"

Alex turned. Crude, and Poachie stepped beside him.

Crude's hand crept over the handle of her sword. "State your peace."

"Easy, darlin'. I want to give ya a warning. UNA is up to something, something big. With those damn labs, they accomplished what they've been trying to do. From all the noise in the upper echelons with the politicians and patricians, it sounds like unwelcome news for anyone considered enemies of the United Nations. Something about ghosts?"

Jo-Jo spoke from the back. "What's that supposed to mean to us?"

"I don't know. All I'm saying is watch your backs. I have a feeling things are gonna start getting lively for both DOR and Anarchy."

Crude's hand fell away as she turned and moved past Alex.

Poachie nodded to the man. "Thanks. We'll keep that intel in mind."

They slipped out of the store. No one said a word. It was as if there was some kind of unspoken rule to not discuss what was said back there. Not yet. But the way that man talked to Crude, the way he talked about the Disciples of Revolution was downright awful. Yet she allowed that man to live.

They began making their way back down the road. There seemed to be fewer people hanging from the crumbling doorways of shacks and huts than before. The building that had those girls dressed provocatively had been cleared, but now there was screaming.

They were a few feet away when two pops of a gun rang from inside. Girls came running out, shrieking at the top of their lungs. As the girls ran out of the structure, some barely dressed, Alex looked away.

A roar of cursing and screaming came from the building as a man yelled about missing money from his trousers. Alex looked up. The man was hefty. A double chin disappeared beneath flabby pink flesh, and his throat hung loose like the wattle of a wild turkey. In his filthy hands clumped between his fingers was the hair of a woman he dragged kicking and screaming into the dirt road.

Five men came out behind hollering and laughing in the doorway.

Jo-Jo took in a sharp breath. "Looks like Pallbearer, Crude."

"It is. Another stunt to strike fear into the crowd." Crude's hands remained in her pockets, unfazed by the commotion before them.

"Can anyone speak on why this filthy piece of garbage found it okay to steal a man's well-earned cash?"

The road began to fill with people, men, women, and children, all eyeing the spectacle before them. Some snickered with broken yellow teeth. Alex looked up at the others who remained calm.

"Anybody have anything to say to this woman before I—" He fired the gun into the air.

Ice ran through Alex's veins. He looked up to the others again. Crude's eyes drifted forward, and she began walking past, the others followed. Alex was lost for words. His hands shivering.

Alex looked back at the woman. He saw the dirty face that was lightly bruised and starting to swell. He saw Nelson in her, and he shouldn't have. But the woman was beyond familiar. Frighteningly familiar.

"Mrs. Tanaka?" Alex yelled sharply.

A hush came over the crowd.

The woman stopped fighting and in her sobs of pain and sadness, looked up at him, and he knew that it wasn't possible, yet … He knew there was no chance it was her because she was behind the walls in Eastern. The Tanakas were somewhere behind the walls, grieving over the loss of two sons.

"Alex," she cried hoarsely. "Please help me."

Alex cupped his mouth, fighting back tears. The crowd was as still as the air. His heart thrashed and bashed in his chest, and he wanted so much to be wrong.

"Please …" her lips quivered, and her teeth chattered as if she had been consumed by a bitter chill. "Help me."

He looked up at Crude.

"We go, now," she demanded.

Their eyes were like knives on him, then he turned to the crowd, and it was the same sharpness. He thought of Nelson. There was no way he would leave his mother for dead. Not Mrs. Tanaka.

Yara shook her head. "Alex, we can't. Don't!"

He turned and looked up at the man. He could feel the prickling of goosebumps racing over his body as he went against the girl who could lop a man's head off with ease, but he could not let a woman he had known most of his life die. Not like a dog, not like this, and not after how he failed to save Nelson.

"Sir, please don't hurt her."

"And who is she to you?"

"She's my mother, sir. She's … my mother."

26

Dried blistered lips pulled revealing the man's yellow stained teeth, a few missing here and there. He stood up strong, straightened his back, and hung the pistol over his shoulder as if he had nothing to prove.

"So you're out with your friends, I see, while your mom works a little?" He pumped his hips. The men in the doorway laughed.

As disgusting as it was, Alex held his tongue and stepped through the crowd. "Please, sir. I'm sorry about whatever happened. I'll pay back whatever she owes."

"Double."

"Okay."

"With interest," he said, then spat at Alex's boots. He stepped closer, towering over Alex. "I can tell you ain't from around here, boy. Otherwise, you'd have kept your mouth shut. You know who I am?"

Alex shook his head.

"Folks call me, Pallbearer. Second lieutenant to the one who runs this region of Outskirts." He threw Mrs. Tanaka's face in the dirt and kicked some more in her face. She crawled over to Alex, and he helped her stand as she sobbed and cried.

She couldn't talk. Her entire body was shivering. "My boss doesn't take too kindly to disrespect. Definitely doesn't take too kindly to thieves and those who protect them."

Kimbo came over and stood by Alex's side. Poachie walked over and held onto Mrs. Tanaka, escorting her out of the crowd. The group of five men came over, bolstering their numbers, and the crowd stepped back.

Alex swallowed, looking around. They were larger, more muscular, and taller than he was. They had experience in their eyes like they'd killed a man or two.

"So where's my double pay with interest, brat?"

Alex stepped back a little. A large hand fell on his shoulder.

"Uh-uh," Kimbo said.

Alex looked up at him, confused.

"I know what you're thinking. You want to bounce. Not gonna happen, brother. You went against orders, direct orders. It's cool that you wanted to save that woman, but you got to walk the walk, even if it means taking a beating."

Alex looked at the large men, who looked to be getting more aggressive by the second. He whispered, "Kimbo, I–I don't have the money."

"I know."

"These guys, they'll tear me limb from limb," he pleaded.

"I know." Kimbo gripped his shoulders. "You're gonna have to take an L, for the team. Keep the balance, remember?"

They both looked around the roaring crowd. He thought of his and Poachie's words earlier about there being some order in the balance. What kind of order failed to be seen?

"Right."

Deep breaths rattled Alex's insides. Kimbo pushed him forward. Alex looked back at the others, who looked on with folded arms. Yara had concern in her eyes, but she gave him a terse nod and a thumbs-up.

What the hell does that do for me? Alex turned facing the men.

The man handed the pistol off to one of the five. He gave a greedy grin. "Let me guess. You don't have that double plus interest, huh?"

Alex gulped and shook his head.

"I appreciate a noble brat who wants to save a woman. A whore though?" Pallbearer sighed. "Regardless, I got to teach ya a lesson."

Alex swallowed and turned back to the group. "We don't have to do this. I'm not your enemy. They are," he said, pointing to the wall. "I'm not the one who has you living in the Outskirts, living off scraps and, and ..." He looked around to see a man biting off the crispy flesh of a roasted rat. *Oh no ...* "Look, we can make this work. Please?"

"Kid don't make me lose all respect for ya. Just take the beating like a champ. I promise, I'll only knock out one tooth, and break a finger."

"But I like my teeth and my fingers. Come on, give me a break."

The man went to grab him. He ducked beneath. The man swung with a growl, and Alex rolled just under it.

The crowd started chanting.

The man threw another punch. Alex stepped in, grabbed his arm, and slung him over his shoulder. He twisted the man's wrist and fell into an arm lock.

He thought about Jo-Jo that time in the armory. The man was fighting to break free, but Alex shifted his hips up, and the man began yelling. His face was on fire.

Four more men ran over. Alex rolled off him and got back to his feet. He turned to Crude and the others. "Help me."

"You got this, bro," Kimbo yelled with a smile.

"No, you don't," Crude barked. "Hurry up and get the crap kicked out of you so we can go home and eat."

Alex snapped forward, ducking beneath another blow. He shoved another man out of the way and kicked another in the face. He didn't know how, but it was like he had known how to fight like this all his life.

"Dude, you're still way too tight. Stay loose," Jo-Jo yelled. "Let it be like second nature to you, like breathing."

"What?" A fist cracked Alex across the face, and he stumbled to the ground. Through the ringing of his ear, he could hear Jo-Jo laughing hysterically from the crowd.

He got back to his feet. The ringing was distracting. The wooziness from earlier returned. He took a deep breath and widened his stance.

They surrounded him.

He went on the offensive. He kicked the first man in the chest, then turned to the other, punched him twice in the face, and kicked him in the chin. A strange ache tensed in his hamstring, and he limped back.

One of the men popped him in the face, another kicked him in the stomach. He gasped for air, before the main guy came barreling forward with his fist drawn back. Alex was already losing his footing. His hamstring was killing him.

As he fell, he looked up to see Crude holding the man's fists. "Enough. You got your point across."

The crowd stepped back.

The ringing faded as Alex got on his hands and knees. As the other five men backed away, the one holding the pistol began raising it toward Mrs. Tanaka, but the man beside him halted his movements.

"It's her. The leader of the Ravens, the One-eyed Devil," somebody from the crowd whispered.

"I had no idea this brat was with DOR I would've never touched him if I knew that." The large man backed off a little. "But he's interfering with Outskirt business and—"

"Tell, Beanie the Butcher it won't happen again, and that the One-eyed Devil owes him a favor."

Alex watched as she released the man. She yanked him to his feet. It felt like Kimbo was on the other end. The moment he got his footing a fist shot forth, and everything went black.

"Never disobey a direct order," her voice echoed in the darkness.

Conversations, the smell of burning wood, and water bubbling fluctuated in the darkness. A sweet smell of herbs and spices filled his nostrils as his eyes opened. He was surrounded by cement walls that broke away in spots revealing brick and mortar. This wasn't headquarters.

His jaw ached as he winced, pressing his fingers firmly over the side of his face. He heard a few giggles not too far off. In front of him, an old green door covered in tawny flaking green paint peeled open with a raggedy screech, and in stepped Big Mah with a wooden bowl.

"Well, look who's up. Heard you caused some trouble deep in Playground, huh?"

Alex sat up on his elbows. "Hey, Big Mah," he said, searching the room once more. A cold breeze crept from the darkest crevice. "Where am I?"

"You at the shop, honey, you at the shop. Sounds like ole Crude knocked you a good one. Might not want to get on that girl's bad side, huh?"

He thought about Mrs. Tanaka and flung his feet over an old thin mattress that cried when he stood. "Sorry, Big Mah," he said, brushing by her and following the conversation down a hallway. He crept down the wooden steps, which creaked and whined; a few were missing. He jumped, catching the attention of the entire group.

Mrs. Tanaka looked up, her face bandaged and a little swollen, but she was fine. "Alex!"

He raced down the stairs, fell at her feet and hugged the frail woman as tightly as she'd allow. He cried. The memories of his childhood in every tear. All that was life, Eastern Suites, the scrapyard, the apartment complexes, Mr. Tanaka, Jason, Nelson, Deacon, Mom, Dad, Olivia … All of them scattered memories. All lingering hopes in a growing fire that filled his belly.

"Alex, I can't believe you're alive. I can't believe you're out here." Mrs. Tanaka held his face up and wiped some of his tears away. "Thank God!"

He wiped the snot from his face. "I thought they got you like the rest of the people they're going to execute."

She nodded and wiped a few tears of her own. "I … I barely got away myself. There were many others that got away, but what's happening is terrible. They're planning on purifying Eastern Suites."

Alex swallowed. "Purifying?"

"Wiping out your neighborhood," said Crude. She was glowing, arrayed by orange flames that burned in a large brick fireplace. She stared ominously. "They haven't done it in a long, long time. But I'm not surprised. They want to make an example. Put fear into anyone who dares to want to help the cause and join Anarchy or us."

Alex's jaw hung open, trying to catch the words banging against the inside of his skull. They couldn't do this. How could they get away with this? It was impossible. There was no way these people were that heartless. No way they … He thought about his mother's death. He thought about Nelson and how he and Yara were going to be tortured and killed all because he stood up to a kid his age.

Mrs. Tanaka rubbed his cheek. "We were so worried about you after … everything that happened." She nodded as if she was trying to accept what was happening herself. "From what your friends told me, they plan on helping you to get your father and sister back?"

He nodded and looked to the others. Jo-Jo sat on Kimbo's lap, scooping brown stew into her mouth with a wooden spoon. Poachie played with the knife in her hand, and Yara was nowhere to be found.

He rose. "Thanks a lot for letting me get my ass kicked. What about being a team, moving as a unit?"

"You broke rank, dummy. Not our fault you risked your life to save someone." Jo-Jo slurped gently. "No offense, Mrs. Tanaka."

She gave Jo-Jo a gentle motherly smile.

Kimbo wrapped his arms around Jo-Jo's waist. "Bro, following orders keeps everyone alive and most importantly, keeps the mission from being compromised. You're lucky things didn't get as bad as they could've."

"My hubby's being nice about it, but you messed up. Bad Lux, bad. The last thing we need is bad blood with a don, especially Beanie the Butcher!"

"What the hell's a don, and who is Beanie the Butcher? I've been here for months, and you guys have never brought any of this up?"

Crude's voice broke from over the crackling fire. "That's because we never had to go into Playground. And don't let my tone be a sign of being soft. If you ever put us in a position where the mission could be compromised again, I swear I'll kill you on the spot. Is that understood?"

"Y–yeah."

"Lux, look, bro. Poachie said it best. There's an ecosystem in the Outskirts. Not even the Ravens, or DOR, for that matter, can mess with that system. Not yet anyway. Every continent has some form of Outskirts, 'cept the Ice Deserts. Dons run specific regions of those Outskirts. They're the bosses of bosses in those regions. They have crazy authoritative power because UNA uses them to keep the peace."

"UNA? Why?"

"As to not rule with an iron fist," Crude rasped. She seemed distracted. "They're like puppets. UNA developed a relationship with the dons, giving them free reign over the Outskirts, only interfering if things get out of hand, or if Outskirt messes bleed into the walls."

"Okay." Alex rubbed his chin. "Why don't you guys get rid of the dons?"

"That's where the balance comes into play, brotha. The dons aren't all excited about UNA's thumb on them. Beanie The Butcher, especially, has built a relationship with DOR and Anarchy to support our endeavors as long as we don't interfere with what he has going on."

He hung his head. "Which is what I did."

"Ladies and gentlemen, something is actually getting through that thick, fat head of his."

Alex wanted to tell Jo-Jo to shut up, but she had every right to talk trash. "What happened to me being a master at hand-to-hand combat or whatever? I should've been able to win. Did I sleep in a coma for two days for no reason?"

Crude turned from the fire. Her eyes glistened from the blaze. "You have the mindset, the techniques. But you lack the physical capabilities. You were warned."

"What about all the training we've been doing these last few months?" He threw his hands out.

Jo-Jo groaned. "Oh, stop crying already. Two months of training isn't going to get you very far, *Lux*. You need to train more, train harder, get your ass kicked a few more times, then you'll have the experience you need."

"How's that going to help with getting my dad and sister back?"

"It's better than nothing," Crude rasped.

Alex looked down at Mrs. Tanaka. If he had followed Crude's command, she'd be dead. And he'd be no different than he was before. "I can't follow orders that don't make sense. How is letting Mrs. Tanaka, or anyone else for that matter, die going to help anything? Aren't we supposed to help people? It's part of the creed. 'We will crush the ones who feed off the meek and innocent. By our blood-soaked hands, we will bring peace and lay down our lives for justice's sake. Our parents are the people who we call our mothers and fathers.' Right? Am I wrong?"

Everyone in the room was silent.

Crude got up from the fireplace and bent in front of him.

Alex threw his hands up when she raised her hand. She moved his arms out the way and gently tapped his cheek. "Get some ice on that when we get back to headquarters."

Jo-Jo's and Poachie's heads perked up. He watched as they both shared a confused glance. He was just as confused as they were. Yara came back in through a hanging tarp. She smiled the moment their eyes met.

Crude knelt down to Mrs. Tanaka. "Mother, we will do all we can to bring back Father. We will do all we can to right the wrong that has been done."

Mrs. Tanaka cupped her mouth as a few tears welled in her eyes. She nodded. "Thank you."

"It's my understanding that Jason Tanaka is your son?"

Her eyes widened, and she began trembling. She held onto Crude desperately. "Yes. Yes, he is. Have you seen him? Please tell me you've seen him."

"It's been a few months. But yes. He's with the Sandstorms, a unit that works the southern border."

Mrs. Tanaka started crying. Her face turned red as she buried her face into Crude's chest. Alex watched as Crude's fingers crawled around Mrs. Tanaka's shoulders awkwardly, then she half hugged, half pushed her away.

Mrs. Tanaka sat back and wiped her face with a shirt still filthy from being dragged. "When Jason left to join DOR, he left us a journal. It had everything from his reasons why he was leaving to giving strict instructions to not go looking for him. Our other son, Nelson, he was angry at first until he read that journal. Then he changed. Right, Alex?"

Alex thought about Nelson's confidence during his time at New Hope and how even though everyone ostracized him, he was steadfast and confident to the very end. Alex nodded.

"Jason would be so proud of his little brother for holding his ground. He didn't give into fear or comfort like everyone else did. He believed in what his brother was fighting for. Freedom. True Freedom. Not this illusion."

Illusion. Alex thought about Jo-Jo's words to him and Yara back in that underground prison. That's what the Suites were. That's what living a life as a Bourgeoisie citizen was. An illusion.

Poachie continued to dig the tip of the blade into her fingernails, scraping dirt away. "Anyone selected for DOR or who plans on joining us must leave a journal if they have loved ones. It gives the reason why and strict instructions not to follow. The journal's written in a way that even if it's turned into authorities, it should make them think about the current way of life. The horrors, the lack of rights and freedoms, and the overall unethical laws put into place that affects those who live below the Exclusive way of life."

Mrs. Tanaka nodded.

"On your feet," ordered Crude.

Everyone jumped up. Big Mah came down and handed Alex a bowl of brown stew filled with bright orange carrots, celery, and bits of brown meat and bone. He started taking the soup in as quickly as possible. Slurping and chewing as Big Mah spoke with everyone. She gave Poachie a bag full of goods, hugged Kimbo tightly, and gave Jo-Jo a peck on the cheek after squeezing her face.

"You babies come back any time, ya hear?"

"You know we will, Big Mah." Kimbo threw up a big hand as he led the way out of the tarp.

Mrs. Tanaka pulled Alex to her and held him tight. "Please promise you'll be careful out there, okay? I can't lose any more sons."

Alex nodded. "Where are you going to go?"

She shook her head. "I'll find—"

"Right here with ole Big Mah," the woman answered. "I need the help, and I need the hands. More hands, more produce, more trade value I always say. Besides, I got plenty of room."

Alex hugged Big Mah. "Thank you so much."

She nodded. "Now do as she says, boy. Be careful out there. That goes to all you kids, ya hear?"

They all nodded.

Alex gave Mrs. Tanaka one more hug. He hadn't seen her smile in a long time. After Nelson, he figured she never would again. But she waved happily, remnants of hope and vigor in her eyes, and a smile to match.

Back at base, Alex sat at the kitchen table with a pack of ice on his face, watching Brain giggle and laugh to his heart's content at some old cartoon. Yara came down from the armory and pulled out a chair.

"Feeling better?"

He pulled the ice packet away and rotated his jaw. "Stiff, but it doesn't feel broken anymore. That's always good."

"I still can't believe she was your best friend's mom. What are the chances? And what was she doing working at a brothel?"

Alex shrugged. But back then, in the middle of that road, he saw the desperation in her eyes. Survival. Mrs. Tanaka was a strong and deliberate woman. She wasn't the type to stroll into a place like that, not for anything, not for anyone. So whatever happened in the Eastern Suites must have been bad. He thought about Deacon and his family.

"Yeah, she must have been desperate. Really desperate."

"That's the game in Outskirts. Desperation. It'll make you do horrible things to survive."

He wanted to block it all out. "Where'd you go, back at Big Mah's?"

"Oh, just the bathroom. Don't dwell too much on what's going on over there. Let's focus on getting our families and the others back, okay?"

He nodded.

That evening, Poachie seasoned some venison with herbs and spices and chopped up some vegetables to make a big dinner. On a full belly, he was feeling a lot better, but his hamstrings and shoulders were tight.

He lay on his bed thinking about everything that had been put into his head by that machine. It was all there, the different moves, the different locks and holds, the body throws, the kicks. He knew it as if he'd spent the last fifteen years of his life eating and breathing mixed martial arts. And that would be fine if it were true. At least then, his body would be used to those kinds of movements.

At least weapons mastery wouldn't be as strenuous. But he needed to get a grip on these skills fast. Time was moving fast, and the date of the public execution wasn't far off. A dreadful chill fell over the room. He could only imagine how Olivia and Dad felt.

27

Shots cracked from the Alpha-9. The weight of the Glock was light, the grip perfect. Alex released the empty magazine and slapped another in, popping off a few more shots. Anything to get the thoughts of what would take place six days from now.

Rounds shredded the green dummy swathed in sentinel armor. The serrated armor piercing rounds were highly effective. Once they broke through armor, three razor prongs entered the body. God forbid they hit bone. In that case, the razor covering spread and cut through anything, causing intense internal bleeding.

"They're the worst to get out too," Jo-Jo said, firing an AR at her target. Every shot hit the same spot over and over again. "The serrated rounds are barbed, so they act like the quills of a porcupine. You get hit, you're out of the fight."

They had been out since seven that morning. Jo-Jo kicked in his bunk room door, ripped him out of bed, and threw a pile of guns in his arms. She carried a satchel of ammo, and they moved to the bottom of a hillside where they always came to test out weapons and improve their marksmanship. Not that Jo-Jo needed it.

She placed the AR on a wooden framed table, browning and falling apart from weathering, then picked up two pistols. She took a quick breath and unloaded. They weren't as tight as the AR, but every round lifted the dummy and armor with impact.

Alex watched, trying to study her unorthodox stance and movements. She would pick up a weapon, unload on the target, then pick up a completely different weapon type and do the same. Every round landed.

"How are you that good?"

A sliver of a smile appeared. "Some of the Anarchy guys say I can shoot the teardrop off an ant. Like I said, I'm a prodigy."

Alex rolled his eyes. "So you just woke up one day and just started picking up a gun and shooting?"

She looked down at the pile of weapons beside her. "No. Actually, my dad started showing me how to shoot when I was a little girl. Shooting became our *us* time. I knew he would never tell me the truth, but I knew he was part of Anarchy's European sector."

"Seriously?"

"Yeah. He would disappear for weeks on end, sometimes months. Mom wouldn't worry either." Jo-Jo picked up another AR and studied it. "Back in the day, there was a highly skilled sniper called Death. He was the most feared assassin and sniper at the time."

"Is that why you're nicknamed the Daughter of Death? Was Death your father?"

She focused, aimed down the sight of the AR, and fired a few more shots. As the smoke cleared, the AR fell at her side. "I'm not the best weapons user, trust me. But I am the best sniper, and I will be better than Death himself. If that man *was* my father, then I'll do him proud."

Alex grabbed an AR, pressed it firmly into the pocket of his shoulder, and fired three precise rounds. They weren't as tight as Jo-Jo's, but he was beyond impressed. That 3CA was incredible. He knew how to handle every gun laid out on that table. That, coupled with the training on proper breathing techniques, body position, and stance, made things easier. He smiled.

"You smile now, but things are a hell of a lot different when you get into a real fire fight."

The thought of killing someone crept in, and his finger shivered on the trigger. He cleared the chamber, released the mag, and sat the rifle down. A sweet blue puff of smoke expelled from the weapons Jo-Jo fired, drifting to the sky. The cracks echoed around the hill, fading into small snaps. *Why can't I fight this awful feeling?*

"Hey, you'll be alright. Got me?" Jo-Jo came and nudged him. "Don't go pissing your pants yet."

"I just don't know if I can do it." He dug his fingers into his scalp. "What if the only way to save them is killing someone? How can I bring myself to do it?"

"I don't know, but the first time is—" Jo-Jo dazed off. She was locked in deep thought, then she blinked hard. "Not so easy."

"Even for you?"

She looked away. "Let's get back to base. Crude's gonna start getting things situated for the plan. It's going to suck not having backup. You're stupid lucky Crude likes you. It's so weird."

His head snapped back. "What do you mean *likes me?*"

She sucked her teeth. "Don't get too excited, Romeo. I mean that she genuinely cares for you, like family. But I've never seen her take to someone so quickly. Never."

"That's funny. Seems like every chance she gets, she threatens to kill me."

"That's her way of banter." Jo-Jo gave a playful bob of her head. "I don't know a lot about Crude. Shit, I don't think Poachie knows a lot about Crude, and she's her second. Valkyrie does, though."

"Valkyrie, the leader of DOR? She led the Ravens?"

"Yup, and the one who put Crude in charge."

Alex thought about the silhouette that hid in the shadows during SITREPS. He never saw her face, never even saw much of her body. To think the commander was that close to Crude. But then again, the Ravens were such a specialized unit that having direct access to the head of the sphere made sense.

Alex wrapped his arms around a bunch of ARs and hauled them back up to headquarters. Jo-Jo dragged the remnants of ammunition in satchels.

Back at headquarters, an array of food had been laid out on the kitchen table. Scrambled eggs, meat patties, fruit. There was even a rigid plastic pitcher of juice.

Alex rotated his neck and stretched his shoulders as he sat down in front of the meal. "Poachie, this looks amazing."

She was behind the counter flipping something. "Thanks. I decided I'm going to go all out for the next few days."

"That's about all we got left, so, makes sense," Jo-Jo said sarcastically.

Alex cleared his throat, but before he could get a word out, Yara came in. "Don't say it that way."

Everyone looked up at her.

"Instead of dreading the next six days, let's train hard and enjoy them." She looked down at Alex. "Right?"

"Right." Alex nodded. It wasn't a coincidence. The last few conversations with Kimbo and Jo-Jo about the mission heightened his anxiety and fear. If what they were getting themselves into had those two worried, it was going to be one hell of a fight.

Seven. Just Seven of them. Well, technically six because Brain couldn't be counted as he ran headquarters.

Hunger dissipated, and the food lost its enticing image. His mom's last words grew heavier and heavier the more the day inched closer. "*Take care of Olivia. Love her with all your heart, no matter what. Promise me you won't let anything happen to her.*"

Clearing his throat to fight the crawling sadness rising up, Alex rose from the table and headed down the hallway to his room.

"Lux, breakfast is almost ready. You can stay and keep me company."

He paused for a moment at the doorway. "I'm gonna go sit for a bit, okay?"

"Well, you can sit—"

"By myself, Poachie. If you … If you don't mind."

He didn't look back. The silence was enough.

He stuffed his hands in the worn camo pants and kept moving. *There's no way we can pull this off. We're going to die. I'm … I'm going to get these people killed.* Alex's hands shivered in his pockets. *What if I fail? What if I get everyone killed, including Olivia and Dad?*

He stopped in front of his door and pressed his forehead against the cool metal frame. His head was about to explode. He fought back tears. The reality of losing Olivia and his dad like he lost his mom frightened him. He thought about Poachie, Jo-Jo, and Crude especially, the ones who'd suffered by losing everyone they loved. His hands reached for the knob as he opened the door and stepped in.

The world froze around him.

Crude's eyes burrowed into him. Strangely enough, he caught the glint of her mahogany brown eyes through her hair, her fingers tight around the rims of her jean shorts, barely over her spandex undershorts as she pulled them up. Her bottom lip quivered as she finished tightening the leather belt around her waist.

His eyes rolled up to the bright red *DO NOT ENTER* sign. He whimpered, "Cr–Cr–Crude, I'm sorry I—"

She grabbed him by the throat. There was nothing but air beneath him as he was slammed onto the floor. Dust, papers and other debris lifted into the air. He could barely breathe.

She stepped over him, the blade pressing deep into his jugular. It was cutting deep. A warmth dripped down his neck. Deep whispers poured out of the blade. Was he going insane?

"How dare you enter my room. My space. Do you have a death wish, Lux?"

Alex was too afraid to move. Too afraid to speak. He mumbled words, letters, anything, really. He scanned the room, the brick wall covered with paintings and rough drawings of people. All of which had deep brown skin. There was a drawing by the bed post done in thick crayon, even oils, of four people, a little girl in the center.

"Don't you dare take your eyes off the one who's about to take your life."

He swallowed, watching her right eye burn a crimson red. The white became as black as onyx. Her pupils thinned sharply like that of a wild feline … a demon. The air became frigid, and a black mist rose from the blade. It even rose from Crude. An unexplainable pressure fell over the room. It was enough to wish he were dead. The whispers, they kept talking, so many, hundreds no … thousands.

Poachie crept in. "Crude … Crude, it's me…."

Crude whipped around with a growl that gurgled from her throat. "Stay. Away!"

Poachie kept coming. "Commander, I can't do that. I need you…. *We* need you to come back to us, okay?"

Every bone shivered. Alex's teeth chattered. No, there was never a time in his life when he felt this kind of fear. Like something was going to consume him, devour him, and he'd be lost forever. That's what he saw in that eye. That awful eye. Hell's eye.

Poachie clapped onto Crude's wrist. "I'm always with you, Crude, you know that. I'm your family," she said, then turned to Jo-Jo, Kimbo, and Yara, who were watching from the doorway in anticipation. "They are your family. So is Lux."

"He needs to die."

"He doesn't," Poachie replied softly. "He doesn't. Put Eerie back. She can sleep now."

Crude shivered as her gaze fell back on Alex. He watched as her eye became normal again. She pulled the blade from his throat. The whispers hushed instantly. She turned and fell into Poachie's arms, and Poachie cradled her like a mother would an injured child.

The pressure, the whispers, all of it vanished.

"Go. Now," Poachie whispered with intensity.

Alex jumped to his feet, blew through the doorway, past the others, and raced down to the gym. He found himself pressed in a corner, knees to elbows, rocking. Jo-Jo, Kimbo, and Yara came rushing in.

Jo-Jo knelt in front of him. "Lux, you okay?"

His eyes searched hers as he rocked. They focused back on the floor.

Yara sat close, inching her way next to him. She wrapped her arms around him. "He's shivering, bad. Really bad. What did she do to him?"

Kimbo shook his head. "Like I tried telling you guys in the beginning, Crude isn't like us. I don't know what UNA did to her; nobody does. Not even Brain. They put something in her, something that gave her crazy strength."

"Not just strength. There's something about that sword. That sword. What is that sword?"

Kimbo swallowed, and for the first time ever Alex saw him bristle with unease. "Eerie's something UNA gave her. I ... I never—"

"There's nothing like it," Jo-Jo said. "Eerie isn't a weapon like anything else I've seen. Neither has anyone else in Anarchy. There's nothing like it in the data we've collected. All the labs we've purged, even the one she was taken from. There's nothing like it existing in the books of UNA. It's off the record."

Yara shook her head. "It's just a sword. Why does it matter?"

Jo-Jo nodded to Alex. "Because it's not *just* a sword. Crude's powerful. She's inhumanly strong and fast. Her reflexes are unreal. But when she has that blade in her hand, she becomes something frightening. You called us monsters, but not even I'm like Crude. I've seen her take down dozens of sentinels in the blink of an eye. Grown men, dismembered, quartered, like a mad surgeon."

Yara looked down at Alex as she held him close. "Sorry. I just don't believe all that. Alex ..." She held his chin up. "I need you. Don't give up now. Don't lose yourself now. Please."

His body rocked on, eyes locked on the flooring of the gym. "The whispers. Those awful whispers. Who were they? I didn't imagine it. The voices were too loud, too real." His eyes rolled up to Kimbo. He felt the sting as he rubbed his throat. A few wet globs stained his fingers. "Was that really her sword?"

Kimbo stood with his arms folded. "Let's put it this way. Crude will be the reason we defeat UNA. And if it wasn't for Valkyrie and the old members of Raven, Crude would've been the reason UNA crushed both DOR and Anarchy. No question."

Yara snapped/ "Well, none of that helps Alex right now, does it?"

Kimbo lowered his gaze. Jo-Jo backed off a bit and pulled Kimbo out of the gym. It was quiet for a while, then Yara laid her head on his shoulder. He shivered. The thought of Crude changed everything about his position in DOR, even the world. This was like some nut job insane scenario that only Deacon could make up.

"You think I'm crazy, Yara?"

"I don't think any of it matters if it doesn't get our families back and free those people."

He tossed his head back. "Yeah. But … I'm not insane. I know what I heard. I heard voices. I can *still* hear them like they're embedded inside my skull. It's like ghosts or something."

"Ghosts?"

"I just … No, you're right." His head fell against his knees. "I need to get it together."

"We only have six days, Lux," She whispered. "Just six days."

28

Alex racked the bar after knocking out a few squats, clothes sticking to him like a second layer of skin and legs burning. He sat down on the edge of the flat bench. It was early. The only people up at this time was Poachie out hunting, and Brain who was providing the overwatch.

The last few days went by fast. Crude had everyone focus on nothing but the plan. Each day was a mixture of rehearsals, training events, then rehearsals again. They spent hours doing that. It was stuffed into his mind to the point that he knew everyone's part.

Knowing everyone's part was paramount in the case one of them died. In that case, someone else could still complete the task. The thought of death brought on a whole new heaviness. But Crude and the others, even Yara, treated it like it was nothing.

Why didn't they value life? To them, life was as simple as biting into an apple and tossing the core into the woods without a care. An ache pressed across his forehead.

He thought of his mother. The world had changed so much since she died. Nothing but shards of lies, pain, and loss that cut deep into everything he knew. The confusion, anger, and darkness seeped out like blood. His only bandage was the hope of saving Dad and Olivia.

He went back to the squat rack, threw on a few more plates, and did as much as he could till the pain went away from within him and radiated down his quads and calves. The physical pain was better. Easier to manage. The pain inside was too much to bear.

"Bro, you've been going overboard these last few days. I'm gonna need you to cut it down a bit," Kimbo said, walking into the gym. He downed a glass of water. "Take it from me. The last thing you need is to be physically exhausted and injure yourself in the middle of a mission."

Alex racked the bar. "That happened to you?"

"Oh yeah." He rubbed his head with a slight look of embarrassment. "Crude had to carry me back."

Alex wanted to laugh, but he couldn't help but think back to a week ago when she manhandled him. The time he heard the voices from that sword. "She tends to do that."

"Anyway, how are you feeling? Sounds like your hand-to-hand has gotten better from what Poachie says, and your target acquisition is good too."

Alex's brows pinched together. "Jo-Jo said that?"

"Not entirely, but something along those lines when we were talking earlier."

I wish I had been a fly on the wall. "Well, I wish I felt as confident as they're making me out to be." Kimbo started pulling off the plates from the bar, and Alex joined. "You guys make it look easy."

"Easy? Hell no." Kimbo laughed. "Bro, I'm pretty sure everyone is crapping bricks right now."

"You guys are confident, even excited. Not what I would consider fear."

"You're stupid and borderline insane if you ain't afraid. I don't want to die, bro. Yeah, I'm willing to put myself on the line to be effective, but death … There's no coming back from that."

Alex let out a sigh as the pressure eased. "What was your first mission like with DOR?"

Kimbo racked the last weight, then patted Alex on the shoulder. He threw his head back with a groan. "Oh man, what a cluster that was. I was with the Lost Boys Platoon at the time. Mostly all boys, we were a mixture of Exclusives, Bourgeoisies, and Pariahs."

"You weren't the only Exclusive?"

"Nah, man, not at all. Just because some of us live in the inner walls with the higher classes, doesn't mean we agree with their systems. Do you agree with UNA?"

"Of course not."

"Well, make sure you answer the same way when a Pariah asks you the same question. Just how you see Exclusives is just how Pariahs see Bourgeoisies. Anyway, it was a weapons cache mission from one of the patrol trucks. My squad waited for the sentinels to jet out. The moment they left the vehicle and went on patrol, we stripped that thing clean."

"That doesn't sound too bad?"

"Well, one of the boys in the squad, codename Shakey, had sticky fingers and couldn't sit still for the life of him.

Well, Shakey got his hands on a sentinel rocket launcher and blew that squad truck to the moon."

"What?"

"Not done yet. With that explosion, those sentinels came running back, and they were pissed something fierce. We got into a firefight, and another patrol truck came in from behind. We got pinned down bad. I'm talking bombs going off, missiles whizzing by, and rounds pinging off brick walls. We were knee-deep in the shit." Alex could see the passion in Kimbo's voice. "Reinforcements finally came through on our end. But we had already lost five guys. Shakey being one of them, the idiot." Kimbo laughed.

Alex gulped. "Doesn't seem like something to laugh about."

"It's not, but … I was there when Shakey got hit. Dude died with a smile on his face. 'Give 'em hell every chance you get. Never let 'em sleep.' Those were his last words."

"Never let them sleep?"

"The Lost Boys motto was, *No rest for the wicked.* Shakey took the meaning as hit the sentinels whenever we had the chance. He was a live-in-the-moment kind of guy. High risk, high output."

"He sounded nuts."

"Yeah, he was my best friend. One of the first in the platoon to believe I was all in for the fight against UNA, and the one who taught me everything I know about survival." Kimbo snickered. "*Almost* everything about survival."

Alex saw the crack in Kimbo's confidence. A blemish of sorrow in the polished hard expression of a soldier. "I hope we all come back alive."

Kimbo nodded. "Me too, brother. Me too."

They both headed to the kitchen area. Yara was watching Gilligan's Island, and Kimbo jumped right on the opposite couch, laughing with excitement. Alex didn't see what they saw in the show, but it caught Yara's attention.

He grabbed some juice from the fridge, then sat at the kitchen table. He dug his finger in the jagged hole created by Crude's sword during their initiation. He faintly heard the whispers again. His imagination more than likely. They weren't the deep voices of sorrow and suffering that swelled in his ears and head.

He forced the thoughts out and focused on Olivia and Dad, his fingers clawing at the table as they curled into fists. *I'm going to get you back, I promise.*

Crude came down the hallway from where the armory and reporting room were. He sat up with confidence and gave her a nod. She squinted deviously, but he didn't look away.

"How do you feel about the plan, Lux?"

He didn't know what to feel. Poachie and Yara's mission was to go beneath the public execution sewer facility and plant bombs for a distraction. Kimbo and Jo-Jo were to cause chaos on the east side of the perimeter, hopefully drawing most of the forces with rockets and sniper fire, while he and Crude were responsible for taking out guards and freeing prisoners in the midst of the chaos.

The mission, by all rights, was a suicide mission from his point of view. Six against a force of sentinels who would be armed with machine guns and who knew what else. Alex swallowed again.

Crude burst into laughter.

He snapped back, rattled by the sudden burst that he wasn't used to hearing from her. He looked over to the couch at Yara and Kimbo. Kimbo was rising to his feet with a raised brow.

Alex couldn't find the humor in any of it. "What's so funny?"

She slapped the table. "No other squad or organization has the audacity to execute what I've approved. But then again, none of those squads or organizations have me." She sighed, a glint of worry in those dark coffee eyes of hers. "Valkyrie's gonna be pissed when she finds out, but better to ask for forgiveness then permission."

"I know you're crazy strong, Crude. I trust you, and I can't thank you enough for this. But are you sure it's safe to execute this mission without backup?" Alex settled in his chair, thinking about Kimbo's first mission, and the death of poor Shakey. "What if we get overwhelmed?"

"I'm the backup." Her cold demeanor returned. "Don't doubt me again."

There was a deep fluttering in his chest. "Y–yes, ma'am."

Her eyes rolled to the couch. "Kimbo, get the others. Rehearsals, now."

Kimbo jumped to his feet. "Yes, ma'am."

Yara threw her head against the couch. "It'll be the fourth time today?"

He watched Crude's right eye roll to him sharply. "*Because* I'm struggling to trust the confidence of the team."

Unbelievable. Alex's head bobbed as he sighed. He scooted back from the table, doing his best to keep his words to himself. "Just bring in backup," he grumbled under his breath.

"What was that?"

Alex looked up to see the white of her eye turn black and her pupil glowed a bloody red. "Nothing. Not a thing…"

Her knuckles cracked at her sides. "Not a thing."

The intensity and pressure of the air dropped on Alex's shoulders. Again he saw the blackness rise from her. A wave of frigid air frothed from her like an icy mist. He jumped to his feet. "Not a thing, ma'am."

The pressure dissolved as Crude sniffed hard. "You better get used to that, *Lux*. Understand?"

"Yes, ma'am."

"Good. Ravens lets go. Rehearsals for the rest of the day."

Deep groans echoed down the hallway but immediately silenced once everyone entered the living room. Jo-Jo glared, Poachie looked with a soft expression of understanding, and Kimbo just shrugged.

Alex didn't bat an eye. With the extra rehearsals, he figured it could only help. They helped him, anyway. The time kept his mind off negativity and pushed the anxiety back into the abyss of his thoughts.

He turned to walk down the corridor and head up to the surface. He needed the confidence now more than ever.

Two more days.

29

A blood-curdling scream shot Olivia out of bed. The echoes of popping gunfire rattled in her ears as she gripped her pillow. "Alex! Alex! Daddy! Alex?"

Where were the comforting words of her big brother, the warmth of his body when his arms wrapped tightly around her to ease her terror? She swallowed her tears, eyes rolling up to the green light that pulsed in the darkness of the corner. Her reality returned in fragments.

The moon's illumination cast through the panes of the window, only pushing the darkness back in slivers. She rolled her legs off the mattress and held the pillow tight, tucking it just beneath her chin. She rocked back and forth.

It was the seventh night in a row of night terrors. Sometimes the voices crept in, and the sharp pops of gunfire were a slice to her ears even though there was nothing there.

Her back slapped the wall repetitively. Nobody complained or banged against the wall to shut up. It's how she knew she was alone in this prison, or at least in this area. She was never allowed to go outside, never allowed to look down the hallways. She didn't even have a mirror on the bolted steel door.

She looked up at the bright red numbers on the calendar. *Two more days.* She shivered. There was still no sign of Alex. No word from Dad either. Was he still alive? She thought about the gun he had beneath the couch. Was Dad really willing to die and leave her and Alex alone in this terrible world?

She hung over the cushioned mattress, fingers pressing against long cheeks and burning red eyes. The moon was bright through the drapes, painting the windowpanes to the shiny tiled floor.

Olivia eyed the pulsing green light in the corner of the ceiling. *They're mocking me.* It had to be true. The only person that came into her room was the woman who served her the three meals a day and cleaned. Nobody else.

Where was Dad? His voice echoed in the pain and loneliness that sliced through the inside of consciousness. "*Do you trust me, honey?*" Her fingers clawed down the sides of her face. "*You still Daddy's little bugaboo?*"

She looked out the window. The world glittered vibrantly with a deep blue, some kind of precious stone she'd only see in her dreams. The towering flood of light that was the Venus Tower was beautiful. She hated to admire it. Hated to be awed by it. The cell was nothing like her home, the awful smell, the rats, the wild animals who stalked the streets. This place … It was like heaven in comparison. It made living in the Suites that much worse. Even Exclusives who broke the law lived better in cells than people like her did in their homes.

Her hands slapped her thigh. She jumped to her feet and jolted toward the window. "He's coming. I know it.

He's coming." Tears fell from her cheeks.. "Alex would never abandon me."

Her heart pounded, and as she brought her hand to her face, she caught how bad she was shaking. She couldn't take her eyes off the window. The tapping of tears smacked the tiles. If she turned, they'd know she was at the edge.

She dropped to her knees and hung her head. "Alex please …" Her plea was a cross between a wheeze and a choppy moan. "Please don't let me die. Please." She could hear his voice even now. *"You and me forever. Right?* You promised, Alex. You pinky promised."

Olivia woke up curled in the corner just beneath the windowpane. Her face wet with tears and drool. The sun was bright, unbelievably bright. She felt it was unfair that when she stood and looked out the window, the grass had never looked so rich as the sea of blades swayed.

Her vision blurred, and her eyes were heavy. Everything was heavy. Almost three months. No Dad. No Alex. No contact with anyone but that woman. Her eyes rolled to the digital count down. *I only have twenty-four hours to live.*

She almost wanted to fall into her bed and go to sleep again, she dreaded watching the hours tick away.

Three hard knocks cracked from the steel door, then it crept open. The tall, broad-shouldered woman came in with her blue jump suit, long braided ponytail, and a tray of food. Maple sausage, scrambled eggs with cheese, a side of blueberry applesauce, toast, and grape jam.

Olivia wanted to throw up. The sourness gurgled from her throat. She sat on the bed.

The woman sat the tray on the desk, turned to grab her cleaning supplies, and came in, scrubbing. "Not much to say today, huh?"

Olivia could barely move her lips or hold her head up. She watched as the woman looked up to the VEN-O, then turned.

"You had so much fire and vigor, so much audacity. But now that you're about to be the youngest girl to be executed in Bourgeoisie history, that cold hand of death has a grip on that skinny neck of yours." There was a tone of victory in the woman's voice.

Olivia watched the wretched smile of the woman pull fiendishly. She sniffed hard, and a tear formed in the corner of her left eye. She hoped it wouldn't fall. *Alex is coming for me. My big brother's coming for me. I know it.*

The woman stood with her hands on her hips, that bitter stamp of ownership shined from her right hand. "I bet you think that brother or daddy of yours is going to save you. That they're gonna come crashing in guns a blazing like they did with those officials at the mansion? But it's not gonna happen. Nobody's coming for you."

Olivia noticed something odd about the woman's expression, the sharpness in her eyes. It wasn't cocky or lazy.

It was watchful as if studying. "DOR is gonna end the United Nations."

"What makes you say that? Do you have information?"

"I—" Olivia paused watching the woman's expression. She was waiting. "Shouldn't you be scrubbing my floors, Exclusive pig?"

"To think this is my last day." The woman snickered. "You know, if you gave me information on DOR, or your brother, they might reduce your sentence to something less severe, like labor in the ore mines."

There was an awful bitterness in Olivia's throat. Anger crawled up and spread from within like a black spiderweb of rage and hatred. The woman's voice was cold in her thoughts. *Nobody's coming to save me. Nobody. Not Dad, not Alex.*

She shrugged. "Nothing? Well, your funeral." The woman propped the door open, then turned to reach for the bucket.

It was a breath in time. A desperate bid for survival. Olivia grabbed the tin tray of food and slapped it across the woman's face, sending her stumbling back. Without hesitation, Olivia grabbed the bucket and heaved the strong fumes and solution into the woman's face. She cried in pain.

Olivia bolted down the silent, empty hallway. The corridors were pristine and white. She curved down another hallway where large glass windows on both sides of the corridor showed high-tech equipment, unmanned with only the color of lights blinking behind the glass. She didn't stop.

A blaring alarm made her insides cringe. She burst through a set of doors and entered a lab. The smell of latex, bleach, and medicine filled her with unease as she crawled behind a metal table. Charging boots rushed behind the doors, and the barks of soldiers echoed down the hall.

Her heart bounced in her chest. She crept to the corner of the table, hoping to get a better look. The sudden whine of the lab door opening made every inch of her freeze. Footsteps, not heavy and clunky like boots and not heavy like the woman, sauntered in soft and subtle.

"You gave General Kaprisha a two-piece." The voice of a young girl giggled. "She's gonna be pissed once she gets those chemicals out of her eyes."

Olivia crawled back, pressing against the table. She looked around, searching for anything to protect herself with. Across from her was an open cabinet filled with a basketful of metal tools wrapped in plastic. She reached for the basket and pulled out the contents.

"I like you. I think you got a lot of spunk." The voice was gentle. The steps creeping ever closer. "You have a raw savageness to you too. We can use that."

Olivia tore through the basket of contents and found a surgical knife. She gripped the thin blade in her hand, her breaths rattling in her chest.

The steps were close now, right on her. Right on the opposite side of the table.

"I get it, you're afraid. Lonely … abandoned. I can help you, Olivia. *We* can help you."

"What makes you think I need your help?

The steps paused. "I was like you once. Confused, angry at the world. If I had been through everything you've been through, I'd be pissed too. Your mother killed in a crappy sentinel raid. A brother who abandoned you to join terrorists. Trust me, we have more in common than you know."

"Not sure what kind of messed up family you have, but my brother didn't abandon me. He's coming for me. And he's gonna save me."

Her cackle echoed over the lab. "You don't need saving, Olivia. What you need is a new perspective."

A metal table fell from the area where the footsteps were coming from. The crash forced Olivia around into the presence of a girl whose chestnut brown eyes locked onto her with frightening excitement. The girl's eyes were almost sadistic.

Olivia plunged the surgical knife toward the girl's face. Excitement intensified in the girl's eyes as she threw her hand out, allowing the blade to pierce clean through her palm. Olivia scooched back, horrified. The girl's devilish cackle echoed through the lab.

"Wh–who the hell are you?"

The girl pulled the blade from her hand, the blood an inky black. No way she was human. The wound slowly filled in, healing before Olivia's eyes, leaving neither a scar nor a blemish. It wasn't possible.

"My friends call me Hyena," she cackled as she crawled toward Olivia. "But you can call me Isabelle."

With the horror and stress overwhelming her, Olivia began crying. This was some horrible nightmare. The girl inched closer, her deep brown skin smooth in the white light of the lab. She looked perfect, beautiful. Like Mom.

Her hair was like thick black ropes, pulled into a ponytail. She was by Olivia's feet when she sat up, still on her knees. "Liv, I'm not gonna hurt you, I promise. See, I always wanted a baby sister, someone I can share things with and even teach her everything I know."

Olivia could see in the girl's intense eyes that there was something off about her, something not too secured. "I don't need a sister. I have—"

"Yeah, yeah, an annoying big brother. I get it. Like I said, I *have* one too." She said it in a way as if the thought of her brother was beyond annoying and a detached inconvenience. "But haven't you always wanted a sister? Huh? Haven't you?" She leaned forward.

Olivia tried to back away from the girl but was already backed into a corner. She was a fly caught in the web of a spider. "Yeah. I guess."

"Great. So it's settled then." She cupped Olivia's hands in hers. "You will be my new baby sister."

Olivia was confused and yanked away from the girl. "I didn't agree to anything. No way I'll accept you as my sister. My mom only had two of us, me and my brother."

Hyena exhaled. "It's okay, baby sis. You just have to have a change of heart, or should I say …" She paused and knocked on Olivia's forehead. "A change of thought."

The girl smiled sadistically as she rose. The lab door shot open as dozens of sentinels poured in, towering over the girl and surrounding Olivia in blackness. Weapons were drawn without hesitation.

Olivia trembled as she looked up at the girl. The white of her left eye became black, and her brown eyes burned a dark red that chilled Olivia to the bone. This girl wasn't human.

"Don't be afraid, baby sister. You'll be fine. I'll be the one taking care of you now, I promise."

30

It was day eighty-nine, and Alex couldn't sit still if his life depended on it. A light jog this morning and hitting the range with Jo-Jo right afterward did nothing to quiet the fear that infected him. It was sickening. The turmoil made the thought of food bitter with bile.

He sat on the edge of his bed in the dark, struggling to concentrate on what they would do tomorrow. What *he* had to do tomorrow. Most of the planning required Crude, Poachie, Jo-Jo, and Kimbo. That pissed Yara off something fierce, but it didn't make him feel any different. Any time to find peace helped Alex relax.

From his understanding of the mission, Jo-Jo was their point of failure, then Poachie. No matter how good of a weapons expert Kimbo was, he lacked Jo-Jo's raw talent with a sniper rifle, and there was no one on the team who knew explosives like Poachie.

He jumped to his feet and headed out to the hall. Poachie was in the midst of dragging large olive-colored containers from her room.

She whipped the two long braids over her shoulder. "You want to see something cool?"

Alex looked down the hallway. He really didn't. He wanted to haul ass down the hallway, climb up that makeshift ladder, open the overhead and run into the forest until his legs gave out. Maybe a pack of wolves or something would get him.

"Sure."

He walked into her room. The smell of oil, sulfur, and almond was heavy. Strewn all over the floor and bed were wires, cords, canisters, and so many rolls of duct tape that Poachie could open a convenience store. On a table taped together were thick bars of what must be clay. They had an off-white coloration, and the wiring alone made Alex nervous.

She gently placed five in a crate. As she did, she cautiously kept checking on the material, wiping her hands constantly.

"What are these?"

"About eight kilograms of fun each."

She snapped the crate closed, and Alex grabbed the handle as they dragged several boxes down the hall toward the armory. The door was pinned back. Everyone was inside, checking their ammunition and weapons.

"What are you guys doing? I thought the pre-combat check was later this evening?"

Yara shrugged. "Nervousness, I guess."

Jo-Jo polished the long pink brass of bullets before slipping them into magazines. "It is, but when you're going into a hive situation—"

Alex cleared his throat. "Hive situation?"

Kimbo slapped a reinforced buttstock onto Missy-E. "She means it's going to be hot, broski."

"I'm starting to understand that," he lied. "Where's the commander?"

Kimbo raised a brow. "In her room. You want to go check?"

The whole room erupted in laughter. A trembling smile stretched across Alex's face, unable to fight the chuckle that followed.

Jo-Jo giggled. "Too soon. Too soon."

Poachie nudged him with a smile as she began stuffing a metal-framed sack with explosives. She filled one to the rim and began filling another. She stuffed thick green cords into one side of the sack and the strange-looking cylinder handles in the other.

"Yo, Poachie. I know we're eating good tonight, right?" Kimbo asked.

Poachie cinched the sack tight and dusted her hands off. "Don't we always eat like kings before a big mission?"

Crude came in, boots clunking at a fast pace. "Did I hear someone say feast?"

Jo-Jo couldn't help but laugh. "Speaking of the One-eyed Devil herself."

"What? Did I miss something?" Crude turned to Alex. "Did you do something stupid again?"

"Nope, not me. Not this time."

"Impossible," Crude replied, monotoned. "But I'll take your word for it. Now, back to this feast talk. Poachie?"

"I plan on doing something big. It'll be a surprise."

Crude's eyes widened, and the smile stretching across her cold, stiff face was uncomfortable to look at. "Good. Alex, come with me, now."

The room grew quiet. The smiles and laughter were replaced with the shifting and clanging of brass and metal. "Okay, sure."

He looked over at Yara, and she gave him a trembling smile.

They walked down the corridor, through the living room and kitchen area, and into the gym. Alex was a few paces behind Crude. Her black hooded jacket, the same one she wore when she killed Principal Krate, dragged behind her. She wore black leggings and camo shorts that had been cut just above the knees and a tactical vest. The red teddy bear holster was so out of place. So was the sword.

Crude turned, and he couldn't help but stare at her. Those mahogany brown eyes were calm but indifferent. There must have been a lot of pain and suffering deep in there. Otherwise, why would a girl like Crude be like … like her?

"You're paired with me, you know?"

"Yes, ma'am."

"You scared?"

"Yes. ma'am."

"Do you trust my plan? Do you trust me to save your family?"

"Y—" Alex hesitated, and his eyes dropped to the floor as the fear of failure crept in again.

She quickened her steps, and by the time he looked up, she was just below his chin, just a few inches away. Her eyes were strong and ferocious. He could barely look at her. "I asked you a question, Lux?"

"Ma'am. I–I don't know if I can trust myself right now, let alone anyone else." His eyes shifted to avoid hers.

A gentle hand fell on his shoulder. "I promise, I will bring back your father and sister. Alive. You understand me?"

Alex nodded.

"We've freed hundreds of prisoners, hundreds of people facing the same situations all over the world. Your family's situation won't be any different. Okay, *Alex?*"

"Yes, ma'am."

Her voice softened. "Everyone who's a Raven is family. You're my blood now, my responsibility, so that makes your family my family ... my blood."

Alex didn't fully understand her statement, but he got the gist of it. He was surprised by Crude's compassion. For the last few months, it seemed nonexistent, but sometimes in these tiny slivers of a moment, something human peeked through. Maybe one day, he'd get to see that part of her more often.

"Hopefully, your sister isn't as much of a pain as you are. If so, I fear I might kill her myself."

"That is a fight I'd pay money to see."

Crude smiled. "Is she strong?"

"Yeah, a spit fire." Alex smiled. "You kind of remind me of her."

"Me? Your sister?" She swallowed, then smiled again. "Really?"

"Y–yeah. Why?"

"Oh, it's nothing. It's nothing. Go ahead. Go back to the armory, get your gear squared away."

Alex nodded and couldn't help but have an added bit of confidence in his step. There was hope again.

"Alex?"

He turned.

"I need you to be at your best tomorrow. You can't give anything less than a hundred percent. There's too much on the table now."

"I'll give my life."

That evening Poachie cooked the biggest meal Alex had ever laid eyes on. Pheasant, moose brisket, venison roast, pork ribs, chicken like the ones he remembered from television, and cooked vegetables and roots. There was buttered corn and candied yams—food he had never heard of. Food he had only dreamed he would eat as an Exclusive. But yet, he was in the Outskirts.

Crude was shoveling food into her mouth. She had ripped the leg off a game hen and stole half a rack of ribs from the plate they laid on. Kimbo demanded a few pieces, and the two argued comically on why the other deserved it. Brain gave a rib to Kimbo, but he denied it, wanting the rack Crude had.

It reminded Alex of the first day he came to Raven Headquarters. Even before a suicide mission, they laughed and talked as if tomorrow didn't matter. He looked over at Yara, who sat just beside him. She looked worried.

He nudged her with an elbow. "Crazy, right?"

"If you say so." Her hands were curled tight on her lap. She took a few bites. He played with a few vegetables trying to keep his voice down and not bring too much attention to their conversation.

"Does your stomach feel like a bunch of garbage going into the dispenser?" he whispered.

"Over and over again. I can barely think."

His fingers rolled over her curled hand and cupped it. "I don't know how, but we're going to do this. We're going to make this work."

She looked down at their cupped hands. "How do you know?"

"Because of them."

Jo-Jo was laughing at Kimbo, who was now in a headlock by Crude. Poachie's face was reddening from embarrassment, trying to talk them out of the dispute. Brain had long given up trying to deescalate and instead watched. Yara started laughing, and Alex couldn't help but join in.

He heard his mom's soothing voice. "*Home and family can thrive anywhere with anyone as long as love and compassion is there.*" That statement had more meaning now than it ever had since she passed.

When Alex stepped out of his room, the morning atmosphere was thick and cold. Goosebumps rolled over his body. Everyone was quiet as they walked down the halls of headquarters. Yara looked up at him with a confused expression but didn't say a word. It was dead silence all the way to the armory until that point. They all wore black.

Like some of the others, Alex wore black sweatpants, combat boots, tactical leather gloves, and a long sleeve shirt made to absorb sweat and keep the body cool. Jo-Jo wore a pink patch over her right eye. Crude was covered in black with a ragged black denim jacket draped over her shoulders, and the red teddy bear was strapped to her back along with her sword.

Brain's intel advised it would help them blend in momentarily if things got hectic. He was right. Alex had never been to a public execution, but when they happened, it was proper respect to those being terminated to wear all black.

"PCCs and PCIs are all good, Commander," Poachie barked, her voice harsher than Alex had ever heard. "Ready for your orders."

Everyone stood up straight, locked tight in step. Alex was surprised he moved like them, even stood strong like they did. Crude walked down the line, checking, tugging away, and eyeing. She stopped and smiled at Alex. Then turned.

"Today, we fly under the radar, Ravens. No backup. No resupply. No additional support." There was silence. With her back still turned, the red teddy bear with a grim stitched smile and black hanging button eyes looked to tease Alex. "We will embarrass the United Nations of America. We'll show that only a thumbprint of soldiers can cause chaos and disrupt their inhuman political system. Blood for blood. Dead or alive.

"We come home heroes!" The room rattled with their voices. Yara and Alex were taken aback by the response.

Crude reached over her shoulders. The gritty grind of the sword leaving its sheath made Alex's skin prickle. But when she raised it to the ceiling, he felt something deep erupt from her. Something cold, heavy, but not frightening like before. "Ravens execute!"

Alex grabbed the MX-23 he had been training with for the last few months. Everything had been customized to his comfort level. It rattled in his hands regardless. He grabbed a large tactical bag. Inside were rations and enough water to last him three days. After that, they would become scavengers.

"What about masks?" Yara asked. Alex had nearly forgotten, too, the horrific masks they wore the day they opened season on everyone at the mansion.

Poachie tried to hide a laugh. "Unfortunately for this mission, we're all going to get hit with some stiff bounties if we get seen."

"No point in wearing masks. We're getting personal on this one. Right, Alex?" Crude turned.

Alex swallowed hard and nodded.

Brain put tiny buds in their ears. "Radio check, s–sound off, Ravens."

Jo-Jo shot him a thumbs up. "Overwatch one, green."

"Overwatch two, golden." Kimbo nodded.

Poachie smacked the large sack on her back. "EO one, read you clear, and riding dirty."

"E–EO two, read you," Yara mumbled like Brain did with a subtle bounce of her chin.

"Warmonger one, on the prowl." Crude growled.

"Warmonger two, on … uh … ready to go."

Everyone looked Alex over in disappointment.

"Ya killing me, Lux," Jo-Jo echoed as they began loading up.

"Read the team loud and clear, Commander. You'll have drone support until you go under, then they're all yours," Brain said, giving Crude a nervous nod. "Your earplugs also have a tracking device where I can give you guidance on your route for local escape routes, but it's up to you to relay the information back if it's a bad call on my part, guys. So effective communication, right?"

Everyone nodded.

"Well, see you by dinner then."

Crude gave a thumbs up. "Ravens, move out."

They lined up in front of the ladder that led to the hatch. With Missy-E slung over his shoulders, Kimbo took point. He lifted the hatch, and the rest of them followed. Alex climbed, his armpits dripping and insides spiraling in a fluttering madness.

The rays poured in from the hatch. Once everyone was on the surface, Alex closed the hatch and covered the entrance up with the netting and added some dirt and branches for good measure. The humming of the drone overhead gave some confidence.

"You guys look clear all the way to the sewer entrance," Brain replied. "Like I said, once you guys go in, I have no eyes, but you'll have my soulful voice for comfort."

They broke through the trees, right out into the shanty towns. Gentle columns of smoke rose here and there, but not much life. Most of the voices echoed from Playground. Enraged drunkards or worse, more than likely.

Alex looked at Big Mah's and wondered how Mrs. Tanaka was doing. He hadn't seen her since everything went down, but Poachie did tell him she was thriving and always asking about him. Of course, she would.

They made it to the entrance of the sewer line. It wasn't like the large opening they came through with dozens of people before. This was a bent-out grate, just big enough for a few people to slip through one at a time. Kimbo struggled to get through, slung Missy-E off and shrugged off the bars. Everyone followed suit.

A red light beamed from the handguard of Missy-E, lighting the rancid darkness of the sewer as they sloshed cautiously through the murky water. It would be a walk of several hours before they got to the point where they all would separate.

Everyone was silent. Alex could only thank Poachie for that, taking him on hunts, learning how to control his breathing and stay hidden. She was beyond just a good cook.

They walked for about an hour. Crude broke away and marked a sludgy pipe with green glowing spray paint. "First rally point."

"You remember what those are, right, Lux?" Jo-Jo snickered in a low whisper.

"Stuff gets crazy before our next rally point. We head back to this spot. I'm not a complete wing nut."

"Just partially."

Crude came back into the line. "Enough. Stay focused."

"Yes, ma'am," both Jo-Jo and Alex replied.

They hit two more rally points before coming to a large opening. Alex remembered as if it were yesterday. The different tunnels. He clearly remembered the tunnel that went back to the mansion.

Crude clenched the leather glove over her right hand. "Alright, everyone has their orders. Poachie, those bombs need to be set and ready to go off in two hours. Jo-Jo, I need the first sentinel to have their scalp peeled back a half hour prior. Understand?"

"Too easy, ma'am."

"Alex, let's go."

Alex turned to look back at Poachie and Yara. He met Yara's eyes, and he thought about his time at New Hope Academy when she was walking away from the apple tree. The difference was her eyes were now locked on him.

She sloshed forward and hugged him. "Stay alive for me ... please."

"All of you better stay alive," Crude added.

31

In the darkness of the sewers, Alex and Crude tactically stalked through the waters, steps hidden in the gushing and rattling of pipes. Their path was brightened by a flashlight that dangled from her vest.

A few rats paddled furiously to the edges of a thin walkway. The tunnels had strange paintings and symbols from a world long since collapsed. Aged posters displaying routes were caked over with black mold, and like old rags, moss dangled from the crevices of ceilings and walls.

Alex lowered his rifle. "This place doesn't seem like a sewer at all."

"That's because it's not." She kept her eyes forward. "It's an old subway station from the old eras."

Alex began to focus more on the peeling mangled paint that seemed to flop away from the wall like slime. He thought about the old tunnels that definitely had a train station type of feel to it. "Crazy to think about the way things were prior to World War III."

"Why?"

Alex was taken aback by her question. "Well, I mean, do you think life is better now than back then? In school, they made it seem like it was hell on Earth leading up to World War III. But I can't imagine things being worse than they are now."

"History doesn't matter."

"Why do you say that?"

"The real history is buried beneath lies and replaced by what the New World Order wants everyone to believe is history. I've come to accept the now and to work toward a future, not the past. The past is dead."

He shrugged, keeping his eyes forward as they continued on. He was nervous being around Crude, but better that than fear. If it wasn't for her statement yesterday in the gym, he'd wonder how their pairing would fair. But he trusted her.

The real question was did she trust him?

The waterway shifted up to a crumbling concrete staircase, wide and slimy. Remnants of a banister remained on both sides, but rust and condensation consumed every inch of it.

They came to the top of the staircase. The flashlight hitting the ghostly fractures of the past gave him goosebumps. Old chairs had been tipped over, some still anchored with spider webs and tangled plant growth. There were bags consumed by mold, a sneaker.... Then the skeletal remains of people.

Alex paused. A trembling crawled down his spine.

Crude turned scornfully. "What?"

His eyes focused on the remnants of two skeletal remains. He made out the long brownish texture through the mud where thin bony hands looked to be wrapped oddly together.

She went over and kicked the skull away from its body.

He grabbed her shoulder. "Why would you do that?"

She glared down at his hands. "Stop focusing on the dead. We have a mission. Right?"

"Yeah. But …" He pulled his hand back and looked down at the remnants that were once human. Even Pariahs got buried when they died. These people, whoever they were, deserved the same. "You're right."

They walked on, coming to a long structure covered with mud, stone, and rusted metal beams. A line of red paint rusted away from the sides, and what must have been a door had been ripped open. More skeletal remains covered the area. Crude's thick black boots crushed bones into a near muddy paste.

"Two more miles."

Alex nodded, unable to keep his eyes off the structures that had rested below his feet all this time. "Is all this really under the Suites?"

"Yes. Like I said, buried beneath lies," Crude said bluntly.

The air changed becoming less musky and pungent, there was a sweet freshness to it. As if a switch had gone off in her head, Crude's walk became predatory, her shoulders dip, eyes locked forward. Alex adjusted to try and match, but this was ingrained into every fiber of her being.

The old world fell away as new concrete surfaced around them as if growing from the old world like plants from fertilizer.

They came to a bolted door. Alex froze. Crude widened her stance at the door, slowly reaching for her sword. The air changed. Pressure that was damn near unbearable came in a harsh wave. Goosebumps came without warning and the flashbacks of the day when she attacked him flickered.

Her head looked to slump low. "Alex, this will be the first time you've seen me work. I chose you to come with me because I need to prove myself to you. What you're feeling right now is the vastness of the darkness, don't be afraid. But when I go to this place, the abyss, I need you to give me thirty yards."

Alex gulped. "Thirty? Why?"

"Because failing to do so will put you in my kill zone." She ripped Eerie from its holster, slashed the door, and had it back in the holster before Alex could gasp. A frightening frigid wind blew in as the steel door peeled away like menacing claws to a tin can. She walked through.

Alex couldn't move. Those whispers were back, and he couldn't take his eyes off the ominous black smog that rose from Crude's ankles, wrapping around her body. The blackness was alive—it had to be.

Thirty. Give her thirty. Do it or die. A bead of sweat rolled into the crevice of his lips. "Yes, ma'am. Thirty."

She looked over her shoulder, and even through the thick black of her wild hair, he saw the glowing crimson eye sharpen with confidence. "Let's go get your family."

Brain came over the radio. "Warmonger one and two, you are two hundred yards from the execution site. Expect light security forces. Two options, bypass or execute on site. Just remember, team EO and Overwatch are ten minutes from their objectives."

Jo-Jo chuckled. "We all know what Crude's gonna do. Why even give the options?"

"Get a move on, Ravens," Crude barked. She bolted down the concrete corridor, Eerie in hand, and blackness pouring out of her like a burn pit. "Alex, head on a swivel and keep running. Got me?"

Her voice jolted him forward. "Yes, ma'am."

In the distance the flashes of her flashlight danced from one point to the next. Up, down, left, right. There was no way Crude could move like that. Not a little girl. Not a human being.

Alex came to his first sentinel. The body was in three pieces. The next was the same. He slapped his hands to his mouth to keep from vomiting. All that came to mind was the mansion. All that blood and carnage. Was this much blood really needed to save lives? To make a change.

As Crude commanded, he kept his head on a swivel, MX-23 at the ready. He grabbed a few mags from a dismembered corpse, slipped them into his cargo pocket, and kept pushing forward, following her bloody footprints. Unlike Crude, he was already slowing down, legs burning from exhaustion. He thought about Kimbo's statement about working out too much. Great advise.

Brain came over the radio. "Looks like Overwatch is in place. Team EO, what's your ETA?"

"Ten minutes," Yara whispered. "We got some company down here."

Poachie whispered, "We got six sentinels. Looks like a specialized unit too. Highly armored and packing some serious heat. I thought it was supposed to be a ghost town down here. Brain, what gives?"

Silence.

Alex didn't like the hesitation.

There was fierce tapping on a keyboard. "Doesn't make sense. It's just an old train station. No strategical value at all to UNA."

Nobody said a word.

"Standby. Wait them out, collect any intel you can," Crude replied. A deep grunt followed. "Alex, get on my six now!"

He hastened his jog to a sprint, the thoughts of Olivia and Dad keeping him moving. They came to another concrete tunnel. Crude was just stepping over a pile of sentinels. They nestled in a corner by a concrete barrier out of sight of anybody that came lurking. The crimson glow of her eye became a mahogany brown as she chewed her thumbnail.

Alex almost hated to ask. "Everything alright?"

"Fine, I guess. Just find it hard to believe that Brain's information was wrong." She tapped the handle of Eerie against the barrier impatiently.

"Poachie and Enyo will be fine. Not like you to worry."

"I worry on every mission. They're my responsibility. *You* are my responsibility. Understand?" She went back to tapping away again.

There was an intensity in her eyes, a glint of desperation. It didn't sit right. "You brought me with you to show me you had confidence, right?"

"Having confidence in me is one thing. Worrying about your family …" She sighed. "Poachie, what's your status?"

"They're working on something. I can't really see, but we're well hidden. Nothing to worry about, Commander."

Crude's eyes burrowed into Alex's. For a moment, he thought she planned to cut him down. She was grinding the handle of Eerie stressfully against the barrier now. "We're moving out."

Brain jumped on. "Crude—"

"We're moving out! Poachie, the moment they're gone, you and Enyo get on setting the bombs on the pillars. You got me?"

"Got it."

"Wait!" Jo-Jo called from the radio.

Alex froze, his heart leaped to his throat. Something wasn't right. Jo-Jo's voice, Crude's composure.

"What is it?" asked Crude.

"I have four groups of six heavily armored sentinels coming from one of the sewer entrances by way of the street. One of the groups is coming right from where we came from. Not liking this one bit. They're popping out all around the public execution center."

"Standby?" Kimbo asked.

Crude pressed her finger to her ear. "Yes."

Brain came back on. "Hate to be the bearer of bad news,

but we're running out of time. We need to make a move or call this mission a wipe."

Alex's blood became fire. "No!"

They were too close now; he couldn't turn back. That was out of the question.

Crude laid a hand on his shoulder. "Not gonna happen, Brain. Everyone, relax." Crude took a deep breath. She looked down at the MX-23 in Alex's hands. "You ready to use that thing?"

"Ready as I'll ever be."

"What's the execution set up like, Jo-Jo?"

"The usual. Eight spots lined up. A sea of black. Exclusives on one side, Bourgeoisies on the other."

"Five minutes till they bring out prisoners. Then that's mission loss," Brain said with a voice as stern as Alex had ever heard come from him.

His heart raced, and his clothes clung to every inch of him after all the running. The radio was silent. Crude was thinking hard; he could see it in her eyes. The tense shift of her jawline, the way she handled Eerie.

"Four minutes."

Thanks, Brain.

"Lux and I are going for the prisoners. Poachie and Enyo, no change to my last order."

"Yes, ma'am."

A shock of cold and an instant heaviness brought Alex to his knees. It felt like gravity had multiplied ominously. The inconceivable force fell on him in waves. His teeth chattered.

A hand reached down.

He looked up, meeting the harsh eyes of Crude. She didn't say a word this time, but her eyes, especially her right, chilled him to the bone. He grabbed her hand, and he was yanked to his feet.

"Three minutes."

She took off down the tunnel. Alex gave her the space needed. He followed the trail of blood and bodies till they came to the city level.

"They're bringing out the prisoners," Jo-Jo barked.

"Jo-Jo, you're free to engage."

Alex waited for the boom. But there was nothing.

"One target down," Jo-Jo said with a deep exhale.

There was an eruption of screams and wails, and the sound of gunfire echoed from outside.

"Two. Three. She's on a roll, ladies and gentlemen," Jo-Jo joked through the radio. "Four. Fi—oh damn, almost five. Got two birds with one stone, but it hit the other Senti in the chest. He's incapacitated, though. No trouble from that one."

By the time Alex caught up with Crude, she had a clean-cut man dressed in a black suit by the throat, pressed against a wall. If it wasn't for the dire situation, it would have almost been funny to see a grown man held up by a girl not even half his size.

Poachie whispered into the radio, "Sentinels moving out. Will immediately began working on explosive implants."

"Where are the prisoners?"

"Not ... telling." The man's face became a shade of a cherry and was quickly becoming a blueberry.

The atmosphere became heavy with a frightening chill again. The cracking of Crude's fingers around the man's throat was beyond unsettling. "Tell me."

"Building, across."

Crude snapped the man's neck and let him flop to the floor. "Thanks."

The radio screeched in Alex's ear. He almost ripped it out. He looked up to see Crude's head jerk hard. "What the hell's going on with the frequency?"

"Not the frequency. Shit! We're screwed. We're so screwed." Poachie's voice wasn't normal on the other end.

"What's going on, Poachie?" Brain broke through the chatter. "You're in the right place. Did those sentinels come back?"

Poachie could barely get the words out. "T-those sentinels planted bombs all over this place. There are enough explosives to bring this portion of the city down to the sublevel. Wh—what are they thinking?"

Jo-Jo jumped on. "What are you talking about?"

Kimbo added, "You're mistaken, Poachie."

"Everyone quiet!" Crude snapped.

Alex pressed against the wall. Sentinels could be heard marching down the streets, taking up fighting positions. The radio from the dead man laying by the wall echoed with chatter. Between him and the dead soldiers below, it wouldn't be long before they came marching in for the kill.

"Poachie, explain the situation. Stay calm."

"I have piles of VNC6. There's enough here to take out the city block. W—wait ..." The radio went silent. "There's a timer too. Forty minutes."

"Crude, this is no longer a rescue mission." Jo-Jo's voice was cross. "This is a pack your bags and get the hell out of dodge kind of mission. Shit has hit the fan!"

Crude turned to Alex.

He started shaking his head. Olivia, Dad. He wouldn't leave them.

Poachie spoke with a trembling voice. "You guys said you saw more sentinels come from the sewers, right?"

"Right," said Jo-Jo.

Poachie's voice strengthened. "Ma'am, I have reason to believe this is a trap. UNA planned on killing everyone here with these explosives, and there would be no proof to show the government had anything to do with it."

Alex pressed against the wall and slipped down. His world was crumbling around him. There was no way this was happening. "They can't do this, right? This ... This is some sick twisted joke. Why would UNA do this?"

Crude came over and knelt in front of him. "I need you to keep it together, Lux. Knuckle up, remember?"

"Crude, what should we do?" Poachie's voice was brittle. "W-we can still try—"

"No."

Alex's heart fell. He looked Crude dead in the eyes. Her right eye glowed, the iris thin as a blade.

"Jo-Jo, how far away are you?"

"Several blocks. Why?"

"Cover us. Enyo and Poachie, head back to our first rally point, now."

"Crude—" Poachie snapped.

"That's an order!"

The radio went silent.

"Yes, ma'am."

Alex rose, steadying himself on the wall. Crude gave him a terse nod. "You ready to die for your family then?"

He thought of the promise he made to his mom, the pinky promise to Olivia. "I am."

They both raced to the building entrance, Alex's heart thumping in his chest. There was still screaming and sentinels yelling. He wondered if they figured out where he and Crude were. His breaths were shallow and deep as his fingers wrapped around the handguard of the MX-23, his finger nowhere near the trigger.

Crude poked her head out, then pulled back. "Not too bad. Twelve, maybe fifteen sentinels."

"Not bad?" Alex choked. He felt the cold grasp of death encroaching around his throat.

"I want you to watch me when I go out, Lux. Let me know if I still remind you of your sister."

Alex nodded.

Crude stepped out, Eerie drawn at her side. The sound of sentinels ushering her commands to stand down were ignored. Alex's eyes widened, his heart pounding in his throat. He could hear the guns ringing, the sound of the pot of spaghetti bubbling. Olivia's shrieks of terror.

Crude. Crude, please don't die....

32

Crude took two strides, then vanished amidst a hail of gunfire. Alex pulled away, the glass windows and doors shattering as the inside of the building was sprayed with a shower of fire. He peeked out, watching blood splatter all over the streets and sides of buildings.

It wasn't possible. Crude's movements. With a single slash, Alex watched a man fall into pieces, his MX-23 with it. The sentinels began firing upon her. Crude reflected a few rounds with Eerie, one hitting a sentinel. Then she vanished again in a wisp of darkness.

Their cries were the only thing not robotic about the sentinels. For an instant, he wanted her to stop. Their screams of agony and pain made them too human, but the memory of him holding his mother as she coughed blood in the kitchen of their home made him watch on. The memory of Nelson dying, one of his eyes half out of its socket, then the screams of fear as they pulled Olivia away, kept him from closing his eyes.

"Alex!" Crude's call over the radio snapped him out of the memory. The firing had stopped. Crude was crouched behind a concrete pillar. The middle of the street was covered in bodies and blood. "Get out here, now."

Every inch of him tensed. The firing, the killing, all the blood. His heart ached as it thrashed against his chest. Move! Move, damn it! His brain was alive, but his body was frozen in time.

"Alex, breathe, brotha. Remember all the training." He heard Kimbo's voice. "Jo-Jo and I got your back. You're clear to go."

Alex couldn't see them. But he trusted Kimbo, and as much as he hated to admit it, he trusted Jo-Jo too. He swallowed, took a deep breath, and gripping the MX-23 as hard as he could, he raced out to the pillar where Crude was.

"Timer on that bomb is down to twenty-five minutes, guys," Brain snapped over the radio. "Poachie, you and Enyo are out of there, right?"

An exhausted Poachie came over the radio. "Yeah. Yeah, we're out of there. Just past the fourth checkpoint. Please, you guys got to get out of there too. When … When that thing blows—"

"You just get to that first rally point, Poach." Jo-Jo chuckled. "My babe and I are bringing the commander and cry baby home, don't you worry."

Crude yanked Alex behind the pillar and peeked out. The wails of sirens and vehicles approaching, groaned in the distance. Helicopters beat the air, getting closer.

"Don't like that," Crude groaned.

"What's that?" Alex asked.

"Birds. Quite annoying. Missiles, machine guns. A pest. Might kill you for sure. Let's end this quickly."

They bolted toward an oversized truck on sixteen wheels, long, black. There was a gun turret at the top. Nobody was up there. Even the streets looked clear. People were still screaming in the distance.

"I don't like this," Jo-Jo came over the radio. "Guys, there's nobody out here. Nobody. There should be a flood of forces by now. Hive style."

Machine gun fire poured in from across the way. It was a patrol truck manned by a sentinel. Four more came out, rushing Crude. Alex peeked out as a few rounds cracked against the concrete pillar knocking out chunks.

Explosions rocked the street, rattling Alex's chest and throwing him forward. He crawled back behind the pillar. He was wet all over and prayed he hadn't pissed himself. Rounds pinging off the street and cracking against the pillar were nonstop.

"Hey, Lux. You want to get a move on already?" Kimbo chuckled. "But seriously, in less than twenty-five minutes, those artillery shells and three sentinels are gonna be the least of your worries."

Alex peeked around the pillar. One of the three sentinels headed for the truck where Crude was. His head shattered into bloody plastic fragments mixed with flesh.

"Sniper! Sniper!" the sentinels cried in a static voice.

"Hurry up, Lux," Jo-Jo demanded.

Alex leaped forward and ran toward Crude, who looked to be trying to get into the large trailer. Gunfire rained over him as he ran the hardest he had ever run. The whizzing of rounds was like angry wasps ripping past his face.

He dove forward and crawled up next to a wheel. It felt like the first day of training all over again. More explosions rocked the streets. The ground trembled beneath him. They were getting closer.

"Screw this!" Crude yelled. "If you can hear me, get back!"

She stood and widened her stance. Alex pressed harder against the thick wheels of the trailer. No way she could cut through. It looked like reinforced steel, the same kind of steel that made up the layers of the outer wall.

With a scream, she cut the trailer open, creating a gaping entrance. She jumped in, disappearing through the gaping hole. Alex's eyes widened. She's a monster, alright. Alex jumped up and heaved himself in.

Huddled in chains were men and women, legs, hands, and wrists bound together. With a flick of her wrist, Crude cut through them easily with precision. Not a drop of blood spilled from the prisoners. Alex began helping and pulling the black sacks from their faces, his heart racing to find his father and sister.

"Twenty minutes, guys." Brain echoed in Alex's ears.

He pulled sack after sack from the faces of men, women, and children. Nobody he recognized. There were two in the back, one figure small and shaking frantically, another broad and bulky. Dad. Olivia? He ripped the sacks away. One a tall, pale-skinned man, the other a young girl about Olivia's age, with yellow skin and short black hair.

An outpouring of thanks fell on Alex and Crude, but he didn't care. None of them were his father or sister.

"Where are they?" He looked around at the dozens of faces frantically. "My father, my baby sister, where are they. Are there more of you?"

The prisoners' faces became frantic. *I overlooked them, that's all.* He pushed through the prisoners again, checking over and over, praying the faces would change to Dad's and Olivia's.

"We… we don't know. There were a bunch more of us. We don't know where they had the others."

"My dearest, rebellious ones, known as DOR…" a voice cracked over the loudspeaker, one that broke over a thunderous explosion, and the cracks of gunfire, a strong voice, smooth as velvet.

That voice, Alex thought. It was familiar, kind, peaceful. He had heard the tone so often, but it had been a while since he last heard it.

"You who shed innocent blood, you who aim to destroy everything the United Nations of America has been built on, you will answer for your crimes against humanity."

Crude growled. "That witch."

"It's … It's the SGUNA, Dalia C. Roberts," one of the prisoners advised with a shaking voice. "Sh–she's actually coming through the speakers."

A blaring alarm wailed from various parts of the city far off. The voice rang loud and clear over the area. "We have found the bombs you planted below the intersection of Eastern and Western. We will do what we can to evacuate, but you will not get away with this. The blood of the innocent is on your hands."

Jo-Jo came over the radio. "Those sentinels just booked it. What is going on down there?"

The words repeated in Alex's head. *Bombs we. … we planted?* Poachie and Enyo didn't have a chance to plant anything because of what the sentinel's had set up.

The prisoners turned to us. "What bombs?"

Crude snickered, then began laughing. "This was a trap. This whole thing was a trap." She looked over at Alex. Her blade raced to his throat. "I don't know how, but they must have known we would come to save the prisoners."

Tears trickled down his face. All he wanted to do was find his father and baby sister before it was too late. "We don't have time for this."

She withdrew her blade. "Can any of you drive?"

A woman raised her hand. "I–I can."

"Grab a patrol truck and drive until you get to the Suites. Get out and hide. Unfortunately, that's all I can give you right now."

They all nodded.

"And tell as many people as you can to get away."

"Yes. Thanks." A man nodded. "But what about you two?"

Crude looked at Alex. "We have to save others. Go!"

The group ran out. There was no gunfire, no more voices from the speakers. Just the beating of helicopters overhead. Alex and Crude jumped out and began searching for other trailers.

"Jo-Jo. Any more trailers like the one we just came out of sitting on the streets?"

"Nothing from what I can see."

"Alright, you and Kimbo, get out of here. Now!"

"Crude!" Kimbo replied.

"That's an order. Go!"

Jo-Jo grumbled on the other side of the radio. "You idiots better get back to rally point one in one piece."

Panic began choking Alex. He could see Olivia as a little girl, innocent, happy and bubbly before their mom died. He even saw his father, someone he admired, no matter how fearful he had become, being as happy and as strong as he used to be. He couldn't lose them. He wouldn't.

"Let's check the center. Stay by my side." They raced, keeping an eye on roofs and windows, her sword at her side. They checked everywhere, but there was nothing.

"Guys, eighteen minutes," Brain's tone trembled. "Poachie, where are you guys?"

"We're at rally point one. Guys you have to get out of there, now. Alex, I'm sorry, but …" Poachie's voice was tear-filled.

Alex's heart raced. He could feel it in his head, in his throat. The world was spinning. They checked vehicles and buildings until they stumbled on a trail of dark red blood. They followed it to a wall where a sentinel lay, an MX-23 in his hand. The rifle fell to his side as he struggled to grasp it.

Crude bolted toward him and impaled him in the opposite shoulder. The man gave a quivering scream. "Where are the other prisoners?"

"Dead," he said on an exhale.

Crude twisted the blade. The man lifted off the ground as he let out a bone-chilling scream. "I said, where are they?"

"Building across from us. First floor. Doesn't matter … You're all dead anyway."

Alex's eyes widened. "You did this on purpose? Why?"

"You're nothing but a bunch of evil, murdering bastards. Ruthless. Savage."

There was a quick whip of wind. The man's helmet cracked against the stone, his head still inside as blood sprayed the wall. Alex stepped back, and the MX-23 fell at his side. *Murdering Bastards?* The thought of someone calling him such a thing shook him to the core.

Crude ripped him away. "Let's go, damn it."

Alex took a few steps back, then turned, running toward the building just behind Crude. They burst through the doors. There was silence in the old government building. With his dying breath, did that sentinel lie? Did he say all that just to waste time?

"Dad! Dad!" Alex ran down a long hallway. "Olivia! Dad?"

"Lux, here!"

Alex raced down the hall from where Crude's voice echoed. She pressed her ear against the door. "You hear that?"

"Ten minutes! You need to find a truck, guys, now!"

Alex ripped the ear plugs from his ears and did the same. The cries of people echoed just enough. "Yeah."

"Move." Crude cut through the door. Though it looked to be made of wood, it was actually thick reinforced steel, along with the walls. "Smart. Soundproof too."

Inside were dozens of people chained down in steel bracelets and linked together like those they found earlier.

Alex started ripping off masks immediately. "Dad! Dad! Olivia?" He ripped off the mask of one. "Mr. Tanaka."

The man looked thin, sickly, his eyes wincing from the light. "Alex … is that you?"

Alex moved to the next prisoner. Ripping off mask after mask. His heart began to sink, his hope dying, the pain crushing. Then he pulled the mask off a tall thin man. "D–Dad?"

The man could barely keep his eyes open. He had all kinds of blisters, scars, and injuries on his face. His brown skin looked fake and pale, and he smelled bad. Real bad. "Dad? Dad, it's me. Alex."

His eyes opened just enough to let tears fall. He fell into Alex, pulling a few people with him.

"Okay, move." Crude cut through the steel chains with a flick of wrist.

Alex's father crumbled to the floor. The once broad-shouldered, muscular man who looked like he could carry the world no longer existed. His clothes were loose and layered, and his face … His eyes were sunken, his cheekbones protruding.

Alex wrapped his arms around his father and cried. "Dad, I'm sorry. I'm sorry. This is all my fault."

A bony hand wrapped around his shoulder. "You fought, Alex," he said, his voice a weak whisper. "Your mom … would've fought. I … was too … afraid." He exhaled. "But, I told them nothing. They would've gotten nothing out of me, son."

"Dad, you don't have to talk."

"Lux," Crude called. She knelt beside him and his father. She lifted up his pants leg, and more of the foul smell flowed from his boots. Both his legs were swollen to inhuman proportions and looked a wet waxy charcoal color.

His father smiled, straining his eyes as he struggled to sit up. "It's alright. Doesn't hurt no more. You found Olivia?"

"N-no, Dad. Where ... where is she?" He looked back down at Crude who went on to remove the boots. She looked back up at him with a cold stare and shook her head.

All of his toes had been gnawed off, and from there infection had worked its way all the way up his legs. Alex looked back up to his father and did his best to keep a smile. That smile that always gave his father confidence.

His father began trembling and laid back. "They took her somewhere else. I haven't seen her since the apartment."

Alex couldn't stop shaking. His eyes rolled around the room for answers. "Dad, we've got to get you out of here."

His father's hand tightened over his shoulder. "You're a man now, kid. You stood up to them."

"Dad, c'mon ..."

"Lux," Crude grabbed his arm. "He can't move, Alex."

"You've got to go. Find ... Olivia. Find her. Take care of her."

"Dad. I'm not gonna leave you here."

Crude snatched Alex's chin, tears welling in her eyes. He hated to see them. He hated to see tears on that expressionless face because he knew. "I'll do whatever you want me to do, Lux. I'll cut both of his legs off, and I'll drag him out of here. The gangrene's rotted to the bone, he won't feel a thing. But no matter what we do … he's dead. Do you understand?"

Tears rolled down his father's cheeks. He coughed, spitting up mucus as his breaths choked out from blistered lips. "You've got this, kid. Show me.… Show me that strong smile."

Alex took a deep breath, closing his eyes. He remembered the family photo that he wished he had right now. That day they all went for dinner, a family event. Mom and Dad were holding each other, he was teasing Olivia, and she was getting frustrated with him, but they were all happy. *Happy. Happy, I'm happy. Force yourself to be happy.* He wiped his eyes and put on that strong face. The same face he gave him before leaving the house for his first day at New Hope Academy.

"I love you, Dad."

His father nodded. "I'm proud of you, my son."

His father's eyes rolled to Crude, who nodded firmly. She rose and yanked Alex to his feet, pulling him away from his father.

"Guys, you need to get a vehicle. ASAP!"

Alex looked down at his father with eyes flowing with tears. After seeing his father's broken withered body, he didn't want to imagine what Olivia must look like. The blood boiled in his veins as he tried to focus on survival.

Crude pulled him out of the building as the other prisoners came bolting behind. A sentinel patrol truck pulled up. Alex kept his eyes on the turret, the MX-23 heavy in his hand, and his whole body weighed down with regret.

Crude drew her sword as the windows came down.

"Heard you guys need a ride?" It was the prisoners they'd freed earlier.

Crude slapped the hood. "Give me the wheel!" Everyone able helped those who weren't to hop in the back. "Alex, I'll take driver's seat. I need someone in the turret, now."

Everyone did as she said. Alex crawled into the passenger side while Crude, stomped the gas, throwing him into his seat. He could feel his soul leaving his body along with the cries of those in the back. He strapped in.

He was sick, his insides swirling with disbelief. Dad ... What happened to Dad. What did they do to him? He thought about the large man who hid his pain behind a smile, a genuine smile, believing the harder you worked, the more you got in return. But not in this world.

This world took everything. It took mothers, fathers, sisters, and best friends. It turned teachers into psychopaths and children into ... He turned to Crude, whose eyes were focused forward.

As the vehicle revved with a roaring engine, all six wheels glided over the streets, jumping barriers, craters, and garbage. His eyes rolled down to the MX-23, heart pounding in his throat now. He never fired a shot. He couldn't.

A massive explosion rocked him forward.

The back wheels of the patrol truck lifted and were no longer at the mercy of Crude's driving. The front end smashed first, then the windshield. Alex braced himself as a quick glimpse showed a massive ball of fire in the distance. Buildings crumbled away in the burst of a fiery black cloud.

The vehicle barreled down the street. The windshield tore away spraying glass and tar everywhere. Crude was thrown out.

"Crude!" Alex threw his hands out, but he never had a chance. His head smacked off the passenger side window, and everything spun into gray fiery blotches.

Flashes of Dad and Olivia flickered. Of Mom. Of Nelson. Of Deacon. Was this real? Were they real? Was … was Dad really dead?

33

"Wake up! Wake the hell up!" a voice ordered overhead.

Alex's blurred vision focused on the dark-skinned girl above him. His eyes watered as a tear broke over the bridge of his nose. Crude's thick black hair was absorbed by the billowing smoke that blew from the buildings in the distance.

"You're alive?"

She wiped her face and pulled him into a sitting position. "People like me don't die."

When she knelt, the ragged clothes revealed blood and heavy bleeding but no wounds. Beside those streaks of blood where wounds should have been, she was scarless. He went to move, but a sharp pain and a grinding feeling in his shoulder halted everything. He winced and gripped his arm.

"Let me see." She tore off his shirt revealing a misshapen shoulder. "Shoulder's screwed. Gonna have to get you back to headquarters."

Sirens wailed in the blackness of the thick smoke. Hell. That's what Alex thought of, if such a place existed. That's where they were.

Eight people huddled in front of the overturned patrol truck that looked like someone had pushed it off the top of a skyscraper. The fact they survived was a miracle.

Mr. Tanaka knelt beside them and helped Alex stand. A stabbing ache forced Alex's right knee to give out, Mr. Tanaka kept him balanced as best he could.

Mr. Tanaka looked up at Crude, barely able to move well himself. "Only eight of us survived. What happened?"

"Explosion. They blew up that portion of the city."

Another survivor blurted without missing a beat, "That's impossible. Insane! That was half of Eastern, some of Northern. Why would they do that?"

"Don't know." Crude shrugged, then cracked her neck side to side and rotated her left shoulder back and forth. "But they're gonna die for it."

Alex put more of his weight onto Mr. Tanaka. "She's right. UNA planted those bombs. We didn't do that."

"No, DOR isn't responsible for this." Mr. Tanaka's eyes slunk away, red with pain. "Those monsters, those ruthless savages who call themselves leaders and pretend they want the best for us are the ones responsible."

Crude tucked Eerie behind her, studying the surroundings. "Follow me. We need to get out of here. Last thing I need is to deal with more sentinels. Plus, I'm starving."

Food? Food at a time like this? Alex sniffled, thinking about his father. He turned to the smoldering black clouds and the orange glow that radiated behind them. He could feel the tears coming, but not a single fell.

They made their way down into the sewers again. Mr. Tanaka and a few others helped him down. The pain in his right knee became a heavy throbbing, pulsing with each step. Thoughts of his dad and not knowing if Olivia was alive or dead brought him to nothingness.

They finally came down the tunnel with the glowing fragments of rally point one. The others jumped up, Kimbo had Missy-E raised. Poachie came running and hugged Crude, then Alex.

Jo-Jo leaned against a pipe. "Cut it pretty close, didn't you? Why weren't you guys answering the radio?"

Poachie stopped Jo-Jo from talking. "Alex, where is—"

Crude's voice was a dry rasp when she said, "I failed." The whispers of the survivors drowned out by her tone. When she turned to face them, Alex saw the glow of her crimson eye. Tears streamed down both sides of her face. "Alex ... I failed you. I-I'm sorry. I broke my promise."

Poachie looked down at Alex and cupped his face, then squeezed tight. She looked around the group. It didn't take long to see the tears in the rest of their eyes and the grief consume them. It was only for a second. "You, okay?"

"I just want to lay down."

Poachie nodded.

Alex limped onward with the group, passing Yara and the others. She was sobbing, by the sound of it, but he couldn't look at her, or he'd fall apart in front of everyone. His throbbing knee and shoulder kept him sane, kept him calm, but as he searched the foul water of the sewer, failure consumed him with a wrenching pain. I let Nelson die. I let Dad and Olivia die … and I let Mom die. The tears fell, dripping silently into the sewer water.

Flashes of his mom covered in blood and his dad as a thin husk of who he used to be made Alex wince.

"*Are you stupid and blind? Are you a UNA dog?*" Nelson's voice echoed in his ears, and his dad's voice came right after. "*Easy street … I know a lot of people who died on that intersection, good men.*"

Alex didn't fight the voices. He didn't deserve to. Everything that happened to his family and friends was his fault. If he had listened to his dad and not accepted the invite to New Hope Academy, the three of them would still be home right now. Eastern Suites would be in some form of peace, and he could've talked Nelson into not going.

Greed. Dreams. All were the catalysts of endless pain and suffering that affected so many people around him. He thought about Principal Krate. A man he wanted to look up to, a man he wanted to admire, only for him to be insane. This world turned people into Principal Krate. Turned them into monsters.

Cold wet fingers slipped between his, and Yara took on his weight even though she struggled some herself. He looked over to see Yara's eyes wide and locked forward, tears flowing. Shocked. Horrified. That's how she looked anyway. But why didn't he feel that way? What happened to all the fear, the terror of failing … of losing Olivia and Dad?

Yara was silent, she gave his hand a gentle squeeze. He didn't have the stomach to return the gesture. His gaze was stolen by the black murky foul soup they sloshed through. The voices in his head kept echoing, torturing.

They made it through the broken bars. Mr. Tanaka and Yara helped Alex through. A massive crowd grew from the Outskirts looking up at the wall. As they came out, Alex turned to see the black columns of smoke, the sirens and helicopters beat the air fiercely.

Mrs. Tanaka came stumbling through the crowd falling into the arms of her husband. The two kissed and hugged passionately. They turned and hugged Alex and gripped him close.

Mrs. Tanaka searched the group. "Where's Doug? Olivia?"

Alex was silent. He looked up, catching the subtle shake of Mr. Tanaka's head. He brought Alex in closer. Mrs. Tanaka began weeping. Her sorrowful sobs reminded Alex of when Nelson died.

Sirens blared from the outer edges of the wall, sending a chill down his spine. He looked over at Crude and the others who began grouping together.

"Lux, we need to go." Crude's voice was gentle.

He looked up at the Tanakas and nodded. "I have to go. Take care of each other."

Mrs. Tanaka clutched onto him. "Alex, you don't have to do this anymore. You can ... You can stay with us."

He looked up at the desperate eyes of the woman. Mr. Tanaka's expression was firm and assuring. The numbness of grief was strangling, there was no hope left, no life.

"Nah," he said, his voice passionless, cold and dead. His eyes rose to the wall and the billowing smoke. A harshness like the bitter winters caused after the nuclear war howled in his insides. And within, planted firmly, were the seeds of his torn family, fertilized by the blood of his best friend and cultivated in an atmosphere of falsehood and lies. "I can't do that anymore."

"Alex, we can help you. We can take care of you. I know it's not the same, but …" Mr. Tanaka tried to explain with hope.

How could he replace Nelson and Jason? How could he replace his own family? He turned and looked up to the wall, smoke billowing higher and higher as the skies became ash.

Crude's voice broke over the growing whispers around them. "This world's broken. There's no unity, no peace, no hope like they promised. Only controlled chaos wielded by a judge who will decapitate and dismember anyone or anything that opposes them."

"Exactly," Alex replied. He turned and began limping toward the others. Kimbo helped him as they vanished into the woods. From behind the gritty grind of gears and iron echoed, the doors of the walls were opening.

Sentinels. They'd fill the Outskirts now.

Alex should've been afraid. He thought of that boy sweating and trembling on his first day at New Hope Academy, that boy with his eyes focused on those bullet holes in his bedroom wall, fearing death. But dying was peace. There were worse things than death.

Epilogue

Hyena walked through the fortified complex that was Mecca, mesmerized by the large marble pillars and white floors, dreaming of skating across them. If they were waxed or covered in blood, it would've been a thrill.

Her team walked a few feet behind. It was the first time they had been let loose since inception, training, and all the fun at the labs. Bubbles of ecstasy rolled from her insides. She wanted to dance, twirl, and leap like the ballet dancers she saw when she was a little girl, but that would have to wait.

They were activated by the SGUNA, the big kahuna herself. She thought about what it would be like to be the leader of the free world, but politics were a drag, and the thought of sitting at a desk, making stupid decisions, and listening to people talk on and on and on—

"Ma'am, what are we doing here?" Ki-Ki asked.

Hyena twirled around, hands tucked behind her straight black hair. She turned to the round-faced girl of East Asian descent, her hair in a tight bun and draped in black and gray camouflage. "I don't know, but if we're in Mecca and we're going to see Dalia, it means something big," Hyena sang with excitement. She jumped, clapping her hands together. "We might see combat soon!"

Tye rolled a lollipop between his teeth. His sharp blue eyes looked down at Hyena with a loathing expression of boredom. "Sheesh, it's about time. It's been what, three years of training? Another four years of schooling."

"Sounds about right," replied Lean. He scratched a bald scalp as his shifty brown eyes rolled over the palace. Even under the light his brown skin looked waxy from sweat. He snickered. "After that attack on Constance and the Suites last week, I'm sure the SGUNA is ready to play her hand against Anarchy and DOR."

"Lean, you think activation is a possibility?" Stanislava spoke carefully in her Russian accent. She was as tall as Tye, with beautiful blonde hair pulled into spiked pigtails. She stood out of the group wearing olive green camo pants and a desert camo top.

Lean nodded. "Better be."

They walked down a flight of steps and at the bottom awaited General Kaprisha. Her face wasn't as red as usual, and she wasn't wearing the shades anymore from when Viper had thrown bleach in her eyes.

Hyena nodded with a deep grin. "General."

The general scowled. "You can say ma'am and salute next time."

"Well …" Hyena threw her hands up as if weighing imaginary consequences.

"Just follow me."

They walked down another corridor beneath gold diamond chandeliers. The walls were lined with fine art, paintings, and rows of marble statues. *Too rich for my blood,* Hyena thought. *Been there, done that.* She hated living amongst the wealthy, too boring and dull. It was no wonder her traitorous brother jumped ship.

The six of them stepped into the elevator. It was impossibly white with a smell of cleaning solution, the kind that would've burned your nostrils if it had been cleaned moments prior. Even the elevator was perfect. Hyena hated it. Perfection, pristine, the environment sickened her. It reminded her of Fort Roberts.

The doors closed with a hiss. The general stepped in front of them and turned.

"You will be silent. You will not speak out of turn. You will not make any unnecessary comments." She burrowed her gaze into Hyena before turning to face the door, hands at her sides and her back straight.

"And why did you look at me when you said, 'unnecessary comments?' "

"You know why."

Hyena huffed. "Whatever. So, how's my sister doing?"

General Kaprisha tightened her fist. "Quite well. Olivia's taking the infusion without issues. Defiant as all hell, but nothing a little mind cleansing won't fix. Again, don't know why you're choosing the sister of a terrorist to join Ghost. It's a terrible idea."

"Well, I'm terrible person." Hyena clapped her hands while bouncing on the balls of her feet.

Yeah, it was crappy that Hyena's parents were dead, and it was a sickening terror staying with the ones who adopted her and her brother. But with her team and the addition of her baby sister, she had her family. A real family.

"Oh, and when we are brought in, kneel before our Secretary General. Understood?"

"Yes ma'am," the team responded in unison.

"Understood," Hyena responded sarcastically. Ki-Ki elbowed her, and Hyena threw her hands up with a sharp whisper. "What?"

"Ma'am, you're embarrassing us," Ki-Ki rasped.

The doors peeled open to a bright room. Everything was white with gold trimming. Minus the clouds, Hyena guessed it might be what Heaven looked like. Quiet, perfect, clean. She wondered why anyone would want to live in a world so boring.

They were greeted by a dark-skinned man with outrageous grayish-black hair, it looked more like a mane then anything. A long, jagged pink scar ran down a milky-white eye. Dressed in a clean, pricey black suit, he clutched a bundle of folders beneath his arm.

Although it was their mission that was in his grasp, Hyena was too distracted by the ominous energy radiating from the man. The black blood running through her veins was going crazy. It only did that around those with power. In his wrinkled face was someone who had seen war countless times. His scar could attest to that. But there was something more, and he didn't have black blood in him, she would've sensed it, so what was he?

Hyena cocked her head to the side. "And who are you?"

"Leonidas. Lord Leonidas to you," he said with a powerful, cracking voice more animalistic than man.

General Kaprisha shot her a sharp elbow. Their gazes met quickly. She was pissed.

"Fine. Fine. I'm calm. Hi, Leo."

"Follow me, please."

They followed Leo into a large bay. It wasn't as pristine as everything else, colder and stonier. No decorations. It was a place where you brought those you wanted to secretly execute. A prickly sensation ran down her arms as an itchiness crept from behind her eye sockets. A devilish grin slipped out. Another test.

"Calm your soldiers, General. They have no need to worry here," a gentle voice broke from behind them.

General Kaprisha knelt immediately, and so did the others. Hyena was the last. She didn't have a chance to look up at the woman, but the clicking of heels echoed in the spacious place. A sweet scent of the finest perfume wafted by with the swift elegance of her stride. An icy wave of terror filled the bay.

A shiver casted down Hyena's shoulders when she turned to follow the voices origin.

"Please, all of you relax." The woman's voice was harmonious.

The television didn't do Dalia justice. Her skin was the color of south sea pearls, eyes like balls of honey. There was no makeup, Hyena could tell by the lack of indifference from the tone of her smooth shoulders showing through a white silk gown. Beauty at its purest. She wasn't tall or intimidating. Dainty really, like someone who needed protection. But that didn't make sense, especially with the cold murderous chill of power radiating from the innocent looking woman.

"You are all here for a reason. Last week was a travesty. Half of the Eastern and Northern Suites were completely devastated along with a portion of Constance. As you know, DOR is responsible. We have also tied Anarchy to this as well." Dalia turned and nodded to Leo, there wasn't a hair out of place as her gesture triggered the man to life. He bowed and handed out the folders. "As you will read in the dossiers, these are all the prominent members of DOR's elite group, and Anarchy's leadership."

"Mission?" Hyena scanned through the documents with excitement. Her eyes fluttered with overwhelming joy when she landed on the face of a stocky brown-skinned boy. *What a coincidence.*

"I'm so glad you asked, Hyena."

S-she knows my name.

"Today is the day that I activate the special antiterrorism squad known as Ghost. All six members have received the black-blood infusion. All of you are UNA's best hope of defense in crushing this threat completely."

The group began whispering with excitement.

"I've got a question, ma'am. You said six. Only five of us had the black blood infusion. General Kaprisha's just a normy." Tye crunched on the remnants of the lollipop. "I hope someone didn't lie to you, ma'am."

"No," General Kaprisha replied. "There were two others who came through The Dark Ones Project before you. One defected. Another has been underground and successfully integrated into DOR"

More whispers followed. Hyena sighed. "So ... that person is the real leader of our operation then?"

General Kaprisha smiled. "You're a smart girl. Yes, for now, You'll lead the field team until the toppling of the insurgency. The true leader, if they survive, will take their place amongst Ghost."

"Whatever. When do we get to kill some terrorists?" Dalia smiled, her hands clasped in front of her. She truly was beautiful, her skin was soft and warm. Hyena wished to peel it off and wear it if she could.

The General cleared her throat. "Mission prep will be three months. You'll be dropped off in South America. DOR has been hitting the agricultural plants hard and stealing food, so neutralizing their operations there would be a great test to your skills and capabilities. From there, work your way through North America. You'll be fed information throughout this operation. Did I miss anything, Your Excellency?"

Dalia's smile brightened the grayness of the space, but Hyena couldn't ignore the malice her beauty hid. "Just one thing. It's something very important the United Nations of America, something I need you to retrieve."

Hyena raised a brow. "And what's that?"

"The original of The Dark One's project, the defector, she has something very dear to UNA. A black Katana known as Eerie." Dalia tapped her finger against her crossed arm. "This weapon is frighteningly powerful and could destroy the world as we know it. At all costs, no matter the sacrifice we need that sword. Failure to retrieve will result in immediate termination…understood?"

Lean spoke up without hesitation. "Why hasn't anyone gone for the sword all this time?"

"Only those with dark blood flowing through them can wield the blade, all others are destroyed the moment their fingers wrap around the handle."

Hyena watched Tye and Lean's gaze of confusion.

"Hard to believe I know, sounds almost magical doesn't it?" Dalia smiled and shot Leo a glance that held secrecy.

"Understood, Your Majesty." General Kaprisha bowed.

Everyone followed suit, except Hyena.

"Isabelle," Ki-Ki whispered, her head still down as she tugged on Hyena's sleeve. She was obviously pissed. Ki-Ki only called her by her real name when she was upset.

But she couldn't help it. This woman before her was beyond them. She didn't have a charagma on her right hand. Not a single scar or blemish, Dalia was doll like, as if there was something fake about her.

Dalia's eyes fell on Hyena, and there was a strange glint of terror that struck even her with unease. With a trembling body, she bowed. "I will execute any mission you give to us, My Secretary General."

Book 2: The Take Over
Coming Soon!!!

Enjoying this book? You can make a big difference

To an independent author reviews are the most powerful tools we have to get are books noticed. At the moment I don't have the backing of one of the big five publishing houses, so you wont see huge ads on billboards, or posters on the subway of Beantown. (Soon though!)

But I do have something much more powerful and effective than that, and it's something that those publishing houses would kill to get their hands on.

A loving loyal mass of readers!

Honest reviews of my books help bring them to the attention of other readers.

If you've enjoyed this book, I would be incredibly grateful if you could spend just five minutes leaving a review (it can be as short as you like) on the book's Amazon page. You can jump right to the page by clicking below.

Have you read the Titans Saga series?

Titans: The Rise of Legends

Elric Blake has more comic books than friends. With his secret crush the only person he can relate to, the fifteen-year-old outcast finds himself about to fight a bully at the Friday night football game. But before anyone can even think to throw a punch, a mysterious portal opens over the field and unleashes an invasion of bloodthirsty beasts.

With the entire town in chaos, the shocked young man discovers he is somehow able to manipulate dark energy and uses it to slay one of the creatures. But with an ominous voice in his head egging him on to continue the carnage, Elric must master his powers if he wants to survive this apocalyptic nightmare.

US UK

Titans: Dark Catalyst

With Blight's crushing defeat, Elric and the others have saved the world from most certain destruction. But life as teenage superheroes aren't what you think. Amidst the crumbling infrastructure of society and going back to high school, regaining any form of normalcy has become impossible. Especially with a dark entity whispering in your ear to destroy everything in sight.

US UK

Titans: Cold Blooded Orphans

Boston. Violet wishes she could wash her best friend's blood from her hands. With their apartment destroyed and their lives in shambles, she relentlessly trains the rest of the team to prevent anyone else from dying. But when they're called to London, she's shocked at the identity of the culprit responsible for a massive explosion.

With their adversary threatening to destroy global government systems, the teenage heroes dive headfirst into a hardened war to save others from deadly violence. But when tragedy strikes again, the Titans must band together if they want to live long enough to avert a diabolical world takeover.

Can these high-schoolers deter the end of days before they're left for dead?

US UK

Titans: Revelations

It's the moment of truth. Light vs. Darkness, and in the middle the world stands. After the crushing defeat at the hands of Elric, Enzo and Rai, Violet and the others have become desperate for hope. With Sage gone, and Elric teaming up with the most powerful Titans yet, hope is found with the return of Jennifer Reeves. But after the destruction of Boston is Elric worth saving? The world has changed, and world governments have put the three teens as international terrorist, and a threat against all mankind. Will Jen be able to turn Elric away from his path? Or will Elric's bloody dream come to fruition?

US UK